Avalanche Pass

Titles by John A. Flanagan

STORM PEAK

AVALANCHE PASS

AVALANCHE PASS

A **JESSE PARKER** MYSTERY

John A. Flanagan

BERKLEY PRIME CRIME, NEW YORK

THE BERKLEY PUBLISHING GROUP
Published by the Penguin Group
Penguin Group (USA) Inc.
375 Hudson Street, New York, New York 10014, USA
Penguin Group (Canada), 90 Eglinton Avenue East, Suite 700, Toronto, Ontario M4P 2Y3, Canada
(a division of Pearson Penguin Canada Inc.)
Penguin Books Ltd., 80 Strand, London WC2R 0RL, England
Penguin Group Ireland, 25 St. Stephen's Green, Dublin 2, Ireland (a division of Penguin Books Ltd.)
Penguin Group (Australia), 250 Camberwell Road, Camberwell, Victoria 3124, Australia
(a division of Pearson Australia Group Pty. Ltd.)
Penguin Books India Pvt. Ltd., 11 Community Centre, Panchsheel Park, New Delhi—110 017, India
Penguin Group (NZ), 67 Apollo Drive, Rosedale, Auckland 0632, New Zealand
(a division of Pearson New Zealand Ltd.)
Penguin Books (South Africa) (Pty.) Ltd., 24 Sturdee Avenue, Rosebank, Johannesburg 2196,
South Africa

Penguin Books Ltd., Registered Offices: 80 Strand, London WC2R 0RL, England

This is a work of fiction. Names, characters, places, and incidents either are the product of the author's imagination or are used fictitiously, and any resemblance to actual persons, living or dead, business establishments, events, or locales is entirely coincidental. The publisher does not have any control over and does not assume any responsibility for author or third-party websites or their content.

PRINTING HISTORY
Random House Australia Bantam book trade paperback edition / 2010
Berkley Prime Crime trade paperback edition / February 2012

Library of Congress Cataloging-in-Publication Data

Flanagan, John (John Anthony)
    Avalanche pass : a Jesse Parker mystery / John A. Flanagan.
        p.   cm.
    ISBN 978-0-425-24540-8
1. Hostages—Fiction.   2. Mercenary troops—Fiction.   I. Title.
    PR9619.4.F63A96   2012
    823'.92—dc23
                        2011039750

PRINTED IN THE UNITED STATES OF AMERICA

10 9 8 7 6 5 4 3 2 1

For Reg and Jane,
who showed us how to ski in Utah

PROLOGUE

TEN YEARS PRIOR

The ground below was a black mass.

By daylight, it would be a rolling ocean of hills and mountains, covered in featureless green jungle. Here and there, the brown snake of a dirt road would wind its tortuous way through the green. The occasional building would be visible—farmhouses, for the most part. And one large sprawling house with a group of outbuildings surrounding it. But now it was just a sea of almost unrelenting black.

Almost.

The F-117 Nighthawk was flying itself up to the final waypoint and Major Nathaniel Pell, call-sign Stalker, took a moment to peer out of the small triangular windows, trying to make out some detail on the ground below him. Far off to starboard, he could see the lights of a small city looming in the darkness. Closer, he saw a group of lights in the sea of black, maybe seven miles ahead of him. Target, he thought.

It was warm and comfortable in the cockpit. With the F-117 set on autopilot he had little to do. At sixty percent power—cruise setting—the twin turbofans behind him provided a subdued, almost soothing background rush of air over the canopy. He yawned. His biggest danger was falling asleep.

Then, almost as he had the thought, a discreet chirp from his instruments brought him wide awake.

The radar warning receiver was glowing in the top right quadrant, the glow slowly fading as the radar beam slid on by, over the Nighthawk. Stalker's eyes narrowed as he watched the instrument. His forefinger went to the stopwatch control on his wrist chronometer, ready for the next warning chirp and flash.

There!

He hit the stopwatch and the sweep hand started around the

watch face. When the chirp and flash came again, he stopped the watch and checked the time.

Twenty-three seconds. That was the time it took for the radar antenna below him to rotate through a full circle, flicking its beam over his aircraft each time it passed. He wasn't surprised to find a search radar out here in the boondocks. Knowing what was down there, he would have been surprised not to find it. And there were almost certainly SAMs as well—surface to air missiles ready to deal with any intruder that might be detected. For the moment, however, they posed no risk to him. The Nighthawk was invisible to the radar. Those below had no idea he was here.

Neither did too many people back home. Since he'd been seconded to this black operations group, he'd breached foreign air spaces half a dozen times without more than a handful of people knowing about it. His orders came in a convoluted chain from the highest authorities. The NSA, the CIA, the DEA, even the White House on occasion, would tell his superiors what they required without ever questioning how it might actually be accomplished. Deniability, he thought, smiling grimly behind his oxygen mask.

The radar passed over him again and he realized he was getting close to the business end of the night. He shifted in his seat to make himself more comfortable, rolled his shoulders to ease out the stiffness of sitting strapped in for four hours and keyed the transmit switch on his radio.

"Showboat," he said. Just one word. The reply came almost instantly.

"Footlights."

He flicked a switch, turning on the forward looking infrared viewer—the FLIR. After a few seconds, an image faded up, enhanced by computer so it resembled a normal TV picture, rather than IF imaging. A large square building, two stories high, without windows or visible doors, it was flat roofed and solid looking. Not solid enough for what it was about to receive, he thought grimly.

With his left hand he reached to the row of weapons selection switches and hit two of them. The display panel lit up to show two laser-guided weapons, ready to drop. He selected a ripple of two and, finally, dialed a separation of five seconds into the system. Now one pressure on the bomb pickle would release the first bomb immediately, with the second rippling off five seconds later. He frowned for a moment. The twenty-three second window between radar sweeps wouldn't be enough to open bomb doors and release both weapons. And when the bomb doors were open, the F-117's low radar signature was seriously degraded. That meant the people below would know he was here.

He shrugged. Knowing it and doing anything about it were two different things. They might see him briefly but they'd have no time for a SAM launch before the bomb doors closed again and he disappeared from their screens. He armed another switch and a set of crosshairs appeared, superimposed over the image of the building. The aim point was a little to the left and below center so he steered the sight to the center of the flat roof with a miniature joystick.

He smiled grimly. "Footlights" was an appropriate call sign. Somewhere in the dark jungle below him, a two-man Special Forces covert team was concealed, illuminating the building with a laser designator. The laser energy reflected from the building would guide his bombs to their final target, as long as the designator was switched on. All he had to do was center the crosshairs, pickle the bombs, orbit gently while they both released, and then get the hell out of Dodge. The laser seeker head on the bombs would do the rest, slaving them to the laser sparkle, so that they steered themselves right into the center of the roof.

And he could watch it all on TV while he headed for home.

On the ground below, Roberto Modesta yawned and rubbed his eyes as the radar completed another sweep. Then, abruptly, he sat up, staring at the scope as a small blip appeared, held, then faded after the indicator line had swept on.

Modesta hesitated. Had he really seen a blip or had it been his imagination? After three hours of watching and seeing nothing, he was prepared to believe that his eyes were playing tricks on him. He knew he should call Alvarez, head of security here at Monte

Verde, and report what he had seen. But what had he seen? He decided to wait for another sweep, and confirm that the blip was still there.

Anxiously, he watched the radial line of light creep around the scope, willing it to go faster.

There! It was there again. But faint. Fainter than any return he had ever seen from a plane before. Even the little Piper Navajo that had strayed above the compound some weeks back had put out a more solid echo than this. Still, there was something there.

He leaned back from his screen and called to the adjoining room.

"Commandante! I've got something on radar!"

Just his luck, he thought gloomily, that the bad-tempered head of security was on duty this evening, and not one of his lieutenants. Odds were that this was a false alarm—a flock of birds or a glitch in the system.

The door to the other room opened and Alvarez entered, fastening his belt buckle. He was a big, fleshy man, a former police lieutenant, and the belt cut into him when he was sitting, dozing.

He scowled at the technician now, hunched over the radar screen again, his finger hovering over a point on the screen.

"What now?" Alvarez said, his ill temper at being disturbed all too obvious.

"A contact, sir," Roberto told him. As the line of light swept over the point, he jabbed his waiting finger where the blip had appeared on the last two sweeps.

Nothing.

The beam swept onward, leaving a blank screen behind it.

"It was there!" he protested, sensing the security chief's anger. The beam swept around again and again; there was no sign of an echo.

Disgusted, the security chief backhanded Roberto across the back of the head. His head jerked forward under the impact, and he cracked his eyebrow painfully against the hood of the radar scope.

"You've been drinking again, haven't you? I've warned you before."

"No! I swear it was there! I saw it! It was . . ."

The room shook as a deafening explosion erupted across the clearing. Then the overpressure hit them and both men were hurled to the floor. A few seconds later, a second explosion shattered the night. This time, it was accompanied by the lurid yellow glow of flames licking at the shattered warehouse.

Fifteen thousand feet above them, Stalker watched it all on TV, and smiled as he rolled the F-117 out of its orbit and headed for home.

"Showtime," he said quietly.

ONE

Jesse was one of the last out of the cable car.

He cleared the wooden landing stage and dropped his battered head radials into the snow. They were several seasons old and they'd seen a lot of work. But they were old friends and he trusted them. Right now, trust was important, he thought. He stepped into them, feeling the satisfying clunks as the bindings engaged and locked onto his ski boots. Stamping them experimentally onto the snow a couple of times to make sure they were securely fastened, he skated a few steps to the edge of the drop.

Eleven thousand feet below, and seventeen miles away, he could make out the straight lines and grid-like layout of Salt Lake City, viewed through a notch in the sawtooth-shaped mountains. He shook his head. The inner anger that had been burning at him for the past few days forgotten for a few moments in the sheer beauty of the view before him: crystal-clear air, a sky so blue that it hurt the eye to look at it and line after line of marching, snow-covered mountains.

A hand touched his sleeve, drawing his attention away from the stunning landscape.

"You ready?"

Larry Allison, the instructor he'd hired for a two-hour session, was waiting patiently beside him. He was the antithesis of the stereotypical ski instructor: forty-one years old, he was of medium height compared to Jesse's rangy six foot one, with a stocky build and the beginnings of a paunch beneath the blue and gold uniform ski suit. His face was round and tanned, becoming startlingly white above the line of the woolen ski cap that covered a balding head. A few strands of his wispy blond hair escaped from under the cap. But for all that, he skied like an angel and was a good instructor as well. Jesse knew that the two didn't always go together and he'd asked around before he'd selected Larry. The instructor nodded at the view, understanding Jesse's distraction.

"Can never resist the temptation to look at her myself. We can wait a spell if you like." He spoke with a slow, friendly Utah drawl. Jesse shook his head briefly.

"No. Let's get going. I'm ready."

The instructor studied him for a moment, unhurried and relaxed. "Well fine then," he said. "We'll head down to the turn-off and stop there."

Jesse followed the direction indicated by the pointing ski pole.

"We're not going down Drifter again?" he asked and Larry pursed his lips, shaking his head.

"Hell, no. Time for something a little harder."

Jesse nodded assent and started off down the trail, skating a few steps to gain momentum, then falling into a relaxed, slumped posture as the skis picked up speed over the perfect snow. Larry watched him as he skied away. He was a good skier. Hell, he was way better than good. He had the totally relaxed and fluid movements of someone who'd grown up on skis. The instructor frowned. From what he'd seen of Jesse so far this morning, there was little he could teach him. There might be a few minor points of refinement he could help with—anyone could use a tune-up from time to time. But the tall, dark-haired man who'd engaged him at the ski school that morning was every bit as good a skier as he was himself.

He wondered about Jesse's reasons. He'd been wondering about them ever since their first run down Drifter, a blue-black run that was moderately challenging and gave him plenty of time to assess a client's capabilities. Larry always took a new client there first. He'd learned early in his career not to accept a customer's assessment of his or her own ability. Most skiers wanted to be better than they were and a lot seemed to think that saying it made it so. Not Jesse, however. He'd assessed himself as "tolerable" when Larry had asked. It had taken maybe twenty yards for Larry to see that he was dealing with an expert.

He shook off the contemplative mood and started after the tall figure. Jesse had reached the turn-off point and was waiting for him and Larry guessed he was waiting impatiently. Clients who shelled out one-eighty big ones an hour for private instruction tended to want their money's worth. Leaving his thoughts hanging in the clear cold air behind him, he took off after his client.

As he'd anticipated, Jesse was moving his feet in impatient little shuffling steps when he reached him at the beginning of the first trail. Drifter curved to the right, snaking under the cable car and winding its way down the mountain. On their left was The Wall.

"Where to?" Jesse asked and Larry jerked his thumb at The Wall below them. Jesse looked and, for a second, Larry saw the quick flicker of apprehension cross his face and knew why he had been approached for this lesson. Jesse was scared of the steep, almost vertical ski run that dropped away. Maybe "scared" was too strong a word, he thought. But he was definitely nervous—more nervous than a skier of his obvious experience and ability should be.

"You can manage it," he said quietly. "Just remember your basics . . . and take it a little easy."

Jesse nodded several times, his eyes fixed on the steep wall of snow below them. His eyes darted from side to side, looking for the trees that framed the narrow, steep run, the rocks that he knew must lie hidden in the soft, inviting snow, just as they had that last time. He felt an electric thrill of pain jangle in his shin—a reminder of the agony that had been his constant companion throughout the previous summer. He licked his lips, noticing that the instructor was studying him intently.

"Problem?" Larry asked. He watched as Jesse hesitated, then shook his head.

"No," he replied quietly. "Everything's fine."

Larry called, "Follow me," and dropped off the edge of The Wall.

It was virtually sheer for the first twenty feet or so. Larry plummeted down, then gracefully poled and thrust into his first turn as the gradient lessened, almost imperceptibly, and he felt the first hint of resistance under his skis. He let go a rebel yell of delight and began a series of short, high-speed turns, sending immense clouds of the light, air-filled powder snow exploding from his skis with each one. For a few moments, he forgot the client waiting at the top of The Wall, watching him disappear down the mountain. For just a brief period, he was free and filled with the swooping, indescribable joy of movement and speed that was as near to flying free as anything he'd ever felt in his life.

Then, reluctantly, a hundred yards down the slope, he broadsided to a halt and looked back up to the crest. The blue-clad figure was still there, stark against the brilliance of the sky behind him. Larry waved one pole above his head in an unmistakable signal.

There was a moment's hesitation—a moment that spoke volumes. Then Jesse dropped off The Wall, following as close to the instructor's pattern of turns as he could. Larry watched, eyes slitted against the glare, nodding to himself.

Not bad. A little tension there, but he'd kind of expected that. The frown returned momentarily as Jesse poled for his turn, slamming the stock into the light snow as if he had a grudge against the mountain.

"Too hard, boy," Larry muttered aloud. Then he nodded approval again as he noted the correct knee action—the high, springing turn that brought both skis clear of the snow so they could rotate easily in free air. But the violence behind that pole plant had him worried. Too often, people used anger as a crutch against fear when skiing. It might work with a beginner but for someone of Jesse's ability it was a retrograde step.

On his fourth turn, Jesse felt himself come down slightly out of balance. The wall of snow behind him seemed to brush his shoulder as he turned. His heart leapt into his mouth as he remembered the last time—the sudden loss of equilibrium and grace as the concealed rock bit into the soft base of his ski, stopping him as effectively as a trip rope would have. Then came the fall, the snow smothering him as he tumbled uncontrollably, then the blinding shock of agony in his leg as he slammed into the young pine. The memories were all there in a rush—not sequentially, but all crowding for his attention at the same time. And, irresistibly, he leaned back—just for a fraction of a second.

On that steep, unforgiving slope, it was enough. The skis slid out from under him, losing their grip on the thin, powdery snow and he was over, rolling helplessly onto his right shoulder, tumbling in the sudden frigid cold.

He felt the icy shock of the snow close over his face as he tumbled uncontrollably. Then he was in the clear again, sailing through the air for a few moments before he came facedown into the snow again. Rolling, falling, rolling: going with it as he felt himself gradually losing momentum. Praying that this time there would be no tree. Telling himself that there was no point in trying to force it. He would slide and roll to a stop when the mountain felt it was ready to let him.

Finally, sensing that the slope was beginning to lessen, he rolled his legs under him, getting his skis downhill until they finally dragged the last few yards of speed off and left him flat on his back, staring up from the hole he'd punched in the snow at Larry's grinning face.

"Well, that's one way to get down."

Jesse lay for a few moments, letting his breathing settle into a normal rhythm.

"I guess I zigged when I should have zagged," he said finally, taking Larry's proffered hand and dragging himself upright.

He was covered head to toe in the light, dry, clinging powder snow. He slapped at it, feeling the inevitable handful slide down the collar of his ski suit and melt instantly into freezing water.

"Anyone can fall on this steep and deep," Larry said. "Don't worry 'bout that. But there's a technique problem. You're attacking it too much and you can't do that in this light stuff."

Jesse removed his sunglasses and ran one gloved finger around the inside of the lenses to clear away the packed snow there as Larry continued. "Be a little subtle. You slam that pole into this stuff and it's going to go all the way in. There's hardly any resistance there to stop it. So straightaway, you're putting yourself off balance." He hesitated, not sure whether he should say what was coming next. Then he shrugged, mentally, and went ahead anyway.

"But someone who skis like you, you should know that."

He waited. And figured now that whatever problems Jesse had with his skiing, whatever it was that he was hoping Larry could fix, they weren't physical. They had to do with fear. And the first step toward solving them might well be to get Jesse to admit to them.

But Jesse refused the overture, replacing the Bolles over his eyes, shutting out the piercing glare of the sun off the snow once more.

Larry gave a small shrug. He'd tried. All he could do now was discuss the mechanical side of things. He demonstrated Jesse's mistake, slamming a pole into the deep, soft snow.

"Now, you do this on all that ice and boilerplate shit they got back east and you'll maybe get away with it. But here, on Wasatch powder, you got to be subtle, okay?"

Jesse nodded.

"Otherwise," the instructor continued, "this mountain's going to say to you, 'Sorry, my friend, but you ain't going anywhere whiles you're pounding those big holes in me.' And then you're gonna end up flat on your ass every time. Understand?"

He grinned easily but there was no response. The dark glasses successfully hid Jesse's eyes, and his thoughts. He simply nodded that yes, he understood. Larry felt a small twinge of frustration. Of course he understood. He was teaching this boy to suck eggs here.

"Okay," he said finally, falling back on the professional good humor that every good ski instructor has to have, "now let's get"— he broke off and put a hand on Jesse's arm—"Hold it a moment," he said.

"What's the pr—" Jesse began, but then his words were swallowed by a sudden, explosive whoomph from a point in the trees fifty yards below them. There was a momentary bright flash and Jesse threw up one arm in front of his face.

"Sorry 'bout that," Larry drawled. "I didn't know they were firing just yet."

He pointed across the valley to the steep, snow-covered cliff face opposite.

"Keep your eye on that spot to the right of the cornice," he said and, almost as he spoke, a white puff flew from the snow to be smothered instantly in a larger explosion of flame, smoke and more snow. The muffled thud of the explosion rolled across the valley to them a few seconds later, repeating and echoing as it rolled and bounced from the walls of the valley around them.

"What the hell was that?" Jesse demanded. Larry kept his eyes riveted on the spot they'd been watching.

"Just keep looking," he said. "Don't see this every day."

Jesse looked back. For a few seconds, there was nothing except the smoke and snow drifting slowly in the light breeze above the cornice. Then he noticed it. A faint stirring in the slope opposite, as if the cliff face itself had trembled. Then a black split appeared suddenly in the hitherto perfect white of the snow and a huge slab of fresh fallen snow slid lazily away from the cliff face and toppled into the valley—perhaps a few hundred tons of it in all.

In a few seconds, it had lost its cohesion as a single slab and become a tumbling, roiling, formless mass that rolled with ever-increasing power down the slope. A deep rumble accompanied it as those few hundred tons rapidly became thousands.

"Jesus," he said softly.

"Avalanche control," the instructor told him briefly and Jesse raised one disbelieving eyebrow.

"You call that control? Didn't look like anyone was controlling that from where I'm standing," he said.

Larry shrugged, acknowledging the point. "True enough," he admitted, "but this way the ski patrol makes it avalanche where and when they want it to. Better to do it now when the area is clear than risk having it come down when there are people under it. Besides, this way, it can't keep building up into a really unstable mass."

Jesse nodded his understanding. He'd done his share of avalanche control with the ski patrol back in Routt County. But there it consisted of placing small satchel charges in the snow and roping off suspect areas to keep skiers away. They didn't have these massive, sheer walls of airy, almost insubstantial powder snow on Mount Werner.

"So what was that they fired at it?" he asked. "Sounded like some kind of mortar?"

"Sort of," Larry told him. "Actually, a 75-millimeter recoilless rifle. It's kind of like an overgrown bazooka, I guess."

Jesse gave a short bark of laughter. "It sure did the job," he said, still looking at the ravaged mountain face across the valley. In the valley, shrouded in white clouds, the massive avalanche was slowly boiling to a stop.

He looked across the slope to the timber platform where the small artillery piece was sited. Two members of the Snow Eagles Ski Patrol, their task completed, were already fastening a canvas weather cover over the gun.

"We've got maybe a dozen of 'em around the mountain," his instructor continued. "Fire 'em on fixed bearings to bring down the bits that are awkward to get at. In other parts, the patrol plants fixed charges and sets 'em off. The whole area is a high-risk avalanche zone, you know."

Jesse nodded thoughtfully as he watched the patrollers skiing away from the site. In the past three days, he had been conscious of the continual dull thumps of explosions echoing around the resort.

"I'd heard that," he replied. "So why build a resort here in the first place? You'd have to have a pretty good reason."

Larry grinned and swept an arm around the entire valley. "Best reason in the world. And it's the same thing that makes this such a high-risk zone in the first place: the best and deepest powder snow in the world. It's great to ski in. Pity is, it's also highly unstable and avalanches if you look too hard at it.

"But don't let it bother you too much," he added. "In the twenty-five years the resort's been here, we've only had one fatality caused by avalanche."

Jesse frowned, remembering a half-buried detail in his mind. "Didn't I read somewhere that you had a major avalanche here ten years back?" he asked, then, as more details came to mind, "Buried the Canyon Lodge, didn't it?"

Larry nodded. "That happened sure enough. The western wall of the valley—behind the hotel building—came down in the spring of 1989. But the resort had closed by then and there was nobody here. The snow was wet and melting and really unstable."

"What set it off?" Jesse asked and Larry gestured skyward.

"Some hotshot air force jet jockey flying too low and too fast. A National Guard F-4 created a sonic boom right over the valley and that set it off. Buried the lower three or four floors of the hotel. Let me tell you, that took a lot of expensive digging out—which the air force paid for."

Jesse nodded. "Fair enough, I guess," he said. Then he swept his ski pole to point back up the way they had just come.

"Any more like that on the way down?" he asked.

"That's the worst of it," Larry said. His tone was easy and light but he was watching the other man, trying to pierce behind those dark sunglasses and see some kind of reaction. He thought he saw a slight lift in the shoulders, a small sign of relief, maybe.

"Well, let's get going," Jesse said.

TWO

It was one of those clear-skied, freezing cold days on Mount Werner. There was no sign of a cloud and the early morning sun flooded the mountain with its eye-searing glare. It was all light energy, however, with no perceptible heat. The air temperature was five below freezing.

Jesse and Lee came off the Storm Peak chair and swung left, heading away from the unloading area. The snow under their skis was firm and dry here in the groomed area. It squeaked slightly as the crystals rubbed together, crushed under their skis.

Lee stopped a few yards from the unloading area, pushed up her goggles, threw her head back and laughed, shaking her hair out in the cold air. She wasn't wearing a hat. She was used to below-freezing temperatures and loved the burning sensation of the frigid air around her ears and cheeks—a sensation that she knew would intensify to the point of pain when she gathered speed traveling downhill.

Jesse stopped beside her, hunched over, leaning his elbows on his stocks.

"What's the joke?" he asked. She grinned at him. She put him in mind of a teenager, with that familiar look of devilment in her clear gray eyes.

"It's a perfect day," she said happily. "And it's all the better because I'm playing truant and shouldn't be here."

"That's always a big part of it," he agreed.

There had been a fall of fresh powder the night before, at least a foot of new snow over the existing base. And, even though the skies had cleared just after dawn, there wasn't enough heat from the sun yet to settle it down into a thick heavy mass. Once they got off the groomed slopes, she knew the snow would be thick and light— blowing away from her ski tips in vast clouds that would hang in the still air behind her, before gradually drifting back to the ground again.

Jesse had arrived in the ski patrol office around eight a.m. There was a pile of paperwork waiting to be done. These days, he thought gloomily, there always was. Although the way things were, he had plenty of time to attend to it.

The phone on his desk shrilled, breaking him out of this dismal train of thought. The bell was set to an excessively loud ringtone, as members of the patrol were often outside and they needed to be able to hear it over the sound of wind and weather. He made a mental note to turn it down when he was in the office. It was the third time that week he'd made the same mental note.

"Ski patrol, Jesse Parker," he said.

"It's a powder day," a familiar voice told him. "Tell the boss you're calling in sick."

He smiled to himself. Lee had always been able to cheer him up when he was feeling down. He glanced around the utilitarian little office.

"I am the boss," he said. "Seth's away at a safety conference in Vail."

"All the better. Tell yourself and save the company a phone call. Let's go skiing."

He hesitated, glancing outside. The snow did look to be perfect and the weather was clear. But still . . .

"Come on, Jess," she said. "We haven't skied together in forever."

Still he didn't commit himself. "I don't know, Lee. I've got a whole bunch of rosters to work out here. I'm up to my elbows in paperwork."

"Paperwork!" she said scornfully. "It's time to be up to your elbows in fresh powder!"

At the other end of the line, she frowned, sensing his reluctance.

It was true, they hadn't skied together recently. As locals, they didn't feel the need to rush out onto the slopes every possible chance. They tended to wait for perfect conditions. Even so, now that she thought about it, she couldn't remember when they'd last skied together this season, if at all. But today, conditions were as perfect as they got.

"Where are you?" he asked. He was stalling for time. He could hear background noise on the line and he knew she wasn't in her office.

"I'm at the gondola terminal. I can be up there in three minutes. So throw that paper in the trash and come skiing. If the sheriff can take a day off, so can the ski patrol commander—particularly the temporary patrol commander."

Again, there was a brief silence on the line. Then he came to a decision.

"Oh hell, why not?" he said.

"Way to make a girl feel special, Jess," she said, but he could hear the grin in her voice. "I'll meet you at the bottom of Storm Peak Chair."

Then she broke the connection before he could change his mind.

The chairs all started running at eight thirty. Most tourists weren't out that early so they should have a clear mountain. Perfect snow and an uncrowded, untracked mountain. What could be better?

Now, as they paused at the top of Storm Peak, she could see she had been right. There were only a few skiers out on the mountain. Suddenly she was impatient to be moving.

"Let's go," she said, poling and skating to get a little speed up and heading toward the chutes. She'd gone maybe twenty yards or so when she glanced over her shoulder to see if Jesse was following. She frowned and stopped, swinging around as she realized he'd turned left and was heading downhill on Buddy's Run—a broad, easy blue run that had been groomed after the snowfall. He was already fifty yards down the run, carving a series of smooth, perfect S turns in the snow.

"What the hell?" she muttered to herself. She jump-turned and went after him, disdaining to turn, simply throwing in a slight check every so often to control her speed.

There was no wind, but her own speed created one and she felt that freezing rush around her face, felt her hair streaming out behind her like a banner. Her forehead started to ache with the intense cold but she gritted her teeth and ignored it, hunching down in the collar of her ski suit for protection.

She was reeling him in fast now, skiing in a straight line, cutting across the smooth rounded curves that his skis had cut in the snow, traveling maybe half the distance he was and moving a lot faster as well.

He was swinging off to the left, down Calf Roper, to head for Four Points Hut when she caught up with him in a drifting cloud of snow. He looked up, a little surprised at her rapid arrival and violent stop.

"Jess? What the hell are you up to?" she said. They were already too low to access the chutes and as far as she was concerned, that meant a wasted run. They'd have to ride up the chair again. He shrugged, but she noticed that he wouldn't meet her eyes.

"Just getting my legs," he said briefly. He turned away to ski off, but her hand was on his arm and she stopped him.

"Getting your legs? You got your legs twenty years ago! We didn't sneak off to ski the kiddie runs, Jess. Let's do some real skiing here, okay?"

She saw his shoulders straighten a little as she said the words "kiddie runs" and he replied with an obvious undertone of anger in his voice.

"Okay fine. Let's get to the chair."

He tried to shake her hand off his arm but she held tight. A worried frown creased the skin between her eyes and she pushed her yellow-tinted goggles up to see his face more clearly. His own eyes were covered by dark brown Bolle aviator glasses, which made it difficult to read his expression.

"Jess?" she asked tentatively, her own voice softening with concern. "Is the leg giving you trouble?" He didn't answer immediately.

"Maybe a little," he said. She could sense the worry in his voice and she shuffled a little closer to him.

"You know the doc said it's fine. It's completely healed. Maybe the muscle tone isn't back to what it was, but that's just a matter of exercise. There's no physical problem."

He looked at her then and she could see she had stung him. "You're saying it's in my mind?" he challenged and she shrugged awkwardly, wishing she could take her earlier words back. How often do we wish that? she asked herself as she tried to pick her words more carefully.

"Well, maybe that's only to be expected," she said. "But so far as I can see, there's an easy way to get rid of any doubt. Just ski the chutes and prove to yourself that you're okay."

"As easy as that," he said in a flat tone. She shook her head in frustration.

"Yes, as easy as that! Jess, what is the problem? You ski like an angel. You know it. I know it. You've been skiing the chutes since you were nine years old!"

"Maybe I don't feel I'm ready for it yet."

She stepped back, looking at the trees and snow around them as she tried to find the right words. She couldn't believe they were having this conversation. Skiing had been second nature to Jesse virtually from the time he could walk. The chutes were a double black run, certainly. But to a skier of Jesse's standard, they should have held no fear.

"This is crazy! You've skied in those trees hundreds of times! Thousands maybe! I tell you, there is no problem Jess. You're fine. You've just got to get over it and believe it, that's all."

"And what if I try it and I can't handle it, Lee? What then?"

She shook her head, scarcely believing what she was hearing. "That's not going to happen. I know it. Sure you might fall, but you've fallen in there hundreds of times—and only once was it a problem." She tried to lighten her tone. "You know what they say, 'If you ain't fallin', you just ain't tryin'.'"

There was a stubborn set to his jaw. "I'm not ready."

"Jesse, this is crazy. You've got to try."

"I *have* tried, goddamn it! And I can't handle it! I start to panic and I can't control the skis and I lose it."

He could see the concern in her face now but he was mistaking it for pity. Once more, she moved toward him.

"Jess, when? When did this happen?"

"It happens every time I go in there. I get maybe one or two turns, then I panic. I lose control."

"But . . ." she began, and then stopped, not knowing what to say.

"I figure I've got to strengthen the leg so I've got confidence in it. Then I'll try again. When I'm ready."

She knew that if he did this, if he waited and put the moment off, he would never be ready. His leg, broken the season before, had set cleanly and fully. The doctors had told him that—and, as his occasional employer, they had told her as well. There was no structural problem with the leg. The problem was Jesse's confidence. And unless he faced his demons and conquered them, he might never regain that confidence.

"You're ready now," she told him firmly. "Come on. Let's ski to the chair, ride up and head across to Chute 2. I'll be with you. I'll help you." She saw his resistance and insisted, "Jesse, you've got to do this!"

"And what if I can't? What if I don't make it?"

Before she could answer, he continued. "Lee, there are only two things I've been good at in my life. I was a good homicide investigator—but I've lost that now. And I could ski. Ski patrol was my backup. If I can't ski the tough runs anymore, there's no place for me on the patrol. What do I do then?"

She took a deep breath. "Well, if that's how you feel, maybe you have to find out, one way or the other," she said.

"Maybe I don't want to find out! Does that occur to you? If I can't ski anymore, what do I do?"

"You could always work for me," she said but he shook his head dismissively.

"That's a part-time thing and you know it. There isn't enough serious crime here to justify you taking on a full-time investigator. The county would never stand for it."

"I'll sign you on as a normal deputy. I could swing that with the county," she said. "There's no call for you to be a homicide investigator."

"And be another Tom LeGros?" he asked.

She allowed a little heat to enter her voice. "Something wrong with Tom, Jesse? Or maybe it's me? Maybe you couldn't work for me."

"You know that's not it. And Tom's a good guy. It's just, I guess . . . It doesn't seem like enough. I'm not cut out to be a small-town cop like him."

The minute he said the words, he knew they were a mistake. But there was nothing he could do about it. He saw the color flare in Lee's cheeks.

"Or like me? You saying what I do just doesn't stack up against life as a big-time investigator in Denver? We're just *small-town cops* here in Steamboat, is that it?"

"That's not what I meant. I—"

"Well, what did you mean, Jesse? 'Cause that's sure as hell what it sounded like."

He spread his hands awkwardly, looking for the right words, unable to find them. There was a long silence between them. Then Lee shook her head slowly.

"Well fuck you, Jesse."

She swung away violently, pushing off and skiing straight down the fall line. Small puffs of powdered snow rose from her stocks as they bit into the ground, hanging in the air behind her. He watched sadly as she disappeared from sight, rounding a grove of trees at the bottom of the run. Belatedly, he took off after her, but she was heading nonstop for the bottom of the mountain and aside from a few fleeting glances, he didn't see her again.

*   *   *

That night, after she'd cooled down, Lee drove up Rabbit Ear Pass to Jesse's cabin to set things right between them. She knew he hadn't meant to insult her or belittle her job and they meant too much to each other to let this drive a wedge between them.

But the windows of the cabin were dark and the door was locked. There was no smoke rising from the chimney and Jesse's battered old Subaru wagon was missing.

He'd gone. And she had no idea where.

THREE

Jesse stood by the window in his room, the heavy curtains pulled wide open. A three-quarter moon had just soared clear of the mountains that ringed the valley where the hotel nestled.

"Goddamn it," he said softly, and futilely, to the white land spread out before him. He'd known, after ten minutes of the lesson, that the instructor had sensed his fear. It was obvious, all too obvious. And he'd known that the friendly Utahan had been more than willing to help. There had been no sense of condemnation, no hint of derision. But when Jesse had spurned each tentative approach, Larry had finally given up and retreated into a mechanical dissertation on technique that Jesse knew backward and forward.

Hell, he knew it so well and he'd known it so long that he didn't even have to think it anymore. It just happened naturally when he was on skis.

Except when it got steep and deep and narrow. Then he started thinking. But the thoughts were dark and dangerous ones.

The chutes on Mount Werner were where the best skiers in Routt County went to challenge themselves. They were steep, deep and narrow and fringed by trees. The trail maps marked them with a double black diamond—the symbol for the hardest trails of all. And they weren't kidding.

But Jesse had skied the chutes hundreds, maybe thousands of times since he was a kid. In Colorado, kids skied the way kids in other places played baseball—every day. He'd had his share of falls, of course. Nobody who skis ever does it without falling. And the better the skier, the worse the falls can be. He'd broken bones before too. But this had been worse. A whole lot worse.

This had been a greenstick fracture, where the bone, instead of snapping clean, had reacted to the twisting force of the fall and splintered like a green, sap-filled stick.

Jesse lay in the deep snow, waves of agony washing over him like an incoming tide. The sun dropped below the rim of the Yampa Valley to the west and the mountain was in deep shadow. Under the trees, where Jesse lay semiconscious and almost buried in the deep, soft snow, it was almost dark.

In a lucid moment, Jesse realized he was dying. His body had refused to succumb to the inescapable pain of the shattered leg but the cold, the inexorable, subzero cold of the mountain, was gradually winning. He would die here before morning, he realized. Quietly. Unnoticed. Futilely.

He tried to rise and the agony surged again, a savage burst of nausea hitting him in the belly as he felt the entire leg come throbbing to life once more—hurting indescribably badly. Hurting more than anything he could ever have imagined. Hurting so that tears sprang to his tight shut eyes and once again he was a little boy calling for his mom, knowing that only she could ease that pain. He whimpered, not even aware that he was doing so.

"Mom's here, Jesse," a voice said inside his head. But it wasn't his Mom. It was Death speaking, tempting him.

"Just let go and relax, boy," it said, "and I'll make the pain go away." And the temptation to do so was so strong . . . to just relax and escape that awful pain.

It was full dark when Pete Tolliver, a buddy from the ski patrol, found him.

They brought him down the mountain in an aluminium rescue sled, pumped full of painkillers and wrapped head to toe in a space blanket. An ambulance was waiting on the snow-covered base, by the chairlift, to whisk him away to the medical center.

That had been eleven months ago. Today, structurally, Jesse was sound as a bell. Unfortunately, the surgeon who repaired his leg hadn't been able to remove one small remnant of the terrible injury. That was a shattered fragment that lay deep in Jesse's psyche. And it surfaced whenever he faced the sort of steep, forbidding ski run that he once used to take in his stride.

That was why, the day after his argument with Lee, he'd phoned for a reservation here at Snow Eagles, thrown some clothes into a bag, packed his skis and stocks into a canvas carryall and driven to the airport at Halley. He had to know if he could overcome this problem. But he couldn't do that in Steamboat Springs. It was something he had to do on his own, away from Lee and friends he had known all his life. If he couldn't solve this problem, he didn't want to be surrounded by pitying looks and well-meaning attempts to help him face up to the fact.

The trip to Utah, he reflected glumly, had been a failure so far. It had been a waste of money and time. Thinking of the money, Jesse glanced around the expensively furnished hotel room. On a deputy's salary, he couldn't really afford to stay in a place like this too long. It was probably just as well he was checking out the following day.

As he thought about it, he decided he might as well head down to the reception desk and settle his bill now. That way he could save time in the morning. As yet he was undecided as to whether he should give The Wall one last attempt or just get back in his rental car and drive to the airport in Salt Lake City. He'd make up his mind in the morning. For now, he'd fix up his bill and make sure there were no loose ends.

He looked at the moon again, and the way it flooded the snow-covered ground around the hotel with a brilliant light. It was a stunning view but it did nothing for his ill humor.

"Goddamn it," he said bitterly.

FOUR

Tina Bowden counted out the last of the bills onto the marble top of the reception counter.

". . . one-eighty-five, one-ninety, one-ninety-five, two hundred. There you go, sir."

She glanced up quickly, smiling. Too quickly for the middle-aged man on the other side of the counter. His eyes were still fastened on the swell of her breasts against the silk blouse she was wearing. Her smile went down to freezing point. There were times when working the reception desk at the Canyon Lodge was a real pain in the ass. She was glad she didn't have to do it often—only in times like these when the rostered girl was down with the flu and the hotel was a little short-handed.

The customer was gathering his bills together as she whisked the four fifty-dollar traveler's checks into the cash drawer.

"Thanks," he mumbled, knowing he'd been caught. She felt herself wishing that at least he might have had the guts to keep looking after she'd caught him. At least that might have shown some strength of character.

"You're welcome," she replied evenly. But her eyes told him he wasn't. Not now. Not ever. Not in his wildest dreams.

Stuffing the bills in his wallet, he shambled away from the desk. She glanced after him for a second or two: overweight, balding and tending to sweat. And firmly convinced that he was God's gift to womankind. She tried to picture him naked but the result was just too ludicrous, too unpleasant to entertain. She laughed shortly.

"Excuse me, miss . . ."

Now he was different. Tall and rangy looking, with high cheek-bones, a thin face and a prominent, aquiline nose. The eyes were a very dark brown and there was a hint of humor lurking somewhere behind them. Hair just a little bit too long, and just a little untidy. The jaw was strong and clean-shaven. She guessed his age around the late thirties. He was tanned and definitely not overweight. Wide shouldered and slim hipped, he would have been a classic light heavyweight build if he'd been a boxer, she thought, remembering a former boyfriend from her time in the Marines. A physical fitness and unarmed combat instructor, he'd gauged everyone by the weight division they would have fought if they'd been a boxer.

"Yes, Mr. . . . ?" She let the word hang there as a question. The man smiled and she liked him even more. The lines around his eyes and mouth crinkled, seeming to accentuate and point to the deep brown eyes. Tina had always liked brown eyes.

"Parker," he was saying, in reply to her question. He continued. "I'll be checking out in the morning."

"Yes, sir. Most of our guests will be doing the same," she told him and saw one eyebrow raise in a question mark.

"Is that so? Nothing wrong, is there?" She smiled reassuringly. A professional smile that she allowed just a little personal interest to creep into.

"Not at all. It's just the way we operate here. Most of the guests come on a week-long package, Sunday to Saturday. We have Saturday as the checkout day and a new group checks in the following day. That way we reduce the congestion at the desk. It also gives us a good break to clean and service the rooms."

He shi .gged. "Sounds logical," he said.

Her smile widened and he grinned slightly in return, sensing her genuine friendliness.

Having a pretty girl smile at you could go a long way toward chasing away the blues he thought, and took a closer look at the girl behind the desk. Late twenties or early thirties, he guessed, with honey blond hair cut short. He had an almost overwhelming temptation to reach forward and run his fingers through it. Slim, with a good figure, but athletic looking and well muscled, she stood around five seven, he'd guess. Her features and complexion were flawless, which he put down to a life spent in the clear mountain air. The wide-set deep brown eyes reflected the same sense of humor that was present in the curve of her full mouth. He thought briefly of Lee, back in Routt County, and felt a small twinge of guilt.

"Believe me, it is," the girl was saying, following on from his comment. "I've worked other hotels and it saves a lot of friction and delay." She leaned her elbows on the countertop, adding, with a slight roll of her eyes, "Checkout time can be pretty horrendous, you see. And the last thing a newly arrived guest wants is to be kept waiting to register while our counter staff are tied up explaining items on a customer's bill."

"Which he can't remember because he ordered them four days ago and he was drunk at the time?" Jesse suggested and she nodded.

"Exactly. Have you worked in hotels yourself, Mr. Parker?" She doubted it. He definitely had an outdoors look about him. But she was enjoying talking to him and wanted to keep the conversation going.

"It's Jesse," he told her, and that easy grin lit up his features again. She was definitely getting interested here, she realized. "Haven't worked in any," he continued. "I've checked out of one or two and you draw a pretty accurate picture."

He noted her quick, professional glance around the foyer to make sure she wasn't keeping other customers waiting while she chatted to him. He liked her for that. Matter of fact, he liked her for a lot more than that and he felt a sudden twinge of regret that he had come down here to check out. It would have been pleasant to have made the acquaintance of the delightful Miss Bowden (he could read her name tag) earlier in the week. Lee's face came to mind again and he pushed it away. No harm just thinking, he told her mentally. She frowned at him and he knew she didn't agree.

He realized he'd been standing there silently for slightly longer than might seem normal. The girl was looking at him curiously, not sure if the conversation was over.

He didn't want it to be. "So, is everybody moving out tomorrow? Surely you must have some guests who want to stay longer than a week?"

"Some. Not many. A week is pretty well the standard ski vacation in these parts." She tapped a few keys on the computer and studied the screen.

"Let's see . . . There's a group from Vermont who got a special deal to stay on till Wednesday; then there are the people who took the two-week package." She looked up quickly in explanation, "Not too many of them this late in the season."

She punched another key and the display changed. "That's about it: maybe fifteen people—a tour group from France, a few singles, oh, and the Senator's Ski Buddies, of course."

Jesse frowned in mild disbelief. "The Senator's Ski Buddies?"

She laughed. "We cater to a lot of groups and conferences here. They often give themselves names. The Skiing Medics was one. The Ski Till You Die Conference was another." She wrinkled her nose in distaste. "Turned out they were a bunch of morticians."

"So who are these senators who like to ski?" Jesse asked.

"Just one senator. Senator Carling, from Washington State. He comes every year, brings a group of businessmen and company presidents—very high-level stuff." She glanced over his shoulder to the gift shop across the lobby, lowering her voice.

"There's one of them now—Mr. Rockley."

Jesse swiveled to look at the man, browsing among the greeting card stands in the gift shop. Sensing their attention, he looked up and smiled politely. It seemed he was accustomed to drawing curious glances from strangers.

"Is he important?" he asked.

"He's rich," she replied. "Mega-rich. So I guess that makes him important. He's Calvin Rockley, president of Rockair Aviation— they make planes."

He glanced again at the tall man. "Yeah," he replied, "I've heard of them."

"So Mr. Parker, you wanted to ask about checking out tomorrow?" she prompted and he nodded as he remembered his original reasons for coming to the lobby.

"Oh, yeah. I thought maybe I'd settle my account now and avoid the rush in the morning."

"Good idea," she said, her eyes down as she punched the keys again and checked the screen. The printer below the desk smoothly ejected a page printed with Jesse's details. She tore it free and handed it to him. He glanced over it quickly. There were few extras on the list. He preferred to pay in cash as he went.

"All okay?" she asked, and he nodded.

"No problems."

She took the Mastercard he handed her, swiped it and typed in the final figures from his bill. She glanced up and smiled as the terminal whirred softly, then approved the transaction and rolled out a payment slip, passing it to him along with a Snow Eagles pen.

"Thanks," he said, and scrawled a signature.

"My pleasure," she replied automatically. She passed him his receipt. Paper flying in all directions, he thought, folding it and putting it in his shirt pocket.

"There's an early shuttle down to Salt Lake City at eight thirty," she told him. "Or we can organize a cab for you if you'd prefer?"

"I've got my own car," he replied. "I'll load it and maybe take a few last ski runs before I get away." Now he said it, he thought that he would definitely take on The Wall again in the morning—and keep doing so until he beat it.

She frowned slightly as she saw something in his eyes—something that had taken him away from their conversation and the here and now.

"Fine then." She punched the computer keys again. "There you go. As of now, you are officially a ghost. You no longer exist on the computer. I'll keep your room keycard activated. Tell them to cancel it when you leave."

"I'll do that. And thanks for your help."

"No problem. I hope you've enjoyed your stay here at the Canyon . . . Jesse."

He flashed that grin at her again, registering the use of his first name. "Why, thank you, Miss Bowden," he said and she grinned back at him as he turned and walked to the lift.

She was still watching him, wishing that she'd noticed him earlier in the week, when Calvin Rockley interrupted her thoughts.

"Pardon me, miss. Can I pay for these here?"

The president of Rockair Aviation laid a spread of postcards on the countertop. Almost apologetically, he gestured toward the gift shop across the lobby.

"There's no one on duty in the gift shop," he explained. Tina smiled at him—a professional smile. No more. No less.

"Surely, Mr. Rockley. Now, how many do you have there?" She fanned out the half-dozen postcards, scanned the bar codes and totaled the bill.

"That's six eighty-five with tax, Mr. Rockley. Do you want me to put it on your room?"

"No. I'll pay now," he said and handed her a ten. She made change, put the postcards in a paper bag for him and handed the change and the cards to him. He nodded his thanks and turned away, heading for the escalator. He'd gone six paces when she noticed the Mastercard on the countertop. At first, she thought it might have fallen out of his wallet and she took a breath, about to call him back. Then she saw the name on the card—J. Parker. She reached for the phone, then hesitated. She was off-duty in ten minutes. It might be the friendly thing to deliver the card in person. She smiled slowly, tapping the card on her palm. From what she had seen so far, she liked the idea of getting friendly with Mr. Jesse Parker.

FIVE

Jesse was in his room, staring morosely at the TV, where a rerun of *Seinfeld* was playing. He should eat, he thought. But the idea of heading down to the dining room and sitting alone at a table, surrounded by diners talking and laughing, didn't hold a lot of appeal. He picked up the room service menu and scanned it. Room service menus seemed to be the same in every hotel he'd ever stayed in. The meals available were always essentially the same, with a few geographical variations. The descriptions were flamboyant and effusive but they invariably left out a few important facts. The meal would take an excessively long time to come and when it did, the food would be lukewarm at best.

Maybe a burger, he thought. Even a room service kitchen couldn't get a burger too wrong. So long as you liked lukewarm burgers and rapidly cooling fries.

There was a light tap at the door and he frowned. Housekeeping had visited the room hours ago to deliver new towels and give the room a quick going over.

He killed the TV, tossed the remote on the bed and moved toward the door, then hesitated. Long established habit made him wary. He'd been a cop for years and that meant there were a good many people out there who didn't have cause to love him. And as the years passed, more and more of them were being released from the penitentiary. He glanced at the backpack beside the bed. His .45 ACP was in there. He never traveled anywhere without it. For a second, he thought of retrieving it and then he grinned to himself. Caution was all very well, but that was a little excessive. Odds were, it was some middle-aged woman from housekeeping who had forgotten to replace the mini shampoo bottle in the bathroom. If he opened the door with a .45 in his hand, she might well go into shock.

The light tap on the door was repeated and he realized he'd been standing here looking at it for some time. He moved to it, lay his hand on the lever and said:

"Who is it?"

"Tina Bowden. From the desk." He recognized her voice. Not a middle-aged woman from housekeeping after all, he thought. The young and very attractive woman from reception. He smiled to himself. He couldn't recall ever sending anyone who looked like Miss Bowden to the Big House. And he was sure that if he had done so, he would remember. Definitely.

"Just a moment," he called, and opened the door.

She smiled at him as the door opened to reveal her. She'd changed from the rather severe trousers and blazer of her uniform. Now she was wearing a short denim skirt that revealed her very good legs and a sleeveless white top whose V neckline did a similar job for her breasts.

All in all, he thought, Tina Bowden looked a damn sight more appetizing than any room service meal he'd ever seen. He smiled back at her, not sure why she was here.

"Did I forget my receipt?" he asked and she shook her head.

"No. But you did leave this behind." She held out his Mastercard and his hand went to his back pocket in a reflex action as he reached for his wallet. Then he realized that there was no need to check. The card was there in front of him, after all.

"Oh," he said, reaching out and taking it. He checked it quickly, making sure that it was his card. "Thanks. There was no need to bring it up personally. You could have phoned."

She shrugged. "All part of the service. I do a delivery run most nights," she told him and he examined her a little more carefully, taking in the impossibly high heels on the slingback shoes she was now wearing. Earlier, in uniform, she would have been wearing low shoes. She seemed a little taller, and the high heels accentuated the excellent muscle tone and shape of her calves.

"Do you always dress up to do it?" he asked. "Or are you heading somewhere special?"

Her smile widened. She was pleased that he'd noticed she'd changed. She did a small pirouette for him.

"You like?" she asked, and he nodded his head slowly.

"Very much," he told her. "Beats the hell out of a FedEx uniform."

She seemed in no hurry to leave so he opened the door a little wider.

"Would you like to come in?"

She inclined her head to one side, studying him for a few seconds, then replied, "Yes. I think I would."

He stepped aside and gestured to one of the chairs at a small circular table by the window. She sat gracefully, crossing her legs. They were very good legs, he thought once more—and they got better the more he looked at them. He wondered where this was heading.

"Drink?" he asked. He nodded toward the side table. "All I've got is Jim Beam."

"That'll be fine. With ice, please," she said. He fixed the drinks and brought them to the table, sitting opposite her. They touched glasses and drank. She leaned forward slightly and he felt a stirring sensation as the movement revealed a little more of her cleavage. Good legs. Good breasts. Pretty. And friendly. What more could a man ask for?

"I was wondering," she said, and he hastily raised his eyes to meet hers. She smiled again, letting him know that she knew what he'd been looking at and it was fine by her. "Did you have any plans for dinner?"

He grinned and indicated the room service menu where he'd tossed it on the bureau.

"I was thinking of a burger," he said.

She frowned in disapproval. "Not the thing to have on your last night in Snow Eagles," she replied. "I'm afraid I can't allow that."

"Well, it's just I don't like eating alone in restaurants," he told her. She tossed off the rest of her drink and stood.

"Problem solved. I'm buying you dinner. Or rather, the hotel is."

He raised an eyebrow at that. "Do the desk clerks here get an entertainment allowance?" She put one elegant finger up to her lips and pretended to look around for eavesdroppers.

"Big secret," she said. "I'm not usually on the desk. I'm the Security Officer here. And since you're a cop . . ."

"I am?" he interrupted and she nodded.

"That's what it said on your booking sheet. You're with the Routt County sheriff's office, right?" He nodded and she went on. "Right. So we can say we were discussing policing and security matters over dinner. That means we both get a decent meal and the hotel pays. I don't know how that strikes you, but it sounds kind of win–win to me."

He smiled. "And will we be discussing policing and security matters?"

"Maybe we'll give it five or ten seconds," she told him, her face mock serious. "So, are you ready?"

The dinner was excellent and Tina was a good companion. It was strange, he thought, but because she was a relative stranger, and a sympathetic listener, he found it was easy to unburden himself a little to her, about why he had come to Snow Eagles, about the accident and about the lingering doubts in his mind.

She listened quietly as he spoke and when he paused, she set down her wineglass and leaned toward him.

"It's logical that your mind would do this," she said. "You just have to build up to it. Don't try to do it all in one hit. Work up to it with ski runs that get progressively harder until you stop thinking about what might happen and begin to do it instinctively again."

He regarded her curiously for a moment. "You sound like you know something about this sort of thing," he said. She nodded.

"Before I did this, I was in the Marines. I joined as an athlete, playing softball. I was pretty close to Olympic selection one year when I fell running between bases and tore up my elbow really badly—tendons, ligaments, the lot. Ruined my pitching.

"Once the medics had patched it up, it took me months to get up the nerve to pitch full out again. At the last minute, I'd back off, afraid I'd throw the whole thing out again."

"So how did you solve it?"

"I built up to it. I'd pitch at three-quarter pace until it had become instinctive again. Then I'd up the pace a little. Then more. Nothing too soon and nothing too sudden—just a gradual increase every few days or so. That's what you should try."

He nodded. It made sense. Up till now he'd been going at it, balls to the wall, trying to regain his former skill and confidence all at once. Maybe he should build up to it after all. Then he made a gesture dismissing his problems.

"Enough about me," he said. "Tell me about you."

She pursed her lips, wondering where to start. "Grew up in Wyoming. Not on a ranch or anything fancy like that. Just in a small town. As I got older, it all seemed pretty dull. The Marine Corps looked like a good way out of it all so I joined up and worked my way into the Corps softball team. Did a hitch in Iraq, with the MPs, then got out of the Corps, planning to get married to my old teenage sweetheart."

"And did you?" he asked. His gaze dropped to her left hand, seeing no ring there. She shook her head.

"Seems he'd linked up with my best friend while I was away in the Marines. So I drifted a while, then got the job here in Security. I like skiing. I like my boss. And the hotel chain seems happy to move me around the network if I want to go. They've got hotels in the Caribbean as well as the northwest. Seems like a good deal."

He nodded agreement and they discussed the relative merits of skiing and scuba diving and the advantages of working in the tourism industry. She was a bright and likeable companion, easy to talk to and, as he had already noted, very attractive. He found it easy to relax in her company and he was a little saddened when the meal was over. They lingered over their coffees as long as they could but by then the restaurant staff were making it obvious that they were keen to close up for the night. Subtle hints, like clearing the surrounding tables, leaving the bill on their table before they asked for it.

Finally, she took the hint. "I think we'd better go," she said. In spite of his protests, she took the bill and signed it. Then she waited while he drew her chair back for her to stand.

"Nice to have a man do that for me for a change," she said.

She walked back to his room with him. As he searched in his pockets for his keycard, she produced her own and swiped it in the lock.

"Allow me," she said, as the lock buzzed quietly and the green light showed. Jesse opened the door, looking at her keycard.

"That's a handy thing to have," he said. She grinned at him.

"Opens any room in the hotel. Sometimes there are perks to being in Security."

There was a long, awkward pause as they both wondered if he were going to invite her in. He thought about it, but he didn't trust himself. They'd shared a bottle of wine and two cognacs after the meal and he wasn't sure he could keep his hands off her. He wasn't sure if he wanted to.

And he wasn't sure if she wanted him to either.

The question was never asked or answered. She moved against him, her arms going up around his neck and pulling his face gently down to hers. She kissed him and he felt her tongue working against his lips. He opened them and let her explore the inside of his mouth.

Finally, they separated. He felt a little light-headed.

"Good night, Jesse," she said and he nodded several times.

"Yeah. Good night. It was . . . nice. More than nice. Thanks for listening to me."

She shrugged. "Listening is easy. Particularly with a nice guy like you."

"Yeah. Well, good night, Tina."

"Good night, Jesse."

She turned away and he stepped into his room, closing the door behind him and moving thoughtfully to the window. He could still feel the softness of her lips on his, the quick, darting urgency of her tongue.

"Jesse," he asked himself, a few moments later, "why the hell didn't you ask her in?"

"I was wondering the same thing myself," she said from behind him. He spun around. She was leaning against the door, the security keycard in her hand. The V-necked top was unbuttoned and she dropped it to the floor, revealing the white lace of her bra and the rounded tops of her breasts. A push-up bra he noticed, but as she shrugged out of it, he could see that the breasts didn't need too much help in the push-up department. He felt himself hardening as she unzipped the skirt and let it slide to the floor after her top. She stood before him, wearing only a lacy pair of bikini panties. He was glad she didn't wear a thong. Thongs did nothing for him. The sight of her body definitely did plenty for him.

"Tina," he began, but she moved toward him and put a finger on his lips to stop him.

"Jesse," she said, "I like you. And I think you like me. Now, I don't plan on following you back to Steamboat, and I guess you're not planning to come back to Utah looking for me, right?"

He grinned at her succinct appraisal of the situation and nodded.

"I guess that's pretty much right."

"Now," she continued, taking his hand and placing it on her breast. He felt the nipple stir and harden and her breath came a little faster. Her other hand was working at the buckle of his belt, then at his jeans. "I've got to tell you that the majority of men I meet these days are either gay or married. I'm guessing you're not gay," she said and her hand stroked the hardness inside his jeans. "So are you married?"

"No," he said immediately. Then, feeling he should, he added, "There is someone in Steamboat who—"

But again, her finger went to his lips, silencing him.

"I don't need to know that. You answered the important question. You're not married. Far as I'm concerned she's crazy to let you run loose. But I figure that's my good luck."

She'd worked his jeans down now and was unbuttoning his shirt. He helped her, then hooked a thumb inside the waistband of her panties, sliding them down over her smooth thighs. He placed both hands on her rounded, smooth buttocks and drew her against him, feeling his erection searching for her. His shirt was gone and her hand was on him, teasing him gently, urging and guiding him.

He picked her up then, hands still cupping her buttocks and her legs wrapped around him as he took the two short steps to the bed. They half fell onto it and his mouth found her breast, rolling the hard nipple around his tongue. Just before he entered her, she chuckled, close to his ear.

"Damn glad I had that keycard."

When he awoke, a little before dawn, she had gone. The place beside him in the bed still retained a little of her warmth so he knew she had left only recently. He smiled at the memory of the night. He felt a slight twinge of guilt, then pushed it aside. He didn't love her. He knew that. And she didn't love him. It wasn't about love or a lasting commitment. But he liked her. And he liked her too much to go feeling guilty about what they had done. Somehow, that would cheapen it, he felt. And that would be unfair to her.

He sat up on the bed, swinging his legs over the side to the floor. There was a note on the side table, torn from one of the pads left in the room. She'd drawn a rough version of the Marine Corps anchor and globe badge. Under it, she'd written:

"Semper fi. Tina."

He smiled to himself. That was one way of putting it, he thought.

SIX

The leading minivan in the three-vehicle caravan dropped back to low gear for the final climb into Snow Eagles Canyon. Kormann, seated beside the driver, checked his watch.

Three-fifteen in the afternoon. Maybe a few minutes ahead of schedule. He hunkered down to check the other two minivans in the outside mirror, considered slowing down for a few minutes, then, even as the thought entered his mind, abandoned it.

Ahead of him, moving down the winding road that led from the higher reaches, he'd caught sight of another group of vehicles. A few minutes later they passed, their occupants glancing incuriously at the three minivans grinding their way uphill. Kormann nodded to himself. Perfect. There had been no reason why the resort should change its normal pattern of operations this weekend. But there was always the possibility that they might. An accident, a blackout, anything could have delayed the departure of the contract cleaning staff.

Even, he thought, with an almost imperceptible twist of his lips, an avalanche.

His driver had slowed fractionally as they'd inched their way past the oncoming traffic on the narrow mountain road. Now the exhaust note picked up again and the eight-seater moved forward a little faster. He craned his neck to look up at the snow-laden mountains towering above them on either side of the road. He nodded in silent satisfaction as he saw the extent of the snow. Plenty there. Plenty of fine powder snow for skiing.

Or for other purposes.

And late in the season as it was, the snow was becoming more and more unstable every day as the warmer weather raised the water content and the fine powder settled upon itself. Just the way he wanted it.

In the main, Kormann was an unremarkable looking man. Around thirty-five or -six, he stood five feet eleven and had a slim build. His features were regular, average, you might say. Neither excessively handsome nor excessively unpleasant. The mouth and nose were normally sized and shaped—plastic surgery had seen to that some years back. In Kormann's line of business, it didn't pay to have features that were too easily remembered or described. His hair was medium length, parted on the side and black, with a hint of gray beginning at the temples.

The one feature that did stand out was his eyes. They were a brilliant blue and plastic surgery could do nothing to disguise them. Tinted contact lenses might have, but much to Kormann's annoyance, he was unable to wear contacts. His eyes were particularly sensitive and anything more than ten minutes with contacts in would see them red and streaming. So his eyes remained the single, memorable feature of the man. At least in snow country such as this he could conceal them behind dark glasses.

The bus finally crested the rise and the huge gray bulk of the Canyon Lodge loomed before them. Kormann gestured quickly to the entrance of the underground drive-in and his driver swung the Dodge into the tunnel. A quick glance behind confirmed that the other two buses had followed suit. A moment later, he heard their engines echoing in the confined space of the tunnel. There was room for the three buses by the automatic doors leading to the hotel interior. He pointed: "There." The driver nodded and pulled past the spot, reversing neatly back into it. Kormann had the door open and swung down, breathing the strange mixture of exhaust fumes and crisp mountain air that pervaded the tunnel. As he walked quickly to the doors, the other buses parked in their turn. Doors slid open and men began climbing down, stretching their legs after the seventy-minute drive up from Salt Lake City.

Three sets of double rear doors slammed open and the drivers and their passengers began unloading bags.

Kormann hurried through into the hotel proper. He twitched his uniform blazer straight and took the escalator to the reception level, one floor up. As he'd expected, the lobby was deserted, with only one staff member—a girl in her early twenties—manning the reception desk. This was something else he'd relied upon. With the previous week's guests gone, and the new ones not due to arrive until the following morning, Canyon Lodge usually operated on a skeleton staff on Saturday evening.

The young girl looked up, a little surprised, as Kormann appeared in the lobby. Then, recognizing the familiar uniform of the Canyon Transportation Service, she smiled at him. Kormann smiled in return.

"Hi. Roger Kormann, Canyon Transport," he said by way of introduction. "Everything okay here?"

The girl allowed herself a slight frown. "Yeah. Sure. Any reason why it shouldn't be?"

"No, none at all," Kormann told her, then, gesturing toward the escalators, "I've got the group downstairs unloading, so I'll just bring 'em up for registration, okay?"

He started to turn away but she stopped him. "Group? What group?" There was a worried tone in her voice. This was something she hadn't been told about. It had the uncomfortable feeling of a foul-up and, in her experience, foul-ups in the bookings had a habit of being blamed on junior desk staff. Like her.

Kormann stopped and was walking back toward the desk. He spoke deliberately, as if not wishing to confuse things further. As if making everything perfectly clear and understood.

"The special tour group. We got permission to bring 'em in a day early because of the heating problem."

"Heating problem?" she repeated, her eyes wandering involuntarily to one of the duct grills set in the ceiling. She hadn't heard of any problem with the thermostat. She hadn't noticed any change in the temperature in the lobby, either. There seemed to be nothing wrong with the heating system as far as she could tell.

"Yeah. Look—," he paused, his eyes searching for her name tag.

"Jenny," she supplied nervously, "Jenny Callister."

"Fine," he said, comfortable now that they were on first name terms. "Now look, Jenny, Ray Archer rang earlier to let you people know. We had this group booked into the Meriton Hotel in Salt Lake City but their heating system had some kind of a meltdown. They've got real problems down there with three-quarters of their rooms having no heat of any kind, so Ray organized for this group to check in here tonight. Weren't you told?"

His easy manner suggested that he knew it wasn't her fault. It was simply a breakdown in communications within the hotel. Jenny wasn't so sure. She shook her head.

"It's the first I've heard of it," she said defensively. Her hand hovered over the phone on her desk. "Maybe I'd better call Ray myself."

Kormann shrugged. "Sure. Go ahead." He shook a cigarette from a pack and lit it, unconcernedly, while she hit the buttons on the phone. Ray Archer was the Day Manager of the transport company. If the call went through to him, it would be the first he'd heard of this arrangement too.

Jenny Callister looked at the phone receiver in exasperation.

"The line's dead," she said. He raised an eyebrow in polite surprise. It wasn't unheard of for the phone line to go down in Snow Eagles Canyon. Usually it was a case of a small, localized avalanche bringing down one of the power poles that carried the line.

"Yeah?" he said. "Well, I guess it won't be down for long."

In fact, it would be down for another forty-five minutes. Then the linesmen who had cut the line a few miles from the hotel would reconnect a bypass line some eight miles down the road before driving back to Salt Lake City and a payment of ten thousand dollars in their bank accounts. He reached into his jacket pocket and produced a slim Nokia cell phone, offering it to her.

"Here. Try this," he said but the girl shook her head, the exasperation mounting.

"They're no use in here. The hotel's in a dead spot."

He'd known that too. But for her benefit, he feigned ignorance and replaced the phone in his pocket. "Look," he continued in a helpful tone of voice, "just check your computer there. You'll see this group is booked in: name of Pallisani. Eleven double rooms."

Quickly, she punched the computer keys. An abbreviated guest list flashed up on the screen before her and she sucked in her lower lip nervously. She really didn't like the way things were going here. There was no sign of any Pallisani group. She punched up the bookings for the next day.

"They're here," she said. "But not till tomorrow."

The Canyon Transportation representative looked at her, throwing his hands out and letting them fall to his sides, with a slight show of exasperation. "That's right. I told you that. They were supposed to be in Salt Lake City tonight but there was a problem. Your list for tonight should have been altered."

"Well, it hasn't," she said, beginning to dig her heels in. Kormann leaned over the desktop and swiveled the computer screen slightly so that he could read it.

"Look, help me out here, Jenny," he said placatingly. "This guy Pallisani has been on my butt all day about the heat at the Meriton. You'd think the whole damn thing was my fault. Could you check it one more time?"

She shrugged. "Well, okay. But it's not going to have changed." She punched the keys again and the display flickered and changed, showing the current guest list. Kormann checked it, hiding the edge of tension he felt. His eye ran down the short list and stopped as he reached the entry "Senator's Ski Buddies." Inwardly, he felt a little surge of relief. He hid the emotion, feigning exasperation instead.

"They're not here," he said and she gave him an "I told you so" look.

"That's all we've got staying here tonight," she told him.

"Now, Roger, is there some kind of problem here?"

It was another voice from behind Kormann. Loud and abrasive. Even Jenny's limited experience in the hotel business told her that this was a voice that didn't like having its plans changed. She looked to the top of the escalators and took in the expensive down parka, casually unzipped, the dark good looks, the iron gray hair, cut en brosse, and the alligator hide overnight bag slung from his left shoulder. Everything about the man simply shrieked money. And it shrieked it in a decidedly bad-tempered way. Another half-dozen or so men, dressed in parkas and casual pants, all carrying shoulder bags, were milling around at the top of the escalator.

"No problem at all, Mr. Pallisani," said Kormann, moving to intercept the newcomer as he made his way toward the desk. Jenny detected a note of nervousness in his voice and her heart sank. This was trouble. A rich client, with a large group of customers and a bad temper, and no record on the computer that she should check them in.

Only too clearly, she could see the problems that would arise.

Check in twenty-two extra guests and that would mean someone was going to have to pay for twenty-two extra room nights. And twenty-two extra included breakfasts. And twenty-two extra God only knew what.

Come the end of the week, it wouldn't be the customers who'd pay. They'd claim their accommodation had been prepaid and at one hundred and fifty bucks a night there'd be a bill for over three thousand dollars floating around with no one willing to pay it. And then all hell would break loose.

Jenny shook her head, coming to a decision. She wasn't going to book these people in on her own authority.

"I'm sorry," she told Pallisani, "but I've explained to Mr. . . . er . . ." She couldn't remember his surname so she slurred over it, "that there's no record of your booking on the computer."

The gray-haired man regarded her as if she were some kind of particularly offensive insect. Then, refusing to talk to her, he swung on Kormann, his dark eyebrows knitting together in an angry line.

"Am I hearing this right? They've got a goddamned empty hotel here," he swept his arm around, encompassing the deserted lobby, "and this . . . person . . . is refusing to check us in?"

"Mr. Pallisani," Kormann began in a placating sort of voice. "I'm sure she doesn't—"

"Because a fucking computer is telling her not to?"

Jenny winced slightly at the obscenity. Not that she hadn't heard it before. Or used it herself for that matter. It was more the vehemence with which the word was uttered.

"Sir, I'm afraid I don't have the authority to do this. I'm going to have to call the manager here to—"

"Fucking-A you are, honey!" the angry man spat at her. "And you can tell the stupid son of a bitch to get here right fucking now!"

Again, Jenny flinched at the language. There was something doubly offensive about it, coming as it did from a well dressed, successful looking businessman like this. Kormann watched the interplay between the two with a quiet sense of satisfaction. The overall confusion, coupled with the embarrassment caused by Pallisani's intentional coarseness, were serving to keep the girl off balance. She reached for one of the internal phones, then hesitated.

"Maybe you and your group would like to wait in the coffee lounge downstairs, Mr. Pallisani?" she suggested. The idea was greeted with an angry negative gesture.

"No. I'm waiting right here till I meet the bozo who's fucked up. Then I'm going to nail his ass to the wall out there. Now I am tired. I want a shower. I want to change. I've been fucked around from here to Salt Lake City and I'm not being bought off with a fucking cup of coffee. Capisce?"

His voice was rising with each word and Jenny looked helplessly to Kormann for assistance.

"Maybe we could wait in the office?" he suggested. Pallisani grunted a surly assent and she nodded gratefully. She'd do anything to get this loud-mouthed, angry customer out of sight. Hurriedly, she raised the lift-up section in the counter and ushered them through to the office behind the reception desk. Pallisani, only a little mollified, paced angrily as she dialed the duty manager's number. The receiver burred softly against her ear. Once. Twice. Oh, please God, she thought, let there be someone there. Then, to her infinite relief, she heard the receiver lifted at the other end.

"Markus. Can I help you?"

The words spilled out of her, almost running over each other in her relief.

"Oh, Mr. Markus, it's Jenny Callister here at the front desk. Well, we've got a problem, sir, and I wondered could you come here right away?"

*   *   *

Four minutes passed in awkward silence. Then the rear door to the office opened and Ben Markus entered.

He was a good-looking young man in his early thirties, with a square face and a strong jaw, and a slightly crooked nose that was the result of a football injury in high school. The gray eyes were behind rimless glasses and they were an inch or two higher than Kormann's, putting him at just over six feet. He was a capable, unflappable professional.

"Gentlemen, I'm Ben Markus, the duty manager. Now what seems to be the problem?"

Kormann and Pallisani exchanged glances. To Jenny Callister's surprise, the two men began to smile, all trace of their previous ill humor seemed to have evaporated.

Pallisani stepped a little closer to the manager, then placed the barrel of a Browning Hi-Power 9 millimeter against his forehead.

"The problem is this, Ben. If you don't do *exactly* as we tell you, we're going to kill you."

SEVEN

Markus froze, unmoving, feeling the cold rim of the barrel gradually warmed by its contact with his flesh. Beside him, he heard Jenny Callister choke back a scream—only a small mewing sound escaped her.

For Markus, everything was a blur, except for the blue-black pistol pressed against his forehead. Try as he might, he could focus on nothing else in the room. He heard Kormann's voice as if it came from a long, long distance.

"Now, Jenny, tell me this: what's the alarm signal for staff in this hotel?"

Jenny shook her head. Her eyes, like Markus's, riveted to the gun against his head. "Signal" she said weakly, "I don't understand."

Kormann stepped toward her and took hold of her chin between thumb and forefinger. Gently, he turned her face to his.

"Yes, you do," he told her patiently. "Now, you know and we know that every hotel has a signal that's used to alert staff to an emergency without alerting the customers. Remember? They taught it to you on your first week here?"

She nodded, remembering.

"Don't tell them," Markus managed to croak through his panic-dried throat.

He felt the pistol withdraw momentarily, then jab forward viciously almost immediately, slamming into his forehead with bruising force. His eyes closed involuntarily as he waited for the thunder of the detonation, the rush of darkness, then nothing. But it didn't come.

The pain of the pistol pressed to his head remained. The sick heaving of his stomach was still there. The gun hadn't been fired, he realized with an immense surge of relief.

"You keep your mouth shut," Pallisani said, very quietly. He jabbed once more, unnecessarily, and Markus flinched again. His stomach roiled and he thought he was going to be violently sick. With an effort, he controlled himself. Kormann was speaking again.

"Now, Jenny, the signal please."

Again, she tried to look to Markus. As before, Kormann's powerful grip wouldn't let her.

"Please," she said. "Please take that thing away from him."

Kormann looked at Pallisani and nodded. Markus took a deep breath of relief as he felt the gun removed from his forehead. Then Pallisani swung the pistol in a short, chopping arc, hitting him just above the left eyebrow. Markus staggered, feeling a sudden rush of hot blood down his face, blinding him momentarily as it ran into his eye. He caught the edge of the desk with his hand and saved himself from falling. Jenny watched, horrified, as he tried to stem the flow of blood.

Pallisani now swung the gun backhanded and caught the manager high on the right cheekbone. More blood. Jenny whimpered as Markus staggered again. The brutality of the pistol-whipping was so casual, so cold-blooded. It almost seemed to be without malice, which made it all the more horrifying.

"Please!" she begged. "Don't hit him again! It's two short and one long."

Markus, dazed by the two sudden blows to the head, made no effort to stop her.

Kormann nodded, satisfied. "Two short and one long what?" he asked. The girl continued to talk, her words tumbling over one another again.

"Two short and one long ring on the fire alarm bells." She gestured uncertainly to a large red button on the wall behind the desk. "We ring it from there. Then we repeat it again after fifteen seconds so everyone will know it's not a drill or a false alarm."

"And where's the assembly point?" Kormann asked.

Now that Jenny had begun to speak, the words seemed almost

anxious to spill out of her. "The lobby, in front of the reception desk."

"Okay. Now, Ben, how are you feeling there?" Before Markus could answer, Kormann continued. "Roughly how many staff have you got on site at the moment?"

Markus' shoulders sagged. There seemed no point in holding out the information.

"Sixty-odd," he muttered.

Kormann's eyebrows rose. "That's all?" he asked.

"That's all," Markus replied, adding, "The others will come in tomorrow from Salt Lake City, before the new guests arrive."

Kormann smiled, without humor. "Not tomorrow, they won't," he said. Then he continued, in a brisker tone. "Okay, Ben, let's ring those bells. Then clean yourself up a little and we'll go out to greet the folks."

EIGHT

On the fifth floor, Maria Velasquez groaned softly as she leaned over the bath in room 546, spraying a generous mist of bathroom cleanser onto the far side. Her back ached and she hated bending and leaning to do this job. She began wiping the enamel with a square of toweling in quick, painful strokes.

In the corridor outside, the fire alarm bells shrilled suddenly. She stopped, feeling a momentary lurch in her heart. Two short, one long. The staff alarm. If it were a test, there would be one long peal of the bells in fifteen seconds. She waited, then heard the alert repeated. This was for real, she thought. She wondered what the danger might be. Her heart began to race as she thought of the possibility of the mountain coming down. That was the thing the old hands always talked about, remembering the time when the hotel had been buried up to the fifth floor. Heart pounding, she gathered her cleaning equipment into a basket and headed for the stairs.

George Kirby was opening a gallon can of tomatoes in the kitchen below the hotel's Mexican theme restaurant.

"Try not to spill them this time," the sous chef said with withering scorn. George, facing away from the sarcastic son of a bitch, mouthed a silent obscenity. The sous chef loved to throw his weight around on a Saturday evening. It was the one night of the week when he was left in total charge of the kitchen.

"And another thing—" he began, then both men froze as the bells rang through the tiled kitchen, reflecting and echoing off the hard surfaces of tile and stainless steel. They both looked at each other.

"A test?" said George uncertainly. Then, as the sound repeated, they both dropped what they were doing and headed for the door. The can of tomatoes teetered for a moment on the edge of the kitchen bench. Then it toppled and fell. Red tomato juice leaked from the half-slit rim, spreading in an ever-widening pool across the floor.

Henry Bolkowski was deep in the bowels of the massive building, inspecting the oil-fired boiler that provided heat for the heating system, when he heard the alarm bells. Henry was sixty-three years old and he'd heard those bells once before. He was one of those people who actually remembered the event Maria Velasquez feared. He'd heard the crash and rumble of the avalanche, felt the entire building, massive as it was, tremble as the thousands of tons of snow and rock slammed into it.

He limped quickly for the service elevator. If it was happening again, he didn't want to be down here.

And so it went all over the hotel. Staff going about their routine duties stopped in mid-task, hesitated, refusing to believe the evidence of their ears the first time. Then, having their fears confirmed, they headed for hallways, staircases and elevators to make their way to the reception lobby.

NINE

CANYON LODGE
WASATCH COUNTY

There were already between twenty and thirty people assembled in the lobby when Markus and Kormann emerged from the office.

An urgent buzz of conversation filled the large room as more and more staff members streamed in. Unlike Henry Bolkowski, the majority had never heard the alarm bells rung in earnest. Now, as they gathered, they wondered to each other what the problem might be. A young room-service waiter, standing close to the reception desk, caught sight of Markus as he emerged from the office with Kormann close beside him. The younger man noticed the adhesive bandage on Markus's eye and the dark bruise on his cheek and wondered if they had anything to do with the current emergency. The manager definitely looked a little rattled, he thought.

"Say, Mr. Markus," he called. "What's going on?"

Instantly, another half-dozen employees echoed his question. A chorus of voices rose and the gathering crowd began to press closer around the reception desk. Markus looked uncertainly at Kormann. The other man stepped forward and held up both hands for silence. Gradually, most of the questioning voices dropped away as people pressed in closer to hear what he was going to say.

"Please, people, please be patient until everybody's here."

"But what's going on?" called a voice from the middle of the crowd. Kormann smiled reassuringly in the direction the voice had come from.

"There's no danger. Let me repeat: there is no danger. We will explain what's happening when all staff are present."

The muttering began again. The crowd was nervous and unconvinced. The young waiter turned to the people around him.

"Who is this guy, anyway? How come someone from Snowdrift Transport is giving the orders around here?"

His neighbors nodded agreement. The young waiter stepped closer, encouraged by their support.

"Mr. Markus, you're the manager. What's going on?"

Kormann turned to face Markus, putting his back to the crowd. He leaned forward, speaking quietly but forcefully so that only the manager could make out what he was saying. He made sure that the reassuring smile remained on his face as he spoke.

"Now you calm them down. Just repeat what I said: they'll find out what's going on soon enough." His hand gripped Markus's fore-arm like a vice as he continued. "And if you don't settle them down, we're going to have a little more bloodshed here. But this time we won't stop at pistol-whipping. Understand?"

His eyes moved around the lobby and, following their direction, Markus became aware of the other men who had arrived in the min-ivans with Kormann. There must have been twenty of them, spaced around the walls, standing back from the central area where the crowd was still gathering.

There was a sameness to the look of them. A hard look. And each of them carried a shoulder bag. Markus had no doubt what would be in those bags. As his gaze passed over them, he caught sight of Tina Bowden entering the lobby. She saw him and started to thread her way through the crowd. But he made eye contact with her and gave a brief shake of his head. She stopped, frowning, then seemed to understand. Tina was listed on the staff roster as a relief receptionist. Her role as security officer was kept secret. There was no sense in letting these people know she was anything but a junior employee. He felt the pressure of Kormann's hand on his arm moving him forward. He obeyed the implicit order and moved to face the crowd.

"Please," he began, then repeated the word a little louder so that it carried over their voices. "Please! Just bear with us. Mr. Kormann here is helping us with the situation. As he told you, there is no danger and we'll just wait until everyone's assembled. Just be pa-tient and stay calm, all right?"

"Is the mountain coming down?" It was a nervous female voice from near the back of the crowd. Markus forced himself to smile, trying to look reassuring. He was sure the effect must be ghastly.

"No. The mountain is not coming down," he replied, forcing his voice to be calm. "I'll say it again. There is no danger. We do have a situation here and we're asking for your cooperation. That's all."

The buzz of conversation subsided a little. They weren't convinced, he realized, but they knew this was all they were going to get for the moment. Markus noticed that Kormann was sweeping his gaze over the crowd, his lips moving fractionally as he counted heads. Seeming to be satisfied, he nodded to the men standing around the walls of the lobby. Without drawing any attention to themselves, half of the men moved away from the walls and headed down the corridor. Markus watched them going. There was nothing in that direction but the main room of the conference center.

Kormann waited another minute, then nodded to the young manager.

"Okay, I think we're about all here. Let's move them to the conference hall, Ben."

Markus frowned at him, uncomprehending. "The conference hall—" he began, then stopped as he saw the cold anger flash in the other man's eyes. He hesitated, then tried again.

"But there's nothing there. We're not set up for a conference," he said. Again, Kormann leaned forward and said in that same forceful undertone: "Just get them in there, Ben."

Their gazes locked for a few seconds. Then the manager dropped his eyes, defeated. He moved a pace away from the other man, as if the physical separation could somehow lessen the threat he felt.

"Okay, people!" he called, and again the buzz of conversation died away. "Let's move out of here. Could you all please move to the conference center, main room."

They complained among themselves, as crowds do. They muttered. They questioned the direction. But they obeyed. Once the first few people drifted from the back of the crowd in the direction of the conference center, the trend was set. The movement became more definite, less haphazard, as those at the front of the room, realizing they were now at a disadvantage, tried to push through to secure better positions in the new location.

"Let's go with 'em, Ben," Kormann said with mock politeness, drawing aside and gesturing for Markus to precede him.

They followed the milling crowd through the double doors that led to the conference center. As Markus had already pointed out, the large room was virtually unfurnished. There was a podium on a raised speaker's stage at the end farthest from the doors, and a large glass watercooler in one corner. Stackable hard chairs were ranged round the walls, stacked four deep in neat rows. The central area, some thirty feet by sixty, was empty floor space.

The conference room was at the back of the hotel, on the western side. The western wall of the room was mainly window area, allowing a view of the small expanse of snow-covered flat land behind the hotel, and the massive cliff face that towered barely forty yards away. Light mesh curtains were drawn across the big windows to cut the glare of the reflected light from the snow outside. For the same reason, the glass was tinted. The diffused light filled the room, obviating the need for internal lighting on a clear day. The other three walls were gray concrete, lined with whiteboards and cork display boards. At the moment, they were bare, except for one whiteboard that still bore a trace of the notes left from a conference the previous week. The words "SALESMANSHIP PLUS!" stared out at Markus. He wondered what the phrase actually meant.

Kormann's elbow nudged his ribs and he headed to the front of the room. He noticed that the ten men who had left the lobby were now ranged around the walls of the conference area. The remaining ten were nowhere to be seen. Now that he studied them more closely, there was an alarming sameness about Kormann's companions. All of them were expensively dressed in casual clothes, as befitted guests at Canyon Lodge. And their same brand name shoulder bags slung over their right shoulders—all with the top zips open and their right hands inside the bags.

It was almost as if they wore uniforms, he thought. And as the thought occurred, he realized that this was probably the reason why they were dressed in such similar fashion. Seen individually, there was nothing to excite comment about any of them. As a group, however, they were easy to distinguish from the staff members who were their unknowing prisoners.

Kormann and Markus had reached the speaker's podium now. The members of the crowd watched them expectantly, knowing that finally they would find out what the hell was going on. One girl near the front of the group raised her hand tentatively and addressed Markus.

"Mr. Markus, are we going to be here long? I've left the switchboard unattended and you know that's against normal procedure."

Kormann smiled reassuringly at her. "The switchboard is being looked after," he said easily and she frowned, not liking what she heard.

"But how? There's nobody left to—"

"One of my men is attending to it." Kormann rode over her protest, then glanced at his watch. "In any event, the line between here and Salt Lake City is down and it won't be restored for another ten minutes."

"How do you know that?" asked a middle-aged woman standing next to the switchboard operator. Several others echoed the question. People were getting just a little tired of this self-important Snowdrift Transport courier, who seemed to have taken control of their hotel. Kormann raised his hands once more, requesting silence and smiling at them all. They ignored the gesture and pressed a little closer, becoming more vocal in their protests. The smile faded from his lips and he raised his glance, nodding at one of the men standing by the wall.

The racketing burst of a machine gun was deafening in the enclosed, concrete-walled room.

Kormann's man had chosen the glass tank of the water cooler as his target. The heavy bullets slammed into it, shattering the glass and sending the entire unit spinning and staggering in a welter of glass shards and spraying water.

Several women in the room screamed and everyone dropped into an instinctive, protective crouch. As their eyes swung to the direction of the gunfire, Markus realized that every member of Kormann's

team was now holding a small, stubby machine gun. Kormann himself had drawn a pistol from a shoulder holster inside his parka.

"Okay, now let's all shut the fuck up!" he roared and the people
dragged their eyes away from the threat of the gunsmoke drifting
in the air and turned back to face him—disbelief mingled with
confusion on their faces. Kormann waited, his eyes roaming the
crowd, looking for the potential leaders, the potential fools, the
potential troublemakers. So far, so good, he thought as none of them
would meet his gaze. They were all cowed by the sudden turn of
events.

"Very well," he began crisply. "My name is Kormann and I'm
taking control of this hotel and its guests." He felt Markus stir beside him, felt the other man's eyes on him, widening in disbelief.

"You're mad," the manager breathed. "You'll never get away
with it."

"Shut up," Kormann told him quietly. Then he raised his voice
again so that the rest of the room could hear him. "If you look around,
you'll see that you are surrounded by armed men."

Instinctively, most of the heads in the crowd turned, even though
they had already seen that what he said was true. He continued.

"None of them will hesitate to shoot if you cause the slightest
trouble," he said. "On the other hand, if you obey orders, if you do
precisely what you're told when you are told to do it, you will be
completely safe." He paused to let that sink in, then repeated it.
"Completely safe. We have no wish to harm any of you and we'll do
our best not to. It's up to you entirely. Is that clear?"

He paused again, his eyes sweeping over them. There was a re-
luctant murmur of assent and agreement. They wanted to cling to
the promise of safety. A few of them nodded fearfully. They were
now subdued. It was time to give them hope for survival. He spoke
deliberately, seeing that hope come alive in every face before him.

"As I said, we have no wish to harm you. Our quarrel is not with
you. Our aim is to hold the guests of the hotel as hostages for ransom. We're not terrorists. We're not political. We're businessmen.
And we know it's good business to keep people alive.

"Accordingly, we'll be releasing most of the hotel staff and allowing you to leave. We'll keep only the managerial staff and a few others to attend to cooking and serving food. We don't need any more of you and we'll begin selecting those who can go in a few minutes."

He could sense the overwhelming tide of relief that surged through them. Muted conversation sprang up again and this time, he allowed it to continue unchecked. People who thought they were about to be released would be less likely to cause trouble, he knew. He smiled briefly, turning to Markus.

"I'm afraid you'll be staying, Ben. Now I want you to pick five others to stay here with us. And Ben," he added quietly, "don't go picking any heroes, okay?"

Senator Ted Carling locked his skis in the ski rack and clumped up the escalator to the reception desk. He stopped, puzzled, as he took in the deserted lobby, the empty tour desks and the lobby drugstore with its closed sign in place. The hotel looked deserted, yet it was barely half-past three in the afternoon.

As he stood, uncertainly, he noticed a tall, gray-haired man behind the reception desk. The senator moved toward him. He didn't recognize the man and he was wearing shirtsleeves and a tie, rather than the usual hotel uniform blazer.

"Yes, Senator Carling? Can I help you?" the man said. Carling wasn't particularly surprised that the other man knew his identity. He was a prominent figure and he was used to being recognized wherever he went. He courted media attention to make sure of it. Being recognized gave a man presence. And influence. And that spelled power. He swept his hand around the deserted lobby.

"Where is everybody? I wanted change for the cigarette machine but the store is closed," he said. His tone of voice, and his body language, said that he expected the situation to be rectified. Whatever the senator wanted, the senator got.

The gray-haired man leaned forward, dropping his voice to a more confidential level, even though there was nobody around to overhear. "Yes, sir. I'm afraid we've had a most tragic event. One of the staff . . ."

"Tragic? What happened?" Carling cut him off. The man behind the desk nodded several times, an expression of deep sorrow evident on his face.

"Well, Senator, it was one of our porters. Somehow, there seems to have been a brief ammonia leak into the heating system. You'll notice that we've had to shut it down?"

Carling hadn't noticed. But now that the other man mentioned it, he looked around and became aware that the ever-present low level hum of the heating system had ceased. He also thought that maybe the temperature was a little lower than usual.

"Yes," he said uncertainly. "Now that you mention it—"

The gray-haired man continued smoothly. "It's only a precaution, sir. I'm sure it's perfectly safe now. But we've had to put all staff to work checking the system in the basement for the source of the leak into the line."

"You mean you haven't—" the senator began but once more he found himself cut off.

"Until we have a clearance, sir, may we ask that you make your way to the gymnasium?"

"The gymnasium?" Carling repeated. "Why there?"

"It's on a separate heating system, sir. It's perfectly safe there and also perfectly comfortable. We've got bar staff up there serving drinks and snacks. If you'd just oblige us, we'll have the situation cleared up shortly."

"Yeah, sure. I'll go on up," the senator capitulated. He moved away, conscious of the other man's unctuous smile as he departed. He glanced nervously at the big, grilled vents above the elevator as he waited to go to the gymnasium on the third floor. He was sure now that it was getting colder. He zipped his ski suit closed at the neck.

Antoinette Deschamps, in room 701, received a similar message when she rang room service to order a pot of herbal tea. She had declined to go skiing that afternoon. Suffering a bout of stomach cramps, she had spent the afternoon sleeping.

Now she climbed painfully out of bed, feeling the ominous beginnings of another bout of cramps. Buttoning her blouse, she headed for the gymnasium.

Like the staff before them, the few remaining guests drifted in, in ones and twos and small groups. As they did, they were directed, politely but firmly, to the gymnasium.

They went there hurriedly, for the most part, anxious to remove themselves as quickly as possible from the threat of further ammonia leaks into the heating system.

They reached the gymnasium with a sense of relief—a relief that changed quickly to confusion, then ultimately to fear, when they were greeted by the ten armed men who waited there for them.

TEN

On the highway, the driver of the ancient shuttle bus connecting Snow Eagles to two other ski fields was mildly surprised to see a tall African-American man flagging him down. It was late in the day and the driver was on his way back to the depot, but he thought he could possibly give the hitchhiker a lift. He pulled to a halt and levered the door open.

"Take me to Canyon Lodge," the man said. The driver was already shaking his head.

"Can't be done, friend. I don't call in there." His eyes widened as he noticed the large automatic pistol that had appeared in the man's hand.

"You do now."

The driver nodded. Bus drivers weren't paid enough to argue with armed hijackers.

"I guess I do at that," he said.

Tina Bowden moved through the crush of people in the conference room until she was close to Markus's side. She had to shove her way through. The manager was besieged by anxious staff members, all of them with the most compelling reasons why they shouldn't be among those selected to stay. Markus ran a desperate hand through his hair and glanced to where Kormann was standing by the podium, deep in conversation with one of his men. The terrorist, for that was how Markus now thought of him, in spite of Kormann's claim that they were businessmen, glanced up and met Markus's troubled gaze.

"Get on with it, Ben," he called, glancing meaningfully at his watch. "You've got seven minutes to pick your people."

Markus turned back to the faces crowding around him. How could he be expected to choose? How could he play God with people's lives, deciding who stayed and who went? A young girl, one of the waitresses from the rooftop silver service restaurant, clutched at his arm, babbling desperately.

"Please, Mr. Markus! I can't stay here! Don't make me stay! Not now I'm pregnant!"

She couldn't have been more than seventeen and Markus looked at her in surprise. A middle-aged receptionist behind her curled her lip in disbelief. "Don't believe that! The little bitch is only saying that so you'll let her go. Me, I've got three kids down in Salt Lake City and no man to look after them. You've got to let me go, Mr. Markus."

Markus shook his head in desperation. A hand grasped his upper arm with surprizing strength and he turned to find himself face to face with Tina Bowden.

"I'm staying," she said, quietly but forcefully. "You know I have to, Ben."

Markus hesitated, then nodded. As part of management, he was one of a limited number of staff who knew that Tina was actually an undercover member of the hotel's security service. She was, in fact, the senior officer on duty at present. He guessed there could be no argument about whether she stayed or went. She stayed.

Counting himself, that made four people selected. He'd already chosen the other two men who were to stay. One was a cleaner and the other ran the lobby drugstore and gift shop. Under Kormann's direction, they were both middle-aged. The terrorist leader had told him he didn't want any "young, gung-ho heroes kept on the premises." Now he had to pick two more women. Another stipulation of Kormann's.

"Five minutes, Ben," came the mocking voice from the podium.

Markus's eye alighted on one of the gym fitness instructors. Fit, healthy, in her mid-twenties, she was unmarried and, as far as he knew, had no ties anywhere local. Then, as he opened his mouth to call her name, he reconsidered. Maybe having an attractive young woman around wasn't such a great idea, he thought. He ran his hands through his hair again. Jesus! Why did he have to be the one? If he picked an older woman, odds were she'd have family some-where in the vicinity, people who depended on her. To hell with it, he thought, the fitness instructor would have to take her chances with the rest of them.

"Lois," he called, and saw her face blanch slightly. She knew what was coming. "I'm sorry, honey, but you're going to have to stay."

That made five. One to go.

CANYON LODGE ENTRANCE
1615 HOURS, MOUNTAIN TIME
SATURDAY, DAY 1

As the group chosen for release reached the underground arrival area, they were mildly surprised to find the old exhaust-and-dirt-stained yellow shuttle bus parked in the tunnel.

The double doors slid apart and one of the guards moved forward to activate the lock that would keep them in the open position. Then he gestured with the stubby muzzle of the submachine gun that he carried, indicating the people closest to the entrance.

"Get moving. Everyone on the bus."

Hesitantly, they moved forward. First one, then two or three oth-ers. Then the herd instinct took over and they began to move as a group, jostling each other as they reached the bottleneck formed by the doorway. The armed men stood well clear; each one avoided standing in anyone else's line of fire.

"Keep moving! Come on! On the bus!"

The commands were taken up from both sides of the moving mass of people.

Now the first few were climbing aboard and again, the group slowed and swelled as they had to negotiate the steps and the narrow doorway. The delay seemed to anger the guards and they moved closer, shouting and yelling, shoving at them, urging them to board more quickly. The shouts became more frequent, with a rising edge of anger and urgency.

"Get moving! Come on! Don't stop! Move!"

It was inevitable that someone would turn to object. It was almost certain that it would be one of the younger staff members. It was a female ski-school clerk who did it. She spun on her heel as a gun barrel jabbed into the small of her back, urging her forward.

"Goddamn it!" she cried. "We're moving as fast as we can! Why don't you guys take a—"

She was right beside the black man who had hijacked the bus when she turned to argue. He saw the rebellion in her eyes, leveled the big pistol and aimed at the girl's head.

Still arguing with the man who had jabbed her, she never saw the movement from her side. The deafening crash of the pistol echoed through the confined space of the tunnel. The heavy slug hit the girl in the back of the skull and exploded out through her forehead in a sickening fountain of red and gray tissue that showered those close to her.

Already dead, she jerked forward, took a few spasmodic steps, then sagged to the cold ground. The woman beside her, covered in blood and tissue, screamed.

Others in the crowd echoed the scream and, in an instinctive, fear-driven reaction, the prisoners huddled closer together. Around the lifeless body, members of the crowd drew back, pressing against their immediate neighbors as they tried to leave space between themselves and the bloody-headed corpse—as if afraid that even touching it would lead to their own destruction.

The black man nodded to one of the other guards, who immediately raised his slab-sided, heavy-barreled submachine gun in a one-handed grip and squeezed off a racketing, seven-round burst.

The shots were deafening in the confined space. The howling of the ricochets, and the echoes they sent up, were terrifying.

Then Kormann's voice cut through the screams of the terrified staff members, reducing them to a frightened silence.

"Now move! Cut the crap and get on the bus!"

Gradually, the panic subsided. Moving once again, and with fearful glances around them, the prisoners began to climb aboard the bus. As the first few climbed aboard, the black man moved along outside the windows, motioning for them to move right to the rear, the threat of the pistol in his hands reinforcing his shouted orders.

There were fifty-five passengers in all—a heavy load for the old bus, with its slipping transmission and worn rings. The driver, still behind the wheel, hoped they weren't heading any further uphill. The bus would never make it.

The black man's next words dispeled any such doubts.

"Okay. Get this load back moving down to Salt Lake City."

The still-warm diesel fired almost instantly.

Spewing black, oily smoke, the overloaded shuttle bus pulled slowly away from the hotel doors. Riding the clutch against the slipping transmission, the driver gunned her up the ramp leading out of the tunnel. The small group of armed men watched it lumber heavily up and out into the late afternoon sunlight.

Behind it, the body of the young girl lay, fair hair already stained to a deep red by her own lifeblood.

ELEVEN

THE WALL
SNOW EAGLES MOUNTAIN
WASATCH COUNTY
1621 HOURS, MOUNTAIN TIME
SATURDAY, DAY 1

The late afternoon sun was low in the west and the shadows were stretching dark across the snow. In the next few minutes, the mountain would block the sun entirely and the ski runs at Snow Eagles would take on the ominous, deserted feeling that came with the end of the ski day. The chairlifts, controlled by automatic time switches that started them every day at eight a.m. and shut them down each afternoon at four thirty, continued to run. But without their cargos of eager skiers, they seemed forlorn and vaguely futile.

Far below, the few remaining skiers were finishing their last runs, the day trippers heading for the parking lot while the on-mountain residents skied toward the bulky, gray, man-made mountain that was the Canyon Lodge. Their bright ski clothes provided a few remaining traces of color in the shadowed, leached-out snowscape. There was an air of emptiness and even desolation to the almost deserted mountain that matched Jesse's mood.

He sat disconsolately in the snow below The Wall, exhausted and defeated. He had given up smoking several years previously but now he reached into the inner pocket of his parka and produced a nearly full pack of Chesterfields, shaking one out of the pack and lighting it with a book of matches he'd taken from his room. The little flame flared, unnaturally bright in the shadows under the pines, and Jesse squinted through the smoke back up the mountain.

The formerly pristine surface of the snow beneath The Wall was churned and tumbled, mute testimony to his repeated attempts to defeat his fear. He'd tried to do as Tina had suggested, building up to it throughout the day, skiing a series of progressively more difficult runs. But finally, he had to face The Wall itself.

Each time, as he stood looking down at the almost sheer slope, the pain would sear through his leg once more and he would feel the familiar jolt of fear deep in his belly. Eight times he had overcome it and launched himself out into space, plunging down the slope, going into a series of rhythmic turns, thrusting with his legs, turning, turning again, defying the mountain's attempts to claw him down. Down the slope, turning and turning, maintaining a constant, flowing motion that harnessed the pull of gravity and the speed of his descent against the bite of his skis into the soft snow and kept him balanced and in place.

And each time, in the moment when he thought he had conquered the fear, it would return, suddenly, jarringly, back to the forefront of his consciousness, manifesting itself in a sudden, well remembered stab of agony that went through his leg and skewered his courage.

In that moment, he would feel the skis slide out from under as he leaned back into the mountain, knowing it was wrong, knowing that he mustn't, knowing what the inevitable result of the fear-driven movement would be, must be. And then he would feel the instantaneous loss of grace and balance as he was turned into a helplessly cartwheeling, inchoate mass of flesh and bone that tumbled and slid and rolled in a tangle of arms and legs and skis until the momentum was gone and he would lie, chest heaving and lungs burning, defeated once again, betrayed by his own fears.

Eight times. Not directly, one after the other, because once he had fallen, there was no way to regain the summit of The Wall until he had skied down to the cable car station and ridden to the very top of the mountain once again. And each time he made that journey, he was mocked by the fact that, on the lesser slopes, he skied perfectly, rhythmically, gracefully, with all the instinctive, unthinking ability that had been ingrained into him since he was a small boy. It was a bitter reminder of what he had once been and what he could no longer be. Because now he knew that every time he ventured to the steep, challenging slopes that demanded the skill and courage of a true expert, he would fail.

The sheer physical effort had exhausted him. On two occasions, he had lost a ski when the bindings, unable to resist the twisting force of his fall, had released, saving ankles and knees from damage. On one of those occasions, he had spent fifteen minutes, thigh deep on the sheer slope, struggling to maintain his position, searching deep beneath the soft powder to find the buried ski. It was tiring work. But as great as the physical exertion had been, the mental and emotional exhaustion was even greater and now he sat, back resting against the skis that he had rammed into the snow as far as their bindings, tasting the harsh smoke of the Chesterfield and the harsher flavor of failure. It was over, he told himself. He had come here to try to regain a lost part of himself.

And he had failed.

He gazed down dispassionately at the hotel. His rental car was in the underground parking lot, his suitcase locked in the trunk. It would take him ten minutes to ski down from here, change his ski boots for the soft pair of moccasins he had left out of his suitcase, and be on his way. Suddenly he was anxious to be gone, anxious to put this place and its memories of failure well behind him.

He hauled himself up, dusting the dry snow from his pants, and heaved the skis clear of the snow, dropping them flat on the ground. He flicked the butt of the Chesterfield away, watching its glowing tip describe an arc until it fell, with a slight sizzling noise, into the snow, melting itself a small burrow before the moisture extinguished it. His boots were covered with the packed soft snow and he kicked one against the other to clear them, ensuring that the bindings wouldn't jam when he tried to close them. Satisfied that the right boot was clear, he poised it above one ski.

Then, distant but unmistakable, he heard the quick rattle of an automatic weapon.

He froze. The sound was strangely muffled. A single shot initially, followed by a sustained burst. Muffled, but with a strangely echoing quality to the sound. Not a heavy weapon, he guessed. An assault rifle or submachine gun. A moment later, faintly through the thin, high-altitude air, he heard the sound of people's voices. Screaming.

His eyes narrowed with concentration as he tried to place the direction from which the sounds were coming. It seemed to him that they must issue from the hotel. There was no other possible source. Yet common sense told him that he wouldn't hear shots and voices from inside the hotel. The same insulating qualities and thick walls that preserved the internal warmth of the building would muffle the sound of shots completely. But there was no trace of movement, no sign of people, outside the hotel.

Which left only one possibility, one that explained the unusual quality he had remarked in the sounds—muffled yet echoing. The shots had to have come from the open-ended tunnel that formed the entrance to the hotel.

His reasoning was confirmed when he heard another sound—the grinding sound of a heavy diesel engine starting and revving up. A truck or bus engine, he figured. And now that he remembered the underground entrance, an open-ended tunnel that would funnel the sound out into the open air, he knew he was right. Cars and buses bringing guests to Canyon Lodge could drive down a ramp to unload their passengers under cover, out of the weather. Guests then took the escalator to the first floor check-in while a second ramp provided an exit for the vehicles once they had unloaded. The bare concrete walls would create that echoing effect.

Belatedly, he drew back into the shadow of the trees. Even now, binoculars could be scanning the mountain for a sign that someone had overheard the shooting. Strangely, as he looked down, he could see no sign of any hotel staff in any of the outdoor areas—the heated pool and spa or the terrace bar. He might have expected the sound of shots to bring people running from both those areas. But there was nothing. The hotel looked deserted. Jesse felt a prickling sensation on the back of his neck. He'd been a cop too long to ignore that feeling. He thought now of the 1911 model Colt 45 automatic that was nestled between layers of clothes in his suitcase. To get to it, he'd have to go through the entrance tunnel—unless he made his way around to an alternative entrance, then took the elevator or service stairs down to the lower levels where the underground parking spaces were. As he thought of his gun, he realized he wasn't going to look for the source of that automatic fire without it.

Now the engine noise that had been throbbing regularly for the past few minutes altered. It rose slightly, then faded as the driver revved the engine and the transmission took the strain. As Jesse watched, the ancient shape of a yellow Snow Shuttle bus emerged slowly from the mouth of the exit tunnel and labored around the turning circle until it was headed down Canyon Road to Salt Lake City.

Jesse frowned. In the time that he'd been here, he hadn't once seen the Snow Shuttle bus come within a quarter mile of the Canyon Lodge. Its normal route took it along the main road behind the cable car terminal, well below the hotel.

That made two breaks in the normal routine, he thought. And one of them, the sound of gunshots and screaming, was a pretty major variation. He could see no immediate link between the two events but experience told him that didn't mean there wasn't one. He watched as the bus seemed to be making hard going of the first shallow rise in the road. It must be heavy loaded, he thought, watching the spurts of black smoke erupting from the exhaust as the driver shifted down through the gears.

No further sound came from the tunnel mouth. He considered the situation. Shots. Screaming. A heavily laden bus going way out of its normal route. Forget that for a moment and concentrate on the shots. Automatic weapon. Somewhere in the hotel. People screaming so people hurt, maybe killed. He shook his head sadly. The world was full of crazies. People were gunned down in schools and churches these days for no good reason at all. Why not a ski resort? The next question was, what could he do about it?

The answer was nothing, until he got hold of his gun. And that meant skiing down to the hotel, across half a mile of open ground, while he was the only thing within sight that was moving. He didn't like those odds. That was asking to be spotted and that was something he didn't want—not while there was some crazy holed up in there with an M16 or something similar. But there had been no further shooting after the second burst. That, at least, was a good sign. The sort of massacres that had happened all too often in recent years were usually characterized by continuous shooting. Not one quick burst and then silence. As long as there was no further shooting, there was no urgent reason for him to go blundering into the hotel. He'd wait until after dark. Or until he heard more shots. Whichever came first.

The engine note of the bus was fading as it reached the first bend in the road, taking it back to Salt Lake City. Jesse watched as the bright yellow, slow-moving vehicle rounded the bend and disappeared out of sight. It would reappear in three or four minutes' time, he guessed, when the winding road would bring it back into view some three-quarters of a mile down the road.

Jesse settled down in the snow again to watch. And to wait for darkness.

TWELVE

The first, uncomprehending shock had worn off. Senator Carling sat on a gym bench, Calvin Rockley close by. The other three members of their party were a few yards away, seated disconsolately on the hard nylon carpet that covered the floor of the gym.

Glancing around, Carling estimated that there must be around forty hostages in the room. Their captors lounged easily against the walls around them. During a career on Capitol Hill, which included many meetings, both formal and informal, with three presidents, Carling had enjoyed ample opportunities to observe the behavior and demeanor of armed, highly trained troops. Now, his relatively experienced eye took stock of the men guarding them. He noted, with a growing sense of unease, that they seemed completely at home with their weapons, showing an air of easy familiarity with them.

Studying the men, Carling came to the conclusion that his captors were highly trained, experienced and thoroughly professional. For the life of him, he couldn't decide whether that was good or bad news.

There seemed to be no common racial link between them. They were a disparate group. Some might have been Middle Eastern, or even southern European in parentage. There were several who were of fairer complexion, including two blonds, and he had already seen one black man among the group. Whether he was African–American or from some other background, Carling had no idea. He didn't see any Asian-looking men among them. Maybe that was significant, maybe not.

Through the picture window behind him, the precipitous, snow-laden wall of the canyon reared high overhead. By now, only the top third of the mountain was catching the light of the low-angled late afternoon sun.

He sensed movement beside him and glanced to where Calvin Rockley had edged a little closer on the bench. The aircraft manu-facturer leaned toward him and spoke in a low tone.

"What do you think, Senator? Who are these guys?"

His voice was barely above a whisper, yet Carling noticed that it drew the immediate attention of the closest of the guards—a slim, fair-haired young man with a look of wide-eyed innocence that was belied by the ugly, squat shape of the machine carbine held comfort-ably in the crook of his arm. The guard shifted his position slightly, so as to keep the senator and his companion directly under his gaze. At the same time, Carling noted, he didn't neglect the rest of the sector assigned to him. Those wide, blue eyes continued to roam across the dispirited group in the gym, ready for instant action at any sign of rebellion.

Not that there was much chance of that, the senator reflected bit-terly. The surprise achieved by their captors had been absolute. As near as he could calculate, every guest left in the hotel had been swept up in their carefully laid net.

Softly, his eyes on the guard, wary for any sign of aggression, Carling answered his companion. "Your guess is as good as mine, Cal. Some kind of terrorist group, most likely."

"Al Qaeda, maybe?" Rockley suggested. Carling shook his head. He'd relaxed a little now. After their first exchange, the guard seemed to have lost immediate interest in them. Obviously, there was no ban on talking among themselves.

"They sure don't look like it," he replied. He inclined his head to-ward the guard, "That one looks like the original all-American boy. And I'd swear the guy on the desk when we came in was Brooklyn born and raised."

The guard had caught the slight head movement and their interest in him. He caught Carling's gaze and glanced meaningfully—once—down to the machine gun. He shook his head slightly—a barely perceptible movement that nevertheless sent a clear message: *Don't start anything. We're in charge here.*

Carling took the hint. He turned slightly so that he was no longer looking directly at the guard. Rockley had caught the interplay as well.

"Whoever they are," he said, "they sure seem to know their business."

The senator nodded slowly, several times. A slight frown creased his forehead.

"Whatever that might be," he said finally.

CANYON LODGE
WASATCH COUNTY
1629 HOURS, MOUNTAIN TIME
SATURDAY, DAY 1

Pallisani noticed the switchboard come back to life. He smiled thinly at the terrified operator still sitting near him, and flicked a switch on the board to answer.

"Canyon," he said briefly. In the headset earpiece, he heard the reply from five miles down the road.

"The line's reattached. You read me okay?"

"Clear as a bell. Now get out of there."

He flicked the switch up to break the connection. The replacement line had been laid several days previously, bypassing a two-mile stretch of the road at Avalanche Pass. He'd hired the linesman who attached it through an intermediary. The technician had been fired by Bell Telephone several years before for illegal wire tapping. He was now twenty-thousand dollars richer and it was unlikely he'd go to the authorities when he found out what was going on here. Even if he did, there was nothing useful he could tell them.

THIRTEEN

The African-American who had hijacked the shuttle bus was lounging comfortably on one of the sofas near the reception desk when Pallisani emerged from the office, dragging a still-distressed Jenny Callister behind him. The girl's incessant sobbing was beginning to annoy him and he had things he had to get on with. Catching sight of his colleague, he called him across to the desk.

"Carter! Over here!"

Carter rose easily and sauntered over to the desk. He didn't care much for Pallisani but he'd agreed, as they all had, that a rigid chain of command was essential for an operation of this scope.

Pallisani jerked the girl's arm and sent her staggering toward the other man.

"Put this one with the others in the conference room," he ordered, a little more abruptly than Carter was willing to accept.

"Yes, Duce," he muttered.

Pallisani swung back to glare at him. "And cut the funny crap. We've got a schedule to keep."

Carter nodded. He understood that. He also understood that he wasn't going to put up with the Italian throwing his weight around unnecessarily. Taking orders was one thing. Taking crap was something else entirely and he hoped the big paisan got the message. He gave the girl a gentle shove in the direction of the elevator.

"Come on, sweetheart," he said, "let's join the others."

Pallisani watched them go. He placed both hands deliberately on the reception counter and took a deep breath. He'd got the message from Carter all right. What's more, he recognized the fact that the big man was right. But dammit, he'd a right to be uptight at this stage of the operation. Things were going to plan so far, but that could change at any minute. He and his companions seemed to be in undisputed control of the hotel but the situation was a fragile house of cards. It could collapse around them at any moment. It was essential at this stage that they maintain their momentum, keep things moving, keep the hostages off balance and wondering what was coming next. Uncertainty was their ally and the longer they maintained it, the firmer their hold over their prisoners became.

He reached into his shoulder bag and brought out a walkie-talkie. It was a piece of equipment that every member of the team carried. He thumbed the squawk button on the side and spoke into the microphone.

"Kormann. You read?"

He released the button and, after a few moments, heard the small loudspeaker in the unit come to life.

"Kormann."

Just the one word. Pallisani thumbed the talk button again.

"Phones are back on line. Let's get moving."

In the conference room, Kormann slid his walkie-talkie back into the leather holder clipped to his belt. He glanced around, caught Ben Markus's eye and beckoned to him to move forward. Hesitantly, unsure of what he might be getting into, the duty manager obeyed.

"Come with me, Ben. We've got some business on the roof and I want you there," Kormann told him.

Markus nodded warily. After all, he had no other choice in the matter. Kormann took his arm and steered him toward the door. On the way, they passed the dejected figure of the assistant chef. Kormann grinned at him without sympathy.

"Tough luck, buddy. Still, things could be worse."

The chef had good reason to look glum. Originally, he had not been among those selected to remain behind. But, as he had been about to move down to the bus, Kormann had noticed the high white toque he wore and realized its significance.

"Just a moment," he had said. "He stays too."

Markus had remonstrated, but without any real hope of success. "But we've already got the five you said."

"Then we'll make it six," Kormann told him. "We're going to be here awhile, Ben, and I don't know about you but I'm a lousy cook. Let's just take out a little insurance in self-indulgence, shall we?"

In a few moments, Kormann thought now, as the guard at the door stood aside to let them through, the chef would be thanking his lucky stars that he'd been chosen to stay.

In a few days, who could tell?

Kormann pressed the call button for the elevator. The left-hand car arrived, its doors sighing open with that peculiar self-satisfied sound all elevators seem to make. Kormann nudged Markus forward and pressed the top button. They rode up without speaking. The only sound in the elevator was the gentle hum of the electric motor whirling them up six stories to the roof. Again, the doors slid open and Kormann nudged the other man out.

The Crow's Nest Bar and heated enclosed swimming pool occupied about a quarter of the flat roof. With panoramic glass windows on three sides, it commanded breathtaking views of the mountain to one side and the ski slopes to the other. Outside, there was a jogging track and an expanse of artificial grass, with lounging chairs and tables set out.

"Move," Kormann said, nudging Markus toward the door. They came out into the crisp, cold, late afternoon air. The sun had already dropped behind the far mountain but there was still a good half hour of light left in the day. Outside the bar, sheltered from the wind by its solid walls, one of Kormann's men was busy setting up an array of equipment. Markus stopped and watched curiously. His captor allowed the delay for a few minutes.

"Twin fifty caliber Brownings, slaved to radar tracking, and a dozen or so Stinger missiles," he said, by way of an explanation to the unspoken question in Markus's eyes. "Just in case you should be talking to anyone from outside, I want you to know that no choppers are going to be coming up this valley."

He paused and Markus looked at him. Then, with a cold glint of a smile in his eye, Kormann corrected himself.

"At least they might come up the valley, but they sure as hell won't be going back down if they do," he said. Markus nodded somberly. The twin mount heavy caliber machine guns might seem to be old technology in this era of missiles and electronic warfare, but he knew that combat in Vietnam and the Middle East had proved the effectiveness of radar-directed small arms fire against attacking aircraft—particularly slow movers like helicopters. He glanced around the roof and saw another twin fifty mount being installed at the opposite side. Between them, the two gun installations covered all approaches to the hotel. And in case there were any gaps, the shoulder-launched Stingers—heat-seeking AA missiles—would fill them in quickly enough.

Evidently, Markus realized, their few moments of communication were over. Kormann shoved him roughly in the direction of the northern parapet. The duty manager shrugged and began walking in the direction indicated. Shivering in his thin blazer jacket and shirt, he walked toward the four-foot high parapet at the edge of the roof. He noted that Kormann had had the foresight to slip on a warm-looking parka. Markus stopped at the parapet, Kormann a few paces behind him.

"Now what?" asked the duty manager. Dully, he looked out over the magnificent view. From here, you could see the massive peaks of the Wasatches all around them, and the heaving panorama of mountains that stretched out before them, all the way back to Salt Lake City. The city itself wasn't visible from this point but at night, when the weather was clear or when there was a low overcast, you could see the loom of the city's lights on the horizon, or reflected on the underbelly of the clouds.

Kormann's eyes were searching the valley below them, looking for something in the near distance. He found the single road that wound tortuously along the canyon and down to Salt Lake City. It was the only route in and out of the valley and its blacktop surface showed up clearly among the white snow cover of the rest of the terrain. It was a stark black ribbon among the shadowed white. His eyes narrowed briefly as he searched along the road, then came to rest on what he was looking for. He pointed.

"There he is. Take a look," he told Markus.

The duty manager followed the direction indicated by the pointing arm and made out the tiny yellow shape of the shuttle bus crawling along Canyon Road. In the clear, cold air, he thought he could even make out a thin, ragged line of black diesel smoke drifting in the air behind the old bus. He wondered why Kormann had brought him up here to see this, then realized that the terrorist was speaking again, virtually mirroring his own thoughts.

"Now, Ben, I wanted you to see this. Just like I wanted you to see those fifties over there." He gestured briefly to the machine gun installations behind them, then looked back to the bus. "Because, Ben, I want you to be very clear in your own mind that we're not just fooling around, blowing smoke up here. You get it?"

Markus nodded doubtfully. He could understand the message implicit in the machine guns and the missiles. What the bus was going to tell him, he had no idea. Still, the edge of mockery in Kormann's tone grated on his nerves. He glanced at the other man with hatred in his eyes.

"You've killed one of my people, you bastard. I'm hardly likely to think you're fooling around."

Kormann had taken the walkie-talkie from his belt. He was in the act of changing the transmission frequency when Markus spoke. He froze, his hands still on the little radio, then stepped a pace closer to Markus, his face only a few inches away.

"Never let your emotions get the better of you, Ben," he said in a dangerously low voice. "Particularly when you don't have the power to back them up. Remember, you're alive—and you really don't have to be."

He held the duty manager's gaze with his as he let the last words die in the cold air. The threat behind them was all too obvious and eventually, Markus felt his own eyes dropping from the other man's. Kormann nodded, satisfied.

"Just speak nice and do as you're told, Ben, and you might survive. Okay?"

Markus nodded, hating himself for his abject acquiescence, yet knowing there was nothing else he could do. Kormann returned his attention to the little radio, selected the new channel and pressed the talk button.

"Kormann. You read?" he said. Markus heard the tiny, muted sound of an answering voice in the earphone against the other man's head. It was too faint for him to make out the actual words.

"How long?" Kormann asked and again there was an indecipherable answer.

"When you're ready," Kormann said into the radio, then clipped it back to his belt. He glanced up and saw Markus's eyes on him. He nodded toward the pass.

"Watch the bus, Ben, not me," he said, deceptively mild in his tone.

Markus turned back to the road below them. He had lost sight of the bus as they had been talking. Now he traced the thin, winding line of the blacktop until he found it again—a tiny yellow beetle struggling along, laboring under the massive, snow-laden cliffs of Avalanche Pass—one of the steepest sections of the mountain.

"Any time . . . now . . ." Kormann said, half under his breath. Sensing that something was about to happen, Markus riveted his attention on the old bus, straining to see more clearly, to make out more detail. But the dying light and the distance defeated him.

Then there was a movement. Not from the bus, but from the cliff face high above it. A sudden fountain of white geysered upward, then another and another, in a line along the rim of the massive cliff, until there were six in all—the snow cloud of the first slowly drifting away on the light breeze as the last erupted into the late afternoon sky. The skin around Markus's eyes tightened as he squinted, trying to see more clearly. There was a small halo of drifting snow hanging above the cliff . . . then a ragged black line zigzagged across the snow, following the line of the fountains they had just seen. Then, for a brief space, nothing.

He glanced down. The tiny yellow bus was directly below the spot on the mountain where the black line scarred the white of the cliff face. Then, dimly to his ears came the reverberating echoes of six short, deep reports.

"Oh Jesus . . ." Markus said softly, the horror of it all suddenly registering as he heard that familiar sound. It was the sound of explosive charges placed in the snow. Markus heard it most days this time of year as the ski patrol on Snow Eagles found those unstable areas of the mountain and brought them down before they could avalanche out of control.

The zigzag gap was widening visibly and now he could sense movement in that mass of white as the entire face of the cliff, millions of tons of snow and loose rock, bulged outward below the line of the explosions and began to slide away from the tenuous grip that had held it there for the past three months of winter.

Now it was a massive, moving wall of snow that thundered down the near vertical slope of the cliff, dwarfing the tiny yellow shape below it. In the mass of it all he could see the dark shapes of trees and rocks, tiny against the ever-growing, roiling mass. Flung snow stood clear and stark above it, like spray above a giant wave, and the avalanche was growing ever-wilder, ever-bigger, feeding on the mountain, devouring it, destroying it and everything in its path as the entire mountain surged on a downward slide.

The deep voice reached him now, a thundering roar that he could almost feel in the pit of his belly, at the precise moment that the massive wall of snow and ice and rock swept over the road, obliterating the bus and the sixty people inside it in an instant, then sweeping on into the valley below the road, unchecked by the tiny obstacle.

Markus watched in silent horror, staring fixedly at the spot where the bus had disappeared, hopelessly willing it to emerge from the mass of snow and debris that had overwhelmed it—and knowing at the same time that it would never happen. The bus was no longer there. Crushed and flattened like a discarded tin can, it was rolling underneath the moving mass of the avalanche, buried deep in the snow and rock that continued to cascade down the mountain into the valley below.

"Now perhaps it's time we told someone what's happening up here," Kormann said. There was a note of satisfaction in his voice that woke a dark instinct within the pleasant-featured young manager. In that moment, he wanted to see the terrorist leader dead.

FOURTEEN

President Lowell C. Gorton looked around at the serious faces that surrounded the coffee table.

"Hostages?" he said, the disbelief clear in his voice. "In Utah?"

Morris Tildeman, director of the National Security Agency, nodded confirmation. "I'm afraid that's right, Mr. President," he said. At least, Gorton thought, he had the grace to look concerned about the whole thing. He didn't like the NSA head and he knew the feeling was reciprocated. That was the problem when you inherited a job like the presidency. You had to accept the functionaries and assistants chosen by your predecessor—at least for the first six months or so. Then you could begin to make changes—slowly and deliberately. Tildeman would be the first of his. But that watershed moment was still two months away.

Gorton had inherited the office when its previous incumbent had been stopped dead, three-quarters of a mile into his regular two-mile morning swim in the White House pool. There had been no warning. President Adam Lindsay Couch had been as fit as a bull—a relatively young man at forty-six, an athlete, a former Green Beret and a fitness fanatic.

Unfortunately, his fitness regime did nothing to protect him against the thin-walled artery that suddenly burst in his brain. By the time his shocked Secret Service guards, floundering fully dressed in the chest deep water of the pool, had reached him, he was dead, his eyes staring in horror at the last thing he had seen—the tiled pattern on the bottom.

And so Gorton had acceded to the presidency. It was a pity that the very qualities that had made him an ideal Number Two for Couch now were so inappropriate for the Number One position in the world. Gorton gave the appearance of being mature and thoughtful, a man who would consider his options before speaking or acting intemperately. This had given the Couch–Gorton ticket, or, as some unkind wits called it, the Couch–Potato ticket, the necessary balance in a political campaign.

In fact, while Gorton appeared to be mature, thoughtful and analytical, he was in reality elderly, querulous and indecisive. As vice president, those failings hadn't really mattered too much. After all, about the only thing a VP was required to do these days was turn up on election day and raise the winning president's fist in victory. As president, it was all too often necessary to do something. To make a decision. To take a stand. And none of these were things that Gorton did well. Now he was faced with the first real crisis of his Administration and he didn't even have the first inkling about how to assess it, let alone what steps should be taken to resolve it.

A more intelligent man might have realized that the Emergency Council established by his predecessor, and now seated around the conference table, could give him invaluable support and advice in situations like these. Couch had selected a group of intelligent, experienced professionals to make up his inner circle. Consisting of the directors of the NSA, FBI, CIA and the current chairman of the Joint Chiefs, they were men, and one woman, who were not afraid to speak their minds and call a spade a spade. His own White House chief of staff and, of course, the head of Homeland Security, made up the numbers. In recent years, the Homeland Security Department maintained an overview on any security-related matter.

A confident and secure person, President Couch had selected a group who were willing to argue and make suggestions. For Gorton, however, their independence and candor were a challenge to his already shaky authority. He regarded them with suspicion and dislike, seeing conspiracy where there was none and regarding discussion as dissent and disrespect.

"They've sealed off the access to the resort, Mr. President." Tildeman was speaking again. "And they say they've placed explosive charges in the mountain overlooking the hotel. Any attempt to rescue the hostages will result in their bringing the mountain down on the whole resort."

Gorton's lip curled slightly at the pedantic NSA chief's carefully correct grammar. Any other person in the room would have said "will result in them bringing the mountain down," but not Tildeman. He interrupted.

"Can they do that?" Gorton asked.

Tildeman hesitated. General Sam Barrett, Chairman of the Joint Chiefs and an air force four-star, nodded gravely. "I'd say it wouldn't be too hard, Mr. President," he said. "Some time back, one of our hotshot pilots came too low over that area and the sonic boom buried the hotel up to the fourth floor." Gorton looked at the military man and shook his head slowly, as if in disbelief that anyone could be so goddamn stupid.

"So I guess we're looking at Al Qaeda here, is that right?" Gorton directed the question at Bennington Traill, director of Homeland Security—a former two-star general who had spent his career in the military justice system. Traill hesitated before he replied.

"We're not leaping to that conclusion straightaway, Mr. President. We've had no indication of any potential Al Qaeda operations in the northwest," he replied.

Gorton snorted derisively. "We had no indication of 9/11 either," he said.

But Traill shook his head. "We had warning, sir. We didn't act on it."

The CIA and FBI chiefs shifted uncomfortably. While neither of them had been the incumbents at the time of 9/11, they still suffered from the fact that their respective agencies had been unwilling to share information—with disastrous results. Traill glanced at them with a hint of apology. He had no wish to rake over past mistakes.

"The point is, Mr. President," Traill continued, "this situation bears none of the hallmarks of an Al Qaeda operation. Or any of the other major Middle Eastern groups."

Gorton gestured impatiently. "How many hallmarks do you want, Mr. Traill?" he asked. "They've taken a group of Americans hostage. That's typical Al Qaeda behavior as far as I'm concerned."

He looked around the group of faces, expecting to see agreement in their expressions. Instead, he saw a few heads shaking.

Linus Benjamin, director of the FBI, decided it was time to take some of the presidential heat off Traill.

"That's just the point, Mr. President. They've taken hostages. And there's been mention of ransom." Gorton frowned, not understanding, and the Homeland Security director resumed the explanation.

"Those people don't give a damn about money. They're getting billions from their Saudi supporters. And they aren't interested in taking hostages. All they want to do is kill Americans in large numbers. If it were them, my guess is that the people in Utah would be dead already."

"That's crap!" Gorton said angrily. "I've seen hostage videotapes. Sometimes it seems those bastards at Al Jazeera are running them back to back."

Traill nodded. "Admittedly. But they're usually the work of fringe groups and they've all occurred in places like Afghanistan or Iraq. This is a major operation, not an ad hoc event where a fringe group of insurgents just happened to get lucky at a roadblock."

"Well if it isn't Al Qaeda, or any of the other Middle Eastern groups, who's holding 'em—the goddamn Mormons?" Gorton asked.

"The hostage takers haven't been identified so far Mr. President," Benjamin told him, although he knew the president was aware of the fact. He was aware of all the facts. A briefing sheet had been distributed before the emergency meeting was called. "We're assuming for the moment that they're a new group."

"After all, new groups are springing up all the time," Gorton said, acid dripping from his tone.

Benjamin thought it was time for the discussion to move on to more fruitful areas, rather than continuing to wrangle over what they didn't know.

"We have a plan of the resort here, Mr. President," he said. He moved now to an easel where a rough plan of the area was set up.

"As you can see, Mr. President, there's just the one road in, which the kidnappers have successfully blocked with an avalanche. There's nearly a quarter mile of the road covered by rock, snow and ice. It'll take weeks to clear it."

"Then why don't we go in the back door?" the president asked. "Isn't that what we've got choppers for?"

Benjamin frowned uncomfortably. "There is no 'back door' as you put it, sir," he said. "The resort is in a huge U-shaped valley. Over the back, there are steep cliffs and heavily wooded slopes. We couldn't move troops up there if we tried. And if we use choppers, odds are the kidnappers will hear or see them coming and start killing hostages." He swept his hand around the horseshoe-shaped ridge that rose above the hotel. "They've said they have men on watch at the top of this ridge here. We've got no reason to disbelieve them."

The president stared fixedly at the diagram. The position was virtually impregnable, he could see—particularly if the kidnappers were willing to sacrifice themselves with their victims. And that was a possibility that couldn't be discounted these days.

"What about the hostages?" he asked. "Where are they?"

The FBI director nodded to his opposite number to take over and then sat down again.

Tildeman resumed the briefing, turning the page on the easel to reveal a plan of the hotel itself: "The hostages are on the third floor," he said. "There's a gymnasium there and the walls are floor to ceiling glass. If the mountain did come down on them, they'd be buried alive in there."

"Jesus Christ," the president said petulantly. "Why would anyone design a building with glass walls?"

There was a brief silence around the room and a few of those present exchanged glances. The question typified the Gorton way of facing a problem, by asking irrelevant questions. "I guess they didn't plan on someone planting explosives in the cliff wall," Janet Haddenrich answered softly. She was the director of the CIA and, like her or not, Gorton knew he could never get rid of her. After a few months in the job, he knew that he wanted the second term in his own right. He also knew that if he fired the first woman ever to head up the CIA, his chances of being re-elected would be diddly shit.

Gorton glanced sourly at her and she remained impassive, her face a deadpan mask. With a loud exhalation of breath to mark his displeasure, he turned back to Tildeman.

"How many hostages?" he asked, "and who are they? Is there anyone well-known?"

That, of course, was another clue to the Gorton approach. If the hostages were nonentities, there would be far less pressure upon him to react to the situation. Tildeman shrugged.

"We don't have a list of names yet," he said. "The terrorists haven't indicated that they're holding any prominent people."

"So we can assume they're not," Gorton said. It was half a question, half a statement. He was actually looking for someone to make the decision for him and put it into words.

Linus Benjamin chipped in with an alternative. "Or we can assume that they may be and they aren't necessarily aware of the fact."

Gorton grunted his displeasure. "What's the name of this hotel again?" he asked.

Tildeman checked the notes in front of him, although he knew the name of the resort. "Canyon Lodge, Mr. President. It's in the Wasatches."

"Well at least we know that much." Gorton replied. "We may not know anything too useful but we know the name of the hotel. I guess that's something."

That was the problem, as Gorton saw it. Nobody seemed to know anything concrete. Yet sooner or later, they'd be asking him what actions they should take. He looked around the faces at the table: Homeland, FBI, CIA, NSA, the Joint Chiefs representative and a crew-cut marine light colonel who had accompanied him to the meeting and been introduced as the commander of the RRTF—the Rapid Response Tactical Force.

As far as Gorton knew, this sort of situation was what the RRTF had been formed for. He nodded at the marine now.

"So what are your people doing about this, Colonel . . . ?" He let the sentence trail off. He'd been introduced to the soldier but he didn't see any reason why he should remember the name of anyone as lowly as a light colonel.

"Maloney," General Barrett interceded, thin-lipped. Maloney hesitated, not sure if the president was going to correct his mistake. Gorton waved one hand in an impatient circular motion, telling the marine to get on with it.

"Ah. . . sir, at this stage, we don't have enough facts to formulate any sort of rescue plan," he said.

The president snorted derisively. "Then what's the point of having the RRTF in the first place?" he asked.

Maloney hesitated again and once more, Barrett answered: "Mr. President, Colonel Maloney is here to observe only. It's not his role to set policy or initiate plans. He'll do whatever we tell him."

Tildeman leaned forward to re-enter the conversation. "In the meantime, Mr. President, we've got forces on the ground there: local police, state police, the sheriff's office and a ranger unit from the Utah National Guard." He glanced at Benjamin. "I assume your people are there by now?"

The director of the FBI nodded. "The local agent-in-charge from Salt Lake City was headed up there as soon as the news broke. We'll reinforce him with whatever he needs as soon as he's assessed the situation."

The president grunted, the sound carrying a weight of disdain behind it.

"Sounds like a jurisdiction nightmare," he said. "Are they at the hotel itself?"

"No, Mr. President," Tildeman answered. "The road is blocked around five miles from the hotel. We've got choppers on site, of course, but the terrorists have warned us that they've got missiles and triple-A set up."

"And we believe them?" Gorton asked sarcastically.

Tildeman shrugged. "No reason why we shouldn't at this stage," he said. "We don't want to risk lives testing their word. Not yet anyway. As for jurisdiction, we've agreed that it'll be an FBI show, with support from the military if it's needed. Linus has one of his senior negotiators already on the way from Washington."

"And your people, Mr. Traill?" Gorton asked. He refused to give the man his courtesy title of general.

"We'll maintain an overview of the situation, Mr. President. We'll coordinate intelligence as it comes in and pass it on. But operational control will stay with the FBI."

The president grunted noncommitally. He gestured to his chief of staff, Terence Pohlsen. Pohlsen was the one appointment he had been able to make already. Even a president-by-default was entitled to appoint his own White House COS immediately.

Pohlsen cleared his throat. "Gentlemen," he said, and they all turned to him as he remembered, belatedly, that Janet Haddenrich was in the room, ". . . and Ms. Haddenrich, of course," he added.

"Mrs.," Janet said flatly, and he smiled and nodded another apology.

"Of course. Mrs. Haddenrich. I suggest at this time we await further contact from the terrorists, and that we spend that time ascertaining who might be among the hostages."

Tildeman and Benjamin both nodded. "We should have a guest list from the hotel chain within an hour or so," the FBI director said. "Plus, if these people run true to the usual form, we'll be hearing from them again within the next eight hours."

Pohlsen glanced quickly at him. "The usual form?" he asked and Benjamin nodded.

"They'll feed us information in dribs and drabs, keep us off balance, keep us guessing. We won't know what they want, the full details, for at least another twenty-four hours. In the meantime, we find out as much as we can and we wait."

Now that a course of action had been suggested, Gorton took the opportunity to look as if he were making a decision.

"That's it then," he said. "We hold a watching brief while we wait for more information. Gentlemen, as soon as anything breaks on this, I want to hear it, understand?"

The department heads nodded. Pohlsen, satisfied that he had given his man a chance to look as if he were in control, now raised a question.

"The press, Mr. President?" he said. He paused a second, then prompted: "I guess we don't want them involved yet?"

Gorton shook his head decisively. As far as he was concerned, not telling the press was always the best course of action in any circumstances. "No need to get them all fired up and asking questions we can't answer. Wait till we have more information and Jimmy can put out a press release."

Pohlsen nodded. "For the moment, we'll keep it simple," he said. "We'll say the road has been blocked by an avalanche halfway up the mountain. So far as we know, everyone at the resort is safe but the phone lines are down and we're working to make contact. Cell phones don't work up there. The hotel is in a dead spot. We'll issue a hotline number where relatives can contact us for further information as it comes to hand. That'll keep it all low-key."

"And it'll give us a line on who's still up there," Benjamin put in. Pohlsen glanced his way.

"Exactly," he replied.

Gorton looked around the table now, then placed his hands flat on the arms of his chair and stood.

"Well, gentlemen . . ." he said and, after just the right length of pause to be infuriating, added, "and Mrs. Haddenrich . . . I guess that's it for now."

Protoc l demanded that as soon as he rose from his seat, everyone must do the same. He nodded to them and swept out of the room on a tide of self-importance, a cavalcade of one.

FIFTEEN

The ski room seemed virtually empty.

Throughout the week, the lockable racks that lined the room had been full of brightly colored skis of widely differing shapes and lengths. An equally diverse range of ski boots had lined the racks set above the heating ducts.

Now the skis were widely dispersed. In a room that would cater to over two hundred pairs of skis and boots, there were barely thirty left, spaced out around the racks that had been assigned to the few remaining residents. The ski room was situated at the rear of the hotel, facing the cliff. A double-glazed door led in and out, forming an airlock that retained warmth inside the building and kept the exterior cold at bay. Jesse had waited till dark and then skied down the broad slope of the homeward run, staying close to the trees and shadows. Once at the bottom of the hill, he had removed his skis and covered the rest of the distance on foot, staying close to buildings wherever possible, until he reached this back entrance.

He'd figured that if there were trouble in the hotel, this entrance would be the one most likely to be forgotten. So far, it seemed that he'd been right.

Conscious of the silence in the room, Jesse leaned his own skis against an unused rack by the door. The packed snow on the skis and in the bindings was melting already, leaving an ever-widening pool of water on the concrete floor. He hefted the skis again and crossed the room, placing them in a rack at the end furthest from the door, slipping the locking bar across and placing the open padlock through the hole in the bar. A quick glance would assume that the skis were locked in place and the puddle of water beneath them would probably go unnoticed by a casual observer.

Leaving them where they had first been, leaning against the end of the ski rack, in a puddle of fresh water, would have been an instant giveaway that someone had entered the ski room in the past few minutes. Why that should be a problem, Jesse wasn't sure. But his instincts were warning him not to take any chances until he knew what was going on in Canyon Lodge. There was no sense in advertising his presence.

Tina's words from the previous night came back to him now. "You're a ghost," she had said when he finalized his bill, and he decided that he would remain that way a little longer. He discarded his goggles, woolen cap and gloves and stuffed them behind the skis. After the piercing chill of the early evening outside, the heat in the room was becoming oppressive but he kept his parka on for the time being. He could see no other parkas in the room and he reasoned that if he left his here, it would be noticed. He unzipped the front of the lightweight padded jacket. For now, that would have to be enough.

His boots were another matter. They were too clumsy to go clumping around the hotel in if he hoped to maintain any degree of concealment. Usually, skiers left their indoor shoes here in the ski room, changing back into them at the end of the day. But Jesse had been planning to go directly to his car in the underground garage and that's where his worn old Timberlands were at the moment.

He knelt quickly and unclipped the ski boots, sliding his feet out of them, unable to resist the small groan of pleasure as the restriction was released from his feet. He grinned wryly to himself. The old adage among skiers, the best part of skiing is taking your boots off, was a definite truism. There was a scrap of threadbare toweling hanging above the boot pegs and he quickly wiped the excess snow and moisture from them and hung them onto two of the thick dowels that stood out from the walls to support them. Then in his socks, he made his way out of the ski room. He cursed quietly as he trod in the icy puddle that his skis had left by the door.

Outside, in the gray concrete hallway, he hesitated. There was an elevator, of course, but there was no way he was taking that. He glanced around, looking for the doorway to the service stairs that he had noticed earlier in the week. It was a few yards from the elevator and he slipped through it, testing it before he let it swing closed to ensure that he could get back through if necessary—that the handle inside wasn't locked. Finding that it moved easily, he allowed the door to click shut. Then he headed down, toward the underground garage, his socks noiseless on the concrete steps.

The fire door into the garage was equipped with a wire reinforced safety window and he peered carefully through it for a few moments, trying to see if there was any movement in the parking lot itself. He could only see a limited area of the parking lot so he eased the door quietly open and slid through, staying close to the wall and moving quickly to a deep pool of shadow.

The parking lot mirrored the air of desertion that he'd seen in the ski room. A vast, low-ceilinged underground cavern, it stretched away before him, row after row of empty parking spaces, with only a few cars in evidence. His own rental, a last year's model Buick, was a quarter of the way down the room. Staying close to the wall, he moved silently toward it, his left hand reaching into his parka's inside pocket for the keys.

And stopped.

Here was a problem he hadn't foreseen. The Buick had an electronic lock, and as soon as he hit it, the indicator lights would flash and the audio warning would chirp twice. In the empty silence of the parking lot it would stand out like a gunshot. Before he tried retrieving anything from the car, he had better make damned sure there was nobody else down here with him.

He scouted the entire basement quickly. It wasn't all that hard, with most of the car spaces empty. He moved quietly around the outer perimeter, the cold concrete chiling his wet feet even further, until he was satisfied that he was alone down here. Then he retraced his steps to the car, stopping in the shadow of one of the concrete pillars some thirty feet from the Buick. If somebody suddenly popped out of the woodwork when he hit the button, it might be a good idea not to be standing too close to the car while it hooted and flashed.

He hit the remote and winced as the car went through its unlocking performance. It seemed even louder and brighter than he'd expected. Pausing a moment, he waited to see if there was any reaction to the light and the noise. Nothing. He edged forward toward the car and opened the driver's door.

There was no shout. No sudden burst of gunfire. No clatter of running feet. He was alone down here. Hastily, he popped the trunk lid and unzipped the battered old soft bag that held his gear. The Timberland moccasins were on top of the folded clothes inside the case and he slipped them on gratefully, then rummaged through the clothes to find a spare pair of socks. As soon as he had a minute, he'd discard the wet pair he was wearing. His hands were running through the layers of clothes and personal items now, searching for the small leather satchel . . . and finding it. He unzipped it and placed it on top of the mussed up suitcase.

The Colt was still there, along with two spare magazines of .45 ACP ammunition.

He slipped the spares into a pocket in his parka, then thumbed the magazine release and caught the magazine as it slid out of the butt, checking to make sure it had a full load. Before he replaced it, he eased the action back a little, making sure the chamber was empty. He remembered leaving it that way when he'd packed it but with guns it always paid to make sure your memory was correct.

He slid the magazine back into the butt and worked the slide once, jacking a round into the chamber. Carefully, he let the hammer down and shoved the safety on. Now, if he needed to fire in a hurry, he simply had to cock the hammer and release the safety where it fell easily to hand by his right thumb. It might be wise to leave the gun with its chamber unloaded for traveling. When you were expecting to run into trouble, it was just as wise to have it ready for action.

He slid the gun into his waistband in the small of his back, then closed the trunk as carefully as he could. Automatically, he was about to hit the remote lock once more, out of sheer force of habit, when he realized he might need to come back to the car sometime later. He left it unlocked.

Taking a moment to get his bearings, Jesse headed toward the western side of the building. There should be another set of service stairs here that would take him up to the arrivals area—the tunnel where he'd guessed the shooting had occurred.

There'd been no further sound of shots since the first. But, some forty minutes ago, he'd been puzzled by a string of muffled explosions that seemed to come from some way off. Maybe they had nothing to do with the situation here. It might just be routine avalanche clearance work. He'd heard enough explosions in the week he'd been here to think of them as a normal background noise.

There was another safety-windowed door leading into the tunnel. Carefully, he checked, pressing hard against the door to give himself the widest possible field of view. Once again, there seemed to be nobody on the other side of the door. Still, he edged it open an inch at a time, peering at the widening expanse of tunnel that became visible, before slipping through and allowing the door to close quietly behind him.

The Colt was in his right hand, safety off and thumb curled over the hammer, ready to cock it. There was nobody here. Then he noticed the small, huddled shape against the outer wall of the tunnel—at first looking like a discarded bundle of ski clothing. But Jesse had seen discarded bundles like that before and he knew it for what it was: a body.

Crouching close to the wall, eyes darting in all directions, he advanced on the body.

It was a woman, he saw, guessing that she was relatively young. He had to guess because the features were a mask of dried blood and a large part of the face was missing.

Knowing it was hopeless, he touched a finger to her throat, feeling for a pulse. The flesh was cold and clammy to the touch. There was no flicker of life there. Kneeling beside her, he cast his eyes around the tunnel and caught a glimpse of bright metal. Crossing to it, he knelt and picked it up—turning it in his hand to see the letters stamped into the brass. It was a 9 millimeter shell case that had caught a stray gleam of light. Now he could see several more scattered around—eight or nine in all. He remembered the sudden burst of automatic fire that he'd heard that afternoon and he realized that he had been correct. This was where the shooting had taken place.

He stood erect, tossing the shell case lightly in one hand as he thought. One shot first. That had most likely been the one that had killed the girl. Then a burst of firing that had left these spent shells by the roadside. To what purpose, he wondered? Obviously, there had been no further killing—there was just the one body left lying forlornly in the road. He shrugged. There could be any number of explanations for the sequence. The important point was that the presence of the dead girl's body established definitely that something very, very wrong was going on around here. When things were normal, people weren't shot and left to lie where they fell.

There was a raised sidewalk outside the automatic doors that led into the hotel. He stepped onto it now, carefully moving to one side to avoid the infra-red beam that would automatically cause the doors to sigh open. Flattened against the wall, he edged to the door and peered around. He had a limited view of the escalators leading from the lobby to the reception area on the first floor level. He hesitated, wondering whether to risk the entrance, then froze as a figure crossed the downstairs lobby, suddenly appearing in his field of view.

The man crossed quickly to the escalators and stepped onto them. He was around six feet, thirtyish and fit looking. Dressed in tan chinos and a rollneck sweater, there was nothing particularly unusual about him. He was the sort of guy you'd expect to see in a ski resort. Except for the slab-sided Ingram submachine gun that he wore, casually slung over his right shoulder.

That was something you definitely didn't expect to see.

SIXTEEN

By now, the hostages, guests and staff members alike, had all been gathered in the gymnasium on the third floor. Kormann entered and swept his gaze around the big room. He'd sent three of the hotel staff to collect bedding and the hostages were setting up sleeping spaces around the room, laying blankets out on the hard nylon carpet that provided only a thin covering for the concrete floor. He noticed, with a wry smile, that as far as they could, they'd maintained a male–female separation.

As he entered the room, he felt the eyes of the hostages upon him and an almost palpable tide of hatred sweeping over him. Word had gone around, as he had known it would, of the fate of the sixty staff members in the shuttle bus. Along with the hatred, he could sense something else—fear. And that was the way he wanted it. Markus approached him now. One of the guards went to intercept him but Kormann said a quiet word and the duty manager was allowed to pass.

"What can I do for you, Ben?" he said quietly. There was hatred lurking behind the other man's eyes, in spite of his best attempts to conceal it. No fear there, he noticed, with some interest. That would bear watching. The duty manager apparently had some starch in his backbone.

The manager gestured to where one of the guests was setting out blankets and sheets. "Is there any reason why we couldn't bring some mattresses in here?" he asked. "We've got two hundred empty rooms full of them," he added. Kormann made a pretense of considering the request, then shook his head decisively.

"Yes, Ben. There's a reason," he said, in that same mild tone. "I don't see why you people should get too comfortable. A little bunking down on the hard floor will do you all good."

He smiled and watched Markus contain the sudden flush of anger that showed on his face. Then the other man turned away abruptly and went back to his spot by the window, where he had spread a pair of blankets and a pillow. Kormann watched with interest as he said something to a good-looking girl he'd noticed earlier. From the way he shook his head, he was obviously repeating Kormann's answer to her. She glanced up once in Kormann's direction. The terrorist leader met her gaze. She was another who might bear watching, he thought to himself. In the meantime, she might as well be put to work.

He beckoned to her. "You," he said. "Over here."

The girl hesitated, then started toward him. She had an athlete's grace as she moved. She was tall, slim and well-muscled. Odds were she was an expert skier. Most of the staff in a place like this would be. She stopped before him, eyebrows raised in inquiry. There was a hint of arrogance to her bearing.

"Get the chef and report to me outside," he told her shortly, turning his back on her and walking away. She hesitated again, not sure what to say to his retreating back. As he reached the doorway and gestured for the guard there to let him through, he glanced back at her. She was already moving to find the chef, who was at the far end of the room. Telling the guard to let them through, Kormann went out into the command center he had set up in the gymnasium offices. Pallisani was there, just hanging up the phone as he entered. Kormann raised an eyebrow in question and the other man smiled.

"Just another call to the roadblock," he said. "I tried to make it sound a little panicky and a little out of control."

Kormann nodded. That was the plan. The more unstable the authorities thought they might be, the less likely they'd be to attempt a rescue. For that reason, he and Pallisani were alternating calls to the county sheriff at the roadblock. They'd decided, for the time being, to insist on speaking only with the elderly Wasatch county sheriff, ignoring the FBI agent who they knew was in charge. It was all part of a deliberate pattern. By refusing a consistent point of contact, they were keeping the authorities off balance.

"What'd you tell them?" he asked, and Pallisani shrugged.

"Not too much. I ranted a little and said we knew they were trying to sneak cops in through the roadblock. Told 'em we'd kill everyone if we saw one cop or one national guardsman coming over that rise there."

Kormann nodded. "Good," he agreed. "Give them another hour and a half and tell them we want to talk to someone who can authorize a ransom, and a chopper out of here."

Pallisani frowned at that. "Shouldn't you call them next?" he asked and Kormann shook his head, wondering why he had to explain details like this to the other man. No wonder Pallisani had never risen too high in the Mob, he thought.

"We don't want it to look like we're taking turns," he said. "Keep it random. Besides, if you keep making more and more unreasonable demands, it gives me room to negotiate more calmly later on."

Pallisani thought that over and nodded. When Kormann put it that way, he could see the logic in it.

"Fine," he said. Then, in response to a knock on the door, he called: "Yeah?"

The girl entered. Kormann remembered to check the nameplate she wore on her uniform blouse: Tina Bowden. He looked at her blankly, letting her make the first move. His silence threw her off balance and finally she had to speak.

"You said to . . . get the chef and come out here," she told him and he nodded.

"I know," he replied flatly. Then: "I see you. I don't see him."

"He's—" She jerked a thumb at the door, indicating that the chef was waiting outside. Kormann put his head to one side, feigning interest.

"Then let's get him—" He mimicked her action, jerking a thumb at the floor in front of him.

Tina hesitated, then turned to the door, opened it and called, "Ralph. Come on in."

The chef entered uncertainly and, Kormann was pleased to notice, fearfully. That was all to the good. Frightened people were a lot easier to keep in control. If they were frightened already, half your work was done.

"So, Ralph," he said pleasantly, "I guess now you're pretty glad I didn't let you go out on that bus?"

The chef went to speak, then stopped, his jaw hanging open. He was around thirty, and, breaking the stereotypical image of a chef, he was a tall thin man with a prominent Adam's apple. Kormann went on before the chef could regain his wits.

"Now I guess you owe me some pretty fancy meals, right? After all, buddy, I saved your life out there."

Ralph glanced sidelong at the girl. Her mouth was set in a tight line as she glared at Kormann. She'd had several good friends on that bus and his joking tone was like salt in a raw wound to her. Ralph read the look on her face and decided it might be better to say nothing. He nodded, a barely noticeable movement. Kormann, pretending not to notice the little piece of byplay, went on in the same light tone.

"So, Ralph, what were you planning to serve up tonight to the guests?" he said, pretending to glance through a pile of printed forms that meant absolutely nothing to him. The chef made a vague gesture, spreading both hands in a kind of a half shrug. His head nodded from side to side.

"Aahhh . . ." he said, "the special tonight was tarragon-coated chicken breasts, char-broiled and served with a Dijon mustard sauce."

Kormann swept the printed forms aside and nodded thoughtfully. "Sounds good, Ralph. Were you doing that with French fries on the side?"

Ralph, on familiar territory, was becoming a little more self-confident. He smiled, a little deprecatingly, at the thought of French fries with his tarragon chicken.

"Well no," he said. "I was going to cream some new potatoes and pipe them around the—"

He broke off in midsentence, his eyes fixed momentarily on the Browning Hi-Power 9 millimeter that Kormann had produced and placed on the top of the desk between them. Then he looked up to the other man's eyes, seeing them hard and unforgiving.

"Ralph, the rule around here is, when I suggest something, you say, 'That's right, Mr. Kormann.' Got it?"

Ralph swallowed hard. Then nodded. Finally, he found his voice. "Yes, Mr. Kormann," he breathed.

Kormann nodded. "Yes, what?" he prompted and the chef's eyes slid sideways to Tina, looking for some kind of support there and finding none.

"Uh . . . yes, with French fries," he said finally, in a small voice. Kormann nodded, satisfied. The Browning went back into the shoulder holster under his jacket.

"And a green salad, I think, with a good French dressing," he added and again the chef nodded, remembering, when Kormann's eyes snapped up to his, to say, "Yes, Mr. Kormann. A green salad would be fine."

"Good," Kormann said, no longer looking at the other man as he checked through the printout of the hotel guest list. "So get on with it. The girl can help you."

Tina started to turn to the door but stopped as she realized that Ralph was hesitating, wringing his hands in fear. Kormann, eyes down on the guest list, affected not to notice for a few seconds, then looked up, frowning, at the chef.

"Yes?" he said.

"Um . . . the chicken . . . it was . . . it was the special," Ralph finally managed to say.

Kormann shrugged. "Great," he said impatiently. "Go get on with it."

Still Ralph didn't move, although every inch of his body said that he wanted to—simply wanted to get the hell out of this room and as far away from Kormann as he could possibly be. The terrorist leader looked up again.

"What are you waiting on, Ralph?" he asked sarcastically, then added, "The next bus out?" He heard the quick intake of breath from the girl but ignored her, his gaze locked on the chef's. Ralph made a few helpless movements with his hands.

"There's not enough for everyone," he said finally. "It was the special. I only have two dozen chicken breasts unfrozen. When it's a special we don't usually have enough for everyone," he explained weakly as he finished.

Kormann let out a short, harsh bark of laughter. "Well hell, Ralph," he said, putting a sneering emphasis on the name. "I didn't want it for everyone. Just me and my men. The rest of you can have stew."

"Stew?" Ralph echoed, relief evident in his voice.

"Yes, Ralph. Stew. You got any cans of stew in that great big pantry downstairs? I'll bet you have."

"Well . . . yeah. I guess so," the chef replied and Kormann nodded emphatically.

"Well, get busy and open some cans, Ralph. No, on second thought, let the girl do that. I guess you can open a can, can't you, honey?" This last was addressed to Tina Bowden, who met his gaze, trying to hide the anger in her eyes and not quite succeeding. She knew he was needling her, knew it was a mistake to let him see how much she hated him. But she simply couldn't help it.

"I guess so," she said, at last.

"Well, get to it," he said, dismissing them with a wave of his hand. "Otherwise you're going to be mighty hungry in that room."

SEVENTEEN

It was a rich man's retreat, Kormann thought, as the silent manservant showed him through to the rear terrace, overlooking the lake. As he followed the man, he noticed the square outline of the pistol under the tail of his shirt, worn outside the black trousers. Big, he thought. Probably a Browning Hi-Power 9. Then, as he took in the rich wooden furnishings of the rooms they passed through, and the mosaic tile work that covered the floor, he amended the earlier thought. It was a very rich man's retreat.

Estevez was waiting for him on the terrace, at a table shaded by a cantilevered sun umbrella. As he emerged from the dim coolness of the house, Kormann squinted slightly in the bright glare. It was hot and humid this close to the equator, but there was the relief of a cooling breeze sweeping up the hill from the lake. Below them, a handful of glistening white and chrome pleasure boats carved their way along the Banana Cut. Further away, a huge slab-sided cruise ship plowed through the Culebra Cut—the commercial channel.

The *Jefe*—as he liked to be called—rose to greet him, a smile creasing his tanned face. The eyes were obscured by dark aviator-style sunglasses, so it was impossible to tell if the smile was genuine or not. He looked cool and comfortable in a linen shirt and trousers. His black hair was brushed so that not one strand was out of place. The teeth showed white against his tanned skin. He was a handsome man, Kormann thought, and he looked much younger than his sixty years. Kormann wondered if the hair was dyed, and decided that it probably was. Estevez had that macho streak in him that would always want to deny the aging process.

"Raymond," he said, offering his hand. "It's good to see you."

Kormann was mildly pleased that he didn't affect to call him *Raimundo*. They shook hands. Estevez's grip was as firm and strong as his own. Then he motioned his guest to a cane chair on the opposite side of the glass-topped table where he had been sitting. He gestured to the servant, who had remained hovering in the doorway.

"Drinks please, Paolo," he said. The servant bowed slightly and withdrew. The *Jefe* studied his guest for a few seconds. He was slightly above average height, lean and well muscled, and he moved like an athlete—balanced and smooth and without wasted motion. He was wearing chinos and a khaki drill shirt that had a vaguely military cut—which was appropriate, considering his occupation. The hair was cropped short. The eyes were a piercing blue above the strong nose. There were crinkles at the corners of the eyes and his face wore a permanent tan, witness to a life spent in the open air.

"You're looking well. Business is good?"

Kormann shrugged. "Business will always be good while Africa is full of politicians trying to kill each other," he said.

There was the very slightest hard edge of an accent. It was almost South African, but not quite. The mercenary allowed his glance to wander around the surroundings—the wide terrace, the green jungle below and the sparkling blue waters of the lake. It was a common mistake to assume that the Panama Canal was like the Suez—a straight, narrow channel cut through the land at sea level. But once ships had passed through the locks at either end, they entered Lake Gatun, a vast expanse of water dotted with islands and traversed by the pleasure boats of rich Panamanians.

"Seems you're doing well yourself," he said. He knew this was only one of Estevez's homes. The *Jefe* never liked to stay too long in one place. There were people in Colombia who would be only too keen to repay what they saw as past insults and affronts. Their task was made all the more difficult by the fact that they could never be too sure where Estevez could be found at any time. Kormann glanced down to the jetty below the house; a high-speed catamaran cruiser was moored there, alongside a perfectly maintained vintage Grumman Gosling amphibian.

Estevez shrugged. "My business is always good too," he replied. He raised one eyebrow as Kormann absentmindedly fished a soft pack of Marlboros from his shirt pocket and shook one out. "You shouldn't smoke," he said reprovingly. "Nicotine is a drug of addiction."

Kormann smiled as he lit the cigarette. "*You're* concerned about drugs of addiction?" he asked.

Estevez shrugged. "Drugs are for business. Not pleasure."

The servant returned at that moment. He set down a tray of drinks and placed an ashtray beside Kormann's elbow. Kormann glanced sideways at him.

"Your man knows my habits," he said and the *Jefe* shrugged.

"He's a good servant. He anticipates my needs and those of my guests. And he knows how to keep his mouth shut."

"And I'll bet he's a crack shot with that Browning Hi-Power he has under the tail of his shirt," Kormann added, and this time it was Estevez's turn to smile.

"Of course. All good servants should be multiskilled."

He reached for the drinks tray and took a bottle, pausing with it over a tall glass, his eyebrows rising in a question. It was an un-branded white rum, Kormann knew, made especially for his host, smoother and more potent than any commercial brand on the market. He nodded and Estevez poured generous measures into two glasses.

"Ice and lime?" he asked and Kormann nodded again.

"That sounds good," he said. He was right. When Estevez passed him the glass, the sides already frosting with dew in the hot, humid climate, the smooth bite of the rum and sharp tang of the fresh limes were a perfect combination. He sipped once, experimentally, then again, deeper this time for enjoyment. He leaned back in the cane chair. This was the way to talk business, he thought, not sweating in tropical heat and swatting at mosquitoes under the palm thatch of an African hut, in the company of a would-be president with psy-chopathic tendencies and delusions of destiny. Again, he surveyed the vast lake below them, dotted in this part with green islands. Estevez followed his gaze, frowning as he saw the cruise ship, still steadfastly making its way across Lake Gatun.

"Look at that," he said distastefully. "Where's the glamour? Where's the beauty? They don't build real ships anymore. They might as well set a city block afloat as one of those."

Kormann shrugged. Estevez had a taste for the old ways, for old-fashioned glamour and style. The restored Grumman at the jetty was proof of that. But frankly, Kormann hadn't traveled halfway around the world to discuss glamour and the lost era of ocean liners.

"It's practical," he said. "But you didn't ask me here to discuss ships."

"That's true," Estevez said. Normally, he expected those he dealt with to defer to him, to allow him to set the pace of their agenda. But Kormann was something more than a subordinate, or even an employee. He was a man Estevez trusted and respected, a professional who had seen the *Jefe* through more than one dangerous situation in the past. He was a colleague—slightly junior perhaps, but a colleague nonetheless.

He reached to a side table now and retrieved a manila file folder. The cover was battered and creased. The file inside had been collated over a long period and added to continually. He opened it and spread out several black and white photos, separating them from the pile of typescript and press cuttings that the folder also contained. Kormann glanced at them incuriously. He knew who the subject would be. The photos were grainy and showed the lack of perspective that meant they'd been taken through a telephoto lens.

He flicked the photos around so that he could view them right side up, then glanced up at the *Jefe*'s face.

"Still him," he said. He saw the sudden rush of blood to Estevez's face, saw the rage that suddenly burned deep behind his eyes.

"Still him. I don't forget. Not ever."

Kormann pushed the photos back across the table. He didn't need to study them.

"Are you sure this is worth pursuing?" he asked. "It must be years now."

"It's eight years. Eight years and two months." Estevez stabbed a forefinger at one of the photos and leaned toward his guest. The intense hatred in his voice was almost palpable. It was all Kormann could do not to recoil slightly.

"And if it were eighteen years, or twenty, or thirty, it would still be worth pursuing. This man attacked me. He chose to become my enemy and I do not allow that to go unanswered. Maybe you don't understand that. You're an anglo, after all." There was the slightest hint of disdain in his voice as he added the last few words.

The mercenary shrugged. Revenge wasn't one of his motivators. Profit was. "It's your money," he said.

Estevez nodded agreement. He took a deep breath, making a visible effort and regaining control after his sudden show of emotion. He leaned back. "And I have plenty of it."

"Which is all I need to know," Kormann told him. Their gazes met and there was a moment of silence between them.

"What I need to know," Estevez said, "is can you put a team together quickly? Say, fifteen to twenty men?"

"How quickly is quickly?" Kormann asked and Estevez paused, considering.

"On two weeks' notice. To be available in the United States within two weeks of your receiving the go ahead. One other thing," he added. "Don't pick anyone you may want to use again. There will certainly be casualties."

He was pleased to see that Kormann didn't even need to think about his answer.

"Not a problem," he said evenly. "Will it be Washington?"

The *Jefe* shook his head. "Washington is impossible these days. Too much security. Too many cameras. I should have got him last time. Things were easier then. But the shooter was incompetent."

Kormann shrugged. "One shooter is never enough if you want to make certain. Too many things can go wrong. Look at Kennedy. It took four to make sure of him—five, if you count Oswald."

Estevez tapped the documents in the folder. "Well, this time, he'll be away from Washington. There's a pattern emerging in his movements that we can take advantage of."

Kormann picked up the half-empty glass. The beads of dew had coalesced into water and it dripped on his trousers as he drank. He ignored it. The material would dry in minutes in this heat.

"Time frame?" he said. "I have a few projects coming up in the next six months."

"There'll be no conflict. I'm looking at maybe eighteen months. Winter in the North."

Kormann smiled. "You certainly plan things well in advance," he said. Estevez didn't return the smile.

"That's how you make sure of things. I learned my lesson last time. I need a little more time to make sure this pattern is permanent. We can talk about fees over the coming months. You know by now that I pay well."

"That's why I came here." Kormann finished his drink and set the glass down on the table. Estevez made a tentative move toward the bottle.

"Another?" he invited. He enjoyed Kormann's company. He liked speaking with someone who didn't live in fear of him. Then again, he thought, with a small inner smile, he liked speaking with people who did live in fear of him as well.

"Maybe not," Kormann said. "I'll call for the boat. He's cruising somewhere down the Banana Cut." He took a utilitarian Nokia cell from his hip pocket and began to hit the numbers. Estevez smiled to himself. Everything about Kormann was unremarkable. No flashy jewelry. No ostentatious phone. Estevez indicated the jetty below them with a sweeping gesture.

"Why not fly back to Panama City?" he offered. "I'll have my pilot take you in the Grumman." But again, Kormann declined.

"The Grumman is a pretty distinctive piece of hardware," he said. "Best if I'm not seen associated with you."

"You may be right. Keep a low profile."

The mercenary nodded. "I always have."

EIGHTEEN

THE PRESENT

Sheriff Cale Lawson took off his small-brimmed Stetson and scratched his head thoughtfully. Above the suntanned face—browned and weathered by years of exposure to the mountain elements—there was a startling white patch of skin where the hat protected his forehead from the sun, surmounted by a thinning thatch of gray hair. Cale was fifty-seven and he'd decided a year back that he wasn't going to be running again for sheriff of Wasatch County. He had another eight months in the job and he wished this damn mess had shown the good taste to wait nine of them. So far, he'd been the main contact with the terrorists in the hotel. Fortunately there hadn't been a lot of it and he felt that, so far, he hadn't made any irretrievable mistakes in dealing with them. But now he was aware of a distinct sense of relief at being able to hand over the responsibility.

"So what do you think?" he said to Special Agent-in-Charge Denton Colby. The FBI agent didn't answer immediately. He was standing in the middle of the road, staring fixedly at the pile of rock, snow and ice that filled it. He was a massively built black man, with a thick, bullish neck, muscle-corded shoulders and heavy features. He was just over six feet tall, but the width of his shoulders and the massive chest made him appear almost squat. He was a remarkably ugly man, and he seemed almost disproportioned. Yet Lawson had noticed that he moved with a certain athletic grace, and a deceptively light step. Vaguely, he remembered the name. He was a boxing fan, had been all his life, and the name Colby was familiar to him. He frowned, searching his memory, but to no avail.

In a day or so, he'd remember that Denton Colby had boxed light heavy in the Golden Gloves and had missed out on silver at the 1988 Olympics when his Polish opponent's intentional elbow, unnoticed by the ref, had opened a deep gash in his left eyebrow, bringing the fight to an abrupt end. Colby could have taken the Pole with one hand. But trying to do it with one eye was a different matter altogether.

Now, the ex-boxer surveyed the blocked road that led to Canyon Lodge.

"Can we clear it?" he asked finally, and Lawson let go a short bark of laughter.

"Hell yes, we can," he said. "But I don't see us doing it this side of a month and by then those boys up at the lodge will be well away."

Colby shrugged. He'd thought as much but it never hurt to make sure. He shifted his frozen feet uncomfortably. He'd flown in from Washington and his thin street shoes were less than ideal wear for this frozen mountain road. He made a mental note to get someone to bring him a thick pair of boots. Maybe the local agent could do that for him, he thought. The damn fool wasn't much use for anything else. He'd been almost pathetically grateful to hand over control of the scene to Colby upon his arrival.

Cale Lawson moved a few paces to get a better look at the agent's face. Colby's features were a mask. He stared, expressionless, at the rubble that blocked the road, his mind's eye soaring far beyond it to the hotel where close to one hundred people were held hostage—for what?

So far, there had been a vague hint about ransom from the kidnappers, one mention only. Usually it was the subject of the first demand—and every other subsequent one as well. His impassive face gave him a stolid appearance, almost an appearance of dullness. Nothing was further from the truth. He was already weighing facts and suppositions, trying to fit the known details and the presumed ones into some sort of pattern.

Lawson, like so many other people before him, mistook the agent's lack of animation for a lack of resolution. Maybe the Washington hotshot needed prodding, he thought, and attempted some.

"We've got the Jet Ranger here," he suggested. "We could try taking a look up the valley some?"

Colby thought about it. He'd seen the Bell 206 when he'd arrived. A similar chopper had flown him from Salt Lake City's airport to the avalanche site. He hadn't even had to deplane through the terminal. The commercial flight had stopped on the runway apron while steps were wheeled up and he disembarked and ran to the waiting chopper. It was lifting off and banking toward the Wasatches even before he had his seat belt buckled. The advantages of priority travel with the bureau, he thought.

"There was some word about Stingers," he said flatly, and Cale shrugged.

"They said they've got 'em," he agreed. "Whether they have or not is another matter."

Colby studied the county sheriff in his turn. He was a small man, thin and gray-haired. The gun belt with its holstered Beretta 9 millimeter sat high on his waist, seeming to cut off his upper torso prematurely, so that his uniform trousers looked to be pulled up way past his waist. Being small of stature, Lawson carried himself erect and straight-backed—making every inch of height count. Colby smiled to himself. He figured the sheriff for a feisty type, maybe a little argumentative and a touch headstrong. Colby found himself thinking of an aging bantam rooster as he looked at the wiry little sheriff. But the eyes were clear and honest, and instinctively he felt he could trust the other man.

"Guess there's one way to find out," he said, and jerked his head toward the sheriff's department Jet Ranger. "You up for a sightseeing flight?"

Together they walked back down the road toward the chopper, passing the trailers that were being deployed, setting up a mobile command and communication post. A group of army six-by-sixes snarled up the hill from Salt Lake City, their diesel exhausts staining the evening sky. Colby saw fresh young faces peering curiously out from under grim kevlar helmets. National Guard, he thought. A state trooper was signaling the lead driver of the convoy, directing him to park a little farther along the road where there was still some space left. With a cliff on one side and a sheer drop on the other, that was becoming a precious commodity.

As they walked, Lawson caught the chopper pilot's eye and made a circling gesture with his right forefinger. The pilot took the hint and Colby heard the high-pitched whine of the starter, saw the big two-bladed rotor begin to turn slowly.

Then as the revs came up and a thin haze of burnt JP4 blasted out of the jet's exhaust, the wind began whipping his long-skirted Burberry coat around his legs. He remembered that his feet were still cold and decided it was too late now to start looking for boots. Instinctively bowing his head a few inches, he moved under the spinning rotor and hauled himself up into the rear seat. Lawson took the seat next to the pilot, stuffing his Stetson behind his seat and cramming an intercom headset on. Colby looked around the rear seat, saw another headset on a hook by the window and donned it.

"Where to, Sheriff?" the pilot was asking. His uniform marked him as deputy in the Wasatch County sheriff's department. The bone dome crash helmet he wore was emblazoned with a deputy's star on its front.

"Let's take her up the valley, Gus," Lawson's voice rasped in the headphones. The deputy did a slight double take.

"Up to the lodge, Sheriff?" he asked and Cale nodded.

"Less you got somewhere else you'd like to go, son," he replied evenly. The pilot pursed his lips.

"Aaah . . . Sheriff," he began uncertainly, "I heard tell they've got missiles up there."

Lawson settled back into the left-hand seat more comfortably and turned a thin smile on the pilot.

"Heard much the same thing, Gus. Now let's pull pitch and go find out."

The deputy swallowed and his hands fell to the controls. The chopper quivered slightly, then rose a few feet from the ground, slewing around to head up canyon.

The sound of the blades whacking the air changed to a less frenetic note as the pitch changed and the little aircraft transitioned from the hover and began moving forward, nose down, with increasing speed.

On the rear bench seat, Colby shifted position so that he was peering between the two men in front, giving himself a less restricted view out of the front windscreen. He guessed that, as the man in charge, he could have taken the left front seat instead of the Sheriff. But hell, he shrugged, it was the sheriff's department's chopper and there probably wouldn't be a whole hell of a lot to see anyway. Lawson and the pilot, with the added advantage of the clear view panels in the front floor, had the best view of the ground rushing by below them.

"Follow the road, son," Lawson told the pilot, adding, "There's no need to get up too high. Keep her below the ridge line as much as you can."

The road below them was still a tumble of rock and snow where the landslide had cut it. Then, after a couple of hundred yards, the black ribbon showed clear again. Looking at the mass of rubble blocking the way, Colby realized that the sheriff's estimation had been right. It would take weeks to clear that mess—and a whole peck of heavy equipment to get the job done.

The chopper twisted and turned, following the snake-like track of the road. The pilot needed no second urging to keep low. He wanted to stay masked behind those hills as long as possible. Unfortunately for their peace of mind, that wasn't going to be for much longer. The valley started to widen out as they approached Canyon Lodge. They rounded a ridge and saw the lights of the massive hotel building a quarter mile away.

"Hold it here a moment, Gus," Lawson said, and the whacking of the rotor blades returned as they went into a hover. "Keep the nose on 'em," he added, and Gus worked the pedals, reducing power to the tail rotor momentarily to slew the nose of the chopper around so that it faced the building. Lawson glanced back over his shoulder at the bear-like FBI agent.

"Those Stingers are short range. And they need a clear look at the heat signature from the tailpipe," he said conversationally. "Figure this way we'll fox them a little."

Colby grunted, then replied, "Good thinking, as long as they haven't got any men on the peaks behind us here." He saw the quick, nervous glance that the pilot flung over his shoulder at him. The distraction caused him to let the chopper slew a little to one side and he hastened to correct the movement as Lawson growled a warning at him.

Colby leaned further forward between the two seats and focused a pair of night glasses on the hotel. Things seemed normal enough, he thought. There was no sign of movement. No sign of any trouble.

"See anything?" Lawson's voice rasped in his headphones.

"Uh-uh," he replied. Then he noticed something moving on the roof, and a light blinking at them. "Wait. Someone's signaling . . ."

"Jesus!" gasped the pilot and threw the chopper into a sideways, skidding dive as a twin line of yellow streaks reached out to them from the roof of the hotel. Colby, who had released his belt to gain a better view, was tossed sidelong on the rear bench seat. He saw streaks of light passing close to the perspex canopy of the helicopter, then impacting the rock face behind them before bouncing high into the air and eventually disappearing.

"Get us out of here, Gus." Lawson's voice was tight. The chopper dropped to a bare twenty feet off the snow as the pilot twisted the throttle wide open, heading for the shelter of the narrow pass once more. The three men were silent as they raced for the narrow gap, fully aware that at any moment the fiery trail of a Stinger missile might reach out for them, homing on the hot gases of their exhaust.

There was a sigh of relief from all three of them as they reached the shelter of the solid rock. Lawson turned to face the FBI agent once more. He pursed his lips reflectively.

"Well, don't know about Stingers," he said, "but they sure as hell have some triple-A up there."

"We heading back down now, Sheriff?" the pilot asked nervously.

Colby grinned to himself, although no sign of it showed on his set features. It was pretty clear which way the pilot wanted them to go.

"Might as well, Gus," Lawson told him. "They ain't going to let us see anything more tonight."

The chopper whack-whacked its way back down the canyon, the pilot bringing it to a landing beside the huddle of sheriff's department cars. Colby noticed how each organization present—sheriff, state police, national guard and FBI—had staked out their own territory. As he stepped down from the Jet Ranger, a state trooper ran forward, holding his Smokey the Bear hat on against the down draft of the rotor.

"Agent Colby?" he shouted and when Denton nodded confirmation, the man gestured to the comms trailer some fifty yards away.

"They're on the line," he said. "Want to talk to whoever's in charge."

Denton nodded and jogged after the man toward the trailer. There was no need to ask who "they" might be.

NINETEEN

The emergency council rose to their feet as President Gorton entered the room.

He glanced around the assembled faces, angry and annoyed, his face flushed. He'd been awakened from the nap that he took every day at this time and he resented it—all the more so when he read the details of the demand that had been passed on from the terrorists at Canyon Lodge.

"Where's Traill?" he asked. The homeland security director was absent.

"General Traill will receive full minutes of these meetings," Benjamin told him, "but he has a pretty full plate at the moment."

The chief of staff leaned forward and spoke in a low voice.

"There's that Florida thing he's been working on, sir," he told the president. Gorton grunted. A series of massive storms had hit the Florida Keys over the past month, leaving tens of thousands of people stranded and at risk. Traill's people had their hands full getting people out, finding temporary accommodation, discouraging looters and ensuring the safety of those left suddenly homeless.

"Damn if we haven't got problems coming out our asses these days," Gorton said, annoyance obvious in his voice.

The annoyance deepened as he recognized a face that hadn't been here before. Truscott Emery smiled back at him as their gazes met. Angrily, Gorton wondered who'd told the special adviser that this meeting had been called. He suspected Benjamin. He knew the bureau director admired Emery's scholastic, analytical mind. As far as Gorton was concerned, Emery was simply another annoying left-over from the previous administration and he couldn't wait for the day when he could get rid of him. To his surprise, his own advisers had counseled against it, so he'd decided to bide his time until his position was stronger.

In the meantime, he had compensated by taking Emery out of the loop as far as possible, excluding him from planning sessions and the cabinet meetings to which he'd been privy under President Couch.

Emery was an interesting study in the politically seething atmosphere of the Capitol. He was an academic, a professor emeritus with Harvard Business School who, prior to his Washington appointment, had spent his time lecturing to short-term students from high-paying corporations around the world. He was also a very practical thinker and his ability to add insight into the most complex of problems had been valued beyond diamonds by Couch. He had secured the services of the professor as a special adviser, with a free-ranging brief to comment on anything and everything that went on in the Oval Office.

But specifically, Emery had been retained for situations such as these: confusing, dangerous emergencies where a clear, incisive mind might cut through the overlying complications and see to the core of a problem, and the beginnings of a possible solution.

Gorton knew that all the other Couch appointees treated Truscott's opinions with deference and respect. That was another factor that annoyed him. To Gorton, he was simply another annoying reminder that too many people in the USA still thought of this as the Couch presidency.

Still irritated by the sight of the smooth-shaven, smiling face, Gorton gestured at the room to be seated. He slapped the report onto the table in front of him as he took his own high-backed chair.

"You all read this?" he demanded. He had skimmed through the report as he dressed. The others all had copies, and he received a chorus of assent from the group.

"Well?" he rasped, his angry gaze sweeping them. He wanted advice. He wanted suggestions. He wanted someone else to commit himself first. Benjamin shrugged slightly.

"Fairly typical first contact, Mr. President," he ventured. "They've shown their hand at last. The ransom demand proves that. The usual threats: Don't try to use force or we'll kill them all and ourselves. We're not afraid to die for our cause. All pretty standard."

"What about this last piece—about no more helicopters?" the president asked. Benjamin looked around. He guessed it was his part to answer once again.

"Apparently, our agent in place took a chopper up the canyon for a look-see," he said. "The response was some very accurate triple-A fire. Agent Colby reports that the terrorists claim to have radar-directed machine guns on the roof as well as the Stinger missiles they mentioned earlier. He's not inclined to doubt them."

The president scowled at his bureau director. "What the hell sort of agent have you put in charge up there, Benjamin? He some sort of cowboy that he's going to take risks like that? Goddamn it, there are close to a hundred hostages in that hotel and I'm not going to have them put at risk by this grandstanding Rambo of yours."

There was a moment's awkward silence. Then Benjamin replied, stolidly, "Denton Colby is one of my best agents, Mr. President. The risk in flying up there was to himself, not to the hostages. He held back at a safe distance. His stance was non-threatening. He received a warning-off and now we know a little more about the situation up there."

"Such as?" The president was looking at the bureau chief but it was General Barrett who answered this time.

"We know that what they say about their defenses is accurate, Mr. President," he said. "Linus's agent has established that we can't try to bust in there with any airborne assault."

Gorton locked gazes with the Air Force General. The ex-fighter pilot met his eyes steadily. In a career that spanned two major conflicts and a lot of brushfire wars in between, Barrett had seen more frightening sights than a frowning, posturing politician. Realizing that the general wasn't going to submit, Gorton switched his angry glare to the table in general.

"So, what do we do? I want suggestions, gentlemen. That's what you're here for."

Tildeman cleared his throat prior to speaking. "Linus might correct me on this, Mr. President," he began, "but I feel the best course now is simply to maintain contact—and to stall them on their demands."

He glanced at the bureau chief for consent or disagreement. Benjamin was nodding. "I agree, Mr. President. In these cases, time is our ally. If we continue to speak with them, we have the chance to negotiate—and to find out what's behind their demands." The president raised his eyebrows at the last words, so the bureau chief expanded the thought a little.

"Who they're working for. What their grievances are—that sort of thing. It all gives us a better idea of how much we can negotiate with them."

Gorton sniffed distastefully. "You're saying I should just sit on my hands and do nothing?" he asked. "While these ragheads dictate terms to me. Is that it?"

"We can use the time, Mr. President," NSA Director Tildeman replied. "Colonel Maloney can get his team to the site. Plus, if we find the terrorists are aligned to any national group, we can start diplomatic initiatives to put pressure on them."

Gorton grunted in reply. The suggested course of action suited him, but he wasn't going to let this group know that. He looked up in annoyance as a new voice spoke.

"Of course, Mr. President," Truscott Emery said in his even, well modulated tones, "there's no evidence so far to suggest that this group is aligned to any of the Middle Eastern States." Emery had noted the president's reference to "ragheads."

The president leaned back in his high-backed chair and looked appraisingly at the Harvard man. "You think maybe it's the Irish doing this? Or maybe the Canadians? They haven't been too happy with us lately," he asked sarcastically.

Emery smiled pleasantly and made a deprecating gesture. "No, sir. I'm just saying we shouldn't jump to conclusions. Odds are, of course, that this will turn out to be an Arab-based group. God knows we've made ourselves enough enemies in that part of the world."

"As I said," Gorton said, dismissing the other man. "Do we have a hostage list yet?" he asked.

Linus Benjamin nodded. "It's being finalized now. The hotel chain will be sending it through to us in an hour or two. They've got a few names left to check on," he said.

Gorton grunted, a noncommittal sound. He glanced up at Chief of Staff Pohlsen.

"I want to see that as soon as we have it," he said.

Pohlsen nodded. "Of course, Mr. President."

Gorton glanced at his chief of staff and made an almost imperceptible gesture for the meeting to be wound up.

"Very well gentlemen—and Ms. Haddenrich—we'll continue to monitor the situation. Colonel, you'll make preparations to get your team out to the site. I assume the RRTF has priority travel, General Barrett?"

Barrett nodded. "The team has its own dedicated transport, sir," he replied.

"Fine," Pohlsen went on. "And Director Benjamin, you'll send me the hostage list as soon as you have it?"

Benjamin nodded agreement and Pohlsen closed his notebook with a decisive snap. "So in the meantime, we make all efforts to find out what, or who, is behind this situation. Let's wrap it up for now and we'll reconvene tomorrow at . . ."

The president was already rising from his chair. The others round the table began to rise too—all except Truscott Emery. The round-faced academic remained seated, a half smile on his face as he studied the briefing paper.

"Does the actual ransom amount strike anyone as unusual?" he asked mildly. The movement around the table stopped. "I mean," he continued, "why nine point seven million? Why not nine point five? Or just nine million?"

There was a moment's silence as all eyes fell on him. He was frowning slightly at the paper, still with the half smile. Benjamin had seen that strange combination of expressions before. It usually meant that Truscott's mind was working full-time.

"Why not ten million?" said the president in a dismissive tone. "Does it really matter? Maybe nine point seven works out to an exact figure in durum or rupia or whatever goddamn currency they think in. The important point is, they want a shitload of dollars and we have to decide whether we're going to give it to them or not."

Emery nodded once or twice, then turned to meet the president's gaze. It was a pity, he reflected, that Gorton combined such a high level of stupidity with his lifelong defensive posture. It made him a much more difficult man to advise and assist.

"The amount might be significant, Mr. President," he said pleasantly, letting no hint of his disdain for the man show in his voice, "if someone were trying to send us a message."

President Gorton let go a short, harsh bark of laughter. "Someone's sending us a message, right enough," he replied, "and it's this: We've got your people. You'll get 'em back when we get your money. That's all there is to it."

He shook his head and turned away. The others rose from their chairs as he left the room. Only Truscott Emery remained sitting, still staring thoughtfully at the figure on the paper before him.

TWENTY

Tina Bowden opened the fourth can of stew and dumped it into the enormous pot she'd set on the gas burner. She glanced into the pan. Although she knew there must be more than a quart of stew in there already, the thick brown liquid barely seemed to cover the bottom of the pan.

Commercial kitchens like this always proved a daunting prospect to the security officer. Everything was built on an enormous scale, as if you'd somehow stumbled into a giant's kitchen. The four cans of Mrs. Blackwell's Canned Mulligan Stew had been in the ready-use pantry. She could see she was going to need more to feed the forty-odd hostages, but she didn't know how many or where to find them.

"Ralph!" she called across the room to where the chef was just searing the first of the chicken breasts on a stainless steel griddle. He glanced up at her. She jerked a thumb at the four empty cans on the bench in front of her.

"How many of these will I need?" she said.

He pursed his lips in thought for a moment. "Maybe ten, twelve more," he told her and, as she glanced around the kitchen to see where she might find them, he forestalled her next question.

"They're in the big pantry," he told her, "on the canned goods shelves in back."

As he spoke, he flipped the browned chicken. The seared aroma of the marinade, rich with tarragon, filled the room. Tina's mouth watered and she glanced disparagingly down at the amorphous brown mass that was beginning to bubble slowly in the pan.

"Where the hell do we serve this crap?" she asked him. After all, the Canyon Lodge had a reputation for fine dining that didn't seem to gel with Mrs. Blackwell's Canned Mulligan Stew. Ralph grinned easily at her. She noticed that he was more relaxed now that he was back in his familiar environment.

"On the mountain," he told her. "We serve it in a bread bowl and the skiers love it."

She nodded her understanding and started toward the pantry door. The armed man who had accompanied them to the kitchen stood up from where he had been leaning against a bench, thumbing through a magazine. He moved to bar her way, his eyes asking a question.

"Pantry," she said, indicating the door to him. He glanced at it, then at her, and nodded permission. He'd had a quick look inside the pantry when they'd first reached the kitchen. It was nothing more than a giant storeroom with only one entrance. He knew the knives were kept on a rack near the chef's work position. He'd already removed all but one, leaving that for Ralph to use as he prepared the meal.

Oddly, Tina thought, he'd allowed the chef to keep the biggest and, presumably, the most dangerous, of the knives. Then she'd realized the logic behind the action. All of Ralph's knives were kept honed to a razor-sharp edge. Any one of them, even the smallest, would be a dangerous weapon. But the biggest one, with a nine-inch heavy blade, would be the hardest to conceal.

Tina had her hand on the pantry door handle when Ralph's voice stopped her.

"Get me a bag of frozen French fries, will you? In the freezer over to the left."

She waved an acknowledgment and let herself into the room. The door, on an automatic arm, swung closed behind her.

The three rows of shelves stretched away on either side. It was like being in a small supermarket, except for the lack of colored labels. It was cooler in here than in the kitchen. She walked along the first row of shelves, heading for the rear of the room where Ralph had said the canned goods were kept. Then she stopped. Something had struck her as out of place—but what?

Frowning, she looked around, then saw it. She was in the narrow aisle between the first and second row of shelves. The first row was attached to the wall adjoining the kitchen, the second and third were freestanding, with the freezers and refrigerators beyond another aisle behind the third row. On the shelf before her, the second row, a piece of bread, topped with a slice of packaged cheese, was resting among the bottles of chili and barbecue sauces. That in itself was strange enough. What made it considerably more so was the fact that one perfectly formed bite had been taken from it. A semi-circular piece was missing, and teeth marks were distinctly visible in the cheese.

She touched the bread with one forefinger. It was soft. It had been freshly cut from a loaf—sometime in the last hour or so. Tina felt her pulse quicken as she glanced along the line of packed shelves. There was somebody in here, she thought. Or there had been, quite recently. Logic said that the most likely explanation was that one of the guards had come in to help himself to a quick snack. But if that were the case, why had he taken one bite and then left?

There was no sound in the room but the steady hum of the refrigerator motors from the left end of the aisle. She held her breath, listening for a sound . . . anything . . . Nothing. She could hear her own pulse, it seemed, beating against her temples.

She turned slowly, looking back along the rows of cans, packs and bottles ranged along the shelves. The hair on the back of her neck prickled. She could feel the presence of someone else in the room—could sense eyes upon her, watching her, waiting for her next move . . .

She shook her head angrily. One cheese sandwich and she was giving herself ESP, she thought. She turned back to the shelf, stooping slightly to reach for the slice of bread and cheese, looking through to the other side of the shelf as she did.

And saw eyes there, staring at her.

Startled, she jerked back, away from them, stumbling and colliding with the facing shelf, catching at it to keep from falling and sending a row of canned pickles tumbling, rolling and thudding to the pantry floor. At the same time, an involuntary cry escaped her lips. There was a scuffle of movement from the other side of the shelves and suddenly she became aware of a face, a finger raised to the lips, and the head shaking in a negative gesture. Now she could make out a shape on the other side—a figure crouched there with his face level with the lower shelf, so that, from her half-crouched position, she recognized him.

"Jesse?" she said. "What the hell are you . . ."

She stopped abruptly as the door to the kitchen opened halfway and the guard peered in suspiciously.

"What's going on?" he demanded and she gestured weakly to the scattered cans on the floor.

"I . . . dropped these . . . that's all," she told him, feeling that her voice was unsteady and hoping that it was only in her imagination. She was conscious of the dark shape on the other side of the shelf opposite and couldn't believe the guard hadn't noticed it. He glanced down, saw the cans—the suspicion instantly replaced by disinterest.

"Okay," he said. "Get on with it." He withdrew from the doorway and the hydraulic-dampened closer allowed it to click shut once more.

Tina stood upright and drew a deep, shuddering breath of relief. She moved forward, closer to the shelf, and said in a low voice: "Jesse? How the hell did you get here? What are you doing?"

He gestured to her now to come around to the end of the row, glancing toward the door as he did so. She got the message. If he came to her, he'd be visible if the guard took it into his mind to check on her once more. She nodded and they both moved to the end of the row, the best point of concealment from any observer coming through the door.

"I was out skiing," he explained, "and I heard gunfire. Now tell me, what the hell has happened?"

She leaned against the end of the row, suddenly feeling exhausted, and shook her head hopelessly. "Armed men," she told him. "They've taken over the hotel. They're holding the guests and half a dozen of the staff hostage."

He whistled softly through his teeth at the news. "How many of them?" he asked.

"Maybe twenty. They've all got handguns and automatic weapons."

She glanced toward the door. "I'd better start collecting the stuff I came in here for. That guy could come looking for me again any minute."

He nodded agreement and they moved to the back row of shelves where she found the extra cans of beef stew that she'd originally come for. He began helping her, stacking them into an empty carton.

"What was the shooting this afternoon?" he asked. She shook her head, the memory still raw.

"They killed one of the staff when she wouldn't get on the bus," she replied.

Jesse nodded. "I figured that's what it was. I saw the body when I came in. But she's the only casualty so far?" he asked.

She looked at him in horror as she realized he had no idea of what Kormann and his men had done. "Oh God, no," she whispered. "The bus that went out? It had maybe sixty of our people on it. He . . . detonated a charge in the mountains and buried them under an avalanche. Over fifty people."

She saw the sudden lance of pain in his eyes. He'd seen the bus leaving and figured that the people on board were safe. Then he remembered that series of dull explosions he'd heard some minutes later.

"Jesus," he said quietly. "Who are these people? Are they some kind of fanatics?"

She paused. "I don't think so. And they say they're not political," she replied. "They're too"—she searched for the right word, then found it—"professional, I guess. Their leader is a guy called Kormann. He's very cold and very smart. They've got us in the third floor gymnasium rooms. He claims they've got more explosives on the mountain behind us and if there's any attempt at rescue, he'll bring the whole thing down on top of us."

The tall deputy hesitated, thinking over what she'd said. She could see her own confusion and uncertainty mirrored in his eyes. "You got any idea what they want?" he asked her and she shook her head.

"They said it's all about money, pure and simple. Ransom, I guess."

"I guess so," Jesse replied. There was silence for several moments as they looked at each other. Then Tina remembered the other item she had to take back.

"French fries," she said and Jesse looked at her, uncomprehending. "I've got to get French fries out of the freezer back here," she told him and they walked the few steps to the big industrial freezer. Jesse slid back one of the plastic lids and she saw a row of plain plastic packs, labeled in blue capitals: "Frozen French fries."

The deputy picked one out for her and added it to the carton with the stew cans. She smiled her thanks.

"I'd better get back," she said and he nodded. She hesitated, then said: "What are you going to do? Maybe you should get the hell out of here." Although she wasn't surprised when he shook his head.

"I'll stick around for a while," he said. "Maybe I'll get a chance to do something. As long as they don't know I'm here, I might come in handy at some point."

The thought struck her that their initial lighthearted involvement was developing into something a whole lot more significant— although not in any direction she might have anticipated. She felt comforted by the knowledge that he was here. He was the sort of person you'd like to have around when there was trouble. There was something . . . dependable . . . about him.

"Here," she said. "Take this." She pressed a plastic card into his hand. He glanced down and saw that it was her security pass card. "It'll open any door in the building. It might come in handy."

He regarded the innocuous looking piece of plastic, tossing it lightly in his hand.

"It might at that," he said and smiled at her.

Another thought struck her. "Room 517 is my room," she said. "You'll find a .38 in the left-hand bureau drawer."

He repeated the room number and nodded at her. "How will we make contact?" he asked and she glanced around the storeroom.

"I guess I'll be helping the chef with meals. Either wait for me here or leave a message under this can." She indicated a can of pickled cactus on the second shelf from floor level. It didn't strike her as the sort of thing they'd be using over the next few days. He grinned as he read the label.

"Good choice," he agreed.

Another thought struck her. "One thing: if I come in here every time we're cooking someone might get suspicious. If you're here, or you've left a message, leave two coffee mugs upside down on the bench beside the big sink."

"Two coffee mugs," he agreed. Then, suddenly fearful, suddenly aware of how long she'd been in the storeroom, she glanced nervously toward the door. "I'd better get out of here," she said. Then she leaned toward him and kissed him lightly on the mouth before she left.

TWENTY-ONE

Cale Lawson and Denton Colby were drinking coffee in the FBI agent's command trailer. The sheriff looked at his companion with a mixture of respect and pity. He was damned glad he hadn't been put in charge of this mess, he thought, particularly now that they'd received the hostages' names. There, right at the top, was Senator Ted Carling, senior senator from Washington state, followed by some of the most important names in the aerospace industry. That piece of information put this whole mess right out of the league of a Utah sheriff, Lawson thought to himself.

"Didn't take the press long to see through the avalanche story," Dent said. The sheriff shook his head.

"They announced the hotline when they released the initial statement. Some bright reporter rang in, pretending to be a relative. They kind of let the cat out of the bag."

Dent sighed and took a sip of coffee. "Bound to happen sooner or later. How's the situation down there?"

"We've set up an information center. So far, nearly three hundred people have been in to find out what's going on. Not that we're telling 'em too much. The important thing is to keep them off the road leading up here. I've had the state police set up roadblocks on Canyon Road. They're turning back anyone who doesn't have a good reason to be here. Including the press."

"Sooner or later, we're going to have to let some of the reporters in," Dent said. "For the moment, I've got a press officer keeping them at bay."

"So, what you going to do about all this?" Lawson asked, jerking a thumb at the hostage list. Colby shrugged.

"Not much I can do right now. Ball's still in their court. We should know soon enough if they know who they've got. Guess if they do, their ransom demand will climb a little higher."

"I guess so," the sheriff agreed. Then, curiously, he asked, "You done much of this sort of thing in the past?"

Colby pursed his lips, selecting his words before replying. "Some," he said at length. "I'm one of the Bureau's three senior negotiators. One of us usually gets called in at some stage in a hostage situation. The scale of this one makes it a little different, of course."

"So what do you usually do in these situations?" Lawson asked him and Colby's heavy featured face twisted into a wry grin.

"Just what we're doing now," he replied. "We wait. And, sooner or later, the perps tell us what they want, where they want it and when they want it by."

"And you just give it to them?" Lawson asked. It wasn't his idea of law enforcement.

Colby shrugged again. "Sometimes," he admitted, "if there's no other way to get the hostages out."

"And how do you know that?" the sheriff persisted. Colby looked up at him and their eyes locked as he answered.

"You can't ever know," he said. "Not for sure. You have to go with what your gut tells you."

Lawson didn't want to ask the next, obvious question. And he sensed that Colby didn't want it asked either. But a mixture of curiosity and professional interest drove him to it.

"What does your gut tell you on this one?" he asked finally. Colby let out a long, drawn-out breath. It was a sound of surrender.

"At the moment, it's telling me this is one of those times," he admitted. He glanced at the narrow cot set against the end wall. The trailer was a normal recreational model, with living quarters, a kitchenette and a shower recess and toilet. In addition to the standard fittings, there was a Hewlett-Packard laptop, with wireless modem connection, printer and scanner and a state-of-the-art communications console.

"Now if you'll excuse me, Sheriff, I think I'll get a few hours' sleep. I figure the time's going to come over the next few days when I'll need all I can get."

He accompanied the words with a small smile, to let the sheriff know no insult was intended. Cale Lawson nodded his understanding, reached for the small-brimmed Stetson that was on the sofa bench behind him and rose, heading for the narrow trailer door. He stepped down the three metal stairs to the road, his breath freezing in giant clouds on the still night air. Above them, when he glanced up, the stars blazed at him out of a clear sky.

"Be a fine day tomorrow," he said. Colby, leaning inside the doorframe of the trailer, grunted.

"For some," he said.

THE J. EDGAR HOOVER BUILDING
WASHINGTON D.C.
2130 HOURS, EASTERN TIME
SATURDAY, DAY 1

The intercom on the director's desk buzzed discreetly. Benjamin looked up from the printout in front of him. "Yes, Lois?" he said. There was no need for him to hit a switch on the intercom. It was voice-activated. Technology, he thought, doing everything possible to conserve his energy so that he could focus more completely on the job at hand.

"Director Tildeman is here, sir." His secretary had a soft Virginia accent that even the tinny tones of the intercom couldn't hide.

"Ask him to step in please, Lois," he said and he rose from behind his desk to greet the national security director as he came in through the heavy, soundproof door that ensured privacy for the head of the FBI.

In times past, Benjamin thought sourly, that privacy had been necessary to preserve the highly dubious reputation of the man for whom the building was named. Nowadays, he hoped, the secrecy served a more worthwhile purpose.

"Working late, Linus?" Tildeman asked and Benjamin replied with a vague gesture.

"Fairly normal hours. You on your way home?" The NSA director's home was over an hour's drive from D.C., set in eight acres of rolling Virginia woodland.

"Not much else we can accomplish tonight," Tildeman said and Benjamin nodded agreement. "What do you make of that?" Tildeman continued, indicating the printout that had come through from Denton Colby's headquarters some time earlier in the evening. Benjamin shook his head wearily.

"It complicates things," he said. "Particularly if these people know who they've got."

"But so far, there's no indication that they do know?" Tildeman said and Benjamin shrugged once more.

"No indication that they don't either," he said. "They could be playing cat and mouse with us here. They know we know who they've got but they're not going to tell us that they know who they've got—that sort of thing."

Tildeman considered the thought. "Is there any reason why they would do that?" he asked. Benjamin sank back into his swivel chair, motioning for the NSA director to be seated. He leaned back, rubbing his tired eyes with a thumb and forefinger.

"Keeps us off balance," he said finally. "If we're not sure how much they know, it affects our negotiating position. Obviously, we don't want to tell them who they've got. At the same time, we've got to move carefully so that if they happen to be testing us out or if they happen to find out in the future, we don't appear to have intentionally misled them. If we do that, we hand them an advantage. We've got to establish a position of trust with them."

Tildeman snorted derisively at the word. "Trust," he said, "with a bunch of gun-toting loony tunes."

Benjamin nodded. "It seems odd, I know," he said. "But we have to establish an appearance of honesty with them. The real skill is knowing when to lie—and to avoid being caught out when you do."

"This guy you've got there—is he good at that?" Tildeman asked, and the FBI director answered with a thin smile.

"Colby?" he said, "Oh yes. He's one of the best. He doesn't look it. That's what makes him so effective."

There was a silence for a moment or two. Both men knew this was a time for waiting, a time to allow events to develop further. But that didn't stop them both chafing at the enforced inaction.

"Jesus," said Benjamin at length. "Why couldn't Carling have gone to Aspen with his buddies?"

"He's a Republican," Tildeman replied, with grim humor. "They still love the Kennedys in Aspen." Benjamin acknowledged the sally with a tired grin of his own. "Who are his buddies anyway?" the NSA director added. "I saw Carling's name and that pretty well stopped me."

Benjamin picked up the printed list and began running down the names. "Rockley you'd know. He's head of the Rockair Group. He's taken two of his people along as well: Bob Soropoulos, his chief designer, and Nathaniel Pell, Rockair's senior test pilot. Antony Beresford is from General Electric—he's a VP in their jet engine division. Then there's Carl Aldiss from Sperry Rand . . ."

"The radar guy?" Tildeman asked and Benjamin looked up at him.

"You know him?"

"Just by sight. He was called to advise a senate committee last month over the horizon radar installations. Some of the work came out of our budget and I went along to see what he had to say. Seems to know his business. So what the hell are they doing there, other than skiing?"

Benjamin sat back and stretched his cramped shoulders before answering.

"It's an idea Carling came up with a few years ago. He's got a lot of the aerospace companies in his electorate and he thought it'd be a good idea to get them together each year in a kind of informal seminar and think tank. This year, the subject is the next generation stealth bomber. Preliminary contracts are under review at the moment. Carling wanted an opportunity to go through the initial test results before he takes a recommendation to the Senate. Rockair has built the prototype and Aldiss and his team have been doing the radar testing on it.

"The thinking is, if he can't see it, nobody will be able to."

"Well," said Tildeman, rising to leave, "one thing's for sure. He can't see it while he's in Utah."

Benjamin walked his visitor to the door. "See you in the morning," he said. There was a conference scheduled at the White House for 8 a.m. They'd all agreed that it was best if the president kept a relatively low profile on this for the moment. They would maintain the outward appearance of keeping him informed and that was all. Any undue interest on his part might alert the terrorists to the fact that they had a VIP hostage on their hands. After all, as Benjamin had pointed out, the Canyon Lodge had television and terrorists watched the six o'clock news like anyone else.

"Don't work too late," Tildeman cautioned. Benjamin laughed softly.

"I thrive on lack of sleep," he said. He opened the door for his guest, punching in a four-figure code as he did so. He could have done that from his desk but Tildeman was a friend as well as a professional colleague and he preferred to see him to the door. The NSA director paused, remembering something.

"Have you heard anything more from Emery?" he asked. Benjamin pointed one forefinger to the floor below their feet.

"He's here, in the basement. I've assigned a couple of guys to him to see if they can see any significance in this message idea of his."

Tildeman pushed out his bottom lip thoughtfully. "You put any credence in that?" he asked. His own immediate reaction was to discount the theory so he was interested to see Benjamin hesitate before replying.

"I'm not going to ignore the possibility," he said eventually. "After all, we've been known to do a little message sending ourselves."

He saw the other man's eyebrows go up a little at that and he went on in explanation. "LBJ spent a good deal of the Vietnam War sending messages to Ho Chi Minh. At least, that's what he thought he was doing," he amended. "When he wouldn't let our guys take out SAM sites before they became active, he figured Ho would think: He could do it if he wanted to. Therefore, by not bombing them while they're being built and they're vulnerable, he's telling me he's a reasonable man and he's prepared to negotiate."

Tildeman's lip curled. He'd done a stint in the Marines during the Vietnam War.

"Pity Ho didn't see it that way. He just kept building them and shooting our guys down," he replied and Benjamin shrugged.

"I didn't say it was a sensible message. Or even a logical one," he said. "Just that Johnson thought he was sending it. Then in Belgrade in the late nineties, NATO planes took out the local television station because Milosovic was using it to rally the Serbs. There was no tactical value in the target. It was a message to him: We can shut you up any time we want to. Now start negotiating."

Tildeman conceded the point, a little reluctantly. It all seemed too much like pie in the sky to him but he had to admit the Belgrade TV station raid had been carried out for the purpose Benjamin had just stated. "I guess he may be right at that," he said. "It certainly won't do any harm to cover that base."

Benjamin held the door open for him. "And at least we know that Emery will cover it thoroughly," he said.

TWENTY-TWO

Senator Michael Atherton waited until the appetizers had been served and the waiter moved away from the discreet table at the rear of the restaurant. He glanced quizzically at the stuffed field mushrooms on the plate before him. Paolo's was a pretty low-profile restaurant in the Washington scene—not one of his usual haunts. But the food was always good.

"I take it from the choice of venue that the president feels disinclined to grant my request?" he said. He didn't add, nor did he need to, that the messenger selected to pass on the news was another indication of the White House's wish to remain detached. His dining companion was a presidential special aide, a position that was just senior enough to avoid insulting the senator, yet sufficiently vague in terms of responsibility to fly under the radar of the Washington press. If the dinner had been with the assistant chief of staff, for example, it wouldn't have avoided notice.

His dining companion, a tall, good-looking man in his thirties, shrugged apologetically.

"It's a bad time, Senator," he said. "We're taking a beating on the gun legislation thing already. If the president comes out and openly supports your stance, we'll be putting out brushfires in all directions. Maybe in six months things might be different."

Atherton nodded. "Funny how the right to lifers and the gun lobby all seem to be drinking from the same waterhole, isn't it?" he mused. Atherton was a firm advocate of the right to free choice. He had never backed away from stating his views publicly. He was a charismatic figure and at one stage he'd been tapped as a possible future presidential candidate. But it would never happen so long as he attracted the hatred of a solid core of rabid right to lifers.

He sighed and pushed the plate away, the mushrooms half finished.

"I know how it is, Ted," he said. "I've been around the hill long enough to understand how these things work. Everyone has their own priorities."

The younger man frowned slightly. He genuinely admired Atherton and he agreed with his stance.

"Of course, sir," he said. "The president will do anything he can to help you—in the way of discreet pressure or influence . . ." he said and let the sentence hang. Atherton finished it for him.

"As long as it remains discreet, I guess?" he smiled wryly. His companion pursed his lips. It was a pretty empty offer, he knew. But it was all he could bring to the table. Atherton knew it wasn't his fault. He'd really had little expectation of any public commitment from the White House and Ted, after all, was only the messenger. He thought it might be time to let the young man off the hook.

"What about your priorities, Ted?" he asked. "Are you planning to stay on at the West Wing?"

The younger man shrugged. "I don't think so. The president is in his second term and if the new man is from our side he's going to want his own people. Of course, if he's not, there's no possibility of staying on. I thought it's time to move on. I'm planning to run for office."

Atherton raised his eyebrows. "The House or the Senate?" he asked.

"Senate. There's a vacancy coming up in my home state and I thought I might throw my hat in the ring while I can still get the support of an incumbent president."

Atherton nodded. "Of course. Senator Ewing is going to retire early, isn't he? Three heart attacks in a year are a good enough warning for any man that it's time to let up a little. Well good luck to you. I think you'll make a fine senator."

His companion smiled gratefully. "Thank you, Senator. It means a lot to have you say that."

"Well, if I can be of any help, don't—" Atherton stopped as the maître d' slipped quietly up to the table and leaned down beside him. "Yes, Emilio?" he asked. The maître d' spread his hands in a little gesture of apology.

"I'm sorry, Senator. We've had a tip-off. It seems that word has got out that you're here tonight. There's a group from the Let the Children Live movement heading this way."

Atherton pursed his lips in annoyance. "With their banners and their bullhorns, no doubt." Then he smiled briefly at the maître d'. "Thanks, Emilio. Maybe we should cancel our orders and get away from here. I don't want your other diners bothered by this."

The waiter frowned angrily. "Stay if you wish, Senator. You're a valued guest."

But Atherton was already shaking his head. "No. We'll go. Besides, it won't serve any purpose to have my young friend here seen in my company. There's sure to be press along with them." He glanced at his companion. "That okay with you?" he asked. The other man shrugged unhappily.

"If it were just me, I'd say to hell with them. But I guess . . ." He paused. He was obviously not pleased with the situation and Atherton leaned across the table and patted his forearm.

"Problem with working for the White House," he said. "You can't indulge in personal statements."

They stood and made for the entrance. Emilio clicked his fingers and gestured for one of the junior waiters to retrieve their coats from the cloak room. As they shrugged into them, Atherton queried the maître d'.

"The bill?" he asked. But Emilio waved his hands in a negative gesture.

"For two appetizers you hardly touched?" he said. "I'll take care of it, Senator."

Atherton smiled his thanks. "I'll make amends next time," he said and the waiter dismissed the need for him to do so.

"I've sent for your driver," he said. "He'll be outside in a minute or two."

"Then that's where we'll wait for him. The mob's not here yet. We'd hear them if they were." Atherton pushed open the door and turned to the younger man. "Can I drop you somewhere?" he asked.

"No need. My car's just down the street." He reached into his coat pocket to make sure the keys were still there. For a second or two he couldn't find them, then realized that he'd stuffed his gloves down on top of them when he entered the restaurant half an hour before. He pulled the gloves and the keys out in one motion. Inevitably, he dropped one glove onto the damp sidewalk. Both men bent instinctively to retrieve it.

ROOM 204
GEORGETOWN INN
WASHINGTON D.C.

The room was in darkness. The window was open just a few inches but it was enough to give the crouching figure a clear view of the entrance to Paolo's. As the two men emerged, he swung up the muzzle of the .308 caliber Springfield M1-A rifle. He centered the scope on his target's forehead, nudging the focus ring gently to bring the image into pin-sharp view.

From a distance of barely seventy yards, the man's head and shoulders filled the scope.

His forefinger took the first pressure on the trigger. He took in half a breath and held it.

And the target suddenly dropped out of the scope's field of vision as he inexplicably bent to retrieve something. Caught by surprise and already committed to the shot, the gunman tilted quickly down after him, reflexively squeezing the trigger, knowing instantly that he'd missed.

He threw the gun on the bed, hurried to the door and let himself out, heading for the rear of the hotel and the backstreet where his car was parked.

PAOLO'S RESTAURANT
GEORGETOWN
WASHINGTON D.C.

Later, witnesses could never agree whether they heard the sound of the rifle shot before they saw Senator Atherton spin around, clutching at the point of his shoulder, where the .308 steel jacketed bullet had slammed against bone.

He stumbled and fell to the ground. His companion dropped to his knees beside him and hunched protectively over him. He looked at the senator's face, contorted with shock and pain, then up to Emilio's horrified gaze.

"Call 911," he shouted.

TWENTY-THREE

ROOM 517
CANYON LODGE
WASATCH COUNTY
0724 HOURS, MOUNTAIN TIME
SUNDAY, DAY 2

THE PRESENT

Jesse woke suddenly. The room was foreign to him and for a moment he wondered where he was. Then memory came flooding back. The previous night, worn out by the cumulative effects of a day's hard skiing and the emotional exhaustion of the subsequent events, he'd crept up the fire stairs and used Tina's pass card to let himself into her room. Even though he was ravenous, the unmade bed beckoned him and the need for sleep was even more urgent. He was out a second or two after his head hit the pillow.

Now, waking, he was instantly conscious of the faint scent of Tina's perfume lingering on the sheets and pillow. The realization made him a little uncomfortable. Hotel rooms were impersonal as a rule but this was her permanent base and there was evidence of her all around him. Her parka was tossed casually across the back of the easy chair by the coffee table and the table itself was host to a half-full plunger style coffeepot and a used cup. The straight-backed chair by the desk in the corner was pushed back at an angle—obviously from the last time Tina had risen from it. Normally, housekeeping would have replaced it squarely in position, but he guessed that as a staff member's room, 517 didn't merit daily housekeeping visits. A bra hung from the back of the chair. He recognized it as the one she had worn the night she had come back to his room. He felt another surge of guilt. Their casual encounter was developing into something much more serious, he thought. Lee's face rose before his mind's eye and he pushed it away.

He tossed back the cover and swung out of bed. The heating system was still functioning in the lodge so the room was comfortably warm. Carefully, he eased the drapes back a fraction, peering through the gap he created. There was no sign of movement around the hotel. No sign of any sentries. Logically, he assumed, they would be on the roof, where they could command a three hundred and sixty degree view of the area. They wouldn't be looking for trouble from within.

He padded silently to the door and put his eye to the wide-angle lens set in the top panel. The corridor seemed empty—as much as he could see of it. There was no reason to suppose that his presence in the room had been discovered, he thought. But there was no reason to believe that it hadn't either. He went into the bathroom and used the toilet, at the last moment stopping the instinctive movement that led his hand to the toilet handle. His experience with hotel plumbing told him that the resultant noise could be as dangerous to him as an alarm system.

His stomach growled and he was conscious of the fact that he'd decided on sleep rather than food the night before. He found the small pantry area in the room that contained the coffeemaker and minibar.

There were two packets of potato chips, a pack of beer nuts and a Nestlé Crunch bar on the shelf. Jesse ripped open the barbecue-flavored chips and crammed a handful in his mouth.

As he crunched them, he twisted the cap off a container of orange juice and washed them down. He crossed to the bureau. There were a few loose sheets of notepaper lying on the desktop, and a Parker ballpoint pen. A slotted metal plate was positioned by the left-hand bureau drawer and he slid the pass card into it, hearing the soft click of the lock disengaging after a second or two.

The gun was there, just as she'd said. It was a Smith and Wesson Model 686, chambered for .38 Special or .357 Magnum loads. It had a three-inch barrel and custom rubber grips. There was also a carton of fifty .357 Magnum bullets and he slid the pack open to reveal five empty spaces and the gleaming brass bases of the forty-five remaining shells. He swung out the cylinder on the pistol. As he'd suspected, she left the chamber under the hammer empty. He flicked the cylinder shut again and considered the weapon. An extra gun mightn't be a lot of use to him, he thought. He was familiar with his own Colt and the feel of the revolver was foreign to him. Plus the custom grips were obviously tailored to her smaller hand. But an extra gun in experienced hands among the hostages might well make a difference a little down the track. He placed the .38 and the carton of heavy slugs on top of the bureau and softly closed the lid again.

He found the TV remote and switched the set on, hurriedly reducing the volume to the lowest audible level as he searched for a news program.

Channel 6 had one. As the digital clock on the bedside unit ticked over to the half hour, the 6 Eyewitness News logo faded up on-screen, accompanied by the usual self-important fanfare beloved by news producers the world over. This was a local station, and the siege at Canyon Lodge was the lead story. The anchor man looked into the lens and intoned in a deep, carefully modulated voice: "Top of the news is the breaking story from Snow Eagles Resort in the Wasatches. It is now believed that the avalanche blocking the road was no accident, and that guests and staff are being held hostage in the Canyon Lodge hotel. Matt Downing has the story."

He swiveled his chair to look at the monitor to one side of the news desk. As he did, the feed cut full screen to the on-site reporter at Canyon Road, in front of an array of vehicles, from sherriff's department cruisers to Army six-by-sixes, parked close by the site of the avalanche that had blocked the road.

"That's right, John. We're now hearing that the avalanche that cut the road in was caused by a series of explosive charges and the Canyon Lodge hotel at Snow Eagles Resort has been taken over by armed men. Over a hundred guests and staff members are thought to be held hostage. It's believed that the hostage-takers have demanded a ransom."

Jesse frowned at the number for a second, then realized that the

outside world had no way of knowing that over fifty of those hostages were already dead, buried under the rubble and snow of the
avalanche on Canyon Road. The reporter continued: "The initial
situation remains unchanged, with the road cut by avalanches and
all access to the lodge blocked. A sheriff's department helicopter,
attempting to survey the scene last evening, drew warning fire from
the hotel, which appears to have been transformed into an armed
fortress by the kidnappers.

"So far, the names of the hostages have not been released. The FBI
spokesperson said that attempts were being made to contact relatives of those people believed to be in the hotel. A hotline has been
set up by the Wasatch County sheriff's department. Contact 801-
8181 if you believe you have a relative or friend in the hotel.

"Last night, we spoke with the FBI agent-in-charge at the scene
here, John. Agent Denton Colby. This is what he had to say."

A shot of the FBI agent faded in on screen. Broad features set on
a thick neck over heavily muscled shoulders. Denton Colby. The
name was vaguely familiar. Then he remembered.

In 2006, the Routt County sheriff's department had been faced
with a serial murder investigation. Colby had been the FBI contact
who provided background information and intelligence. He and
Jesse had communicated by phone and fax several times, although
they had never met.

"Small world," he muttered to himself. He wondered if the FBI
agent would remember his name. He doubted it. But he'd surely
remember the case.

He watched the man answering the reporter's questions. The authorities were watching events carefully, Colby said. He assured the
kidnappers, if they were watching, that their safety and the safety
of their hostages was his primary concern and he expressed his will-
ingness to talk with them at any time.

"Call the FBI office in Salt Lake City," he was saying. "They'll
patch you straight through to me. I'm here and I'm ready to talk to
you." The phone number was superimposed over the bottom third
of the screen. For a moment, Jesse was tempted to take it down. Then

he thought of the crazies who'd be screened out by the local FBI office. Only the kidnappers would get through to Agent Colby.

The screen faded back to the reporter at the avalanche location. Jesse rubbed his chin thoughtfully. His prior contact with the FBI agent was a lucky break and he thought he could see a way to get around the screening.

"A White House source said today that there is no indication that the ransom demand is connected to Al Qaeda or any other known terrorist group. The situation is regarded at the moment as an internal criminal activity and is being handled by the FBI, although the president's emergency council will continue monitoring developments. The spokesman stated that the White House had total confidence in the FBI team on the spot.

"Rumors that the rapid response tactical force has been despatched to the siege site were still unconfirmed. John?"

The slight upward inflexion told the anchor that this was all the reporter had for him at this stage. He swiveled back to face the camera as the location shot reduced down to the monitor beside him once more.

"And we'll bring you further developments on this breaking story as they arrive. In other news, the secretary of state today was welcomed in Beijing by the premier of the People's Republic of—"

Jesse had no wish to hear what the secretary of state had said to the Chinese premier. He switched off the set and sat thoughtfully for a few moments. It seemed that the outside world knew very little about the situation here. He was one up on the FBI, he realized. At least one of the hostages was a US senator. There'd be hell to pay when that news got out. Unless, he thought, the authorities already knew it and were keeping it quiet. After all, a United States senator would make a powerful bargaining tool for the group who had taken over the hotel.

He stretched out on the bed, considering his options. Perhaps, he thought, the most useful role he could play would be to keep the authorities aware of what was going on in the hotel. He had a cell phone in the glove box of his car. He could . . .

Then he remembered. Earlier in the week, he'd tried to use the phone and discovered that the Canyon Lodge was in a dead spot. Probably an intentional one, he had thought at the time, as it meant customers would have to use the room phones, with their usual one and two hundred percent charges for calls. The phone systems in hotels these days were handy little profit centers.

Of course, he could always try the room phone. The hotel had an automatic switch that would allow him to dial an outside line. But the switch could be monitored and he wouldn't take the risk. Maybe he could find a phone outside the hotel itself, he thought. There was a payphone near the base of the chairlift, he remembered, and there would be other phones in the adjoining buildings. Potentially, there was the same problem with those phones, of course. Chances were they would all go through the same central switchboard in the hotel. The cell phone would be best. He'd just have to find a spot where its signal wasn't blocked. There had to be one somewhere on the mountain.

TWENTY-FOUR

Most of the usual group was assembled although this time, Benjamin noticed, the marine colonel was absent. He assumed that he was on the way to, or was already at, the siege site with his rapid response tactical force. Following the decision to keep the president's involvement as low key as possible, they'd moved the venue for these meetings to the cabinet room. The Oval Office, after all, was the president's principal workplace and a constant gathering of this group in the Oval Office, along with the disruption it would cause to his normal schedule, might have aroused the sort of media attention and speculation that they didn't want on this case.

President Gorton swept in on a wave of self-importance, followed by Chief of Staff Pohlsen. He made a half-hearted gesture to prevent them rising from their chairs—which, had they obeyed it, would have brought his displeasure down on each and every one of them. He dropped into his own high-backed chair at the head of the table and glared at them all.

"Now what the hell is this about Carling?" he grated.

Benjamin cleared his throat and answered. "Ah . . . Senator Carling was chairing a kind of informal conference with a group of aerospace executives from his constituency. Does it every year," he replied. Gorton frowned, trying to place the name. He didn't know the senator from Washington but the name rang a bell in his memory.

"Carling . . . Carling . . ." he muttered to himself. Then memory cut in. "He was involved in some kind of shooting a few years back, wasn't he?"

"Only by chance, sir," Benjamin told him. "He was a White House aide at the time. He simply happened to be dining with Senator Atherton when there was an attempt on Atherton's life."

"Atherton? The abortionist?"

Mentally, Benjamin rolled his eyes at the president's propensity to sum up a person in one overarching, and usually inaccurate, phrase.

"He's a free choice advocate, Mr. President, yes. The assassin's bullet hit him in the shoulder. Carling had dropped his glove and they both bent to pick it up at the moment the shot was fired."

"Mmm. Pity." Gorton said. "So, as to Carling. Do the kidnappers know his identity?"

"They've shown no sign that they do, sir."

The president rubbed his fingers across his smooth shaven chin. At this early hour of the morning, the skin was sleek and shiny from the close attention of his razor. Later, the gray stubble would begin to spoil the effect. Gorton usually shaved two or three times in a day, depending on his schedule of commitments.

"So what do we do?" Gorton demanded of the room in general. "How do we get Carling out of this goddamned mess he's got himself into?"

Janet Haddenrich answered this time. "We feel it's best to keep a low profile on this one sir," she said smoothly. "If they know who they're holding, they have a real bargaining card."

"How can they not know?" General Barrett interrupted. "All they have to do is check the hotel registration."

Benjamin shuffled the printed sheets in front of him, containing the list of fifty names of the hostages. "There's a good chance that Senator Carling was incognito," he began and, as the general looked askance at him, continued. "It's fairly normal procedure. And it would account for the fact that the terrorists haven't mentioned his presence."

"Maybe," Barrett said doubtfully. His opinion of the senator from Washington was that Carling, like most elected officials, would never travel incognito. They craved the limelight. That was what kept getting them elected, after all. "Or maybe these damned terrorists are just jerking us around, waiting to see if we'll admit he's in there."

Linus Benjamin lifted one shoulder in a small shrug. "Could be," he agreed. "But we just have to play it by ear until we find out more. In the meantime—" he turned back to the president—"we feel the White House should maintain its current low profile. Too much interest from the president might start the terrorists looking harder at the hostages' names."

There was a general muttering of agreement around the table and Gorton paused, pretended to think the matter over, then nodded decisively.

"Okay," he said. "We'll play it that way for the time being."

General Barrett voiced the question that all of them wanted answered. "Do we have any line on these people yet?" he asked Benjamin.

The FBI director turned both hands palms up in a negative gesture. "Nothing so far," he said. "Homeland security has nothing on them and neither do we. Whoever they are, they're playing it real close to the chest."

"Our sources are showing nothing so far, either," chipped in Haddenrich. "There are a couple of possibilities—long shots. We're checking them out. But so far these people look as if they're new kids on the block."

"These guys are professionals. Look at the equipment they've got," Tildeman added. "Radar-slaved fifty caliber, heat-seeking missiles."

Pohlsen held up a hand to interrupt. "Stingers and machine guns?" he said skeptically.

"That's pretty low tech for this day and age, surely."

But General Barrett shook his head in reply. "That's just the thing, sir," he said. "Professionals usually stick to the KISS principle." He noticed Gorton's frown of incomprehension and elaborated. "Keep it Simple, er . . . Sam," he said, at the last moment changing "Stupid" to "Sam" as he realized that the president could possibly think the word was aimed at him.

"Low-tech equipment is reliable. There's less to go wrong. The past few decades have shown simple triple-A is often more efficient than more complex missile systems." He turned now to Hadden-rich. "Surely we've got *something* on them?"

The CIA director made no reply. She raised one eyebrow at the general and shook her head. They might be pros, the gesture said, but we still don't know jack about them.

"Well we need answers, goddamn it," the president rasped. "Get more people on it and keep them working on it till we know something. We have to know who we're dealing with."

There was no answer to that. Several pairs of eyes around the table dropped and there was a low mumble of acknowledgment. Both the FBI and the CIA were frustrated by their inability to pin the blame to any individual or group. The fact that Gorton could then use their inability as a way to needle them made it even more galling.

There was an apologetic cough from the bottom of the table and Truscott Emery leaned forward, his well-manicured hands resting on a small stack of computer printouts.

"Um . . . we might have a possible lead," he said softly and the table turned toward him. His hesitant tone brought an instant frown to President Gorton's face.

"Are we talking facts or supposition here?" Gorton asked, and his predecessor's special adviser hesitated once more before replying.

"No facts yet, Mr. President. Just a theory we're working on," he said.

The president heaved a deep sigh. "Well let's not waste any of our time on it until you have some facts, okay?" he said unpleasantly.

Emery nodded several times, looking down at the notes in front of him.

"Of course, Mr. President. It's just that—" The president's hard gaze cut him off midsentence.

"Facts, Mr. Emery. That's what we need to deal in here. We go off half-cocked on any of your wild-eyed theories, we could be putting a lot of people in danger. This is the real world. Not some hypothetical one you used to study at Harvard. Understand?"

The special adviser made a half bow from his seated position. "Of course, Mr. President," he said, his even tone giving no hint of the rage he felt inside at the vain, stupid man sitting at the far end of the table. "I'll refine the theories a little and present them then," he said.

Again, the president's gaze bore into him. "Present them when they're facts, Mr. Emery," he said shortly. Then, dismissing the man, he asked the table at large, "Anything else?"

Heads shook around the table. One or two of them looked sympathetically to the annoying little special adviser, he noticed. Well, that was their bad luck. It was time he reined in some of these leftovers from the former administration. Time they knew that President Couch was dead and gone and not coming back again. He rose, waited until they all stood with him, then left the room. Pohlsen delayed a few seconds.

"Anything breaks here, Benjamin, let us know ASAP," he said. "You too, Ms. Haddenrich," he addressed this last to the director of the CIA, who nodded. "Otherwise, another briefing tomorrow, same time." He glanced at his watch and hurried out after the president. Benjamin, Tildeman and Janet Haddenrich all exchanged wry glances. Then Benjamin looked down the table to where the chubby special adviser was replacing his notes in his briefcase, the careless way he was stuffing them in was the only clue to the rage that was burning inside him.

"What have you got, Trus?" he asked quietly. Emery looked up, realized that the others were still sitting around the conference table, waiting for him, and stopped packing his notes away. Benjamin glanced meaningfully around the room.

"Perhaps we should—" He began, jerking his head toward the door. The others all nodded assent. There wasn't a meeting room in the White House that wasn't wired for sound, as everyone who could remember the Nixon era knew all too well. Only Truscott Emery stood his ground.

"It doesn't bother me who's eavesdropping on this," he said, with a definite note of acidity in his tone. "After all, it may well be the only way to get an idea heard at the top levels these days."

Benjamin shifted uncomfortably in his chair. The sarcasm in Emery's voice would be picked up by the tapes, he was sure. Also, most of them made a polite pretense of not knowing that tapes were running everywhere in 1600 Pennsylvania Avenue these days. Then he shrugged. If it didn't bother Emery, why should it bother him?

He looked at the others. Tildeman and Barrett both shrugged in return. Janet Haddenrich, he realized, was smiling approvingly at the plump ex-Harvard man.

"Okay, Truscott, why not?" he said.

Emery busied himself with removing the notes from his briefcase once more. He'd stuffed them in angrily, creasing several of the sheets, and now he took his time smoothing them out. He cleared his throat, glanced quickly at his first page summary and began.

"Are any of you familiar with Operation Powderburn?" he asked. He glanced up at them and saw the blank looks on all their faces. He nodded briefly and continued.

"I thought maybe not. It was before all our times, of course. It was a clandestine operation in the early 1990s. But it made use of air force resources and I thought maybe General Barrett may have heard rumor of it?"

The burly ex-fighter pilot shook his head, his face blank. "Name means nothing to me," he said. "Powderburn?" he repeated. "It doesn't sound like the sort of operation name we'd use. Most of them are computer-generated these days—just random words."

Truscott Emery smiled. "That's true. Unless of course we're talking important, self-serving names that include words like Freedom and Liberation and so on. Part of the reason for using computer-generated codenames is that there's always the risk of someone choosing a name that gives a hint about the purpose of the operation. The concept of a computer doing that with a randomly generated name is pretty thin. However, in this case the operation name was intentionally chosen to do just that."

General Barrett shook his head in disbelief. "That's contrary to all good planning policy."

Emery nodded his agreement. "That's true, General. Unless . . ." He let the word hang for a moment or two, until he was sure he had their attention. "Unless you want the enemy to get some idea of the purpose of the operation."

Janet Haddenrich frowned at the benign, smooth-cheeked face. "Why would anyone in their right mind want to do that?" she asked. Emery favored her with a nod, as if he were talking to one of his brighter pupils back at Harvard.

"Exactly, Mrs. Haddenrich," he replied, and she smiled at his acknowledgment of her married status. "The only logical reason one would do that would be if one were intending to send a message."

Benjamin and Tildeman exchanged quick glances. "In this case," Emery was already continuing, "the message was to a Colombian drug lord named Juan Carlo Estevez. He was an independent, operating outside the Medellin cartel."

Haddenrich shook her head. "Dangerous thing to do," she said, and Emery glanced at her.

"True. But he was big enough not to worry about them. He'd built himself a virtual fortress in the mountains. His men were well armed and trained and he could afford the latest equipment. He controlled access into the mountains where he was based and he was planning a large-scale operation. He was preparing for a major blitz aimed at San Francisco. This was his plan. He was going to hit one city at a time and dominate it. Then, once he had that market tied up, he'd move onto other major cities. He'd built up a stockpile of cocaine, buying up supplies from the smaller independents, whether they were willing to sell to him or not. He had ten million dollars' worth of it piled up in a warehouse in the mountains. He'd invested all his available cash in the venture."

He paused, then elaborated. "That ten million dollar figure, of course, was his cost price. It would have been closer to fifty million on the street, even given the fact that he planned to undercut the cartel's price."

Tildeman whistled softly. "A sale like that would have caused the cartel quite a headache."

"That was the idea. But apparently, we got word of his plans. I'll let you imagine who it came from."

"The cartel?" Barrett asked and Emery nodded.

"Exactly. We might not have wanted Señor Estevez peddling his product on our streets but they wanted it even less. The upshot was, those in power decided to send a message to Estevez—and to any others who might have similar ideas in the future. Hence Operation Powderburn."

He leaned back, steepling his fingers. He had no further need to refer to his notes. He knew the details by heart from here on in. He glanced quickly around the table to make sure he had their attention, then continued.

"There was a top secret black operations group formed in the early 1990s for precisely this sort of purpose. It was an inter-service group with a team of Special Forces troops under its command, along with Navy SEALs and small boat forces. There were also several air force pilots seconded to it, along with two F-117 Nighthawks and their support crews. Stealth fighters," he added, in case anyone around the table didn't recognize the name. Several heads nodded. "They could have been purpose-designed for the Group. That's all it was known as, by the way, the Group.

"The command structure of the Group was, to put it one way, convoluted. People kind of knew it existed but nobody needed to admit to it. But the CIA, FBI or the DEA could let it be known, by various devious routes, that they wanted a certain result and it would be carried out. On occasions, the 'suggestion' came from the White House itself. In all cases, operations were totally clandestine, totally deniable. No permanent records were to be kept by anyone."

"One moment, Mr. Emery," Tildeman interrupted. "If this . . . Group . . . was so top secret and nothing was put on paper, how did you come to know all this?"

Emery smiled at him. The chubby face and the smooth pink cheeks gave him an expression of almost cherubic innocence, Janet Haddenrich thought.

"There's always a paper trail, Director. I said it was forbidden to keep any permanent records but we all know that people don't always obey orders like that. The compulsion to cover your ass is an all-powerful one in this city."

There were a few glances exchanged around the table. All of

those present knew that at different times in their careers, they had kept records that technically should have been destroyed. Then General Barrett spoke for all of those present as he gestured for Emery to continue.

"Okay. Point taken. Go ahead," he said. Emery met his gaze and nodded once or twice. Then he resumed his narrative.

"The decision was taken to destroy Estevez's stockpile. He had his mountain headquarters protected by radar and surface to air missiles so the F-117 was the logical choice for the job. A two-man special forces team was parachuted into the area. They didn't need to penetrate his perimeter at all. They simply occupied an adjoining hilltop and acted as designators for the Nighthawk."

Barrett ran his hand through his close-cropped hair.

"We're talking Colombia, right? That means the F-117, if it had launched from Florida, must have crossed into the airspace of at least three countries?"

"Exactly, General. As I said, that's why the operation was so perfectly suited to the Nighthawk. It simply flew through borders as if they didn't exist. As if it didn't exist, in fact. And to all intents and purposes, it didn't."

Barrett nodded understanding. He was pragmatic enough to accept that violating another country's airspace was a fair practice—so long as you didn't get caught doing it. Emery continued.

"Once the ground team targeted the warehouse with a laser, it was a simple matter for the F-117 to release two laser-guided bombs. The first was a standard five-hundred pound explosive device. The second, following a few seconds later, was a napalm bomb. Bomb number one opened up the roof of the warehouse. Bomb number two fried the cocaine stored there. It took less than a minute to put Estevez out of business."

"I should imagine the Medellin cartel were delighted," Tildeman said heavily.

Emery nodded agreement. "Of course they were. But from our point of view, at least we continued to face the devil we knew—not some newcomer who might provide us with some unpleasant surprises down the track. We sent a message to Estevez and to anyone else who might plan to follow his example: Don't consider it. No matter where you are or how big or well protected you may be, we can reach you and put you out of business."

Emery had leaned forward again as he told his story. Now he sat back, looking around at the assembled faces, waiting for the obvious question. As he had expected, it came from Haddenrich.

"Professor," she said slowly. "You said the ransom amount was significant—nine point seven million dollars. Where's the connection?"

Emery smiled. "It was the odd amount that first set me looking. Nine point seven million dollars. As the president said, why not nine point five? Or ten million? It seemed such a strange amount. So we began a search to see if anything turned up a similar figure." He nodded his thanks to the FBI director. "Director Benjamin was kind enough to lend me some staff and facilities. I even considered the president's rather simplistic suggestion that it might be a figure converted from a round number in some other currency, but nothing matched."

Several people around the table, conscious of the ever-present recorders, winced at the phrase "the president's simplistic suggestion" but Emery seemed not to notice.

"What we found, eventually, was Operation Powderburn. Estevez had ten million dollars' worth of cocaine in the storehouse. But a small proportion had been moved to a second room. It was protected from the initial blast and from the napalm. Our Intelligence told us later that he was able to recover a few hundred thousand dollars' worth of cocaine. Three hundred thousand, to be precise."

"Leaving a loss of nine point seven million," Linus Benjamin said softly.

"Exactly." Emery smiled at him. He was always delighted when other people reached the same conclusion he had.

"So you're telling us that because we burned his cocaine stockpile in 1993, Estevez is behind this attempt to extort money from us?" Benjamin asked. Emery shrugged.

"It's a theory, Director Benjamin, nothing more, nothing less. I'm saying it's a possibility, that's all."

"But why not go for the street value he lost—fifty million dol-

lars?" Tildeman asked, and the professor inclined his head thoughtfully.

"Aaah, that's the whole point, you see. We set out to send a message to Estevez and his like. Now he's doing the same thing right
back."

"You mean he wants us to know it's him?" Haddenrich asked and
Emery shook his head.

"That's the beauty of it. This way we'll know it's him but we'll
never be able to prove it. As far as the rest of the world is concerned,
the Arabs—Al Qaeda, Hezbollah or one of the other militant
groups—will be behind this. We could never convince them that
it's a grubby Colombian drug baron."

Morris Tildeman shook his head wearily. It was a bizarre idea, he
thought. But his years in public office had taught him that bizarre
ideas were all too often correct.

"I still think it's odd that he didn't ask for the full amount," he
said.

Haddenrich shook her head in disagreement. "If Professor Truscott is right, the amount of nine point seven million is significant.
Fifty million is a round sum—we might never see the connection."

"So who cares about the connection? Fifty million is a lot of
money."

"Maybe he doesn't want his money back," she said. "Maybe he
wants revenge. And he wants us to know he's taking it."

TWENTY-FIVE

Tina Bowden shoved the kitchen door open and reached to the side to turn on the rows of overhead lights. As the fluorescents flickered to life, she glanced quickly at the big rinsing sink and felt her pulse rate increase slightly. The two coffee mugs that she'd left there that morning after preparing the breakfast were turned upside down.

Casually, she walked past them and turned them right side up again. It was an unimportant movement and the armed guard who had accompanied them took no notice. She thought that for once, the normally efficient Mr. Kormann had made a small mistake—small but significant. It seemed logical to assign the same guard to her and Ralph each time they came to the kitchen to prepare a meal. But by doing so, Kormann had allowed a situation to develop where a familiar routine was established—and with familiarity came a certain lack of attention.

This was the third time the same man had accompanied them. He was used to them now, accustomed to their moving around the kitchen, fetching ingredients from the pantry. Now he was beginning to take such actions for granted, where a less familiar sentry might have questioned their every move and even supervised their trips to the storeroom.

As usual, Ralph had been assigned to cook for the kidnappers, Kormann having ordered a meal of veal valdostana from the suggestions that Ralph had put forward. It seemed that the leader of the kidnappers enjoyed toying with the chef's sensibilities, making him suggest meals and then insisting that, no matter what they might be, they should be accompanied by French fries. Tina had noticed that Kormann rarely ate more than one or two of the fries. He was fucking with Ralph's mind, she knew, making sure the chef was constantly reminded of who was in charge.

As Ralph started selecting veal fillets from the meat fridge, Tina caught the guard's eye and motioned toward the storeroom door.

"Need some cans of meatballs in sauce and some pasta," she said and he nodded easily.

She pushed the door open and stepped inside. The lights in here came on automatically with the kitchen lights and for a moment she looked around the brightly lit racks and shelves, seeing no sign of Jesse. Then he stepped out of the shadows beside the big upright freezer at the back of the room and he realized she had been waiting to make sure she was alone. She raised a hand in greeting and moved quickly to the back of the room.

"Hi again," he said quietly. "I got this from your room."

"This" was her .38 Special. He placed it on the shelf beside them, then put the carton of fifty slugs with it. She reached out and picked up the gun, feeling the custom grips conform instantly to her hand. For a moment or two, the temptation to take it back into the gymnasium and empty all six chambers into Kormann's sneering face was almost irresistible. Then she steadied herself and looked around for somewhere to conceal it. There was still the possibility that she and Ralph might be searched when they returned to the gym, she realized. Jesse read her thoughts and took the gun from her, wrapping it in Saran wrap and shoving it deep inside a large bin of rice. The box of slugs went the same way.

"Best leave it here until you know you want to use it," he said quietly and she nodded agreement. He'd obviously had time to think of a hiding place for the gun. She began to collect cans of meatballs in tomato sauce as they talked, knowing that her time was strictly limited.

"What are you planning on doing now?" she asked.

He hesitated for a second before answering, "I thought I'd try to make contact with the federal guys out where the road's blocked," he said. "Strangely enough, I kind of know the agent-in-charge. If

I can keep him abreast of what's going on in here it could give him an edge."

She nodded. Having an observer in the enemy's camp could be a big advantage for the FBI negotiators. Any piece of information could be of value in this situation. Then she saw the doubt in Jesse's eyes. "What's the problem?" she asked and couldn't help grinning to herself as she heard the words. Here they were, held in a hotel by twenty armed men, with explosives all around the surrounding hillsides, and she was asking "what's the problem?".

Jesse saw the irony of the question too and for a moment there was an answering gleam of dry humor in his eyes, then he shrugged. "Can't risk using the phone lines in here," he said. "I was wondering if there might be another line in the terminal or over to the ski school that didn't come through this switch?"

He'd barely finished the question when she was shaking her head. "No use," she said. "They took out the main phone line when they came in. From what I've heard, they laid their own line over the mountains and they've plugged into that." A thought struck her. "How about a cell phone? There's one in my bureau drawer?"

"No use," he replied. "I've got my own but we're in a dead spot here."

He stopped, realizing she was shaking her head again.

"Here, yes," she said quickly. "But up on the mountain there's coverage. At the top cable car station you've got a clear line of sight to an antenna halfway back to Salt Lake City." She saw the protest rising in his eyes again and forestalled it. "I know. You can hardly go up in the cable car without being noticed. But the chairlifts should be working. The entire chairlift system is on an automatic time switch—they come on and off every day. You can ride the chairs up to Eagle Ridge, then hike around to the cable car station. It's a hundred or so feet higher up, but it's not impossible."

Jesse thought about it. It seemed possible. "It's worth a try, I guess," he said. "Is there anything else you've found out about these guys that I can pass on?"

Tina chewed her lip thoughtfully. "The more I see of them, the more I'm sure they're not terrorists," she said finally. "They're just in it for the ransom. I overheard their leader telling Senator Carling that as soon as the money was paid, he'd be back on Capitol Hill. There's been no talk of any other conditions, any political prisoners they want released, any concessions to be made—you know the sort of thing that usually goes with a terrorist group. Just the money."

"So they don't strike you as a bunch of crazies?" Jesse said and she shook her head.

"Just the opposite. They're so damn controlled and sure of themselves that it's scary. Right from the start they said they were here for business reasons only—and I believe them."

She glanced toward the door, conscious that she had been here too long already. Jesse gestured for her to go. She grabbed up several packets of dried spaghetti noodles as she went and exited into the kitchen.

Jesse watched her go, waited for a few minutes to be sure the guard hadn't decided to check the storeroom, then started prowling through the shelves, looking for something to eat. He had the feeling it was going to be another long day.

CANYON ROAD
WASATCH COUNTY
FIVE MILES FROM CANYON LODGE
1540 HOURS, MOUNTAIN TIME
SUNDAY, DAY 2

Agent-in-Charge Denton Colby stepped down from the humvee outside his command trailer. He nodded to the marine colonel who was behind the steering wheel.

"Thanks for the tour, Colonel Maloney," he said. "I can see your unit's reputation isn't exaggerated."

Marine Colonel Maloney had suggested that Colby inspect the RRTF encampment, talk to the men and assess their readiness. Colby had been impressed. The rapid response tactical force troops were intelligent, highly trained and dedicated. Most of their officers and senior non-coms carried combat decorations. Now, in response to Colby's words, the colonel gave an informal salute, one forefinger raised to the peak of his fur-lined cap. "Just wanted to be sure you knew what you had behind you, Agent Colby," he said. "Don't want to look like I'm pushing. I know you're the man in charge. But if you decide you need to use force, we're ready. We'll go on your call."

Colby said nothing for a moment, standing with his hands on his hips and looking toward the mountains, where a series of peaks blocked the Canyon Lodge from sight. Earlier that day, he'd sited a television camera on one of the peaks, dropping the crew off below the ridge line, and out of sight of the lodge, and leaving them to hike uphill for the last fifty feet. The camera, with a fifty-to-one digital zoom lens on it, was linked to several monitors in the camp, including one in Colby's command trailer. It provided a constant surveillance picture of the hotel.

"It may come to that, Colonel," he said. "If so, I know you and your men will do everything you can to get it done quickly."

"Give me the word, sir, and once we've cranked our choppers, I can put fifty men on that roof inside five minutes." The colonel spoke quietly, confidently. He wasn't boasting. He was stating a fact. Colby nodded several times.

"You'd lose quite a few of them on the way in, Colonel," he said and the marine nodded, acknowledging the fact.

"Every one of my men is a volunteer, sir," he said. "Every one of them knew what sort of duty they were volunteering for. It's our job to take casualties and make sure the hostages don't. We all know that. We all accept it."

"And you'll go in the lead ship?" Colby asked.

Again, Maloney nodded. "That's the way we train. That's the way we'll do it."

"Let's hope it doesn't come to that," Colby replied. Then, hearing his name called, he looked around to the comms trailer parked on the shoulder of the road. One of his communications technicians was in the open doorway, calling to him and beckoning.

"Looks like I've got a call. Maybe this time they'll tell me what they really want."

So far, conversations with the hotel had been a series of frustrations. They had threatened the lives of the hostages and demanded the ransom. But they had steadfastly refused to begin to negotiate a handover method, threatening instead to open fire on any aircraft or vehicle that entered the valley surrounding the lodge. When Colby pointed out that he would need free passage for some kind of vehicle to deliver the money, they had angrily shouted that he was trying to trick them and hung up.

Even though the behavior sounded irrational, Denton Colby was beginning to believe that it was totally intentional, a ploy being used to keep him off balance.

He jogged now to the comms trailer and mounted the steel steps, dropping behind the desk where a gooseneck microphone was connected to the phone line.

"This is Colby," he said. "Who's talking that end?"

He'd spoken to two of the terrorists so far, never knowing which of them would make contact. One of them seemed to be totally irrational, ready to fly off the handle at the slightest provocation—real or imagined. The other was calmer, but no more easy to deal with. When the voice answered, he recognized the calmer of the two.

"This is me," the voice said from the small speaker mounted over the desk. The slow-turning wheels of tape recorded every sound in the trailer.

"It'd be a lot easier if I knew your name?" Colby suggested, for perhaps the tenth time. There was the usual short bark of laughter.

"You do keep trying, don't you, Agent Colby?" said the voice.

Colby shrugged. Even though he knew the other man couldn't see him, he felt body language helped the tone of voice in a negotiation.

"Just a first name. It helps when we're talking. After all, I'm willing to negotiate. I've told you that."

"You've told me. It's just that when it comes down to it, you're not willing to negotiate anything meaningful." The voice was sarcastic.

"I'm willing. You just won't tell me how we can effect the handover." He had to be careful here. If he sounded as if he were blaming the other man for the present impasse, he could easily break off communications. And a continuing dialogue, Colby knew, provided the best chance of survival for the hostages.

"Figure it out, Colby. You're a clever man." Now there was a trace of suppressed anger in the disembodied voice and Colby backed off.

"I'm trying. Believe me, I want to get this whole mess straightened out. I don't want anybody hurt. Not the hostages. Not me or any of my men. Not you or any of your men."

"Sure. You'll let us walk with the money, won't you?"

"If that's what it takes, yes," Colby said.

"Christ, man, it sounds almost as if you believe it yourself. That was really smooth. I'm impressed." The anger was back now, and rising, and Colby sensed that once again, a conversation with the kidnappers was going to end in sudden disconnection.

"I do mean it. I'm telling you . . . look it'd be a lot easier if I had a name—even a first name . . ." he hesitated, waiting to see if there would be a reaction.

"No deal. Call me mister. That'll do. And stop trying to trick me here with your smart-ass 'I want to be your friend' shit."

"Hey, it's no trick. And okay, maybe I don't want to be your friend. But I do want to be able to negotiate with you. I want us to be able to trust each other."

"Well, okay, maybe we could do a little something to establish trust. I'll tell you what, you can call me Roger."

"Hey, that's fine," said Colby. "Now we're getting somewhere, Roger."

"Glad you think so, Dent," the other man replied, laying a sarcastic emphasis on the name. "Now you can do a little something for me to show we can trust you."

"Name it. If I can do it, it's yours," said Colby.

"Good. Well here's the pitch, Denton: the British government has just arrested four Irish freedom fighters in Liverpool."

For a second or two, Colby was speechless. The night before, the TV news had carried an item about a bomb squad from an ultra right

Irish breakaway group being caught in the British seaport city. He hurried to regain his composure.

"Yeah . . . right . . . I saw that on the news last night, Roger," he said, wondering where the hell this was going.

"They're our comrades in arms. We want them set free. See what you can do or you can kiss four of these hostages good-bye."

"See what I can do? They're in Britain for Chrissake—" Colby began desperately. But the loudspeaker above the desk was silent. The other man had broken the connection.

TWENTY-SIX

President Gorton swept an angry gaze around the assembled group.

"Irish patriots?" he asked, the sarcasm thick in his voice. "A bunch of bog stupid fucking Irish thugs and none of you had the slightest idea who we were dealing with? Gentlemen, I am speechless, totally speechless, with the absolute lack of meaningful intelligence coming to this office from your organizations."

He paused, waiting to see if any of them might choose to defend themselves. There seemed to be nobody willing to say anything so he continued, belying his earlier claim to be totally speechless. "Now if any of you think for one minute that I am going to go cap in hand to the British Prime Minister and beg his help in this matter, you have another think coming. So when you finally collect your wits and decide to suggest some course of action to me, don't make the mistake of including that one. Do I make myself clear?"

Again, his eyes swept the room and again he was greeted by silence. Even Haddenrich, he noticed with a small thrill of pleasure, who usually maintained an unruffled and sardonic demeanor in these meetings, seemed chastened by the failure of her organization to have seen the hand of the Irish rebel group behind the attempted extortion bid.

He had been leaning forward in his chair as his voice flailed them. Now he sat back abruptly, the springs and leather creaking under the sudden impact.

"If any of you have any ideas, any ideas at all, I'd be willing to listen to them."

Linus Benjamin cleared his throat. It was, after all, his principle responsibility. "Mr. President," he said. "We can't be totally sure that these people are aligned to the Irish situation—"

The president's sharp voice cut him off before he could finish the statement. "Is that right, Director Benjamin? We can't be sure? Well, I'd say a message that says 'Give us nine point seven million dollars and turn loose our Irish comrades' might give us a pretty broad hint that they are, wouldn't you? It also tells us what they want the money for. They'll have it earmarked to buy weapons."

He glanced down the table and singled out the smooth-cheeked face of the Harvard professor. "Which also seems to blow your ridiculous 'message' theory out of the water, Mr. Emery."

Emery shrugged. He knew there was no point arguing. Benjamin, however, felt that he should make another attempt.

"Mr. President," he said. "It's not unusual in these situations for the terrorists to try to muddy the waters on us. After reflection, that's what our man on the spot thinks is happening. This is the first time any mention has been made of any link to the Irish. Besides, this group in Liverpool are a one-off bunch of crazies. The IRA has given up on that sort of thing these days."

"Jesus Christ, Mr. Director, will you have the grace to admit you are wrong! These people have slipped under the guard of the FBI, the CIA, the NSA and just about everybody else with a set of initials to identify them as intelligence experts, and you choose to simply deny their existence?"

"Sir, that's not exactly—" Benjamin began but again he was cut off.

"Now I'm sorry if your collective egos have been bruised here. But so far, the only knowledge we have of these people is that they hold the whip hand, they are demanding money and they are aligned to the Irish . . ." he paused, looking down at the notes on his desk.

"Irish Action Group" Pohlsen reminded him quietly and he nodded quickly in acknowledgment.

"Exactly. Now, until we find out that they are not so aligned, we will proceed on the assumption that they are! Is that a reasonable course of action?"

"Yes, sir," Benjamin answered, speaking for the group. "I was merely saying that we should keep our options—"

"Thank you, Mr. Director. I'll give that advice the consideration it deserves. By tomorrow morning, I want your recommendations as to what course we should follow in this matter. And we will proceed on the assumption that we are dealing with representatives of the IAG. Is anyone among you too distressed with that premise to continue?" He glared at them all, challenging them. Nobody spoke. He noticed, with some anger, that the special adviser, Emery, met his gaze coolly, refusing to let his eyes drop before the president's anger, refusing to try to mask the hint of scarcely veiled criticism in his expression.

"That will be all," Gorton said shortly and, as the group began to gather papers together and prepare to leave, he added, "Emery: I'll trouble you to stay for a moment." Several of the others exchanged glances. Truscott Emery inclined his head gracefully in a half-bow.

"Of course, Mr. President," he replied.

Gorton waited impatiently, fidgeting with a mother-of-pearl-handled letter opener while the others left the office. When he, his chief of staff and Truscott Emery were the only ones remaining, he spoke. "Mr. Emery," he said, refusing to give the man his academic title of doctor, "I was willing to retain you on my staff in memory of my predecessor, and in accordance with what I am sure his wishes would have been."

Emery noticed the conditional nature of the opening statement. He nodded, watching the president closely, seeing the barely concealed satisfaction that underpinned his words.

"However," Gorton said, "your attitude has left me with no alternative but to discontinue your activities in the White House."

"My attitude, Mr. President?" Emery said, with a look of feigned surprise that served only to goad the small-minded man opposite him.

"I demand loyalty, Mr. Emery, as I'm sure President Couch would have. And I'm afraid I'm not getting it from you. You've shown your utter disregard for this office, in your attitude and in your words."

He reached for a control console on the side of the desk and pressed a switch. There was a brief hiss from hidden loudspeakers in the room, then Emery's voice, clear and unmistakable, after the electronic filtering and digital enhancement that had been carried out on the original tape could be heard.

"It doesn't bother me who's eavesdropping on this. After all, it may be the only way to get an idea heard at top levels these days."

Gorton hit the switch again and the tape stopped. He raised one eyebrow at the academic.

"Well?" he said.

Emery shrugged. "I see no disrespect there," he said evenly.

"Well, that's where we differ, Mr. Emery. How dare you accuse the President of the United States of eavesdropping? You make it sound as if I were kneeling with my ear to the keyhole. You made reference to me making a 'simplistic suggestion,' I think the term was. Not only that, but you disobeyed my explicit wish, in promulgating your ridiculous 'message' theory to my senior advisers.

"And I'll point out, Mr. Emery, that subsequent events have demonstrated how mistaken that theory was, and how correct I was in directing you to stop wasting your time and the time of my council with it. You see no disrespect, do you? Well let me tell you, I have seen little from you but disrespect for this office since I assumed the presidency."

Gorton stopped, leaning forward in his chair, stabbing the air with one forefinger to emphasize his words. Emery held his ground, his head tilted slightly to one side as he regarded the seething man across the desk from him. He realized that his time in the White House was finally at an end and, with a sense of surprise, he recognized the fact that he was relieved that it was.

"Believe me, Mr. President," he said calmly, "my respect for the office of the presidency is unwavering—regardless of how I might feel about some of the people who have filled that office."

The words hung in the air between them, their meaning all too clear. Gorton regarded the smooth-cheeked, harmless looking little academic with something very close to hatred.

"You're finished in this office, Emery. Get out. Get out now!" he spat. Emery rose, and again gave that half-bow.

"You'll have my resignation by the end of the day, sir," he said calmly.

"I don't need it!" Gorton spat back at him. "You're fired. Terence, make sure his security passes are invalidated as of this moment. He is out."

"Yes, Mr. President," the chief of staff murmured. He had seen this moment coming and felt no sympathy for Emery, whom, he had always felt, looked upon him with a kind of intellectual contempt.

"I'll be gone as soon as I clean out my desk," Truscott Emery said, addressing the remark to the chief of staff.

But it was the president who answered. "You'll be gone right now! As of this moment, you have no security clearance here and you no longer have any business in the White House. Your files are government property. Any personal items you may have will be sent to your apartment."

He felt a savage stab of satisfaction as Emery raised his eyebrows in surprise. Finally, thought Gorton, he had cut through that imperturbable facade. Then Emery recovered his poise and, turning his back on the President of the United States, he left the Oval Office for the last time.

TWENTY-SEVEN

It had been a long, uncomfortable night. Jesse had left the shelter of the hotel around 11:40, a few minutes after the moon had set over White Eagle Ridge.

He had decided that moving across the open ground between the hotel and the chairlift system during daylight was simply too risky. He had no idea what sort of lookout was being kept from the roof and all it needed was one man looking down and seeing a figure moving in the open to give the entire game away.

Consequently, he had decided to make his move in darkness, spend the rest of the night in the chairlift terminal building and take the first chair up the mountain once they started running in the morning.

He'd collected some food from the pantry and used Tina's pass card to let himself into several of the other rooms on the fifth floor, where he helped himself to the minibars, taking a few bottles of soda and as many of water as he could lay his hands on. He'd loaded his supplies into a small skier's backpack that he found in one of the rooms, then spent the remaining time fashioning a poncho-like garment from one of the hotel's white bedcovers. With the white poncho draped over his head and shoulders, his dark-colored ski clothes would be less visible as he moved across the snow-covered ground to the chairlift terminal.

That nerve-racking journey was one of the longest in Jesse's life. He pushed off from the sheltering bulk of the hotel building, gliding smoothly on his skis across the flat, white ground. It was about one hundred and fifty yards to the terminal and for every inch of it, Jesse's shoulders twitched expectantly, waiting for the shout to come from above and behind him, followed by a hail of automatic fire. Even without a moon, the snow-covered ground provided a terrifyingly bright light. The white camouflage provided by the poncho seemed pitifully inadequate. It was only when he finally glided into the dark shadow of the terminal building that Jesse realized he had been holding his breath, in a ridiculous attempt to make himself less conspicuous. His upper body was soaked with nervous sweat.

The terminal was simply a large metal shed, open at either end, where the chairlift ran in from the mountain, disconnected onto a slow speed bullwheel while skiers took their seats, then reconnected to the fast-moving cable to speed away up the mountain again. The sides and roof were intended to provide a certain amount of cover for the skiers and the lift attendants during bad weather. But it definitely wasn't designed as a place to spend the night in below-freezing conditions. There was a small, enclosed cabin for the lift attendants. The door was locked but Jesse rammed an elbow through the glass window and let himself in. He huddled down on the floor of the little cabin, wrapping the poncho around him, cursing the sweat that was now clammy and freezing on his body.

Eventually, he slept, cramped and uncomfortable. He was roused with a jerk by the sudden clash of gears as the timer cut in and the chairlift's giant electric motor came to life a few yards from him. He groaned and tried to move, his cramped muscles protesting. He'd slept with his head twisted to one side and he could barely turn his neck. That was going to make skiing a lot of fun, he thought ruefully and then gingerly moved his head in a circle to try to loosen the muscles.

Outside, the chairs were slowly parading past the hut, then connecting onto the drive cable to go dancing away up the mountain as the impetus of the sudden start-up sent the whole system bouncing against the spring of the cable. Jesse took a swig from one of his water bottles, and ate a Hershey bar. Along with his cell phone, he'd collected a small pair of folding binoculars from his car the previous night. Taking them now, he moved to the edge of the terminal shed to a spot where he could see the hotel building.

Staying back in the shadows, he focused the binoculars on the rooftop, scanning for any sight of a sentry or a watcher looking in his direction. Nothing was visible, but that didn't mean nobody was watching. They could be in any of the top floor rooms, he realized. There was no need for them to stay out in the cold to keep watch. Only the gun and missile crews would need to be actually at their posts through the night.

Still, there was no point worrying about observers who might or might not be there. He waited for a gap between chairs and made his way back to the hut. He slung the backpack once more, then draped the white poncho over his head and shoulders. He clipped his skis together. He didn't plan to ride the chairlift sitting up with his legs dangling. The quad chair was long enough to accommodate him lying down, and the perspex bubble should shield him from view as he made his way up the mountain.

A chair clattered past the hut and he stepped out behind it, waiting for the next in line. It moved smoothly up to him and he blessed the fact that this was a detachable chairlift. It gave him time to get settled and out of sight before he was out in the open. Clutching the skis to his chest, he lay sideways on the chair, feeling the jolt as it moved from the bullwheel to the high-speed cable, and whipped away from the station in a series of giant swoops. He glanced back over his shoulder, his neck muscles protesting fiercely at the movement. As he had foreseen, the perspex weather cover, which was automatically tripped open when the chair reached the station, lay open behind him, effectively screening him from view. He settled back and made himself as comfortable as possible, listening to the hum of the cable and the repetitive rattle of the chair passing over the pylons en route.

He'd ridden this chair many times in the previous week and when he judged he was nearly at the top, he swung himself upright in the seat. The hotel was far below him now and the chance that he might be seen was a very small one. He stretched his neck again, moving his head in ever larger circles, despite the pain that screeched at him. Then the chair was passing the last marker and sliding into the top terminal. He felt the jerk of deceleration as it disconnected onto another bullwheel, then he stepped off and walked clear.

His cell phone was in his parka's inside pocket and he checked it now, only to read the message "No signal" in the tiny screen. He shrugged. Obviously, he would have to climb the last hundred and fifty yards to the summit, and ski around to the top of the cable car station to get a clear line to a cell aerial.

Getting to the top of the ridge took him another twenty minutes, side-stepping up the slope through the deep, soft powder, and often having to detour to get around thick-growing groves of trees. At least now there was no fear that he might be seen from below, as the hotel was well and truly screened from view by an intervening ridge. Fit as he was, he paused, breathing heavily, at the top. His legs felt like lead and the muscles were on fire. Later, he knew, they'd warm up and the pain would lessen. But for now, the lactic acid in his muscles was torture. He had a breather at the top of the ridge and took another swig of water. Ridiculous how, surrounded by millions of gallons, frozen in the form of snow, a man's throat and mouth could become so dry and parched in this atmosphere. Again he checked the phone, but the same message was still glowing on the screen. He hadn't expected otherwise.

There was an access path here at the top of the ridge that led around from the cable car. Of course, it was an uphill slope for him, being intended to cater for traffic moving in the opposite direction. But herringboning up the groomed path was a lot easier than side-stepping up the steep and deep of the ridge. He swung into a smooth rhythm, driving with the inside edge of each ski, planting the pole just behind the foot for maximum effect. Another eight minutes' effort saw him glide out to the top of the cable car station.

It was another brilliantly clear day and, without meaning to, he stopped to look at the magnificent view, looking back through the sawtooth tops of the mountain range to the haze that hung above Salt Lake City. It all looked so peaceful, so unchanged. He shook his head in wonder and skied forward a few yards until he could just see the hotel in the valley below.

He unlatched the skis and then moved into the sheltering shadow of the cable car terminal building, focusing the binoculars on the roof of the hotel far below him.

From this vantage point, he could see small figures moving on the roof—maybe half a dozen men, he figured. There were two pedestal mounts set up, each with twin fifty-caliber machine guns, and a radar dish. Several long, narrow drab olive cases were in evidence. They had a military look to them and he figured them to be the cases for Stinger missiles.

Nobody on the roof seemed to be looking his way. He swung the glasses toward Canyon Road, where he could make out the huge rift in the snow caused by the avalanche two days ago. Somewhere beyond that, he knew, the police, FBI and army had set up their base. At the thought of it now, he reached for his phone and switched it on.

He punched in a number and hit the send button, waited a few seconds, then heard the muted burr that told him the phone at the other end was ringing.

SHERIFF'S OFFICE
STEAMBOAT SPRINGS
COLORADO
0930 HOURS, MOUNTAIN TIME

For the third time that morning, Lee began to word a memo about overtime hours. She rewound the microcassette recorder to the beginning to erase her previous effort, pressed record and tried again.

"Denise, this is for the financial controller at the county administration office, with copies to the mayor and members of the town council." She paused, not sure how to begin, then shrugged angrily. Just jump in, she told herself.

"Regarding recent overtime hours submitted by members of the sheriff's . . . make that the Routt County sheriff's, Denise . . . office staff . . . make that personnel . . . sheriff's office personnel . . . *Routt County sheriff's office personnel*," she corrected herself savagely, "in particular with regard to activities regarding the recent Olympic ski-jump trials . . ." she tailed off uncertainly. She sensed that she was saying "regarding, regard and recent" a hell of a lot in that first sentence. She clicked the stop button, rewound and played back what she'd dictated so far.

"Oh, for Christ's sake," she said, then threw the recorder violently against the office wall. It slid to the floor, the spring-loaded cover snapped open and the cassette half-ejected on impact.

The door opened a crack and Tom LeGros put his head around the edge.

"You call me, Lee?" he said. He was a little nervous. The sheriff had been like a recently woken grizzly these past few days. She glared up at him for a second, then realized it wasn't his fault that she was on edge and waved her hand in a negative gesture.

"No. I'm sorry, Tom. Just a bit keyed up is all."

He nodded, saying nothing. Everyone in the office knew that Jesse had taken off but nobody knew why and nobody was keen to discuss it with Lee. Tom swallowed. He wished there was some way he could help but he'd known Lee long enough to realize that wishing and doing were two different matters.

"Okay, then," he said. He withdrew his head and closed the door quietly behind him. Lee kept looking at the closed door for several seconds, then shook her head wearily.

"Damn it, Jess. Where the hell are you? Why do you have to run off whenever you've got a problem?"

It was a continual source of frustration to her. Put Jesse in a dangerous situation where lives might be at risk, and she couldn't think of a more steadfast, dependable person. Jesse was the companion you'd choose to go into the trenches with, she thought, remembering her father's dictum on how to judge another person's worth. If you were in trouble, he'd move heaven and earth to help you. But when anything threatened his personal space, he had a tendency to run away from the situation, hiding away like a wounded animal while he tried to heal the wounds by himself. He'd done it when they were teenagers, and again after that shooting incident in Denver. It seemed that when he had a personal crisis, he just couldn't accept outside help from anyone.

"Not that you offered much help," she muttered to herself, uncomfortably aware that her parting words to him were to "fuck off" and "get over it." "You know what he's like. You should have taken it a bit easier."

The phone on her desk pealed and she hooked the receiver out of the cradle.

"Sheriff Torrens," she said, her mind still on the problem of Jesse. Then she stiffened in her seat as she heard his voice.

"Lee? It's Jesse."

"Jesse! Where the hell are you? What are you—" She forced herself to stop, hearing the overtone of anger in her voice. This was not the way to deal with him. She'd just been telling herself that. Jesse needed careful handling when he was in this mood and here she was trying to jump down his throat—as usual.

"Lee, I'm in Utah," he began.

She frowned. "Utah? What—" Then with an enormous effort, she stopped the outburst that was threatening to erupt down the phone line. She took a deep breath, calmed herself.

"Okay, Jess. You're in Utah," she said.

"Lee, I need your help. You been watching what's going on at Snow Eagles Resort?" he said and she felt a cold hand of fear wrap itself around her heart.

"Yes," she said. She couldn't say more than the one word. She had an awful sense she knew what was coming.

"Well that's where I am. Came here to ski and . . . sort a few things out."

"You're a hostage?" she said and he hurried to correct her.

"No. No. I'm in the clear. I was out skiing when they took over the hotel. I've been hiding out ever since. They don't know I'm here."

"Then get the hell out of there, Jess. Get out right now before they find out!" she said. She felt a terrible sense of helplessness. Jesse was in danger and she was powerless to do anything about it. But

Jesse's voice continued, calm and determined now. She reflected on her earlier thoughts. Now he had a situation to focus on, he was the Jesse you'd go to the trenches with.

"Can't be done, Lee. There's no way out at the moment. And besides, I think I might be able to help these people if I stay around."

"One man, Jesse? What can one man hope to do?" she asked. She was desperate for him to get out of that ski resort, any way he could.

"I can keep the FBI informed as to what's happening," he said quietly and she stopped her protesting as she realized how valuable it would be to have an observer on the inside in a situation like this. It made a lot of sense for him to stay put, she thought. More importantly, she realized that, in his place, she'd do the same thing.

"How can I help, Jess?" she said quietly.

He sensed the change in her tone and was grateful for it. "The agent-in-charge is Dent Colby. Remember him?" he asked.

She scratched her cheek thoughtfully. The name rang a bell. As she paused, thinking, he reminded her.

"I had contact with him during the Mountain Murder thing. He was advising us. Never met him but had a few faxes and phone calls to him."

"I remember," she said. "You want me to contact him?"

"Figure you'll have a better chance to get through than me. If I call the FBI, I'll be shunted aside with all the crazies—and I don't have time for that. I've only got a limited time when I can make contact. The phones are monitored in the hotel and the valley is a dead spot for cells. Only place I can make contact is from the top of the cable car."

"That's a problem," she agreed.

"I want you to get through to him, tell him the situation and give him my cell number. Get him to call me, okay? I'll wait another two hours. That should give you time to get through to him. If he doesn't call today, I'll get up here again tomorrow, same time. Okay?"

She paused, trying to think if there was anything more she could do to help him, then decided that there wasn't. Best she could do for him was do what he asked.

"Okay, Jesse. You've got it," she said.

"Lee? Don't mention this to anyone, okay? Word of this gets out and the press mentions it, I'm toast. They'll come looking for me."

"I understand." She hesitated, there was a lot she wanted to say but somehow this didn't seem the time to say it.

"Lee?" he said, in the pause. "I better go. This cold weather plays havoc with the phone battery and I don't have a lot of power left."

"Okay, Jesse. You hang tight and I'll get onto this Agent Colby." Again, a pause. Again the sense that she should say more. Eventually, she said: "Jesse? You take care now. I need you back here."

"You bet, Lee. I better go. Tell Colby I'll switch the phone off for an hour, then I'll turn it back on again, in case he's calling."

"Take care, Jess."

"You said that already." She was sure she could hear the grin in his voice.

"I meant it. 'Bye." Abruptly, she jammed her forefinger down on the phone button, breaking the connection. She waited a second or two, then pressed the intercom button on the phone.

"Denise? Get me the FBI in Salt Lake City."

TWENTY-EIGHT

Large as it was, Linus Benjamin's office was crowded with people. The FBI director had called in all his senior operatives, deputy directors and controllers to canvas their opinions on the Canyon Lodge situation.

It was a preferred method of the director. He figured that he had on his staff a group of highly paid, highly intelligent, professional law enforcement officers and it only made good sense to turn their collective experience and intelligence loose on any large problem that the bureau faced. The age of the men and women around his office ranged from the early thirties to several who were, in reality, long past retirement age. Benjamin, however, wasn't prepared to lose the years of experience and maturity that such people embodied and as long as they wanted to stay in harness, the bureau was delighted to keep them on.

They sat on the sofas at his coffee conference table, some perched on the arms. His visitors' chairs had been the first claimed, and several additional ones had been brought in from his PA's annex outside the door. The only face in the room that didn't belong to a bureau employee was that of Truscott Emery. Benjamin hadn't been surprised when he'd heard how the president had dismissed Emery. Rather, he saw it as the thin end of the wedge that would break up the tight-knit little band of advisers assembled by President Couch. Sooner or later, he knew, he would go the same way as Emery. For the moment, he valued the other man's intellectual and analytical abilities and had invited him to join the general session.

Opinions through the room had been divided—as was predictable. There were those who advocated the Strike First, Strike Fast option—use the RRTF and go in fast and hard. Hit the terrorists quickly while they thought negotiations were still possible. This was the best time to do it, the proponents argued. As the siege went on, the terrorists' expectations of military action would inevitably become higher and higher.

The opposite view had its advocates as well. Keep negotiating, give a little more each time and wait for the best opportunity to strike.

All in the room agreed that there was little to be gained by appealing to the British to release the Irish terrorists. As Deputy Director Sandy George had said only a few minutes earlier, "Let's face it, guys, if the Brits asked us tomorrow to let the Unabomber go so that they could get a bunch of hostages freed, we'd politely tell them to go fish."

The inevitable result was to continue to wait. To be prepared to cut loose Colonel Maloney and his marines if necessary and, if the chance arose to do so with minimum risk, but otherwise to wait. To keep talking, keep trying to establish a sense of trust, keep trying to whittle down the demands. Maybe to get some of the hostages released.

The more time went by, experience told them, the greater the chance of a positive outcome. It was frustrating but it was the best option. At heart, even those calling for an immediate rescue bid knew it. There was, however, another element added to the mix now, and it was the disembodied voice from the starfish conference phone on Benjamin's coffee table that pointed it out.

"We've got one thing extra going for us now, guys," said Denton Colby. He had joined the conference from his command trailer in the Wasatch mountains, listening to the opinions put forward by his peers and fellow agents, agreeing with some, disagreeing with others, but for the most part remaining a silent listener. Now he spoke. "This new demand actually gives us a chance to buy some extra time. They can't expect us to negotiate a release for these Irish guys overnight."

"Dent," interrupted Senior Agent Edith Carswell. "You don't seriously believe that they give a damn about these Irish guys do you? It's a blind. It's just something they're throwing in to put us off balance."

Several of those present murmured agreement. Dent Colby waited till comment had died down before he spoke. After a second or two, Colby replied. "Maybe so. But even if we don't believe it, they don't have to know that. If they think they've got us chasing our tails, all the better. It gives us time. These guys are watching the TV news. If they see a report that our ambassador has called on the Brit prime minister, and there's a certain amount of speculation that we might be asking for cooperation, it'll buy us a few more days. I can say we're trying to be good guys, trying to be cooperative. None of that will do us any harm. And it puts the ball back in their court to drop the demand."

Some of the people around the room exchanged glances, nodding agreement.

Agent Carswell voiced the general consensus. "Yeah, you could have a point there, Dent. Anything we can do to drag it out will help."

"And if they are faking on this one and they back down, it'll cost them momentum," Sandy George added. They all knew that in negotiations of this kind, as in a chess game, momentum was all important. There was a rhythm to this sort of dialogue. You tried to keep going forward. If you had to backtrack, it cost you. Again there was a low chorus of agreement.

"One problem," Benjamin broke in. "The president won't go for any attempt to ask favors of the British. He thinks it'll make him look weak."

There were a few muttered comments about the president's weakness, real and perceived, around the room. Benjamin glanced up angrily and silence fell. He might agree with the sentiments but he knew that to allow such comments to go unchecked would, in the long run, have a negative impact on morale.

"We don't actually have to ask the Brits anything, do we, Mr. Director?" That was Dent Colby again. "Can you pull any strings with State? Just have our guy go see their guy about anything at all. Then, if we deny that the visit has anything to do with the Irish prisoners, the press is bound to pick it up and run with it."

Benjamin smiled. Colby was a devious bastard. It would be a simple matter to plant a question with a friendly reporter about meetings between the state department and the British ambassador. And the surest way to ensure press coverage would be to deny any connection between the meetings and the hostage situation in Utah. A few of the others in the room were grinning too.

"Good thinking, Dent," he said. "I'll speak to Alan Walinsci at State, see if we can get something organized." He glanced at his watch. "I guess that's it for now. Thanks for your time, people. And Dent, keep us up to date and let us know if you need anything."

"I'll do that, Mr. Director. Thanks for your suggestions, guys." The last was addressed to the room in general and a few of those present replied with personal farewells and good luck wishes to their colleague. As the room began to clear, Truscott Emery stepped forward for a quiet word with the director.

"Linus," he said, "I was wondering . . ." Benjamin held up a hand to stop him.

"Truss, if you were going to ask if you could keep looking into this downstairs, the answer is yes. Any help you can give us would be welcome."

The professor's face broke into a smile. He nodded his head in thanks. "I appreciate it, Linus. I still feel I have something to contribute in this thing."

Benjamin laid a hand on the other man's shoulder. "Well how about you get down to that computer and start contributing. I've asked Lois to get you a temporary ID and access card. Right now, I'd better talk to Alan Walinsci—see if he can organize to invite the British ambassador around for drinks."

CANYON ROAD
WASATCH COUNTY
1005 HOURS, MOUNTAIN TIME
MONDAY, DAY 3

Dent Colby leaned back from the microphone and stretched his stiff
shoulders. The conference with the other FBI personnel had been
useful, he guessed, if only to confirm that he was already following
the best course. There was a knock at the trailer door and he rose to
open it, stepping down into the bright, cold sunlight. The trailer
was well heated and he was wearing only a plaid shirt. In spite of
the bright sun, the temperature here was barely above freezing and
he shivered.

The communications technician who had knocked was standing
with a message form in his hand, the paper fluttering in the stiff
breeze. The man looked a little nervous.

"What is it?" Colby asked him and the technician handed him
the form.

"This came in while you were in conference, Mr. Colby," he said.
"At the time, I didn't know whether to interrupt you or not. But
then I did some checking and I think it could be important."

Colby took the piece of paper, frowning as he read the name. "Lee
Torrens? Who the hell is he?"

"He's a she, sir. She's the sheriff over at Steamboat Springs, in
Colorado. Contacted the Salt Lake City office saying she has confidential information for you that might help with the situation here.
They checked her out and she's genuine, so they passed the message
on," he added.

Colby frowned thoughtfully. The place name had rung a bell.
"Steamboat," he mused. "I did some work on a case there a few years
back." He looked down at the note again. "I'll call her. Sure can't do
any harm."

TWENTY-NINE

TOP STATION
FLYING EAGLE CABLE CAR
SNOW EAGLES RESORT
WASATCH COUNTY
1010 HOURS, MOUNTAIN TIME
MONDAY, DAY 3

Jesse stamped his feet in the snow, trying to keep the blood flowing. While it was a bright, sunny day, the temperature up here on the mountain was below freezing and standing around in the ankle deep snow for the better part of an hour was a great way to get frozen feet.

He swung his arms in great arcs, driving the blood out to the fingertips. His breath hung on the still air in clouds. For perhaps the tenth time, he moved to the side of the tram terminal and leveled his binoculars at the hotel. He counted half a dozen men on the roof, most of them sitting at ease by the quad fifties and the radar dish. Two of them, however, maintained a constant watch on the pass to the northwest, and occasionally scanned the mountains surrounding the hotel. As one of them swept his glasses in the general direction of the cable car terminal, Jesse froze against the building's shaped steel side. The glasses swung past him and continued sweeping, covering the ridge lines and the trees through a three hundred and sixty degree arc.

Jesse estimated the straight line distance to the hotel as maybe three quarters of a mile, although going cross-country would almost quadruple that distance. Given a high-powered rifle and a good scope sight, he figured he could stop those guys getting off too many rounds from the fifty calibers. And he could make it pretty damn unhealthy for anyone trying to line up a Stinger on an inbound aircraft. He shrugged. The chances of getting his hands on a rifle were slim to none, he realized.

The sudden burr of his cell phone drove away these random thoughts. He fumbled in his pocket for it, clumsy with the gloves he was wearing, and slid it open. "This is Parker," he said.

"Deputy Parker?"

"That's right. Who's this? Is this Colby?"

The voice was deep and authoritative. It matched the heavyset man he'd seen on television.

"This is Special Agent Dent Colby. Deputy Parker, exactly where are you?"

The voice had a strange echoing tone to it and Jesse guessed that he was talking on a speaker phone.

"How many people can hear me there?" he said cautiously. He didn't want the world to know where he was and there was always the chance that there might be a member of the press within hearing.

"Just me and my comms tech, Deputy," Colby assured him. "You can speak freely."

"Okay. I'll make it fast. I'm on the mountain above Canyon Lodge, at the top of the cable car station. I've been in the hotel and I've seen what's going on. They don't know I'm here."

"Records show you checked out night before last," Colby said. He still wasn't totally sure about this. Parker might be calling with a gun to his head. It could be a trick on the part of the terrorists— another way to keep him off balance.

"I did," Jesse said impatiently. "I settled my bill and stayed the night. I was having one last ski run when these guys took over the hotel and all hell broke loose."

"Okay," Dent said carefully. "Deputy Parker . . ."

"Call me Jesse, for Chrissake," Jesse broke in.

"Okay, Jesse. You understand I have to make sure you are who you say?"

CANYON ROAD
WASATCH COUNTY
1016 HOURS, MOUNTAIN TIME
MONDAY, DAY 3

Colby said the words very deliberately, hoping that the other man would read the underlying message—I have to make sure you're not under duress. He glanced at the notes the technician had give him, seeing one salient fact there that he could use. If Parker had his wits about him, and if there was a gun at his head, Colby would give him a chance to reveal that fact by giving a false answer—one that the terrorists wouldn't detect.

"I understand."

Colby frowned at the small loudspeaker, trying to detect some sense that the other man knew what he was talking about. He thought maybe it was there but then he shrugged. Maybe he was just hoping it was.

"Okay, the sheriff in Routt County is Lee Torrens. What can you tell me about him?"

This time he was sure he could detect a grin in the man's voice as he answered.

"I can tell you he's a she for starters. You testing me, Colby?"

Dent let go a pent-up breath, suddenly conscious of the tension in his shoulders. He nodded at the loudspeaker.

"Just making sure you're able to talk freely, is all." He said. "Okay Jesse, what can you tell me about the situation up there? You're not a hostage?"

"No. Like I said, they don't know I'm here. I've been sneaking around the hotel for the past day and a half, keeping out of sight."

Colby drummed his fingers on the desktop for a few seconds, thinking fast. This was a real break. Now all he had to do was work out the best way to exploit it.

"Let me get this clear. You're free to move around?"

"Within limits. I had to get up to the peak above the cable car to get a signal for the cell phone. The hotel is in a dead spot. I've made contact with one of the hostages. She's the security officer, name of Tina Bowden."

Jesus, thought Colby, this was getting better and better by the minute. To the microphone, he said: "Tell me everything you can about what's going on up there."

Jesse paused, collecting his thoughts. Then he began. "They're pros, Colby, real pros. The girl says there's a military feeling to them. They're organized, disciplined. They know what they're doing. And they're totally ruthless."

Dent Colby frowned. The picture Jesse was providing didn't gel with the impressions he'd been given in his telephone contact with the kidnappers.

"Parker, this isn't the picture I've been getting. When I talk to these guys they're coming across as a bunch of terrorist crazies."

"Then they're messing with your head. These guys aren't crazy. They're very calm and collected. According to Tina, they say they're in it for the money and nothing else. They seem more like mercenaries than terrorists. There's no particular racial group here. No political agenda." He hesitated, then concluded, "If you're thinking of these guys as a bunch of loony-tune fanatics, forget it. They're cold, hard and organized."

"You haven't seen anything that might tie them into any sort of Irish operation?" Colby asked. He was pretty sure the Irish connection was a red herring, but it wouldn't hurt to check.

"Irish?" Jesse said, puzzled, "First I've heard of it. Why d'you ask?"

"Never mind. Just keep telling me as much as you can. The hostages are all safe so far, right? Nobody's been injured?"

This time the pause was longer. Much longer. Dent felt a sudden premonition of bad news, then Jesse's voice was back on the loudspeakers again, quiet and with a note of disbelief to it.

"Jesus, you mean you didn't know? They've killed maybe fifty people already."

The words hit Colby like a kick to the stomach. He actually recoiled slightly from the microphone in front of him, staring in horror at the speakers, as if he could see the man behind the disembodied voice.

"What?" he said, the words barely above a whisper.

"There was a bus . . . it was full of people from the hotel that they'd released. The bus was halfway down Canyon Road when they brought the mountain down. It's buried there somewhere under that avalanche. Fifty, sixty people," he repeated.

Colby was struck dumb by the news. There had been no hint of this in any of the conversations he had had with the terrorists. He had been proceeding under the normal rules of hostage negotiation: keep the lines of communication open, give way on a few small concessions, stall for time and try to establish a rapport with the man at the other end. Above all, do everything possible to make sure the hostages remained unharmed. And now this.

This changed everything. This was outside anything in his experience. Sixty people, simply wiped out. It was staggering. It was beyond comprehension. As he stared at the loudspeakers once more, he knew the immediate question that would be asked of him when he reported this news to his superiors. And he knew he had to ask the question now of Jesse.

"Jesse, the people on the bus . . . who were they?"

"I don't know names. But they were all hotel staff. They kept a skeleton staff to run the place, and sent the rest down."

"So, as far as you know, the guests are okay?" Colby didn't want to ask directly about Senator Carling. If Parker didn't know his identity, there was no point in risking telling him about it. His next words dispelled that thought, however.

"The senator's still okay, if that's what you're asking." The flat tone was discernible, even through the speakers. With over fifty people dead, Jesse wasn't too impressed with Colby's obvious focus on one senator. Colby shrugged. That was too bad. This was the real world.

"Do they have any idea who he is?" Colby persisted. This time, Jesse's tone was more matter-of-fact. As a lawman, he could understand the significance of the question, and the value of the senator as a negotiating tool.

"I don't know." Then his memory kicked in and he altered that statement: "Just a moment. Tina said she heard their leader telling him he'd be back on the Hill as soon as this is over, so I guess they do know who he is. Look, Colby, this cold weather is playing hell with the cell phone battery. I'm getting a battery flat signal constantly and it could cut out any time now."

Colby felt a sudden chill at the words. He'd heard the warbling chirp on the line but hadn't registered its significance. This could be his only contact with the deputy and there were still so many questions he needed answered.

"You got any way to recharge it?" he asked, dreading the answer.

"Yeah. I can plug it into the car socket overnight. Now look, from where I am, I can see those guys on the hotel roof. They've got two twin fifty-caliber mounts down there and they look like they're slaved to a radar system."

"That's right. Plus they tell us they've got Stinger missiles. You see any sign of those?"

"Can't be sure but there are cases down there that could hold 'em. I'd say they've probably got 'em."

"How many men, Jesse? Any idea? And how are they armed?"

"I figure around eighteen to twenty. They've all got automatic weapons—the one I saw looked like an Ingram—and probably sidearms. I'd say they . . ." The next few words were obscured and Colby leaned forward, calling urgently.

"Jesse? You still there? Jesse?"

The reply was a little garbled but he could make it out. "Still here, Colby. I think the battery's just about dead. Could go any moment now. If I cut out, I'll call again tomorrow or the next day. Your number will be in the phone memory now."

"Jess!" Colby cut in urgently, "If you can contact this"—he checked the notes he'd been taking as they spoke—"Bowden girl, see if she can tell us who's running this thing. Name, description, anything you can tell us, okay?"

"Got it. I'll try to make contact with her this evening, see what she knows. Let me know if—"

The line went dead midsentence. There was a slight hissing noise from the speakers in the trailer. Colby stared at them, then at the monitor again.

"Jesse? You there, Parker?"

He waited a few seconds. There was no further word. The technician was checking his instruments, shaking his head.

"He's gone, sir. The connection is broken."

TOP STATION
FLYING EAGLE CABLE CAR
SNOW EAGLES RESORT
WASATCH COUNTY
1021 HOURS, MOUNTAIN TIME
MONDAY, DAY 3

Jesse cursed as the phone went dead. He looked at the display window. The green light was out. There were no symbols visible on the screen. Dead as a dodo. That was the problem with this below freezing weather, he knew. It would kill a battery quicker than anything, cutting its endurance to a fraction of its normal charge life.

There was a wooden bench by the side of the terminal building and he slumped onto it, thinking through the logistics of the next few days. He couldn't risk moving back to the hotel before dusk. The chances of being spotted in the open during daylight were too great. That meant he would be cutting it fine to make contact with Tina this evening. He'd need to make his way to the car and plug his phone battery into the car charger, then get across to the chairlift again before dawn the following day. Assuming everything worked out, he might be able to contact the FBI agent again tomorrow morning—Tuesday morning, he reminded himself. But if just one part of the schedule went wrong, it would be Wednesday before he could phone again.

Suddenly, he felt very tired and he leaned back against the steel side of the building, closing his eyes for a few moments and feeling the warmth of the sun on his face. He was in that position when there was a massive crash of machinery from the building and the wall shuddered against his back.

He came up off the bench in a second, his right hand fumbling with the zip on his parka as he reached for the Colt. Then he stopped, his heart racing. He didn't need the gun right away. But as he realized what had caused the noise, he knew he'd have to get out of sight, and quickly.

Someone had boarded the cable car at the bottom station. Whoever it was, he was on his way up the mountain right now and he'd be here in less than ten minutes.

THIRTY

Jesus," said Morris Tildeman as he studied the printed sheet of notes the FBI director had prepared for the meeting. Benjamin had just finished expanding on the notes, repeating all that Dent Colby had passed on to him. Tildeman, Janet Haddenrich and Truscott Emery had been summoned to the FBI building for an emergency briefing.

"Have you taken this to the president?" Haddenrich asked now. Benjamin shook his head.

"I'm doing that directly. He's been tied up with the G8 meeting this morning. He's due back in the White House at 1:15. I've told Pohlsen that there's been a development but we thought it best to let the president keep his normal schedule.

"We don't want the bad guys getting any idea that we've heard anything out of the ordinary. We want to keep things looking as normal as possible. As far as they know, the White House is concerned, of course, but not involved."

The others nodded. It only needed one nosy reporter to figure out that the president had canceled an important session with the G8 council so he could confer with the FBI, NSA and CIA directors and they'd have it linked to the situation in Utah. And then the kidnappers might start wondering why the White House was showing such an interest in the matter. After all, as Jesse had pointed out to Colby, the kidnappers were keeping track of events on TV.

"The question is," Benjamin said now, "what sort of difference does this make?"

"Jesus, fifty people dead? That's a pretty big difference, Linus,"

Morris Tildeman answered, shaking his head over the summary once more.

"It changes the entire scenario," Emery put in and they all looked at him. He shrugged and spread his hands. "In a normal situation like this, the kidnappers leave themselves an out, right up to the point where they kill someone. Short of that point, they know the authorities will negotiate. Once that line is crossed, they know that there will be no real negotiation, no matter what is said. Once they've killed any of the hostages, they know that we can't trust them to release the others. And these guys crossed that line on day one," he added.

The FBI director nodded. "That's the way I see it too. These guys are mass murderers. Simply no way we can let them get away with that. There's no way we can realistically try to negotiate a solution and they'll know it."

"Except they don't know we know," Haddenrich put in. "At least that lets us keep up an appearance of negotiating."

"More and more, I'm wondering whether they really want to negotiate, at all," Emery said. "I can't get rid of the feeling that there's something more behind all this—something we're not seeing."

"The president isn't going to buy your message theory now, Truss," Benjamin told him.

The professor shrugged. "Doesn't mean it's not right," he said.

"Christ, what a mess," Benjamin said quietly. He looked around the assembled group. "I'd better get this to the president, see what he says. Anyone got any bright ideas before I go?"

"Keep up the negotiations. Keep stalling all we can until this guy can get us more information. That's the one card we've got now." It was Tildeman who spoke but the others nodded their agreement.

"What do we know about this Parker guy?" Haddenrich asked.

"We've checked his background. Seems like he's a good cop. Was a top flight homicide detective with Denver PD, then he had some kind of trouble in a shooting and moved back to Steamboat. Been with the sheriff's department there for the past two years."

"And the girl?" This time it was Tildeman who asked.

"We've pulled her records too. She's ex-Marine Corps. Went in to play softball and was assigned to the MPs. Got a good record. Nothing outstanding but a good solid record. Came out of the service and took a job with the hotel in security." He spread his hands. That was it. "What more can I tell you?" he said.

Nobody answered. Then Janet Haddenrich spoke. "I guess we better make sure Maloney and his guys are ready to go on a moment's notice," she said.

Benjamin's expression was pained. "We'll stand to lose a lot of men if we send them in. And we could lose all the hostages," he reminded her.

She sighed. He wasn't telling her anything she didn't know. "We may lose them anyway, Linus," she said.

TOP STATION
FLYING EAGLE CABLE CAR
SNOW EAGLES RESORT
WASATCH COUNTY
1026 HOURS, MOUNTAIN TIME
MONDAY, DAY 3

The cable car came to a halt at the top station, rocking back and forth on the pendulum of its massive single support arm as it slowed, then stopped, after its ten-minute haul up the face of the mountain. The automatic trip set the sliding door open and the single occupant stepped out.

Slim build, maybe five eleven, black hair going slightly gray at the temples. Regular, average features, the sort of guy who would be virtually impossible to pick out of a line-up. Utterly unremarkable, Jesse thought as he watched from the small loft window above the coffee shop at the rear of the terminal. The man was wearing a parka and sunglasses. He reached into the parka now and produced a cell phone. He looked around, saw the same bench Jesse had been sitting on a few minutes earlier and moved to it, punching numbers into the phone as he went.

It was fortunate that there'd been no fresh snow in the past three days, Jesse thought. His tracks were just one set among many around the cable car terminal. He edged a little closer to the window, which he'd carefully worked ajar while he waited for the car to arrive.

"This is Kormann," he heard the man say. Obviously, someone had answered at the other end. He paused briefly, obviously listening, then said one word:

"Friday." Another pause, then: "You got that? As long as George stays on schedule, Friday is the day . . . good."

He snapped the phone shut, breaking the connection, then turned back to the cable car once again. A few seconds later, Jesse heard the clunk of gears connecting and the rising whine of the massive electric motor as the tram moved out from the loading dock and began its swaying journey back to the valley floor.

Jesse frowned. It seemed like a hell of a long way to come simply to tell somebody Friday.

THIRTY-ONE

CANYON ROAD
WASATCH COUNTY
1513 HOURS, MOUNTAIN TIME
MONDAY, DAY 3

The main problem with hostage situations, thought Dent Colby, was boredom. You spent so much time sitting around waiting for the other side to do something, say something, demand something. And then you reacted to it. Or not.

But in between, the hours of waiting, of inaction, the feeling of impotence, got you wishing that something—anything—would happen. Then, all too often, when it did, you wished it hadn't.

He was stretched out on the cot in his trailer trying to catch a nap. It was a futile attempt. The facts of the case whirled around inside his head, refusing to fit into a neat pattern and refusing to let his mind relax, along with his closed eyes.

Fifty people killed. Another forty to fifty held prisoner—under the threat of a terrible, suffocating death if the charges in the mountain were fired. Kidnappers who seemed panicky and irrational when they spoke to him, yet were totally in control according to their captives. Professional. Calm. Businesslike, Parker had said. It made no sense at all. Nor did the demand that the Irish terrorists be released.

He thought about the geography of the situation. Somehow, the kidnappers planned to get out when this was all over. Maybe they'd demand a helicopter and take hostages with them. That was the most likely way, the safest way, for them. There was no other way out of Snow Eagles Canyon. The road literally ended there. Behind and on three sides, there were thousands of square miles of wild, mountain country. The fourth side was the road back to Salt Lake

City—up until the time when it had been blocked by the avalanche, the only ground route in and out.

Dent and Colonel Maloney had already discussed the possibility of trying an end run: sending choppers in low over the wild back country, following the valleys and canyons on the far side of the canyon, popping up over the final ridge a bare mile from the target. But even that short run would expose them to the deadly accurate triple-A from the hotel roof. Besides, thought Dent, if he were the leader of the kidnappers, he'd have some kind of surveillance set up on those back ridges—maybe a remote-controlled camera like the one Colby himself was using to keep a visual on the hotel.

The Colorado deputy's presence on the mountain was an enormous stroke of luck, of course. And, judging by the way things were shaping up, Dent was going to need every stroke of luck he could find.

The telephone on his desk burred quietly. He glanced up at the telltale screen above it to see the number displayed, then rolled quickly off the bed as he saw the number for Canyon Lodge.

"This is Agent Colby," he said.

"What are you trying to pull here, Colby? What are you trying?" It was the second of the two men who usually made contact, the one who was normally the least excitable. Now, however, there was an edge of hysteria or anger in his voice. Dent's immediate reaction was to assume that they'd captured Jesse. His pulse raced as he hesitated, not sure what to say.

"Trying?" he said finally. "We're not trying anything here."

"Oh, is that right? Is that right? Well maybe you think we've gone blind in here or something. Would that be right? You think we've gone blind?"

"I'm sorry," Dent said slowly. "I don't know what you're—"

"The airplane, Agent Colby. The airplane that flew over here not five minutes ago. You think just because it's high we're not going to see it? Those things leave con trails, man! Did you think of that?"

"Just a moment." Colby stepped to the trailer door, taking the cordless with him and switching off the loudspeakers. He glanced outside, looking high above them and, sure enough, there was the

‐

feathered remains of a jet's contrails, up at maybe thirty thousand feet, gradually dispersing in the stratospheric winds.

"You think we don't know you Federals have got cameras that can look down on us from that sort of height? We're not stupid, Agent Colby. So don't go thinking we are!"

"Wait, please," said Dent. "That aircraft has nothing to do with us. It's a normal commercial flight."

"Don't you try playing me for a fool, Colby. Don't try it."

Dent's eyes narrowed as he made his way back to the desk and sat down. The behavior, the repetitive patterns in the speech, the almost high-pitched excitement, would normally have him suspecting that the caller was on some kind of drug high. Maybe cocaine or some other stimulant. But that didn't sit with what Jesse had told him. Now that he listened more carefully, he began to suspect that it was a put-on, an act. All for his benefit.

"I guarantee you," he said slowly, "that plane had nothing to do with us. You have my word on it."

"Your word? Ha! Your word is worth nothing to me! Nothing!"

"That's not true. We've done what you asked. The money is being collected but you demanded notes in random numbering patterns and in twenties, fifties and hundreds. It's nearly together. And we're doing all we can about the Irish prisoners. Watch tonight's news and you'll see." He closed his eyes briefly, hoping that Benjamin had been able to organize the phoney news story.

"Well your word had better be good, Agent Colby, because here's how we want this thing organized."

Dent sat up straight all of a sudden. This was something new. He glanced at the indicator on his control panel to make sure that the conversation was being recorded, and pulled a pad and pencil toward him.

"Go ahead," he said.

The man at the other end sensed the heightened interest in his voice.

"That got your attention, didn't it? Okay, here's the pitch. Sunday morning at ten a.m. you send one Chinook helicopter up the valley. You know the Chinook?"

"I know it," Colby said. The Chinook was a big, twin-rotor troop carrier. From memory, Colby guessed you'd fit around forty people in one of them.

"Okay. The money is to be on board, in the sort of notes we've told you. Any variation, any suspicion that you've marked those notes, and one of the hostages gets it. We want a crew of two on the chopper. No more. We see one extra person when that chopper puts down and we start killing hostages. You got that very clear in your mind?"

Colby guessed he was expecting a reaction. "Got it," he replied.

"We'll go out of here with our men and ten of the hostages. I want a flight plan cleared to Salt Lake City Airport and I want a Dash 8 ready there, fully fueled, ready to go. If everything's fine, and I see no Federals around, no snipers, no SWAT teams, we'll give you back five of the hostages."

Colby frowned. A Dash 8 was a small twin-turbo prop that was used by most of the feeder lines servicing the ski resorts in the area. It'd carry maybe twenty-five people but wouldn't have the range to get the kidnappers anywhere out of the country—except maybe the Canadian border.

He quickly made a note to find out the range of a Dash 8. Beside it, he jotted the words "rough airfield." A good pilot wouldn't need a sealed runway to put a Dash 8 down.

"You still with me, Colby?" the voice said sarcastically.

"Yeah. Sure. Sorry. I'm making notes, making sure I got this right."

"Sure you are. Why not just check the tape afterward?"

"I'll do that too."

"I bet. Now one thing, we've got scanning gear and I'll be going over that Dash 8. If I find any trace of a bug, any kind of electronic tracer on board, you're going to say good-bye to one of the hostages. Got that clear?"

"There'll be no bugs," Colby assured him. He figured the terrorists were planning to go out at low level, below the radar, and lose themselves somewhere in the mountains. He frowned. It wouldn't be too hard, he thought, to have a high-flying air force surveillance plane—an AWACs, for example—keep track of them.

"I'd better tell you that we've got an RWR device as well," the kidnapper told him, almost as if he'd read Colby's thoughts. RWRs— or Radar Warning Receivers, were carried by military aircraft to alert them in the event that they were under radar surveillance. This was getting tougher by the minute, he realized.

"What about the last five hostages?" he put in now, knowing what the answer would be.

"We'll keep hold of them until I'm sure there's nobody following us. No radar surveillance. No bugs. Once I know we're in the clear, so are they. Oh, and one other thing . . ."

"Yes?" said Colby, sensing from the casual tone of voice that this was going to be the real crux of the whole matter.

"That Dash 8, make it one of the United Express fleet. And make sure there are five other identical birds in the hangar, fueled and ready to go."

There was click as he hung up, then Colby was listening to the high-pitched tone of a broken connection.

THE OVAL OFFICE
WASHINGTON D.C.
1530 HOURS, EASTERN TIME
MONDAY, DAY 3

"Fifty people?" President Gorton repeated. His face was gray, the blood drained away with the shock of what Benjamin had just told him.

"At least fifty, Mr. President. Maybe more," Benjamin confirmed. The president stood and walked around to the massive French doors, looking out to the Rose Garden.

"Fifty people. Wiped out like that." All the usual bluster and false confidence was gone. "My God, Benjamin, what are we going to do? What are we going to tell the families of the hostages? How can I tell them that one of fifty could be their brother, or husband, or daughter?"

Benjamin looked up quickly. For the first time since this affair had begun, the president wasn't trying to assign blame or take credit. He was genuinely affected by the shocking news. He was actually asking for help and advice. In the past, Benjamin knew, there had been more than one unworthy occupant of this office. But often, the man grew with the job. Maybe there was a chance that this was going to happen here.

"We can't say anything to them, sir," he replied firmly. "If word gets back to the kidnappers that we know about this, they'll know we've got a man on the ground up there."

Gorton nodded wearily. "Of course. I hadn't thought of that. What about him?" he added. "Can we depend on him? How reliable is he?"

"He's a cop, sir. A deputy sheriff. Colby thinks he can trust him and that's good enough for me. At least now we're not working in the dark and we've got a chance to learn a little more about these kidnappers."

"Yes. Yes. That's one thing on the positive side. So, you've spoken to the others?"

"Yes, sir. Less than an hour ago. Our consensus is to keep talking to the kidnappers, keep trying to look as if we're cooperating, and find out as much as we can about them. In the meantime, we want to bring Colonel Maloney's team to full alert status."

Gorton thought about it. "Yes. I agree," he said finally. "Do we have any word on the senator?" he added.

Benjamin hesitated a fraction of a second. "They know his identity, sir. We can only assume that he'll be one of the last five hostages they release."

The president frowned. "But they haven't mentioned his name so far?" he asked, and Benjamin shook his head.

"Not a word, sir. I can't figure it. They must know what a trump card they're holding there."

The two men looked at each other, each seeing the puzzlement in the other's eyes. Then the president gave a hint of a shrug.

"Okay. Let me know as soon as you hear anything." He turned to his chief of staff. "I want to be informed on that score as soon as we hear anything, Terence. Clear?"

"Yessir, Mr. President," Pohlsen said. Gorton looked up at his FBI director.

"Benjamin, we haven't agreed on a lot of things in the past. But this is too big now to let personal feelings intrude. You have my full support in this matter and I want you to know that. Do whatever you can."

"Yes, Mr. President."

"And keep me informed."

"Yes, sir. Mr. President . . ." Benjamin hesitated and President Gorton looked back at him.

"Yes, Director Benjamin?"

"I . . . uh . . . want you to know sir that I have engaged Professor Emery as an adviser on this. I think his ideas have merit and I thought I should tell you so."

Gorton nodded several times. "Sure. Damned man is a pain in the ass. Personally I can't stand him. But if you think he might be able to contribute something, go ahead and use him. We can't afford not to use every resource we've got now."

"Thank you, Mr. President. I'd better . . ." Benjamin gestured toward the door and Gorton nodded agreement.

"Go ahead. And as I said, keep us informed."

He turned away again toward the view of the Rose Garden, as if seeking some kind of solace there. He was shaking his head slowly. It might have been in sadness or it might have been in disbelief, thought Benjamin. Or maybe it was a combination of the two.

THIRTY-TWO

Tina Bowden leaned against the outer wall of the building, sitting on the hard carpet, while she assessed the group around her. If push came to shove, she was going to need help and she wanted to get some idea where she might find it.

Exactly what she might achieve, she wasn't sure yet. But the fact that she had the gun stashed in the rice container at least gave her some chance of taking action if it became necessary. She studied the guards in the room. There were three of them and by now she had established that they worked a four-hour shift. She'd figured three different shifts so far—nine men. She guessed the remaining terrorists were assigned to the weapons that were sited on the roof. The guards in the gym patrolled the room, their hands always on the stubby machine guns they carried, slung over their shoulders.

For their part, the prisoners had fallen into a strange malaise resulting from a mixture of conflicting emotions. Boredom was the most obvious and immediate. There was nothing to do, nothing to see other than the snow-covered wall outside the picture windows—and the web of detonating cord that covered the windows, set to shatter the tough glass a few seconds before the main charges brought the mountain down on them. It was a constant and all-too-visible reminder of the danger that hung over them, every minute of the day and night.

There was no reading material, no television or radio. Kormann had banned any form of distraction. And there was no physical activity allowed—ironic when you considered that they were being held in a fully equipped gym. But lying just beneath the boredom was the gut-gnawing tension of fear and uncertainty—and the frustration of being totally helpless. They knew that the men who held them captive were killers. Knew they would kill without the slightest hesitation. The young ski instructor, shot so casually outside the hotel, was one example. And the fate of the bus passengers themselves was another. Ben Markus had said nothing about what he had witnessed, but Kormann made sure the remaining hostages knew what had happened. And Ben's tight-lipped silence when he had been questioned by the others was answer enough.

This was why, she reasoned, Kormann allowed them no form of diversion. He wanted the tension to prey on their minds, wanted their guts churning with uncertainty, wanted their nerves fraying. And that was definitely happening. Already there had been several altercations among the prisoners, one of them leading to actual violence. Ben Markus had stepped in quickly each time, calming things down. He'd done a great job so far, but he was looking drawn and strained. He believed that the responsibility for all their lives rested on his shoulders and it was a heavy weight. By unspoken agreement, Tina had made no particular contact with him, other than what might be expected between a junior employee and the hotel manager. It wouldn't do for her to draw too much attention, to single her out as one of the leaders of the hostage group. Senator Carling, on the other hand, had provided Ben with some valued backup and had done a lot to keep the prisoners' morale from sagging into the depths. But his ability to do so was severely limited. Kormann was quick to rein him in if he thought the senator was raising the hostages' spirits too far.

Thankfully, sanitation arrangements had been adequate. This was a gym, after all, and it had showers and toilets in an adjoining room. But even then, Kormann had continued to emphasize his control over them. The showers were only available for use every two days, and only eight towels had been distributed. The prisoners were allowed to use the toilets every four hours, for a period of fifteen minutes only. Inevitably, this meant that some missed out but there was nothing to do but wait for the next fifteen-minute period. Ben had established rosters for both showers and toilets but, even so, there were arguments. The people were dirty, uncomfortable, bored and frightened all at the same time.

And Kormann watched them and smiled in satisfaction. He'd set the thermostat so that the temperature in the gym was higher than normal. They were hot and sweaty and frightened and argumentative. They were concerned by relatively minor problems like full bladders or the desire for a hot shower. It kept them off balance. And he knew it would keep them from planning or plotting or organizing.

At least it would keep most of them that way. Not Ben Markus, of course, or Carling. They were people who needed to be watched carefully at all times and he'd impressed that fact on his men. But he hadn't recognized Tina as a potential threat, and that might prove to be a costly mistake.

She studied the guards, flicking her eyes from one to the other, measuring angles and distances between them as they patrolled. She was confident that, with surprise on her side, she could drop two of them in rapid succession. The first one would be easy. He would never see it coming. She saw in her mind's eyes the movement as she slid the .357 out from under her jacket, leveled it and squeezed off a shot, then swung in one movement to the second guard as he looked for the direction of danger, taking him out even as he realized that she had the gun.

But the third man . . . he was the problem. There was always one man out of her line of vision. Their patrol pattern around the room kept one of them behind her. He'd have time to locate her and take her out before she could swing around to him. Maybe if she moved to the very back of the room, she'd have all three in her sight at once. She considered the possibility for a few minutes, then discarded it. Such a move would mean she'd be firing the full length of the gymnasium for the first shot and she couldn't count on accuracy at that distance.

From where she sat, halfway down the room and to one side, she had two shots of less than thirty feet and she knew she was good enough to make them both. It would be the third man who would get her. She turned now to check his position. He was a few yards from the senator and his friends. She glanced back at the other two guards. They were in the optimum position for her, so that's where number three would be.

She waited as they patrolled again, changing positions, scanning the dejected, sullen faces of the hostages. Each time the pattern was the same. When two of them were within easy range for her, the third was always behind, close to the senator and his friends. She looked at the small group, assessing them. One of them might be the man she was looking for, she thought. She knew she could count on Ben Markus for help but Ben wasn't the physical type. He was brave enough, sure. She'd seen plenty of evidence of that in the last two days. But somehow she couldn't see him tackling an armed man and keeping him out of the argument. Besides, she had other tasks in mind for Ben.

She stood now and stretched. As soon as she moved, all three guards stopped and turned to face her. She met the gaze of the closest, shook her head slightly and made a negative hand gesture. No trouble here. She took a few paces across the room to one of the guests—an older woman who had been showing some signs of distress earlier in the evening. She dropped to her knees beside her now.

"Mrs. Patterson?" she said quietly. "How are you feeling?" Out of the corner of her eye, she saw the nearest of the guards walking toward her. She ignored him.

"Oh, not so good, Miss Bowden," the woman replied. "I have my special medication, you see, but I only had a few pills in my handbag and now they're gone."

Tina patted the woman's shoulder. "I'll see what I can do," she reassured her. She smiled at the woman, then stood. As she did so, the guard was standing over her.

"What're you doing?" he asked.

"I'm checking on people," she said. "They're still my responsibility. I'm still an employee of the hotel. You want people getting sick in here?"

She'd prepared the answer. It was natural for her, as a hotel employee, to check on the guests' welfare. It drew a certain amount of attention to her, but not enough, she figured, to spotlight her as a threat. Besides, she'd selected a time when neither Kormann nor Pallisani was in the room and she doubted that any of the guards would see her activities as worth mentioning to their leaders.

The guard hesitated. He had no real objection to her moving around. He just didn't want it to become general. If they all started milling around, anything could happen. Kormann had told them to keep the hostages sitting in one place. Still, this girl was the one who served the food to them, so she was already allowed to move through the room. He shrugged.

"Okay," he said, then, looking around the room, "but the rest of you stay put."

She nodded and began moving from one group to the next, checking how things were, seeing if people were coping okay, occasionally making a note of individual requirements that she might raise later with the guard. All the time, she moved closer to the group of men at the far end of the room.

As she came closer, Senator Carling looked up expectantly. She nodded and smiled, greeting him briefly. But it wasn't him she wanted to talk to. She'd picked out one of his group, a fit-looking man who was probably in his late thirties. His receding hair was cut short and she was willing to guess there wasn't an ounce of fat on him. He was medium height and he had alert gray eyes that followed her as she approached.

She dropped on one knee beside him. "Hi. I'm Tina Bowden, with the hotel."

He nodded. He'd noticed her as she'd served the food. "Can't say I think too much of the room service so far," he said dryly, and she allowed the ghost of a smile to show. He held out his hand. "Nate Pell," he said.

They shook hands. She'd singled him out because he stood out from the rest of the senator's group. They had the slightly overweight, soft look of businessmen or technicians or, in the case of the senator, politicians. This man was harder, with an athletic look to him.

"You been in the services, Nate?" she asked, trying to look casual about it. He nodded.

"Blue suiter for fifteen years. Now I'm senior test pilot with Rockair." That explained the fit, athletic look. A jet pilot had to stay in top physical shape, she knew. She felt a small twinge of disappointment when she heard he was ex-air force. She'd been hoping for maybe army or Marines—someone with a bit of experience in close-in combat.

"Uh huh," she said, still maintaining the outward casual appearance. "I'm ex-Marines myself." She glanced at him to see what his reaction might be. He inclined his head slightly, his eyes showing signs of interest.

"Figures, I guess. Thought you weren't the run-of-the-mill reception clerk. I guess you're really security, right?"

"Right," she told him. "Thing is, Nate, the time could come when we have to do something about these bastards. If that's the case, I'm going to need someone to take care of one of them. Jump him, put him down. Get his gun away from him."

She studied him for a second or two. The gray eyes were assessing her. She could see a light of satisfaction behind them. "Just one?" he said, with a slight mocking tone. "What about the other two?"

She smiled and patted his shoulder as she'd done with half a dozen other captives as she'd moved around the room, looking as if she were merely spreading a little reassurance and good cheer.

"I figure I'm good for them," she said simply and his answering smile never reached the gray eyes.

"Is that right? And just how do you plan to do it?"

She shook her head, a small movement only. "I'll go into that later. At the moment, I'm just seeing if there's anyone here I can count on to back me up."

He studied her for several moments and she met his gaze evenly. Then, seemingly satisfied with what he saw, he nodded several times.

"Then count on me for the third man," he said. She started to rise to her feet.

"I'll be in touch," she told him and this time, when he grinned, the eyes joined in.

"*Semper fi,*" he said softly.

*   *   *

It was long after dark when Jesse made his way back to the hotel. He'd decided against skiing all the way back. The chances of a single moving figure being spotted on the otherwise deserted mountain in daylight were too high and skiing in the dark had its own, obvious risks. In the end, he'd traversed back to the Eagle Chairlift and downloaded, lying flat across the chair as he'd done before. Once down, he'd concealed himself in the lift attendant's shack until darkness fell.

He realized that he was too late to make contact with Tina Bowden again tonight. He'd try to make contact in the morning, although he knew that the breakfast preparation gave her little reason to go to the storeroom. It was odds on that he wouldn't see her before the midday meal. He shrugged. He'd just have to try for both.

He left his skis and boots in the ski room, on the principle that a forest was the best place to hide a tree. Retrieving his Timberlands, he made his way down the concrete stairs to the parking lot. His rental car was where he had left it and he clipped the cell phone back into the cradle to let it charge for a few hours. Luckily, the cradle was permanently connected to the car's electrical circuit and there was no need to leave the ignition on. He thought about making his way back up to Tina's room but the thought of soft footing it up five flights of service stairs suddenly seemed too much. The car, parked deep in the shadows of the parking lot, was as good a place to spend the next few hours as anywhere else. He still had some food and a bottle of water in his backpack and the roughly fashioned poncho to wrap himself in. In the morning, he'd make his way to the kitchen before anyone had risen and hope to make contact with Tina. But for the moment, there was nothing more he could do tonight.

He settled down in the back seat of the Buick, wriggling around to make himself comfortable. Within ten minutes, he was asleep.

THIRTY-THREE

THE KITCHEN
CANYON LODGE
WASATCH COUNTY
0745 HOURS, MOUNTAIN TIME
TUESDAY, DAY 4

Tina followed Ralph into the kitchen, the guard a few paces behind
them. It was becoming a well-established routine now. The lines
of lights over the workstations came flickering to life and before
they had settled, Ralph was already firing up the burners on the
massive range that dominated the room. Tina moved to the far end
and began filling the four big coffeemakers with water and fresh
coffee packs, turning on the power to each one as she had it ready.
Within a minute or two, the water began to gurgle and drip down
and the rich smell of fresh coffee filled the room.

The guard, as ever, called to her. "Get me a cup of that as soon as
it's ready."

She nodded. He expected no reply. Even his request was part of
the morning routine. The one thing that wasn't was the sight of the
two coffee cups turned upside down beside the sink. Her eyes had
gone to them the moment she reached the coffeemakers, checking
to see if there were any sign that Jesse was waiting in the storeroom.

Casually now, she started toward the storeroom door.

The guard glanced up at her. "Where you going?" he called. He
was a slim man with olive skin and dark hair and eyes. She thought
he looked Hispanic—just another racial type among the mix repre-
sented by the guards. Today he was obviously in a foul temper. Usually, he was fairly disinterested in her movements but unfortunately
for her, he'd lost a bundle of cash playing poker the night before.
He was still sore about the loss, principally because he was convinced that Alfredo, the guy who ran the poker school among the

guards, was cheating. Exactly how, he didn't know. But then, he guessed, if he'd known how, Alfredo wouldn't have been able to cheat him in the first place. Truth was, the guard was a lousy poker player and had no idea of the odds involved. All the others knew it and made sure nobody told him. He was a pigeon ripe for the plucking as far as they were concerned.

This morning, still chafing over the loss, and Kormann's strict rules that forbade any drinking, even during off-duty hours, he was ready to be objectionable and to make life difficult for the two hostages who were preparing the breakfast.

"Just getting eggs," Tina told him casually, then cursed silently as Ralph interrupted their conversation.

"No need. I've got plenty here."

He indicated the ready-use fridge, where there were half-a-dozen cartons of eggs. Tina hesitated. She knew it could be dangerous if the guard sensed that she wanted to get into the storeroom. If he became suspicious, that could be the end of everything. She shrugged and turned back to her workstation.

"Fine," she said, trying to sound casual. "Saves me a trip."

She took one of the loaves of bread that Ralph had baked the previous night and set it in the automatic slicer. Again she cursed quietly to herself. Now it would be at least five hours before she had a chance to speak with Jesse.

The first pot of coffee was nearly full. She poured a cup for the guard, added the two spoons of sugar she knew he liked, and took it to him. He grunted as he accepted it from her. She was relieved to see that he was no longer interested in the storeroom. She went back to the coffeemakers and cleared away the used packs of grounds. There were half a dozen unopened packs on the shelf facing her and, glancing over her shoulder to make sure the guard wasn't watching, she scooped them into the big trash bin, tossing the used packs in on top to cover them.

At least now she would have a reason to go to the storeroom at the next meal break, she thought. She weighed the value of talking to Ralph when they returned to the gym, and telling him not to contradict her like that again. Then she realized that if he got any hint that she was planning something, there was an excellent chance that he'd give the game away—either intentionally or otherwise.

Ralph was a good chef. But he was also, she knew, an abject coward. Casually, she turned the two cups right side up. At least now Jesse would know she had seen them.

LEARJET N-451987
VIRGINIA EN ROUTE TO SALT LAKE CITY
0926 HOURS, MOUNTAIN TIME
TUESDAY, DAY 4

The Learjet belonged to one of Truscott Emery's former pupils, a man who had used what he'd learned from the professor to make a considerable fortune in grain futures. Ever-conscious of the debt he considered he owed, he made his company aircraft available to Emery whenever the professor needed it. This was one of those times.

With Benjamin's blessing, Truscott Emery had decided to visit the site of the crime and talk to Dent Colby. Deep in the professor's mind there was a vestigial stirring of thought. Somewhere, just out of reach, was the link that he was looking for. He was still sure that this was no ordinary hostage case. The reports from Colby had only strengthened the impression when he had described the discrepancies between the kidnappers' apparent behavior and the impressions of the deputy sheriff from Colorado.

Now, as the Learjet cruised steadily at four hundred knots, he sat back in the comfortable leather seat, frowning to himself as he tried to puzzle through the situation. His laptop was on the polished wood writing table in front of him and he scrolled quickly through his notes.

The names of the staff and guests who had been at the hotel on the Saturday when the terrorists arrived formed the first item. Sadly, he looked at the list of names, shaking his head slightly as he realized that at least fifty of them were no longer alive. Fifty staff members, he realized. The deputy sheriff had said that the people buried alive under the avalanche had been staff members. That pointed toward the fact that the real targets were among the guests. Carling, of course, was the most obvious choice, yet so far there had been no mention made of the senator from Washington State. He would have expected the kidnappers to have played such a valuable and powerful card by now. Perhaps the senator's presence was a coincidence after all. The Canyon Lodge was a relatively expensive resort and it would be a fair assumption that any guests there would tend to have influential friends and relatives—unlike the staff. Thirty or forty wealthy people, even if they were relatively anonymous, would make an excellent hostage group.

Scrolling down the screen, he highlighted the staff names and patched them to another part of the document, leaving only the guest list on the screen in front of him. He hit another key and added whatever background details he had already been able to glean about them.

There was a polyglot mix of titles and professions. Two dentists, a McDonalds' franchisee, the owner of a Cadillac dealership in Maryland, a scattering of accountants, attorneys and businessmen. The senator's companions were all listed as aerospace executives, most of them credited with degrees in differing fields of engineering. Of course, there were also a lot of gaps—names against which there was no information. Any one of them, he knew, could be the key to the riddle.

He yawned softly. The bright sun striking through the Learjet's windows was warm and the seat was comfortable. The combined effect was soporific in the extreme. He shook himself awake and opened another file. This one held details of the long ago raid over Colombia—Operation Powderburn. Deep down, Emery was still convinced that this held the real key to the riddle he was facing. The coincidence of the money amount was too striking, the amount itself too odd to be a mere chance.

He spooled through the details of the operation again. There were the bare facts—the flight plan, transit times, altitudes, fuel and bomb loads. He noted wryly that the aircraft was listed only as carrying "special weapons." In addition, there were side notes on the performance of the F-117 Nighthawk and the debrief papers from the anonymous pilot.

There was also a related article from *Newsweek*, showing several pilots grouped beside one of the black, angular fighters. This had nothing to do with the actual Powderburn raid. In fact, it was dated a few years earlier and was a general news item on the effectiveness of the F-117 that his wide ranging search had thrown up. It concentrated particularly on the raids carried out over Baghdad during the first Gulf War—where the Nighthawks had come and gone seemingly at will, undetected by the city's massive defense network.

He studied the group photo. Three pilots were grouped around a fourth, their leader. They were all in flight suits, with helmet bags beside them. A chart was spread out on the ground before them and all of them were on one knee, studying it. These were some of the elite pilots who had been selected to fly the Nighthawk, the article said—the best the air force had, serving with the 152nd Tactical Fighter Wing based in Florida.

He smiled wryly. He doubted that pilots like these waited till they were on the flight line to study their charts. The photo was obviously a posed one for the benefit of the media.

But once again, as he read the caption, he felt that infuriating twinge of recognition. There was something there . . .

Abruptly, he closed both files and scrolled the cursor to the list of programs loaded into the computer. There was one that was his own design and he double-clicked it. In a moment of whimsy he'd called it Common Ground, and he waited now till the program opened. It had proved invaluable on more than one occasion in the past. He had designed it to sift through several different files at the same time and find any common ground between them—any synchronicity of times, dates, names or events. Now he typed in the names of the two files he'd just been studying, plus another that the FBI research staff had provided, dealing with previous terrorist hostage situations.

There was a muted whirr from the laptop. The screen was suspended, showing only the hourglass icon that told him the program was running. He leaned back, stretched and yawned again. Then a series of soft chimes told him that the computer had found several matches. As the results began to appear on screen, he leaned forward to read them, feeling his pulse quicken as he saw the connection that he had been sensing all this time.

"Well I'll be damned," he said softly. He saved the search results to a new file and then, as a memory struck him, he began a new search, seeking the names of senior White House staff at the time of the Powderburn raid. The screen filled rapidly with photos, names and brief career details, starting with the then chief of staff and working down. Five from the top was the name he was looking for.

"Well I'll be double damned," he said.

THIRTY-FOUR

Dent Colby looked up at the skies over the Wasatch mountains. The wind had got up in the last hour and the clouds were dark and heavy bellied, driving in low over the mountains, rolling toward the wild country beyond Canyon Lodge. Beside him, the marine colonel tilted his close-cropped head back, staring at the clouds as well.

"Looks like it's going to snow," he said and as the words were uttered, the first big, fat flakes began to drift down. The good weather that had held for the past three days seemed to be over and done as the mountains reverted to their true nature. The snow was coming faster and thicker already and the strong wind sent it swirling around them. Colby glanced down the road to where the support vehicles and the mess tent had been set up. Though they were barely fifty yards away, they were becoming increasingly difficult to see through the rapidly mounting blizzard.

Both men were thinking the same thing and finally it was Colby who voiced it.

"Maybe we could go in this," he said. Maloney eyed the swirling snow critically.

"They'd sure have trouble seeing us coming," he replied. "Mind you, their radar might not be troubled too much."

That was the problem, of course. The heavy, swirling snowfall would hide the choppers from view until the last moment, and might even mask the sound of the rotors—although the wind would be behind them. But they'd show up bright and clear on the radar screens that controlled the fifty calibers on the hotel roof. And they'd also be clear targets for the heat-seeking heads on the Stingers.

"If they know we're coming," the colonel continued, "chances are we'll lose a lot of men. And they could bring the mountain down anyway."

Colby nodded unhappily, although he doubted the last statement. He was becoming increasingly convinced that the erratic behavior exhibited on the phone was nothing more than a ploy to convince him that the terrorists weren't rational, that they were prepared to sacrifice themselves along with their hostages if any attempt was made to storm the lodge. His conversation with Jesse Parker, and the deputy's description of the cold, calculated attitude of the men in charge were at odds with that picture.

Problem was, Colby thought, he couldn't be more than sixty percent sure—and sixty percent left too big a margin for error. If he were wrong in his assessment of the situation, a lot of innocent people would die. Still, the inactivity chafed at him, particularly now that he saw the deteriorating weather conditions providing an outside chance for some kind of action. Deep in his heart he sensed the hostages were doomed anyway. These guys had already killed fifty or sixty people. They wouldn't hesitate to kill another thirty or forty. After all, they could only go to the gas chamber once.

But sensing and knowing for sure were two different things and he knew he couldn't gamble with the hostages' lives on a mere supposition.

All th. same, he might as well explore every possibility. "Maybe we could go in low, hugging the ground and the ridge lines. Might keep us off their screens," he said. But Maloney was shaking his head before he'd even finished the sentence.

"I understand how you feel, Colby," he said, "but this wind will be swirling and shearing all the way up the valley. If we get below their radar coverage, chances are we'll stay there permanently."

He didn't add that the last quarter mile would be over open ground, without any concealment from the radar. He didn't have to. Dent Colby already knew it. The heavy-set agent swore softly to himself.

"Pisses me off," he said. "Just sitting here on our asses while those bastards give us orders."

The marine laid a hand on his shoulder in a gesture of empathy. "Know how you feel. But it won't do us any good getting our men killed, and the hostages blown away as well. Just hang in there, Colby. Our turn at bat will come."

Colby eyed him balefully. "Yeah? When will that be? After they've taken off in one of those Dash 8s on Sunday?"

The colonel shrugged. "I don't see that we can let them get that far," he said.

"I don't see that we can stop 'em," Colby told him.

Along with Sheriff Lawson, they'd brainstormed the kidnappers' demands the previous night and they were pretty sure they knew the overall scheme the terrorists had in mind. The general agreement was that the Dash 8s would all be compelled to take off together, and fly in a group so that the one containing the kidnappers and their hostages would be all the harder to keep track of.

If Colby were running the escape, he'd make sure the radios and ID transponders in each of the aircraft were disabled and, at a prearranged time, organize for the aircraft to split up in six different directions. It would be simple enough to give each pilot a different heading to turn onto at a given visual signal or at a given time. Then all hell would break loose as the authorities tried to follow one aircraft out of a group of similar types. There was no way of knowing which of the six aircraft the kidnappers were going to use. They might even split their forces and the hostages and fly out in two or three of them.

As Colby ran the possible scenarios through his mind, he had the sinking feeling that the terrorists had a damn good chance of getting clear if they ever reached Salt Lake City Airport. There were going to be just too many variables to keep track of and, of course, the pilots' compliance would be assured by the fact that any divergence from their orders, any failure to follow instructions, would result in the death of one or more of the hostages.

On the other hand, these men had already killed fifty people. There was no way the government could countenance letting them get away scot-free.

"Jesus," said the FBI agent, "what a fuck-up."

The sound of an engine made them both turn. A Jeep station wagon was pulling to the side of the road a few yards away from them. As they watched, a small, rather portly man, smooth cheeks ruddy in the cold air, stepped down from the passenger's side. He looked at the two of them, the marine colonel in camo fatigues and the big African–American in jeans, Timberlands and a parka. It was obvious who the FBI agent-in-charge was. He stepped forward to Colby, his hand outstretched.

"Agent Colby?" he said, smiling pleasantly. "My name is Truscott Emery." He glanced around the windswept road, the thick snow already clinging to his gray-blond hair. His eyes settled upon Dent's command trailer. "I wonder is there somewhere we could talk?"

CANYON LODGE
WASATCH COUNTY
1440 HOURS, MOUNTAIN TIME
TUESDAY, DAY 4

The storm hit the hotel fifteen minutes after it had swept in over the control point on Canyon Road. By then, it had gathered its full momentum and there was no initial scattering of snowflakes. It hit with the full driving force of the wind behind it, in a white wall of flying snow.

On the roof, the watch commander quickly radioed a report to Kormann, describing the conditions to him. Kormann wasted no time heading for the rooftop elevator and a few minutes later he stepped out into the whirling, freezing cold. The watch commander greeted him and together they hurried to the small, canvas-walled enclosure that contained the radar receivers. The operator looked up as they entered.

"How is it?" Kormann asked. The technician shrugged. The sets were good and he'd tuned them himself. The blizzard was causing a little disturbance to the screen, but nothing he couldn't tune out.

"No problem," he said laconically. He was a Korean-American

and he'd spent the first fifteen years of his life working in his father's electronics business. This was child's play to him.

"They could try to make a dash in here using this storm as cover," Kormann warned him. The technician allowed himself a small smile.

"They'll be in big trouble if they do," he said. "They put a chopper in the air, I'll see it clear as day. Look here."

He indicated the screen in front of him and Kormann bent to look into the display, hooded to keep side light from reflecting on the screen. As the dish outside rotated through a one hundred and eighty degree sweep, he could see the effect of the snowstorm. It showed up as a low-level interference on the screen, like white specks of dust, with thicker flurries providing a slightly heavier imagery. Then the tech tapped the screen as the beam swept over something solid and a bright green blip showed up, distinct and unmistakable.

"See that? It's one of the pylons for the cable car. Shows up clear as a bell, even through all that crap out there."

Kormann felt a slight lessening of tension. He'd assumed as much and they'd discussed the effect of a blizzard like this when they'd planned the operation. But seeing it proved beyond doubt was a whole lot better than assuming. He slapped the Korean-American on the shoulder.

"Good work," he said. "Keep a close watch." He turned to the watch commander who was crowded into the canvas and timber-framed hutch with them. "You even think they've put anything in the air, open fire as soon as you've got a lock. Don't wait for my say-so."

The watch commander nodded his understanding. "I'm bringing the visual lookouts in for a while," he said. "There's nothing much they can see in all of this and the radar will tell us if anything major is happening."

Kormann thought about it, then nodded agreement. There was no point in keeping the men out in the open unnecessarily in this weather.

"Bring them into the pool area," he said. The roof had a heated indoor pool set behind full-length glass windows. "But keep the gun crews out there. Change them every fifteen minutes." That would give the men an hour and a half inside the shelter of the pool area for every fifteen minutes they spent out in the wind and snow. That was plenty. The commander nodded again.

"You got it."

Kormann turned back to the Korean again. "You let me know if there's any problem, okay?" The technician shrugged. He was beginning to think that Kormann was obsessive about this but what the hell, he was being well paid.

"Won't be no problems. Long as we keep the snow from building up on the dishes, and we've got guys with hot air blowers to look after that."

Kormann stepped out into the wind again and glanced around the roof. Satisfied that things were under control, he headed for the elevator again, hunched over against the keening wind.

"I'll get back downstairs and ring that damned federal agent again," he said. "If they're even thinking of trying something, I want to have him on the phone, talking to me."

THIRTY-FIVE

Colby looked around at the former professor as the connection to the Canyon Lodge was broken. The phone conversation with the man he now referred to as Roger had followed the usual pattern—accusation, threats, seeming paranoia and, in between, very little in the way of real communication. He had also noted that the original pattern of calls coming from both Roger and his companion had changed lately. Roger was now the main contact.

"So what do you think?" he asked, and Emery shrugged.

"Sounds like normal behavior for this sort of situation," he said. "He's keyed up, excited, unwilling to trust you or anything you say. Hell, you've done this before, what do you think?"

Colby shifted uncomfortably. They'd barely reached the command trailer when the phone had begun its muted chirping and he'd been tied up in a conversation with Roger ever since. Truscott Emery had listened silently throughout the exchange.

"It's how I'd expect a terrorist to behave. That's what troubles me. It's all so pat. There's something about it just doesn't ring true. I'm getting one picture when I talk to Roger, and it simply doesn't gel with what Parker has told us."

He stood and moved to the coffeemaker on a bench along one wall, pouring himself a cup. He glanced at Emery, eyebrows raised, and the other man shook his head.

"So," Dent said finally, "what brings you out here?"

Emery shrugged in his turn. "I wanted to get the feeling for this on-site. I've been kind of fired by the president from his advisory council," he added. He wanted Colby clear on that point. The FBI agent smiled briefly.

"From what I've heard, that could be in your favor," he said.

"But Linus Benjamin has kept me on in an advisory capacity. We both thought I might be of some value out here." He hesitated and Colby nodded. Emery was relieved to see the positive response. There had always been the possibility that Colby might see him as intruding on his authority. He continued: "Point is, there's been something worrying me since this started. Like you, I feel something just doesn't ring true. Did Linus mention anything to you?"

"Not specifically. I knew he'd asked you to stay involved after the president blew his top. He didn't say what you were up to in any specific terms."

The trailer shuddered as the wind gusted up to a new level. Colby stooped to look out through the window. The clouds were still scudding low overhead, the snow still flying. It was difficult to tell now how much of the snow was falling and how much was just blowing. Either way, it formed a thick white curtain.

"Let me tell you what I was working on then," said Emery. "I was looking into an operation called Powderburn that happened just over ten years ago."

It took Emery five minutes to give Colby a quick outline of Operation Powderburn. The FBI agent listened with a frown on his heavy features. The whole thing seemed so long ago and far away, it couldn't possibly have any bearing on events here in Utah. When he finished, Dent shook his head slowly.

"It's thin," he said. "Very thin. You're saying this Estevez guy is behind this because we blew up his drug cache over ten years ago? Jesus, you're hanging the whole case on the odd amount of the ransom."

Emery shook his head. "No. That was just part of the message. That was to make us look more carefully. There's another link that I hadn't seen until I was on the flight out here. Look at the article about the F-117. Particularly the photograph."

Dent did so, scanning quickly through the details.

"Now," said Emery, "look at the hostages' names."

And there it was, buried in the middle of the list—one of Senator Carling's party, listed as an aerospace executive working for Rockair Aviation, with a degree in aeronautical engineering. But what wasn't so obvious was that he was more than a company executive with a nine-to-five desk job. He was Rockair's senior test pilot, and he'd had fifteen years in the air force. He was the leader of the group of pilots in the photo—the ones described as the best the air force had.

"Well I'll be damned," Dent Colby said quietly, as the man's name leapt off the two lists. "You think that he . . ."

He hesitated and Emery concluded it for him.

"Do I think he flew the Powderburn operation? I phoned General Barrett and he ran a check of Pell's records. There's a twelve-month gap—listed as special duties. It coincides with the time of Powderburn. And now here he is in Utah, still involved in developing stealth technology.

"Now all of that could be a coincidence. But then I did some more checking. Seems that when Powderburn was planned, there was a special presidential aide in the White House called Ted Carling."

"Carling? The senator?" Dent sat up a little straighter. But Emery shook his head.

"Not then. That came later. But his role in the White House is listed as 'Special plans aide to the president on internal security'—or, more specifically, the much vaunted 'War on Drugs.' You see where this is going?"

"Carling was the one . . ." Dent began, then hesitated to make sure he wasn't leaping to a false conclusion. But Emery finished for him.

"Pell might have been the pilot on Operation Powderburn. That's a possibility. But one thing is definite. Carling was the one who planned it and ordered it carried out. He's the target in all of this. The very fact that they haven't mentioned him or used him as a bargaining tool confirms it. They want to keep us guessing."

Right then, before Colby could say anything, the phone rang.

TOP STATION
FLYING EAGLE CABLE CAR
WASATCH COUNTY
1551 HOURS, MOUNTAIN TIME
TUESDAY, DAY 4

The storm had been a blessing. With visibility reduced to a few yards, Jesse had taken the chance to make his way to the chairlift once more. Shrouded in the white poncho, he figured he was virtually invisible in the whiteout.

It had been a successful day so far. He'd managed to make contact with Tina Bowden again when she and the chef had arrived to prepare food in the middle of the day. This time, she had engineered a reason to come to the storeroom and he wasted no time putting the questions that Colby wanted answered. In clipped tones, as they moved through the storeroom, piling another carton with the requirements for the lunch break, she had given him the answers. How much Dent would make of them, he had no idea, but now, at least, he knew for sure that the terrorists were aware of Carling's identity, and he had a good description of the man in charge—Kormann, she had said his name was. When the storm hit, he realized that he had a chance to get this information to Colby immediately, without another overnight wait for the chairlift.

Now, at the top of the mountain once more, armed with his own cell phone and one he'd found in Tina Bowden's room, he hit the redial button for the FBI's 1-800 number.

As soon as he identified himself he was patched through to Colby's phone. The eagerness in the other man's voice was unmistakable.

"Jesse! I didn't expect to hear from you until tomorrow!" he said.

"Don't know if you've noticed, Agent Colby, but there's a storm blowing. I used it for cover to get up here. Now listen up. I managed to speak to Tina again and here are some of the things you wanted to know.

"The leader of the mercenaries is a guy called Kormann. Around five ten, five eleven, medium weight and build—say one-sixty pounds. Dark hair going gray, so he may be in his late thirties, early forties. I saw him up here the other day and he looks pretty fit. What I didn't see was something Tina mentioned. He has amazingly blue eyes—piercing blue." He hesitated. "You getting this?"

"I'm recording the whole thing," Dent told him. "Keep going."

"Okay. I've been thinking some on this. They've got Carling and they know it. But they're not using him as a lever to bargain with you, right?"

"That's right, Jess. Where you going with this?"

"Just hear me out, Dent. Next up, they've spun you some story about Irish terrorists they want set free. But nobody in here has heard one word about that. On the other hand, this Kormann guy said right at the start that they were businessmen and they're here for ransom."

"With you so far," Colby said. He and Emery exchanged glances. The man on the other end of the phone was beginning to reflect their own thinking.

"It's just I think this whole terrorist thing is a blind of some kind, is all," Jesse finished. "It's not political. They're in it for the money, pure and simple."

"Nine point seven million is a lot of money," Colby agreed.

"Nine point seven?" Jesse queried. It was the first time he'd heard the sum. "Why'd they pick a figure like that?"

"That's what's got us all wondering. You got anything on any of the others besides this Kormann type?"

Jesse hesitated slightly. He thought briefly about what he'd told Dent the previous time they'd spoken. The group was disciplined, efficient, businesslike. There wasn't a lot more to tell. Except one other detail.

"The second in command is calling himself Pallisani," he said. "Sure to be a false name but Tina says he looks like he's got an Italian background and he sounds like he was born in the U.S. Maybe Brooklyn, but she's not certain."

Colby jotted down the details. Jesse was sure to be right. The name would be a phoney. "Anything else on him, Jess?" he asked quickly.

"He's a bit easier to describe than Kormann. He's tall, maybe six one or six two, with gray hair and prominent cheekbones. He's maybe fifty and he's very thin, Tina said." He hesitated, then added apologetically, "Sorry I can't give you more."

"That's fine, buddy. You're doing great. Anything else spring to mind?"

"Yeah. This one I'm not sure about. It may mean nothing. But have these guys given you any sort of deadline so far?"

Dent Colby hesitated. Then he realized there was no reason why he shouldn't give Jesse the details of the ransom demand. "So far, they're asking for the money and they want a chopper in there on Sunday. They say they're taking ten of the hostages with them and we've got to provide a plane out of Salt Lake City. If we screw up, they'll start killing hostages."

"Sunday?" Jesse said, uncertainty obvious in his voice.

"That's right. Does that mean something to you?"

Again the deputy hesitated. Colby knew he was a man who considered his words carefully, never made a statement that he hadn't thought through. "It's just . . . I told you this guy Kormann was up here the other day. He came up in the cable car after we'd spoken."

"He was looking for you?" Colby prompted, suddenly concerned that the kidnappers might have some way of monitoring Jesse's cell phone conversations. Jesse hurried to dispel the fear.

"No. He'd simply come up here for the same reason I did—to use his cell phone."

Again, Colby and Emery exchanged puzzled looks. Why would Kormann, who Colby guessed was the man he knew as Roger, need to travel all that way to use the phone?

Emery leaned forward and said softly: "Maybe he didn't want the call monitored. The line runs through here."

Colby nodded but at the sound of the unfamiliar voice on the line, Jesse was instantly alerted.

"Who was that? You got someone else in there?" He was reasonably confident Colby wouldn't be dumb enough to let anyone from the press listen in but he wanted to be sure. After all, it was his life on the line up here if Kormann's men ever realized he was on the loose.

"It's a guy name of Emery who's here with us, Jess," Dent reassured him. "He's okay. He's a presidential adviser." He made a small moue at the professor as he added this last. It wasn't technically true anymore but it was the quickest way of reassuring Jesse. Emery nodded his understanding. Jesse's voice, when he spoke again, sounded mollified.

"Okay then. Thing was, this Kormann guy just said one or two words. He said Friday's the day. There was something about depending on someone called George . . . then he repeated it: Friday."

"Friday?" Colby said. "That was it?"

"That was it. Mean anything to you guys?"

Again, Colby and Emery exchanged puzzled looks. "Not so far, Jess," Colby said finally. "We'll think on it some. You got anything else for us?"

"That's about it for the moment. I'd better call it a day. I want to get back down the mountain while this storm's still blowing, and the chairlifts shut down at four thirty. Anything else you need to know?"

"Just a few things," Colby said dryly. "Starting with what the fuck this is all about. But for the moment, that's it. Good work, Jesse, and stay safe."

"I'll work on it," Jesse told him. "I'll try to get back to you tomorrow or Thursday. I'll see if Tina has heard any mention of something happening Friday, okay?"

"Okay, Jess. Stay in touch."

There was a brief beep as the cell phone disconnected. Colby shook his head, trying to make sense of all the disparate pieces of the puzzle. Already, Truscott Emery was typing the description of Kormann into his laptop, to send back to the research team at Quantico. At least that was somewhere they could start.

THIRTY-SIX

Kormann wiped a crust of bread around the rim of his plate, soaking up the last of the gravy. The veal had been excellent and he had to admit there were side benefits to hijacking a luxury hotel. Ralph had excelled himself tonight, he thought, pushing away the separate plate of French fries that he always insisted on and never ate.

He glanced up at Pallisani sitting opposite him in the gymnasium office. The other man had finished his meal several minutes before Kormann. He bolted his food, wolfing it down without taking time to appreciate it. Still, he thought, what could you expect? Regretfully, his mind dwelled for a few moments on the excellent wine cellar maintained by the hotel restaurant. He would have appreciated one of the fine reds that were stored there to go with the meal. But he'd set the no drinking rule from the start and he felt it was only right for him to adhere to it if he expected his men to.

Pallisani belched softly. Kormann wrinkled his nose in distaste. He wished the Italian had chosen to wait until he'd finished his meal. Pallisani didn't notice the fleeting expression. He wasn't big on subtlety, Kormann thought, either giving or receiving.

"So, looks like they're going with the plan on Sunday?" Pallisani said now, and Kormann nodded.

"Not much else they could do," he agreed. "They can't take the chance that we'll kill the hostages."

"You think they bought that Irish thing?" Pallisani asked and Kormann shrugged.

"Maybe. Doesn't matter if they didn't buy it completely. They can't totally ignore it and it keeps them looking in another direction. If they think we're terrorists or political fanatics, it'll make it that much harder to find us after it's all over."

"The news tonight said they were talking to the Brits about it. I guess that means they believed it," Pallisani said thoughtfully. Kormann studied him for a few moments.

"That could have been a snow job. Maybe they believed it. Maybe not. As I say, it's not too important. They've got to give it some credence at least and the doubt in their mind is what matters most."

Pallisani nodded several times, although Kormann was willing to bet that the Italian had no real idea why the doubt was the important thing. As Kormann had observed before, Pallisani was no genius. He was a good operative and good at carrying out instructions. But the concept of mind games, of keeping the other side off balance and denying them any hard knowledge of who they were dealing with, was beyond him. Original thought was not his strong point. He was content to play his part and take the money at the end of it.

Which, after all, was why Kormann had recruited him in the first place. The last thing he wanted was a second in command who might guess what he really had in mind.

"So, what are you planning to do with your three million bucks?" Pallisani asked now. He was in an expansive mood and he wanted to discuss the prospect of the money that was coming to him. As Kormann had explained it to him, there was two hundred thousand for each of their eighteen accomplices and three million each for him and Pallisani. Leaving one hundred grand for incidental expenses, that totalled nine point seven million dollars. It was a perfectly logical reason for the odd amount and that was why Kormann had recruited eighteen men, along with Pallisani.

As far as the men themselves were concerned, the price of the ransom was determined by the number sharing in the proceeds and that was what he kept them believing. Kormann couldn't help a small flicker of a smile as he wondered what Pallisani would say if he realized that he, Kormann, never planned to collect the ransom money. By Sunday, everyone still in the hotel would be dead.

"I guess I might get out of this business," he said now, in reply to the question. He had no intention of getting out of the business. He loved the buzz, loved the power, loved the challenge of living by his wits. But Pallisani believed him and was nodding in agreement.

"Me too," he replied. "Maybe settle down, get a little ranch some- where. Somewhere warm," he added, "not some ass-freezing dump like this."

"Yeah," said Kormann, bored to tears by the other man's conversa- tion. "That'd be the life all right."

Suddenly, he couldn't wait for Friday to come. He glanced at his watch, then shoved his chair back from the desk he had been using as a table and rose to his feet.

"Time to check on the roof," he said. "Keep an eye on things here."

Pallisani nodded. There had been no need to tell him that but it made it easier for Kormann to leave alone. In his present expansive mood, Pallisani might have suggested keeping him company. As Kormann walked through the outer reception room for the gymna- sium, he noticed that five of the guards were taking their meal break. That would mean three were on patrol in the gymnasium itself, where the hostages were finishing their meal. He smiled to himself again. Another variation on stew. The girl doing their cooking cer- tainly didn't have Ralph's touch in the kitchen, he thought.

He went through the outer room, a kind of reception room where guests would have waited for their turn on the complex exercise ma- chinery, and several of the men nodded to him. He acknowledged their greetings and headed for the elevator bank.

Tina Bowden saw him leave. The outer room was separated from the gymnasium proper by two heavy glass sliding doors. Tina knew the glass was almost half an inch thick and was shatterproof. That meant it was pretty well bulletproof—particularly if you were using one of those 9 millimeter machine carbines or pistols that the guards all carried. Maybe a 30-06 or a Magnum might crash its way through, she reflected. But she hadn't seen any of them around.

Except for the one she now had secreted under her bedroll on the floor. She'd collected the gun earlier, when she and Ralph had pre- pared the evening meal, tucking it into the waistband of her skirt under the white blouse. At the same time, she'd stashed a dozen of the shiny brass magnum slugs into her boots, carefully concealing them when she returned to her bedspace against the wall.

Eighteen slugs in all, counting the six that she'd loaded in the pistol. It wasn't a lot to be taking on ten armed men. But she hoped to supplement her weapon with one or two of the Ingrams that the guards carried, if push came to shove.

Casually now, she let her gaze roam around the room, watching the movement of the guards, mentally rehearsing the movements she would make and forcing the thought of the third man from her mind. When the time came, she knew, she would have to blot him out of her consciousness and trust Pell to take care of him. She wouldn't be able to let any thought of him distract her from the task in hand. No matter how tempted she would be, she mustn't glance in his direction until the first two men were down. And by then it would be too late, one way or the other. She figured that in the confusion of it all, after she'd taken out the first guard, she'd get one free shot at the second. But by the time she'd taken it, the third man would have her well and truly located. She wished she knew a little more about Pell. She would be putting a hell of a lot of trust in him.

She now turned to see where the third guard was and located him at the back of the room. Her eyes rested on him for a few moments, then looked to where Pell sat beside his companions, just a few yards away. The pilot had been watching her and as her gaze fell on him, he met it and nodded, almost imperceptibly.

THE J. EDGAR HOOVER BUILDING
WASHINGTON D.C.
0105 HOURS, EASTERN TIME
WEDNESDAY, DAY 5

Deep in the basement of the FBI building, research technician Brady Temple watched the names and photos of known terrorists, mercenaries and political activists as they scrolled across his computer screen in a flickering blur, faster than the eye could follow. The computer was on a probability search, into which he'd fed the parameters, such as they were, that had been emailed to them from Utah by Truscott Emery.

Age, height, build, hair color and, of course, the most salient detail of all, those piercing blue eyes that Jesse had mentioned, were all fed into the computer as it tested and rejected hundreds of names and profiles every minute. Temple had even programmed in the initial letter of the surname Kormann. All too often, he knew, when people assumed false names, they stayed with the same initials. It seemed to make things easier to remember. Or maybe it gave them a link with some kind of reality in the shadow world they inhabited.

Temple wasn't really interested in the motivation. All he knew was that it occasionally gave him an edge on a search like this one.

At irregular intervals the computer would beep softly and pause as it found a candidate whose specifications matched the search parameters. The search would stop momentarily and a face and dossier would appear on screen. The dossiers, more often than not, were nearly as scant as the parameters that Temple had to work with. People on these files spent a lot of time keeping their details from being too widely known—particularly by organizations such as the FBI.

As the computer paused at each suggestion, Temple would hit a command key to transfer that dossier and that photo to another, smaller file. He yawned, wondering whether it was worth going to the canteen for a cup of coffee, then decided not. He checked the indicator on the side of the screen and could see that the program was almost finished. There couldn't be more than a couple of hundred names left to sort through. The computer chimed once more and he glanced curiously at the latest suggestion.

"Kavel, Raymond," he muttered, reading the name under the picture. It was a completely nondescript face, with no outstanding feature. Pleasant, certainly, but not so good-looking that an observer might remember it from one moment to the next. Even features, brown hair, mouth not too wide, not too narrow, nose neither too long nor too wide, a face that was totally, irrevocably, average in every way—except for one.

The eyes seemed to blaze out of the screen at him, brilliant blue, with a burning intensity. For a moment, Temple was taken a little aback by those eyes. After all, in feeding the search parameters into the computer, he had only been able to specify eye color—there was no way the computer could make a subjective judgment as to the intensity of the eyes. To a computer, blue eyes were blue eyes.

But these were something different, and as Temple copied Kavel's details to the other file, he couldn't help feeling that this was the man they were looking for.

He glanced at his watch, realizing for the first time that a new day was already more than an hour old. As he did so, the computer emitted a series of short beeps, telling him that it had finished the sorting process. Temple yawned again and stretched, easing the cramped shoulder muscles that were the result of too many hours sitting hunched forward at the computer screen. There was time to email the compiled list to Emery tonight, he decided, then he was going home.

THIRTY-SEVEN

Colby walked with Cale Lawson along the side of the road, their boots crunching in the gravel. The FBI agent looked up at the broken cloud overhead, where patches of blue sky showed through. After the storm weather of the previous two days, this was a welcome change. The wind was still blowing keenly, of course, but it was nowhere near the speeds it had reached during the storm.

"At least the weather has improved," he said to the sheriff. Lawson raised his eyes to the skies, squinted and frowned.

"Enjoy it while you can," he said, with a local's eye for the weather. "Ain't going to last much more than another day. There's another storm front coming in from the west, should hit us tomorrow night sometime."

"Just what I need," Dent said gloomily. "More wind and snow. I'd kind of hoped that was it for a while."

Lawson smiled at him as they stopped to watch a squad of Maloney's men abseiling down the cliff face on the upper side of the road.

"What's the matter, son," he asked. "Don't you ever watch the Weather Channel? They've been predicting this pattern for days. All thanks to some hurricane in the North Pacific, so they tell me."

"Is that right?" Colby asked absently, still watching the marines as they moved forward, flanking their practice target—one of the trailers set up for accommodation. The colonel, he noticed, was in the lead group. He kept his men training day and night, and wasn't afraid to mix in with them.

A cell phone shrilled its ring tone and Dent automatically

reached for his pocket, then realized it was the sheriff's phone. Lawson answered it. As the caller spoke to him he glanced curiously at Dent.

"Hold on, Connie," he said into the phone. Then, lowering it, he asked Dent: "You know some woman called Torrens? Sheriff from out Colorado? Says she was speaking to you a day or two ago," he added.

Dent nodded. "She's our contact with Parker." He waved a hand in the general direction of Canyon Lodge. "The guy who's on the loose up there. He's one of her deputies. What does she want?"

Assuming she was on the phone, he held out a hand for it, but Lawson shook his head. "She's down at the roadblock. Wants to come on up. That okay with you?"

Dent thought for a second, then nodded consent. "Why not? Could be a handy person to have around."

Lawson raised the cell to his mouth again. "Bring her up, Connie," he told his deputy, then snapped the phone closed.

They waited, watching as a sheriff's department cruiser weaved slowly through the staggered vehicles that were blocking the road below them and headed uphill to the control center. It stopped some twenty yards away and the passenger side door opened. Lee stepped out, blond hair blowing in the wind, long-legged and athletic. Even the heavy sheriff's department parka couldn't conceal the fact that she was a very attractive woman.

"How come I got you instead of her?" Dent said quietly to Lawson. The Utah sheriff grinned in consolation.

"Luck of the draw, son." He stepped forward as Lee approached. "Sheriff Torrens? I'm Cale Lawson, Wasatch County sheriff. This here's Special Agent Dent Colby, from the FBI."

Lee shook hands with the two men. Her keen eyes measured them, evaluating them. Lawson was a typical northwest sheriff. An outdoors man, his face tanned and the corners of his eyes creased from years spent behind the wheel of a cruiser looking into the snow and sunglare on the backroads of Utah. Colby was something else. She took in the massive shoulders and chest. He was a powerful-looking man, not at all the type she'd expect to see as a negotiator. Somehow, Lee thought of negotiators as academics. Colby looked like he'd crush a kidnapper with his bare hands sooner than reason with him. She decided she liked the look of both of them.

"Call me Lee," she said. "Any further word from my deputy?"

"Spoke to him earlier," Colby told her. "He's still safe and he's doing a great job. He's a good man."

"He's the best," she said firmly. He looked at her a moment, then nodded.

"I guess he is at that. Let's get in out of the wind and I'll fill you in on the latest developments."

He gestured toward the mess tent that had been set up for the marines. There was hot coffee available there all day. As they headed toward the tent, Lawson noticed a figure hurrying toward them, waving a sheaf of papers in his hand.

"Looks like your buddy from Washington wants to talk," he said.

Colby halted until Emery reached them. He introduced Lee to the professor. She couldn't help thinking that Emery looked more like a negotiator than Colby did.

They walked into the mess tent. It was virtually empty at this time of morning, and there were petroleum gas–fueled heaters placed at strategic locations between the tables. Dent Colby chose a spot near one and they sat down.

Quickly, Dent brought Lee and Cale Lawson up to speed on Emery's theory that the entire scenario was revenge for the top se-cret Operation Powderburn ten years previously, beginning with the connection between the ransom amount and the money Estevez had lost, then going onto the fact that Carling had probably planned the raid and Pell was most likely the pilot of the F-117.

"So this Estevez has a good reason to hate Carling and the pilot who flew the mission. And they both happen to be here," she said. Emery nodded.

"You can push it a little further," he said. "He has a good reason to hate anyone associated with stealth aircraft in general, and he has a whole swag of those people here as well. People who build and test them."

"How's that, Mr. Emery?" Sheriff Lawson asked. Emery glanced quickly at him.

"That's why Carling is here. For the past five years or so, he's organized an annual seminar up here, with representatives from the aerospace industry. They talk some business and tie it in with a ski vacation. This year, they've been finalizing contract details and specifications for the next generation stealth bomber."

"One question," Lee said. "How would this Estevez have found out about Carling's involvement with Powderburn?"

Emery smiled at her. "With enough time, money and computer power, you can find out most things. That's the beauty of the computer age—nothing ever stays completely secret. Of course, all the evidence that points to Carling's role is circumstantial. But it's pretty compelling and you can find it if you look hard enough."

"As you did," Colby said, and Emery glanced quickly at him.

"Precisely." He tapped the sheaf of papers he had laid on the mess table. "Now, speaking about information, I've got something more for you. I think we have a reasonably good take on our friend Roger," he said and turned the first page over. Dent looked at the face staring off the page at him. It fitted the description Jesse had given them—nondescript in every way except for the eyes—a piercing, intense blue.

"Raymond Kavel," he read softly, seeing the name under the photo. Emery nodded.

"Or Roger Kormann. The initials are the same. Sometimes makes life easier if you spend a lot of time under assumed names. He's the closest match to any of the ones the computer threw up at us."

"What do we know about him?" Cale Lawson chipped in. Emery's face showed a trace of chagrin.

"Not a lot. But that goes with this territory. He was born in Rhodesia. He's around thirty-eight or thirty-nine and served in the Rhodesian army before Mugabe and his thugs took over. Kavel got out at the last moment and spent a few years in South Africa—he got himself a commission in their army quickly enough. Then he drifted into the mercenary business. The Congo, Angola, even Eritrea—the usual round. Not a lot of detail but there were rumors that he was involved in the Sierra Leone war a couple of years back. Nothing definite, mind you. People like him try to keep their names out of the headlines.

"Again, unconfirmed reports placed him in Fiji during the rebellion there. Some of the white expatriates, Australians and New Zealanders, were offered the services of a 'professional protection force' and our boy Raymond may well have been at the head of it."

Colby held up a finger to stop Emery's flow, thought for a moment and then said: "Let's cut to the chase here, Truscott. This guy doesn't sound like a terrorist."

Emery shook his head definitely. "Nor a radical. He's a mercenary straight and simple. And, unlike a lot of mercenaries, he doesn't even have a basic code of honor or sense of loyalty to one side or another. He's strictly a pro. He'll work for anyone if the money's right."

"Okay," Emery continued. "So here's what we've got. We have a hostage situation up there where the kidnappers are demanding a ransom and the release of Irish terrorists. Yet we know their leader isn't a terrorist, doesn't have any political connections and is a long way from being a suicidal radical. You've said that something rings false in the way he's been behaving, Dent."

Colby shrugged. "It seems a little too pat," he said. Emery nodded agreement as he went on. "He's given you a deadline of next Sunday. Yet your friend, Parker," he glanced at Lee, "has told us that something is going to happen on Friday."

Lawson looked up at that. Like Lee, he was hearing this information for the first time. "Friday? What's supposed to happen Friday?" he asked quickly. Emery shrugged.

"We don't know. This guy Kavel, or Kormann as he's calling himself, was overheard saying 'Friday's the day.'"

"He also said something about George playing his part . . . or 'if George is on time,'" Colby added.

"My guess is—" Emery paused momentarily, as if unwilling to commit himself fully, then plunged on—"that Kormann is working for Estevez. He's been hired to kill the hostages, including the Carling group who are the real targets. I think he's set us up with this elaborate ransom plan for Sunday when in reality he's planning to blow those charges on Friday, and get the hell out of Dodge before we realize what's happened."

There was a long pause. Dent finally broke it. "You think he'll blow the charges with his own men still there?" he asked, and Emery nodded.

"It'd be too hard to get them out. I think he's planning to double cross them. He'll blow those charges and bring the mountain down on the hostages and his own men, then get out. Maybe he's got a chopper coming in low over the back country. The most likely time would be in darkness and the fact that there's bad weather forecasted for Friday night only makes it seem more likely. The whole thing will look like a terrible accident—as if the kidnappers suddenly lost it and blew the charges. It's just the sort of thing we all fear in a hostage situation. The media will go mad with it, which will suit Estevez's purposes. He wants a circus like this. And we could never prove any different. Hell," he added as they considered his words, "we wouldn't know any different if it weren't for your guy up there, Sheriff Torrens."

"But how will he collect the ransom?" Lawson asked and Emery shook his head impatiently.

"He doesn't give a damn about the ransom! The ransom was designed to get our attention, with the amount carefully selected as a clue to tell us what this is all about. It's Estevez telling us, *You pissed me off. Now I'm returning the favor.* But of course, he's doing it in such a way that we can never prove his involvement. We'll know it but we can never accuse him without appearing to be paranoid."

He paused and sat back, spreading his arms in a questioning gesture. "So tell me," he said, "am I crazy or does this make any sense at all?"

Lee hesitated before speaking. She was a new arrival here and things seemed to be moving a little fast. What the smooth-shaven professor was saying was outlandish in the extreme. But all too often, Lee knew, outlandish was the way things turned out. Plus there was one other small item that Emery seemed to be unaware of—one that added another small piece of credibility to his theory.

"Have you given any thought to who this George might be?" she said, and Emery shrugged.

"That I can't even guess at. Maybe he's the chopper pilot who's going to bring Kormann out."

He stopped as he realized the Routt County sheriff was shaking her head.

"You said that bad weather Friday night would help this guy get out," she said. "Well, that's George's role. George isn't a pilot. George isn't even a person. It's the typhoon in the North Pacific that's caused the weather patterns we'll be getting for the next four days."

Suddenly, thought Dent Colby, Emery's wild-sounding scenario was starting to look all too plausible.

THIRTY-EIGHT

This time there had been no attempt at subterfuge, no time to try to disguise the fact that the president was meeting with his principal security advisers. If the press got hold of it, Benjamin thought, that was just too bad.

An outline of Truscott Emery's scenario had been circulated to all present. Now, as President Gorton paced the room, he appealed to them to give him some reason to reject Emery's findings.

"It's too fantastic," he said, a note of frustration obvious in his voice. "It's all circumstantial. I've had Terence digging back through the records and there's no solid connection between Carling and this Operation . . . Powderburn. There's no record of the operation that he can find. It could have happened and Carling could have been involved, but that doesn't prove he was. It's all conjecture. There's not one solid piece of evidence here to sustain his idea."

Years ago, in his capacity as a district prosecutor, Gorton had built and won many a case on circumstantial evidence. He knew how convincing it could be. But, by the same token, he knew that it never provided one hundred percent doubt-free proof. As a prosecutor, it had been his job to dispel reasonable doubt. As the president facing this dilemma, he had to deal in certainties. Too many lives were in the balance.

He turned to Janet Haddenrich. "Have your people found any inkling, any sign at all, that Al Qaeda might be behind this? Is there anything that can link them to it?" If he could find hard facts confirming even one part of the theory, that might make a difference.

Haddenrich shook her head sadly. "I'm sorry, Mr. President. We've heard nothing. Of course, our human resources in the Middle East are virtually nonexistent these days."

There was a hint of criticism in the last words. Years before, previous administrations had elected to forego human resources in the troubled area and rely largely on electronic resources—satellites, radio intercepts and the like. Haddenrich knew that these were valuable. But nothing did the job like a pair of eyes and ears on the ground, in the middle of things.

Morris Tildeman shook his head as well, forestalling the president's next question. "We're hearing nothing from our international sources," he said.

"What about the Israelis?" Gorton asked. "The goddamned Mossad have agents everywhere, don't they?"

Tildeman shifted uncomfortably in his chair. "The Israelis aren't saying anything, Mr. President. But they're pissed with us over the whole West Bank business."

"Jesus," said Gorton bitterly, "with friends like that, who needs fucking enemies?"

He began pacing again, his frustration growing. Benjamin exchanged glances with the others around the table. He could see no help there. Emery's theory was plausible. It was possible. But, as Gorton had said, it was built entirely on circumstantial evidence. The strongest argument in its favor was the fact of the multiplying coincidences involved—there seemed to be just too many here. Yet everyone in the room knew that chance was a strange thing. It was possible for someone to toss a coin ten times in a row and toss ten heads. It was possible for a dice player to roll twenty sevens, one after the other. It was unusual. It was even fantastic when it happened. But it did happen.

Gorton stopped abruptly. "I'm sorry," he said to the room in general. "I can't go along with it. There are too many uncertain factors here. Too much theory, not enough fact."

Briefly, Benjamin wondered what he would do if he were in Gorton's position. It was all very well for him to be critical of the president for his unwillingness to act or take tough decisions. But could he, Linus Benjamin, take the decision to order an armed assault in a case like this? Uncomfortably, he realized he didn't know. He thought maybe. But maybe wasn't definitely.

"Mr. President," Tildeman spoke again, "at least there's the matter of the leader—this Kavel guy. Our people are confident that from the description and the behavior patterns, it really is him."

The president met his gaze for a second, then gave a short bark of laughter. "The description, Mr. Director? The description, as I read it, is mainly a lack of description: average height, average build, average hair color, average features. The only positive feature is that he has blue eyes. For Christ's sake, how many average looking people are there in this world who have blue eyes?"

He dropped into the replica of the JFK rocker that his predecessor had installed in the room. Even his furniture was inherited, he thought bitterly. He rubbed both hands over his face and realized, with a horrible flash of self-honesty, that this job, the requirements of this job, were beyond him. He had hit his peak as vice president, the appointment being a just reward for long, faithful but uninspired service to the party and the congress. He could not make a decision like this. He could not risk the lives of the hostages on such a web of circumstantial, coincidental evidence. He thought back to the courtroom days again and realized that if he were trying a capital case with the death penalty involved on circumstantial evidence like this, he wouldn't give himself one chance in four of getting a jury to convict. And in this case, he was looking at fifty capital cases and fifty death penalties if he got it wrong.

As that realization hit him, he felt a certain relief. At least now he could come to a decision. He looked up at the circle of advisers.

"I'm sorry," he said, "I cannot give the order to attack."

He was surprised to sense a certain empathy in most of the reactions around the room, even more surprised when Haddenrich spoke.

"Mr. President, for what it's worth, I don't believe any of us here would do any differently. If we get this wrong, we'll have fifty dead bodies buried under a mountain."

"We've already got that," General Barrett reminded her and she turned to him with a flash of anger in her eyes.

"Then we'd better be damned sure of ourselves before we let it happen again," she snapped. It was Benjamin who held up a hand to stop them before the exchange went any further.

"Okay, people. The important thing is we know what we're not going to do. Where do we go from here?"

At least now, he thought, they could get on with planning an alternative strategy, based on the kidnappers' demands for the ransom and their escape aircraft. He turned to the president again.

"We've currently found three agents who are checked out in the Dash 8. We have another three who are pilots, undergoing familiarization on the type now. We figure that each of the planes can have an agent on board as copilot and our technicians are working on installing homing units on the five Dash 8s."

"I thought they said they'd sweep the planes electronically?" Pohlsen put in. It was unusual for him to contribute to these meetings.

"They can only detect an active homing device," Benjamin pointed out. "And we doubt they'll continue sweeping once they're in the air. This way, our guys on board can activate the homers when they think it's safe to do so."

"When they know it's safe to do so," the president corrected him, and he nodded in acquiescence.

The president looked around the faces once more; he read the message in their eyes. The best they could do wasn't a hell of a lot. And they all knew it.

THIRTY-NINE

The snowstorm that hit Snow Eagles Resort had been short but less intense for its lack of duration. It had also been almost totally local—five miles down the canyon where the road was blocked, the weather was clear.

Jesse was in Tina's room when the first wall of white swept in, blotting out the terminal buildings at the foot of the high-speed quad chair. As the snow and pellets of ice spattered against the window, he realized that this was an opportunity to make contact with Colby once more. Hurriedly, he left the room and made his way down the service stairs to the ski room, grabbing his skis, gloves and poles from the rack and heading out the rear entrance of the hotel.

He was vaguely surprised that Kormann and his men had done nothing to secure this exit so far. Then he realized that, as far as they were concerned, everyone who had been in the hotel when they arrived was already accounted for.

The white curtain was still driving across the open space when he exited the hotel and clamped his feet into the bindings on his skis. As before, he had the makeshift white poncho draped over his shoulders and, had there been anyone watching him as he skied away from the shelter of the building, they would have lost sight of him before he'd gone five yards.

This time, he skied straight into the chairlift entrance and out between two chairs. There was barely a pause before he was on his way up the mountain again. He sat upright in the chair, ready to roll sideways in case the short storm cleared. It didn't happen till he was well and truly away from the hotel and out of sight. The wind gradually eased and with it, the snow. He brushed off the thick coating of dry powder that had collected on him and rode the last quarter of the chairlift in a milky, weak sunshine. As the chair took him behind the ridge line, the remaining wind died away to nothing.

He wasn't totally sure why he had suddenly decided to make his way to the top of the mountain again. Maybe it was simply to make contact with someone else on the outside—another human being. The tension of being alone among enemies was beginning to tell on him. He guessed that maybe those agents who were dropped behind enemy lines during World War II felt much the same way.

There was a practical side to his actions as well. If anything was going to happen on Friday, this might well be the last chance he would have to speak to Colby. The necessity of moving to the lift terminal during the hours of darkness, and the uncertainty of his ability to make contact with Tina, made the whole business incredibly ponderous and time-consuming. This way, he could speak to Colby today, and if there were any messages to pass on to Tina, he might even make contact later this evening. Or, at worst, when she came to the kitchen to prepare breakfast the following day. Anything that sped up the process would be a benefit.

On the other hand, if Colby had nothing new to tell him or ask him, then there was no harm done. He wasn't exactly loaded down with things to do. As an experienced cop, he was used to the enforced boredom of stakeouts. A large amount of a working cop's time was spent sitting and waiting. But never before had he done so in such potentially dangerous surroundings and as a result, he found himself wanting to speak to Colby—to hear a voice from a more normal and a safer world.

On the flat at the top of the mountain, the wind had built up again and he moved into the shelter of the lift building as he took the cell phone from his jacket's inner pocket. Once again, he went straight through to Colby's phone without delay. It was reassuring to hear Dent's deep voice and picture the heavyset, capable man at the other end of the connection. Maybe, Jesse thought, he was getting a little stir-crazy.

After the first few words of greeting, however, the reassurance ebbed away as the FBI agent detailed Truscott Emery's theory.

"Jesus," said Jesse softly when the other man had finished. "Do you believe this?"

There was a long pause and Jesse could sense the uncertainty at the other end. Finally, Dent replied: "I think it could be on the money. I've felt right from the start that there was some hidden agenda here. But you've seen the situation up there firsthand. How do you read it?"

Now it was Jesse's turn to hesitate. He had to admit that the professor's theory sounded logical. It sounded possible. Hell, when you got right down to it, it was more than either of those. It was the most likely reason behind the entire operation. These men were not fanatics. They had proven themselves to be cold-blooded and disciplined.

But, like Dent Colby, Linus Benjamin and the president himself, Jesse balked at the jump between probability and fact. The penalties for guessing wrong were too huge, too unconscionable.

"I just don't know, Colby," he replied. "It seems to match all the facts up here, particularly if this Kormann guy is who you say he is. But if we're wrong . . ."

He let the sentence hang. Colby picked it up. His voice was heavy with a sense of defeat. "If we're wrong, they could bring the mountain down on those fifty hostages."

"And if this professor guy is right, he's going to do that anyway, come Friday night." Jesse put in. Again there was silence on the line and he knew Dent Colby had already considered that possibility, over and over again.

"So, whose call is it?" Jesse asked. "Do you make the decision, Dent?"

"It's already out of my hands," Colby told him. "It's gone all the way to the top and the president has refused to authorize an assault.

The thinking is we should go along with the ransom arrangements and hope for the best."

"He's probably right," Jesse said thoughtfully. He could sense Colby shaking his head in frustration as he replied.

"Probably. It's the safest way to go, that's for sure. But Jesus, if he's wrong . . ."

There was the muffled sound of another voice in the background. Jesse recognized it as the Harvard professor. He'd been listening in to the conversation.

"Just a moment, Jesse . . ." Colby said to the phone.

He obviously covered the receiver then, as he spoke to the other man. Then, after perhaps a minute, he resumed the conversation.

"Jess?"

"I hear you."

"Emery has a thought here. If this guy Kavel, or Kormann or whatever you want to call him, is planning to blow the mountain Friday night, he's going to have to do it from up where you are now. He can hardly bring an avalanche down on himself, right?"

"Right," Jesse said thoughtfully, wondering where this was going.

"Plus we're assuming he's got a chopper coming in over the back country to pick him up, and the cable car station is the most logical place for a landing site."

Jesse looked around the surrounding peaks. There were other cleared areas, but he had to admit that the cable car top station was the spot he'd pick if he wanted a chopper to get in and out in a hurry.

"So far I'm with you," he said.

"Okay. So here's the thing. How long does that cable car take to reach the summit? I'm figuring maybe ten minutes?"

"At least that," Jesse agreed.

"Okay. Let's assume we're here on standby on Friday, ready to go, locked and loaded in the choppers, with the engines running. We can be in there in five minutes, catch Kormann on the way up. We figure any avalanche is going to take down the cable car pylons, so Kormann will have to wait till he's out of the car before he blows the mountain."

"He can still be up here and bringing it down while you're trying to secure the hotel, Dent. It's too tight," Jesse protested.

"Maybe. But Maloney has two choppers here for flak suppression: Apaches armed with Maverick missiles. We send one of them in the lead to take out the cable car with Kormann in it. He'll never know what hit him."

Jesse thought it over for a few seconds. It might work. But it was going to leave the hotel assault exposed to the defensive fire from the roof. By diverting one of the Apaches to the cable car, Dent was halving his chances of taking out the triple-A crews. When he said as much, Dent's reply was matter of fact.

"Chance we'll have to take," he said grimly. And Jesse knew he meant "we." Dent Colby would be in the first chopper to touch down on the hotel roof, he knew.

"What we need from you is two things, Jesse," Dent continued. "We need some kind of signal if it looks like Kormann is making his move. We've got a camera trained on the hotel. Is there any way you could signal us? A flare, maybe? Anything?"

Jesse thought. There must be flares somewhere in the resort. Maybe Tina would know where he might find them. Then he'd have to get to a vantage point to . . . he stopped, as realization hit him.

"No need, Dent. If the balloon goes up, I can phone from the hotel. The switch is automatic, so I can dial out from any of the rooms. By then it won't matter if they realize I'm here."

"Okay. That's good. Now the other thing is Kormann's men. They won't know he's pulling out on them and if we hit the hotel, their first action is going to be to try to secure the hostages. If they can do that, we're checkmated. Is there anyway you and this Bowden girl can hold them off till the cavalry gets there?"

"I think she's got something like that in mind," Jesse told him. "She figures there's a way of blocking the doors to the gym for a short time. How long are you going to need?"

"Half an hour, tops," Colby told him. Jesse took a deep breath before he committed himself. He could be making the biggest mistake of his life, he thought.

"Okay. We'll figure a way. Oddly enough, you know," he added, "this guy Pell you're talking about is one of the people she's got helping her."

"I guess that's only fitting," Colby said with grim humor. "If he'd been more careful where he dropped his bombs, we wouldn't be in this damn fix."

"Let's just hope we're wrong about this," Jesse said. "Let's hope Friday comes and goes and I don't have any reason to call you."

"I'll keep hoping, Jesse," Dent told him. "But I'll have those choppers running and ready to go, just the same."

"I'll try to get back to you before then," Jesse told him. "See if Tina has any hint that something might be about to go down. In the meantime, I'll warn her she'd better start getting organized. Time I wasn't here, I guess," he added, glancing at the rapidly lowering sun. The chairs wouldn't be running much longer and if he missed the last one he'd have an uncomfortable ski down in the half light.

"Stay safe, Jesse," Dent told him. He could almost hear the crooked grin on the deputy sheriff's face in the reply.

"Exactly how d'you suggest I do that, Agent Colby?" asked Jesse. Then he broke the connection.

FORTY

The strain was beginning to get to Tina Bowden. Another mealtime had gone by without her having an opportunity to speak to Jesse. He'd been in the storeroom while she and Ralph had prepared dinner for the hostages and their captives, but once again, she'd had no excuse to go in there to speak to him.

As she left, carrying the heavy pot loaded with beef stew, she'd glanced back at the coffee mugs on the sink—the signal that he'd been waiting in the storeroom and wanted to make contact. As ever, she'd turned them right side up to let him know that she'd seen the signal.

The meals in the gym had settled into a routine by now. She set the stew pot up on a folding table that one of Kormann's men had brought in from the nearby conference room and the captives filed past, their bowls ready, while she served them. The guards, and Kormann and his Italian-looking companion, were served their separate meals by Ralph. Tonight, they were having veal chasseur, with a Neapolitan sauce and the inevitable French fries. Not for them the food for the common horde. It had occurred to Tina that this separate menu regime offered an opportunity. If she could only get her hands on some really virulent, totally tasteless poison, she could probably wipe out the entire force of guards—if she could convince Ralph to let her put poison in their meals.

And if she could persuade the guard to turn his back while she did so. And if there were some really virulent, unnoticeable poison available in the first place.

Good plan, too many ifs, she decided.

She started collecting the used dishes. Ralph had been delayed when he served Kormann. As ever, Kormann had chosen to give him a hard time over the French fries and the chef was still finishing his own meal. Tina was finished eating so she began clearing up—at least it gave her something to do and an excuse to move around the big room. Being near the exit to the gym office, she went to collect the dishes from Kormann, Pallisani and the three guards on duty there. She walked into the office as Pallisani and Kormann were in the middle of a conversation. They both looked up at her and then Pallisani, ignoring her, said, "Why move them? What's the point?"

She saw the fleeting expression of anger on Kormann's face, directed at Pallisani, and realized that the Italian had said something that she wasn't supposed to hear.

She tried to appear nonchalant and disinterested as she reached for the plates on the desk. The fact that Kormann had said nothing in reply to his subordinate's question strengthened her feeling that she had overheard something significant.

The silence in the room was becoming untenable. She looked at Kormann, forcing herself to look bored and ill-tempered, anything to prevent her eagerness to hear more being apparent.

"You finished?" she said, in as sullen a tone as she could muster. Kormann nodded curtly at her and she took the plates, managing to clash them together clumsily as she piled them. As ever, she saw the French fries on Kormann's plate were untouched. Then she turned and walked out of the room, back into the main section of the gym.

As she left, Kormann turned his anger on Pallisani. His voice was low but it cut like a whip and he lashed the other man with it.

"We'll move them because I say we'll move them. Got that quite clear?" he demanded. Pallisani nodded with ill grace. Kormann continued. "Because it will keep them off balance and because if they have been planning anything, if any of them have any idea of trying to pull some kind of stunt, we'll take them by surprise."

"Yeah, yeah, okay. I get it," the Italian said in a surly tone. Instantly, Kormann's temper went to white heat and he leaned across the desk, his eyes boring into Pallisani's.

"But Gino, you dumb fucking wop, we will not throw them off balance or take them by surprise if you blurt out the fact that we're going to move them in front of that girl. When she is in this room, you keep your fucking mouth shut. Understood?"

Pallisani's mouth set in a thin line. His resentment was plain to see but Kormann knew that he couldn't let this small challenge go unnoticed.

"Understood?" he repeated and finally Pallisani had to meet his gaze and nod briefly.

"Yeah. Okay."

Kormann held his eyes for few seconds, then allowed a more conciliatory tone to come into his voice.

"Besides, if we put them in the Atrium restaurant, the threat to them is heightened."

Even Pallisani should understand that, he thought. The Atrium restaurant was two stories high, with floor to ceiling glass on the wall facing the main mountain—the mountain where they had laid charges to bring down an avalanche. It wasn't as easy an area to secure as the gym but Kormann didn't plan to keep them there long. He'd planned all along to move them there in the last few hours, to make sure that there was no chance of survival in the avalanche.

What Pallisani didn't realize, of course, was how close to the end they were. He still thought the deadline was Sunday. He had no idea that he'd be in the Atrium restaurant with the hostages when Kormann brought a couple of million tons of snow, ice, rock and trees crashing through those big picture windows.

As she piled the dishes on the trestle table, Tina Bowden was frowning to herself. They're moving us. She thought. Why are they moving us?

The two men had been talking about moving something or somebody. The fact that Kormann had shown that brief flash of anger that it had been mentioned in front of her was a strong indication that they planned to move the hostages. Of course, they could have been discussing the guards on the roof or the Stinger missiles, or any of a dozen other details. But why shut up in front of her if that were the case? Why move us, she wondered? And where to?

Maybe Jesse would have some idea, she thought. She hoped she'd be able to make contact the following morning. A worm of doubt was eating at her as she realized that any move could jeopardize the plan she'd formed with Pell. A different location would mean a different set of circumstances. Here, she was confident that they could secure the heavy glass doors and hold the guards at bay—at least in the short term. They'd have her pistol, and the weapons they could take from the three guards, each of whom carried a sidearm in addition to the stubby Ingram machine carbines. That was a total of seven weapons. But her plan depended on the fact that there was only one entrance to the gym, and one that was easily defended. That was the reason Kormann had held them here in the first place, she reasoned.

But the advantages that the gym held for the guards would also apply to the hostages, as long as she could take out the three patrolling in the room. If they moved somewhere else Kormann might change the guard detail as well. She could be faced with half a dozen men patrolling and she knew if that happened, she'd be helpless. She might take out two men, with Pell handling the other. But any more than that and it was all over.

She shook her head hopelessly. She needed to know more. Once again, she found herself hoping that she'd get a chance to speak to Jesse the next morning. Friday, he'd said, was the day they might try something. And now that was only a day away.

FORTY-ONE

Jesse heard the outer door open and shut and saw the line of light go on under the bottom of the storeroom door. Almost immediately, the fluorescent lights in the storeroom came to life as well, triggered by the same switch. As the light flooded the room, he twisted the Maglite to off and slipped it into his pocket.

He'd been here since five in the morning, using the time to get something to eat other than the potato chips and chocolate bars that he'd been taking from minibars in the rooms. Not that the choice was too appetizing here, he thought moodily. He didn't dare risk cooking, or even heating any food, so his selection was limited to cheese, crackers and a large pressed ham that he'd found in one of the fridges.

He heard footsteps and voices in the outer room, then distinctly heard Tina call, "We're out of coffee."

He grinned slightly at that. One of the first things he'd done when he entered the kitchen, over two hours previously, had been to find the packs of coffee ready for the drip filter machine and take them all back into the storeroom.

In the kitchen, Ralph looked up with a frown as he heard Tina's statement.

"We can't be," he said in an annoyed tone. "I put three packs there yesterday."

Cursing him silently, realizing what had happened, Tina tried to look casual as she shrugged at him. "That was at lunch," she said. "I used them last night, remember?"

The guard had glanced up at the exchange. He was disinterested for the moment but that could change at any time. Ralph was moving to where the drip filter coffeemaker stood, looking increasingly annoyed. Disagree with a chef in a kitchen, no matter what the circumstances, Tina thought, and he'd start feeling put upon.

"It wasn't lunch," he said. "It was last night. Remember?"

Tina found herself reviewing her former plan. If she had a non-detectable, virulent poison, she'd put it in Ralph's meal along with the guards', she thought. She shrugged at him as he stared at the empty bench.

"Well if you did, where are they?" she asked, with undefeatable logic and he had no answer to that. The bench was bare. He went to speak but the guard, thoroughly pissed by now, interrupted.

"For Christ's sake, who cares? Just stop whining and get some fucking coffee on, okay?"

It had been a good move on Jesse's part, she thought. The one thing that the guard didn't want delayed was his coffee. She gave Ralph an "I told you so" look and shoved past him toward the storeroom door.

"Get me some extra eggs and butter while you're there," he said. She might have known that once he had lost one argument, he would try to reassert his authority in another area. Again, the guard contradicted him.

"Fuck that. Get the coffee going first. Then get the other shit," he ordered and Tina shrugged, trying to look annoyed. Inwardly, she felt a quick surge of satisfaction. She now had two reasons to go to the storeroom, on two different occasions.

She shoved the spring-loaded door open and went into the storeroom. Jesse was waiting for her by the cold cabinet, the three coffee packs already in his hand. She took them and, feeling ridiculously pleased to see him, stepped forward and hugged him briefly.

"Can't stay long," she said, "but I'll be back in a minute. I think they're planning to move us."

She saw the quick frown of concentration on his face as she said it.

"Any idea where to?" he asked, and she shook her head. She was backing toward the door and he followed her for a few paces. Incongruously, she noticed that he had cracker crumbs on his shirt.

"No idea. I'll be back in a few minutes," she said.

She emerged into the kitchen and heard the grunt of pained satisfaction from the guard.

"About fucking time. Now let's get that coffee."

It occurred to her to tell him that if he'd bothered to fill the coffeemaker with water while she'd been gone things would move a little quicker. But there was nothing to gain by antagonizing the man so she kept the thought to herself and got the coffee brewing.

He snatched the pot off the hot plate as soon as there was a cupful in it and poured it into a mug. The stream of brewing coffee fell, hissing and spitting, onto the hotplate. Quickly, she placed another pot under it and managed to wipe most of the spill with a sponge. The rest bubbled and burned off.

Ralph was glaring at her from his position at the big multiple cooktops.

"Eggs and butter," he demanded. "And get some white wine vinegar while you're at it." Kormann had demanded eggs Benedict this morning. The hostages would have more stew. She pretended to look annoyed at him.

"Okay, okay. Keep your shirt on. I'm going," she said. She knew there was no risk he'd go to fetch the items himself. He was reestablishing his territory.

As she entered the storeroom, Jesse already had the eggs, butter and vinegar ready for her.

"You can't let them move you," he said immediately. "Odds are, they're planning to put you in a more exposed position."

"That's what I figured," she replied. "Besides, God knows what the situation is going to be if they move us. They might increase the guards. They might put us in a spot out in the open."

Jesse hesitated. Then he seemed to come to a decision. "Colby figures they can be in here in ten to twenty minutes," he said. "I guess it's going to come down to this: if they look like they're moving you, we're going to have to trigger things ourselves."

She glanced at the door. She'd been in here too long already but they needed more time to discuss all this. She pointed to the back of the room.

"Get under cover," she said. Then, as he hesitated, she shoved him gently in the direction she wanted. "Go. I need to buy more time here."

Understanding, he moved to the back of the storeroom, squeezing himself into the narrow space between the refrigerator cabinet and the end wall. She could just see him, but she knew he was there. She decided the cover was good enough. She opened the pack of eggs and let them drop onto the floor, at the same time letting out a shriek. Then she dropped to her hands and knees and let the container of vinegar and the butter roll across the floor as well.

"Shit!" she yelled at the top of her voice. A few seconds later, the door flew open and the guard came in, in a half crouch, his Ingram ready. He relaxed as he saw her on her hands and knees, surrounded by the sticky ruin of a dozen eggs.

"I slipped," she said angrily and he grinned.

"I can see."

Dusting herself off, she stood up and retrieved the butter and vinegar. She gestured toward the eggs on the floor.

"I'll get some more of these. Then I'd better clean this up."

He nodded and waited while she went to the dairy cabinet for more eggs. Then he stood aside as she took them out to Ralph. The chef grinned unpleasantly at her as she set the items down beside him. He'd overheard the exchange.

"You better clean up your mess," he said and she nodded angrily.

"I'll get to it," she said. She didn't want to appear too eager to go back to the storeroom. "I'll get the stew heating first." It took her five minutes to open six cans and dump them into the stew pot. Ralph, as she'd hoped he would, couldn't help rubbing it in.

"Don't forget to clean up in there," he called, swirling vinegar into the pan of simmering water he had ready to poach the eggs.

"Okay!" she yelled at him. "I said I'd do it!" Out of the corner of her eye, she could see the guard enjoying the little spat between them. He had his coffee and was munching on a Danish that he'd warmed up in one of the microwaves. He could afford to enjoy himself. Looking sulky, she headed back to the storeroom, grabbing a sponge and a roll of paper towels as she went.

Inside, she found Jesse had already cleaned the mess up, a wad of sodden paper towel in his hand. She leaned against one of the shelves and let go a pent-up breath. He grinned at her. "You're doing a great job," he said and she shook her head wearily.

"Keep telling me. I feel like shit." She shook her head again. "You really think that professor guy is right, don't you?"

Jesse didn't hesitate this time. "We've got to assume he is. It's the most logical explanation. You're going to have to take those guards out and barricade yourself in the gym. We've got plenty of time. If this Emery guy is right, Colby says Kormann won't make his move until it's close to dark. We figure he's got a chopper coming in to pick him up and he won't want that to happen in daylight. So we're looking at some time late tomorrow afternoon."

"But he could move us any time before then," Tina protested and Jesse nodded.

"Yeah. I thought of that. If you get any idea he's going to do it, I guess you're just going to have to start the party and I'll call for help. Once I've called Dent, I'll try to divert some of their attention from you."

She considered his words. "I guess you're right," she said. "But Jesus, what if we're wrong on this?" They looked at each other for a long moment. Then Jesse shrugged. "It's the best we can do," he said. "Just be ready to move if there's any sign of a change in their routine. Colby can't do anything to start things moving," he told her. "The president has forbidden it. If push comes to shove, it's up to us."

"Christ, I hope we're good enough," she said.

FORTY-TWO

CANYON ROAD
WASATCH COUNTY
1104 HOURS, MOUNTAIN TIME
THURSDAY, DAY 6

Dent Colby put down the phone and glanced up at Maloney and Emery, his eyebrows raised in a question. He had just spent ten minutes on the phone with Roger, in which time the leader of the kidnappers had demonstrated a growing sense of paranoia, accusing Colby of trying to infiltrate men over the back ridges and of more overflights.

In addition, the kidnappers' leader had accused Colby of stalling over the release of the Irish prisoners. In spite of Colby's protests that things were moving as fast as possible, Roger had added a further demand. In the early nineties, a small group of terrorists—a surviving splinter group of the Bader Meinhoff movement, had been arrested after exploding a bomb in the main square of Kassel, killing half a dozen people and injuring over twenty others. The four surviving members of the group—three had been killed resisting arrest—were serving a life sentence in Nuremburg prison. Now Roger had demanded their release as well.

But it was his closing words that sent a shiver of premonition down Colby's spine. Before breaking the connection, Roger had told the FBI agent that he had moved the prisoners to a new location in the hotel.

"I've put them in the Atrium," he had yelled down the line. "You've got a plan of the building, I'm sure. Take a look at it and see what that means!"

Then he'd hung up.

"Well," Colby said to the two men, who'd overheard the entire conversation, "Do we buy it?"

Emery was shaking his head. "The bit about the Germans? I don't think so. Where does that come from? Nobody gives a damn about them—not even the other revolutionary groups. They were loose cannons and at the time the PLO, IRA and all the others were damned glad to have them out of the way. It's another feint."

Colby nodded. He was inclined to agree. The yelling, the paranoia, the accusations, they all seemed so much at odds with the behavior described by Jesse.

"What about his claim that we're sneaking men in there?" he asked.

Again Emery looked skeptical. "Could be a pointer to the fact that he's really planning something for tomorrow," he said. "If he gets us treading lightly, and being extra careful about spooking him, it could make life a lot easier for him if he's planning to get out of there."

"One thing's for sure," Maloney put in. "If he has moved them to the Atrium restaurant, the risk is heightened."

Kormann had been right. They did have a plan of the building and the marine colonel had been studying it. Now he pointed to the plan of the Atrium restaurant.

"To the left of the gym and facing the main mountain," he said. "And it's glass from floor to ceiling. If the mountain comes down on them in there, there's no chance anyone will get out alive."

Colby and Emery moved to the table where he'd spread the map. Dent frowned thoughtfully. "It's a big open area. Not the easiest place to keep prisoners confined. Jesse told us they have three men in the room with the prisoners at the moment. In a room like this, with possible exits everywhere, he'd need eight or nine to keep an eye on things. That doesn't leave too many to man the roof defenses. Plus they've all got to sleep sometime. He's stretching things pretty thin."

"Maybe that's why he's left it till now," Maloney replied. "If he's going to make his move tomorrow, it's not going to matter too much."

Dent looked at him for a moment, then at Emery. The professor's usually smooth-cheeked face was drawn from lack of sleep. Dent knew that he'd been awake into the small hours, tossing every possible combination of circumstances around, trying to find an answer to the enigma that faced them.

"It fits," Emery said simply.

Colby let go a long breath. "Okay, okay. I'll pass it on to Washington. But we all know what they're going to say: Sit tight and see what develops." He pressed the intercom buzzer for the sound tech who'd monitored the phone conversation. "Get that last tape to Washington for analysis," he said. All conversations with Roger were digitally recorded and then transmitted via satellite to Quantico, the FBI building. Trained vocal specialists analyzed the conversations, using computer models to assess Roger's speech patterns and mannerisms. The claim was that they could detect nuances of behavior—alterations in rhythm, pitch and tone—that could determine whether a subject was lying or acting a part. So far the results had been depressingly indeterminate. With Roger, they thought maybe he was. But then again, that meant they thought that maybe he wasn't.

Maybe, thought Dent Colby heavily, was the word of the week around here.

"Let's go check those choppers again," he said. At least that would be better than sitting around here waiting.

THE OVAL OFFICE
WASHINGTON D.C.
1600 HOURS, EASTERN TIME
THURSDAY, DAY 6

"Your man thinks he's lying," President Gorton said. It was somewhere between a question and a statement and Benjamin nodded.

"Yes, Mr. President, he does."

Gorton turned and walked to the big full-length windows, looking out to the Rose Garden. It was something he did, Benjamin realized, when he was considering a tough problem.

"Tell me about this Agent Colby," he said now, his back to the FBI director. Benjamin considered for a few seconds.

"He's a twenty-year man. Came up through the ranks. Former Olympic boxer and an impressive academic record. He's got a masters in psychology—did it when he was in his late thirties. He's one of our best negotiators—been involved in maybe half a dozen kidnap-hostage situations . . ."

The president turned from the window at that and Benjamin hesitated.

"What's his record like there?" he asked, and the director shrugged unhappily.

"About fifty-fifty, I guess. But that's pretty much par for the course in these things, Mr. President. You're dealing with unstable people who are operating under pressure. It's not the negotiator's fault if things don't work out."

"So let's analyze this," the president continued. "By your own say-so, you wouldn't expect a better than fifty-fifty result from one of your best men in a situation like this. Correct?"

Benjamin started to prevaricate, then realized that the assessment was a fair one. He nodded. "I guess so, Mr. President."

"And how about your voice experts? What can they tell us about this Kormann person?"

"I guess they're split fifty-fifty too. They can't determine whether he's genuine or not."

"That's what I figured. So maybe this Kormann guy is going to double cross all of us some time tomorrow and maybe he's not. Maybe he's willing to go ahead with the negotiations and take the money on Sunday. And maybe, if he does that, we'll get most of those hostages out of there alive. Maybe all of them."

It was a lot of maybes, Benjamin thought, unknowingly duplicating Colby's reaction. But he had to admit the president was presenting the situation fairly.

"On the other hand, if I send Maloney and his men in, we're relying on two people inside to keep the hostages safe. A security officer and this deputy sheriff from Colorado."

"Dent says this Parker guy is a cool head, sir. I trust Colby's opinion."

"Other people might disagree," the president said flatly and Benjamin looked at him in surprise. The president gestured to a manila folder on the desk. "I've had Tildeman's people finding out whatever they could about these two. The girl first. She has a good service record but she never rose higher than corporal in the Marines. She's intelligent, loyal, talented. She qualified as expert with both rifle and pistol, which might be handy if she had a gun. She's got a good record with the hotel company. All in all, a good choice as a security officer. But not exactly the background you'd want in someone making a decision of this magnitude."

There was more coming, Benjamin knew. "Now Parker. After all, he's the only one we've had contact with. We're gauging everything on his opinions, on his reading of the situation. Right?"

The president flicked open the folder and glanced down at it briefly, as if refreshing his memory on a couple of points.

"Here's what his lieutenant in Denver said about him: He was a good, solid type. Good cop. Dependable. Got on with the job and got it done. He was one of their top investigators, right up till a shootout went wrong and an officer was caught in the cross fire— Parker's partner, as a matter of fact. Some people even said that Parker himself shot him—accidentally, of course. Point is, Mr. Director, that Parker had something of a breakdown over it. Tossed in the job and went back home to become a ski bum. He's *part-time* deputy for the Routt County sheriff's department."

"Now, last year, part-time Deputy Parker was badly injured in a skiing accident and since then, folks around Routt County say he 'hasn't been quite himself.' He's fine physically but people seem to think he's got something on his mind. He acts a little weird. Nothing important, mind you. He's not racing around saying the Martians have landed. But he's not what you or I might call totally stable." The president paused and offered the file to Benjamin.

He took it and glanced quickly at the section Gorton had highlighted with a yellow marker. The comments from people who lived and worked with Jesse Parker were all there and he had to admit Gorton was right. You had to have some doubt over Jesse Parker's stability.

"Now I'm looking at a situation with a whole bunch of maybes and one guy who's been traumatized twice in the past five years. My decision is, we sit tight and continue to wait."

Benjamin said nothing while the president moved to the far side of the desk and sat down in his high-backed leather chair. "That's my decision, Director Benjamin. Now you tell me, in all honesty, would you do it any different in my place?"

You didn't get to be director of the FBI without being a keen student of human behavior and Benjamin looked up at the president now. Interesting, he thought. Gorton had announced his decision before asking for Benjamin's opinion. It was a direct reversal of the way the president usually behaved.

Maybe he'd been right and this crisis was the catalyst that would help Gorton grow into the job. In the yin and yang of life, perhaps this situation, as ugly as its outcome might be, would be instrumental in providing the country with a president who could be forceful and decisive. He smiled sadly at the president, who was still waiting for an answer.

"No, Mr. President," he said. "I wouldn't do it any different."

FORTY-THREE

It was cold and uncomfortable on the fire stairs and Jesse shifted his position again on the unyielding concrete. He'd spent the night here, deciding that Kormann could try to move the prisoners at any time. If that happened, Tina would be forced to put her plan into action and he'd better be around to hear it happen. From the fifth floor, all hell could break out down in the gym and he'd never hear a thing, so he'd moved to the landing where he now sat uncomfortably, half a flight above the fire door that led to the floor where the gym was located.

He'd brought a blanket from the room but after half an hour sitting on the cold concrete in the unheated stairwell, he'd begun to wish he'd brought two or three. The cold ate into him, seeming to go bone deep and numbing his feet and hands from the inside out. He was cramped and stiff after the first hour. By now, after twelve hours, he was totally miserable.

And totally bored.

Yet, at the same time, there was a hard lump of apprehension in the pit of his stomach. He was exposed here, as he hadn't been at any stage so far. Kormann and his men were only a matter of yards away and at any moment one of them could decide to walk into the stairwell and check it, or maybe take a shortcut between floors. It wasn't likely, he knew. If he were one of the guards and had to move to another floor, he'd use the elevators. There was no reason not to, particularly when you considered that with less than twenty people moving around the hotel at any given time, the elevators were easily able to cope with demand.

Still, it was possible that someone could come in here and discover him. For that reason, he'd had to keep his equipment to a minimum. If he heard or saw that door beginning to open, he had to be able to gather everything immediately and head upstairs in a hurry, keeping out of sight. He'd chosen the upstairs landing deliberately. If someone were going to use the stairs, odds were best that he'd be going down. The only reason the guards had to go up was to head for the roof and that was fifteen floors away. If he was wrong about it, he'd just have to get well ahead of whoever was coming upstairs, then use Tina's keycard to open the door into one of the higher floors.

The potential need for silence was another source of discomfort. He'd left his Timberlands off and was wearing socks only and now his feet felt like blocks of ice. As a member of the Denver PD, Jesse had spent many hours on stakeout, cold, bored and uncomfortable. And around Steamboat Springs, he'd done his share of hunting, waiting in hiding for his quarry to come first into sight and then into range. So he was used to the discomfort, the cold and the utter boredom of it all. But being used to something and enjoying it were two different items altogether, he thought. In fact, the more time he spent in situations like this one, the less he liked it.

He wished now that he'd thought to bring one of the pillows from Tina's room. The concrete was getting harder and harder with each passing minute. He wriggled his butt for what must have been the thousandth time, finding a few seconds of relief from the new position before the hard concrete asserted itself once more. He yawned. He'd made a pot of coffee the night before and emptied it into a used soft drink bottle—a systematic search of Bowden's room and the two adjoining ones had failed to turn up any sign of an insulated container. There was a grainy, cold mouthful left in the bottle and he swigged it morosely, hoping the caffeine hit would do something to revive his spirits. He yawned again. Apparently not, he thought.

Such was the dulled state of his reactions that the fire door was halfway open before he registered the fact that someone was coming through it.

It was too late to run now. Any movement would be seen. Cursing himself for letting the conditions relax his attention, Jesse quickly stood and tossed the blanket to one side, out of the man's line of sight, and began walking down the half flight of stairs toward the door. The man who entered the stairway now was a tall, well-muscled African-American. Jesse had a second to wish that he'd been a small, thin Italian-American but now the man was looking up at him in surprise. He hadn't expected to see anyone else on the stairs. Before he could say anything, Jesse spoke.

"Where the hell have you been? Have you got the seeker unit?" He forced himself to sound exasperated, like a man who has been looking all over for the person he's just confronted. Carter, the African-American, hesitated. Jesse was dressed in jeans and a parka, much the same sort of clothes that the guards wore. That, and his words, created a moment of doubt in Carter's mind. There were nearly twenty men working for Kormann and he only knew maybe five of them—and another eight or nine by sight.

"Seeker unit?" he repeated now, wondering what the hell Jesse was talking about.

"Goddamn it! I told Kormann that one of the Stinger seeker units was acting up. He was sending a replacement twenty minutes ago." The exasperation was plain in his voice now. That, and the mention of Kormann's name, served to allay any possible suspicion on Carter's part. He shrugged. He knew nothing about any seeker unit. He'd been heading down to the ground floor level to check the layout of the Atrium restaurant. It was only two floors down and he'd decided it was quicker to use the stairs.

"Sorry, buddy," he said. "I don't know anything about it." He stood aside, assuming that the man wanted to go through the fire door into the hotel proper. Then, as Jesse hesitated, Carter realized that he had subconsciously registered something unusual about the man before him. Now it hit his conscious awareness.

"Where are your shoes?" he said, realizing in the same instant that he had let the man get too close to him. He tried to back up but the edge of the half-open door stopped him and he glanced around involuntarily to see what the obstruction was and that was when Jesse hit him.

It was a hard, straight left with all Jesse's body weight behind it and it landed with crunching force on Carter's nose. Tears sprang into his eyes in an unavoidable reflex as the bone and cartilage gave way. He reeled away from the door, hitting the concrete wall of the stairwell, blinded by the tears, clutching the air in front of him as Jesse grabbed desperately at his throat to stop him calling out. Carter felt his head bounce off the concrete as Jesse jerked him backward and forward, keeping him off balance, slamming his head repeatedly against the wall.

Jesse fought grimly to maintain his advantage. The man was bigger than he was and if he let him recover from the first attack, he would inevitably get the upper hand. In addition, Jesse had to keep him silent, while the other man had no such problems. He could yell the house down for help if he got any respite. At the moment, his entire being was focused on survival. Jesse slammed the man's head against the wall again, then felt hands gripping at the collar of his parka. The .45 was in the parka pocket and he had no chance to reach for it. Besides, a shot would be heard all over the second floor and he couldn't afford that. He jerked the man forward and back, hitting the wall again. He could see the eyes beginning to lose focus. Carter fought for his life, but his knees were buckling and his consciousness was beginning to waver.

Carter felt a sudden surge of fear as the face in front of him began to blur and he knew he was losing the fight. The fear turned to desperation and he rolled sideways, still gripping the other man's collar, taking him with him as they plunged down the half flight of stairs, spinning so as to bring Jesse underneath as they hit the hard concrete.

They rolled in a tangle of arms and legs down the stairs, each losing his grip on the other, coming to rest side by side on the landing below. Jesse gasped for breath. His ribs had taken the force of the stairs, with Carter's weight on top of him in the first fall, and he could barely breathe. The other man was in worse condition, however. He was dazed. He'd cracked his head against the iron pipe stair railing as they fell and rolled and now he lay with his head through the rail, supported by the lower rung.

Blinded and disoriented, Carter groped in his belt holster for the Beretta Model 92 that he kept there, clawing it free of the jacket that was in his way. Dimly, he was aware that his assailant was regaining his feet, just a yard or so away, and he knew if he didn't get the pistol out in time he was finished. He felt a wave of relief as the pistol came free and he pointed it vaguely at the fuzzy shape near him and pulled the trigger.

Nothing.

The Beretta was fitted with a double-action trigger. Once a round was chambered, all you needed to do was pull on that trigger to cock the hammer and get the first round away—as long as you also released the safety at the top left of the grip. Dazed and disoriented, Carter had forgotten that vital step. Now as his thumb sought the little grooved lever, Jesse had come to his knees beside him.

Carter sprawled across the stairwell, his neck supported by the iron railing, his throat and chin exposed. Jesse heard the small metallic click as the safety on the Beretta released and knew he had maybe two seconds to act.

One was enough. He struck forward with the heel of his right hand, thrusting at the raised chin before him, fingers spread to stiffen the impact. His hand caught the exposed chin and jolted Carter's head violently back over the railing. His neck, trapped as it was, couldn't take the sudden impact and snapped like a twig.

As he died, his right hand clenched in a reflex movement and the Beretta went off, the report loud and ringing in the concrete walls of the stairwell.

"Shit!" Jesse exclaimed, ducking for cover as the 9 millimeter round cannoned off the concrete walls. The shot had been deafening in the confined, echoing space. It had to have been heard outside the stairwell. He staggered upright, shaking his head. The adrenaline was still pumping, for the moment masking the pain of the bruises and contusions he'd suffered as they rolled down the stairwell. He figured he had a couple of minutes to get the hell out of here, and the way was down. His ski boots and skis were in the lower ground floor ski room. He'd use the time he had to get to them, then get the hell out and head for the chairlift.

There was no time to recover his shoes and anyway, he realized, he wouldn't be needing them. He pounded silently down the concrete stairs for the lower level. Behind him, he thought he heard muffled shouting. He was three flights down when he heard the door into the stairwell open, back on the second floor. Then the shouting was a lot less muffled as whoever it was saw the sprawled body on the landing. A voice echoed down the stairwell to him.

"It's Carter! He's dead!"

He kept going, unaware of the fact that his shoes, and the blanket he had been using, had brought him precious extra minutes.

Seeing them on the stairs above the body, the man who found Carter naturally assumed that his attacker had gone that way, abandoning shoes and blanket as he went. He started up in pursuit, then hesitated. His reaction had been an instinctive one, now reason came into play. Why would you attack a man, then abandon your shoes and a blanket as you ran away, he wondered. He stopped, uncertainly. From several floors down, he heard a door open, then bang shut. He grabbed the radio from his belt and thumbed the talk button.

FORTY-FOUR

"What the fuck was that?" Kormann sat bolt upright in his chair at the sound.

Pallisani, relaxing on the couch opposite, swung upright at the sound too. Both men looked at each other. Kormann was already thumbing the talk button on his radio, while he unholstered his own Beretta.

"All stations, report your status," he said. There was no need to identify himself. They knew his voice.

"Roof. Nine men," came the laconic reply from Mosby, in charge on the roof. They'd heard no shot fired and he assumed it was a routine check.

"Gym. Three men." That was the patrol leader in the room with the hostages. Kormann added quickly. Twelve men. Plus him and Pallisani made fourteen. Three more in the ante room outside the gymnasium, where he could see them. One of them raised his eyebrows interrogatively. He was looking around as well. He'd heard the shot too. Seventeen men reporting.

"Harrison, ground floor, patrolling." Eighteen.

"Alston, second floor, patrolling." Nineteen. "Thought I heard something from the stairwell," the last voice added. Nineteen accounted for, thought Kormann. That left one . . . he thought, picturing the faces of the men in the different positions who had reported in.

"Where's Carter?" he asked suddenly. Pallisani replied, easing the slide on his own Beretta to make sure there was a round chambered.

"He went down to the ground floor to check out the Atrium," he replied. Kormann thumbed the talk button again.

"Carter, report in . . . Carter . . ." He waited but there was no sound other than the hiss of the carrier wave. Then they heard a click as someone depressed his talk button, and Alston's excited voice, shouting down the radio link.

"It's Carter! He's dead!"

Kormann jerked his head to Pallisani. "Let's go," he said. Outside, the three men who had been relaxing in the ante room were waiting for them, Ingrams ready slung. The three on patrol in the gym would stay where they were, Kormann knew, and he led the way to the stairwell.

He hit the radio again. "All stations, we've had a shot fired and Carter is dead. Roof, you got any sign of inbound traffic?"

There was a brief pause as the sentries above scanned the horizon with a deal more care than they had been doing. Then the reply:

"Negative."

"Okay. Keep your eyes open. Anybody off-duty up there, give them a pair of binoculars and get 'em on watch. This could be the start of something. Or it could be an accident. Let's assume it's the first, okay?"

He heard a double-click as someone acknowledged—he assumed it was Mosby. Then they had reached the stairwell and Alston was waiting for them.

"His neck's broken," he said simply and they crowded into the stairwell, standing over the sprawled body that hung over the rail.

"He wasn't shot?" Kormann asked quickly, moving down the stairs to kneel beside the body, checking to see if there was any sign of a gunshot wound.

"No. His neck's broken. The shot was from his gun."

The Beretta was still clasped loosely in Carter's dead hand. Kormann took it, prizing the fingers apart, and raised it to his nostrils. There was the distinct smell of burnt powder around the ejection port. A gleam of brass caught his eye and he saw the ejected shell case lying on the next half flight of stairs. He touched the back of

Carter's head and his hand came away sticky with blood. He looked up at Pallisani, who indicated the wall by the door, where he could see unmistakable smears of blood.

"I found these on the stairs up here," said Alston, and showed the way to where a blanket, a pair of battered Timberland moccasins and an empty soft drink bottle were lying on the stairs. Kormann surveyed them, a worried frown on his face. Who the hell had been sitting out here on the stairs, he asked himself. He sniffed the neck of the bottle and smelled coffee grounds. Someone had been keeping watch out here, he realized.

"Then I heard a door slam down there," Alston continued, pointing down the stairwell. Kormann rounded on him instantly, fury in his eyes.

"You dumb fuck! Why the hell didn't you mention that before?" he raged. Alston's mouth worked silently. He knew what Kormann could do in one of these rages. He was saved by the radio.

"Kormann, this is Mosby. We've got a guy just broke cover from the hotel. He's heading across the open space!"

"Stop him!" Kormann yelled into the radio. Then, turning to Pallisani and the three men who had accompanied him from the office, he pointed down the stairwell. "Get after him!"

Pallisani might not have been one of the world's great thinkers, but he was ideal in a situation like this. He plunged down the stairwell, the three men following him, their feet clattering and echoing from the bare walls. Kormann turned back to Alston. The man was cowering away from him, keeping as much distance between them as he could manage. Kormann took a pace toward him. He had no idea what he was going to do but he wanted to smash his fist into the stupid face before him. Then his priorities changed in an instant as he heard shots from the gymnasium.

One thing that Tina Bowden had learned in her time in the Marines was the value of surprise. And diversion. If you could distract an enemy, then hit him when he least expected it, where he least expected it, you stood a good chance of coming out on top, even if the odds seemed to be stacked against you.

She'd spent the last few days trying to figure a way to take the guards by surprise, a way to distract them so as to give herself a few invaluable extra seconds of time. Now she realized she didn't have to. It had been presented to her on a platter. She had no idea what had caused Kormann, Pallisani and the three men in the ante room to light out the way they did. Here in the gym, with the heavy glass doors shut, the gunshot had been all but inaudible. Had she been listening for it, she might have heard a dull, muffled thud. But the sounds of the people around her, coughing, talking or just moving restlessly where they sat, had effectively covered the sound.

All she knew was that the men outside had gone, leaving only the three inside guards. She might never again have a chance as good as this one, she realized, and as she did so, she acted upon the thought. She glanced around, looking to see where the guards were, catching Nate Pell's eye and nodding surreptitiously. The ex-fighter-pilot had recognized the potential of the situation as well. He returned the nod, looking sideways to where the third guard was only a few yards away, his back turned.

Tina took a deep breath, slid her hand under the bedroll and closed it over the hard grips of the Smith and Wesson. The furthest of the two guards was looking in her direction, although not directly at her. He'd be the one she'd take first, she thought. She was surprised to notice how calmly her mind was working, how smoothly her body was following its directions. Sitting with her knees drawn up under her, she raised the gun in a two-handed grip, thumbing back the hammer as it came up, and sighted with both eyes open, down the barrel, centering her sight line on the man's chest. She heard an indrawn breath and an exclamation of surprise from someone nearby as they saw the gun in her hands. The guard heard the sound too and was looking around to see what had caused it. But she hadn't raised herself above the mass of prisoners and he didn't register the gun aiming at him until it was too late. She saw the final moment of realization on his face as she squeezed the trigger, then fired a second shot double action.

Both slugs hammered into the man's chest cavity and he went down like a stone. Now she rose to her knees. People were screaming all around her and things were moving in slow motion as she swung the gun smoothly through an eighty degree arc to the second guard. He'd seen her all right and he was fumbling with the Ingram that was slung over his shoulder. But the sling had tangled and he wasted precious seconds clearing it. She fired, double action again, to get a shot away quickly, then thumbed back the hammer for a second, more deliberate shot.

The first bullet went low and right and hit him in the left hip, spinning him around and dropping him to his knees. He was numb from the waist down on one side of his body and the Ingram was pointing at the floor as he struggled against the shock of the impact. The bullet, with a magnum load behind it, had smashed into the large bones of his hip, causing massive trauma. Instead of passing through the soft tissue of the body, it had transmitted the full force of the bullet to hard, resisting bone, jarring, smashing and shocking its way through. It wasn't a killing shot but it was a completely disabling one. As he fought to retain consciousness, Tina's second shot took him in the chest cavity and everything went black.

There was panic in the room and now Tina came to her feet, turning to face the direction where the third guard had been, fully expecting a burst of automatic fire to tear into her. Instead, she saw the grinning face of Nate Pell, holding an Ingram in one hand and a small dumbbell in the other. As Tina had fired her first two shots, the guard close by him had turned toward the noise. Pell and two of his companions had leapt upon the man, using the small, heavy exercise weight as a bludgeon. He was down before Tina fired her third shot. Senator Carling watched in fascination as Pell and Carl Aldiss, the Sperry Rand radar expert, hurried to secure the unconscious man's guns. Pell took the 9 millimeter automatic, while Aldiss was running his hands over the Ingram with an appearance of utter familiarity.

"You know what you're doing there, Carl?" said the senator. Aldiss smiled at him calmly. Pell and he were good friends and the pilot had taken him into his confidence the day before.

"I don't spend all my time in dark rooms with a CRT, Senator," he said. As a matter of fact, Aldiss was a keen hunter and an expert shot, not that you'd know it from his mild, bespectacled, studious appearance. But Pell knew it. That was why he had instantly turned the Ingram over to him.

As the two men, accompanied by Bob Soropoulos from Rockair, made their way through the confused crowd of hostages to where Tina stood, the security officer was doing her best to calm the panicky hostages around her.

"Quiet, people! Please! Quiet!" she glanced around, caught Ben Markus's eye. The manager was a quick thinker and he could be depended upon to stay calm in a crisis. "Ben, give me hand barricading this door, will you?"

She began dragging one of the heavy weight benches toward the door, to block its opening. Markus lent a hand and snapped at several of the other hostages to join in. Suddenly the dam of uncertainty broke and there were willing hands on all sides as people realized this was their chance. Now they had a tangle of weight benches and Nautilus machines stacked in the doorway and Tina waved the other people back out of a direct line.

"Get back along that wall," she yelled, gesturing with the gun to back up her orders. Gradually, the milling crowd fell away, as Pell and his two companions began stacking heavy punching bags against the barricade. Tina caught the senator's eye and moved toward him. "Senator Carling, I'm Tina Bowden, security officer for Canyon. Could you please take charge of the people back there while we secure the room, sir? Just get them to move as far back into this blind corner as they can, and stay there. Maybe they could stack more of the machines there as cover."

Carling nodded. He was still a little taken aback to find that the attractive girl, whom he'd thought of as a receptionist, had taken out two of the terrorists within the space of five seconds and four carefully aimed shots. But he moved to carry out her suggestion, his air of authority invaluable in calming the excited hostages and bringing some semblance of order to things.

Ben Markus finished wedging the stainless steel bar from a barbell set between the two handles of the doors, then turned back to survey the result.

"They won't come through there in a hurry," he said, and Tina nodded grimly.

"That's the general idea. With any luck, there's a rescue assault on the way now. All we have to do is hold them off for a few minutes." Jesse had told her half an hour but she thought it sounded better her way. Besides, now they were committed. Markus looked worried momentarily.

"What if they blow the charges on the mountain?" he said.

Tina laughed harshly. "With them still here?" she asked. "Let me ask you, Ben, do these guys strike you as suicidal fanatics?"

Markus hesitated, thinking it through. Then his expression hardened as he saw the reason in her words. "No. As a matter of fact, they don't," he replied. Then, in a brisker, more decisive tone, "So what can I do to help?"

Tina held out one of the automatic pistols they'd taken from the guards. "Give us a hand holding the line. Can you use one of these?"

He took the big pistol, turning it over in his hands. "Not very well," he admitted, "but I'll hang onto it until you can find someone better."

Tina flashed him a smile and turned to the group of hostages huddled back away from the doorway. She held up the third pistol and one of the Ingrams and called out:

"Anyone here know how to use one of these?"

To her surprise, the first person to step forward was Ralph, the chef. "Don't know about the machine gun," he said, "but I've fired a pistol some." She nodded and handed him the Beretta, watching as he expertly dropped the magazine out of the butt, then eased the slide to make sure there was no round chambered. He slapped the magazine back in, worked the action and then set the safety.

"I guess you have at that," she said, and he looked up at her, his eyes angry.

"Let that son-of-a-bitch stick his head around that door," he said. "I'll give him fucking French fries."

FORTY-FIVE

Jesse was halfway across the cleared space to the chairlift building
when he heard the first rattle of automatic fire from above and
behind him. The snow to his left came alive with fountaining spurts
as the bullets whipped home—not in a straight line, the way they
do in the movies, when a special-effects man pumps a blast of air
down a perforated hose, but in a rough, elliptically shaped killing
field created by the movement of the Ingram's barrel as it recoiled.

He cursed to himself as he redoubled his efforts, poling more
savagely to gain a little extra speed. This was all going to hell in a
handbasket, he thought. He hadn't had time to warn Dent Colby
that the shooting had started and now there was no way he could
phone the FBI agent until he reached the top of the mountain.

More shots from above him and more bullets zipped into the
snow. But visibility was poor in the heavy falling snow and the range
from eight stones up was a little too much for the short-barreled
Ingrams. The second burst went even wider.

He'd heard the shouting behind him as the body of the man he'd
killed had been discovered and he knew his only chance was to make
it to the chairlift. His skis and boots were in the ski room and he'd
slammed in there, dragging the boots on in a fever of panic. Of
course, that had been a mistake. His foot jammed in one of the
boots, refusing to go in properly as a clip caught and the boot
wouldn't open fully. Desperately he thrust at it, his efforts only serving to jam the clip even tighter. In the end, he had to stop, calm
down, force the clip open, back off and try again, slowly. When he
did it that way, his foot slid easily into the boot but it had all cost

him precious minutes. Learning from his mistake, he donned the other boot carefully and without haste, then tossed his skis flat on the snow and stepped into the bindings.

There was no time to fasten the boot clips and he skied with his boots gaping open. That was no real problem as the ground was even and there was barely any slope. He skated as fast as he could, waiting for the inevitable moment of discovery. Now he was barely twenty yards from the chairlift terminal and there were at least three automatic weapons firing at him from the roof.

He skied under the overhanging eaves of the terminal and halted for a moment, breathing heavily from a mixture of fear and exertion. The men on the roof couldn't see him now and he paused to get his breath. It was a mistake. A volley of shots from ground level spanged into the metal stanchions supporting the terminal roof and he looked back to four men running from the hotel toward him.

"Shit!" he muttered and skied straight to the chair line, dropping awkwardly into a chair just as it made the connection to the main cable and swooped up the mountain. Behind him he heard more shouting, and a bullet screeched off the metal pylon that supported the chairlift cable. He squirmed around in the chair and saw the four men behind him, waiting to load on one of the chairs. Unused to the mechanism, they selected one of the slow-moving chairs on the disconnect bull wheel. Then, as the line of chairs leveled out, they were blocked from his sight.

He figured they were maybe fifteen chairs behind him and that was too damn close for comfort. He bent down and began fastening the clips on his boots. He might manage the level ground between the hotel and the chairlift without having them fastened, but sidestepping up through the thick ungroomed snow at the top of the chairlift would be another matter altogether—with the boots unfastened, he'd probably step clear out of them. He remembered that the men had been running across the clear ground and that meant they had no skis. That should hold them up when they hit the thick, thigh-deep snow at the top of the chair, he thought grimly. He wondered if it would be a big enough delay.

Knowing it was a futile gesture, he checked the cell phone but there was no signal, only the inevitable message that the phone was "searching." He put the phone away in his parka pocket, tapping his other pocket to make sure the Colt was still there.

CANYON LODGE
WASATCH COUNTY
1121 HOURS, MOUNTAIN TIME
FRIDAY, DAY 7

This was all starting to come badly unraveled, thought Kormann, as he led the way back toward the gym. He thumbed the talk button once more and called:

"Gymnasium, report."

He paused, waiting to hear a reply but none came. Cursing, he hit transmit again.

"Mosby, did you get that guy?"

"Negative. Pallisani and three of the others are still after him. He got on the chairlift and they followed."

Kormann slammed his fist against the wall in anger. Once the intruder had reached the chairlift, Pallisani should have given the chase away. He was no good to Kormann halfway up the mountain and he'd reduced his available forces seriously—particularly now that the three men in the gymnasium seemed to have been disabled. He transmitted again.

"Pallisani. Come in."

There was a pause, then Pallisani's voice came back at him.

"Pallisani. We're on the chairlift behind this guy."

"Get your asses back down here! I need you. All hell is breaking loose here."

"We'll ride the chair around, Kormann," Pallisani told him confidently. "I've checked a trail map and there are only two ways down from the top of this chair. They both go right under the chair line, so whichever way he goes, we'll have a close range shot at him."

Which was a logical mistake to make. Everyone knew you went

up a chairlift in order to ski down again. Pallisani assumed that the man he was chasing had boarded the chair in a reflex attempt to escape—in other words, it was the quickest available escape route. When he came off the chair, he'd be faced with two trails down and they both ran close to the lift line for the first couple of hundred yards—one on either side. After that, they split off in half-a-dozen different directions. But he could see that when Jesse started down, he'd have to stay close to the chairlift long enough for them to nail him.

It never occurred to him that Jesse was planning to keep going uphill when he left the chair.

"Okay," Kormann said, accepting the inevitable. "Don't waste any more time on him. We've got problems here . . . oh shit."

The last two words came out involuntarily as he reached the ante room to the gym. The two heavy glass doors were piled high on the other side with leather and chrome gym equipment—weight benches, treadmills and heavy bags. Somehow the hostages had overpowered the guards and barricaded themselves inside the gym. Which meant they had the guards' guns. Which meant . . .

He flung himself sideways just in time, as three heavy reports thumped out from the doorway, the slugs slamming into the concrete wall behind him. Alston dived for cover in the opposite direction. More from frustration than anything else, Kormann leveled his Beretta and let go four shots at the door. The bullets starred the heavy shatterproof glass but didn't penetrate. Now he could make out a dim shape crouched among the jumble of equipment that barricaded the doorway. The two doors left a gap of maybe half an inch where they met and the man on the other side had placed the muzzle of his gun right into that gap in order to get off his shots. It would take an incredibly lucky shot from this side to penetrate the gap.

"Mosby," he said into the radio. "I need more men down here."

"Are you kidding, Kormann?" said the incredulous voice. "We need them here in case there's an attack."

"There's already an attack and it's down here! The hostages have taken over the gym and they've got guns. There's just me and

Alston to keep them in at the moment. If they realize they've got us outnumbered and out-gunned, they might just decide to break out. Now get me three men down here right now!"

There was a pause as his words sank in. The man in charge on the roof assessed his needs, worked out which three men he could best spare, and replied:

"They're on their way."

"Make it fast," Kormann said. He hit the radio again and contacted Harrison, still patrolling the first floor, ordering him to come to the gym. Alston, he noticed, had taken cover behind an angle of the wall opposite the entrance to the ante room. From there, he could see the door leading into the gym and he had the Ingram ready, covering it. Now that he considered the position, Kormann realized there was little chance of the captives breaking out. They had no way of knowing how shorthanded he was. Besides, if they were planning on escaping from the gym, they would have hardly piled all that crap in front of the door in the first place. He relaxed a little, realizing he had time to think.

The elevator doors sighed open and the three men from the roof arrived to join them. Figuring he now had more than enough bodies to keep the situation under control, he sent one of the men back to the roof and positioned the other two to support Alston. The third man departed, muttering inaudibly for the most part, although Kormann made out the words "make up his fucking mind" quite clearly. He needed time and space to think, so, denied access to the gymnasium office, he took over one of the rooms down the corridor, using a master key he had taken from Ben Markus.

It might still be possible to salvage something out of this mess, he thought. After all, he was being paid five million dollars to pull this off. Half the money was already in a Swiss account and the other half would go in when word reached Estevez that the hostages were dead. It would mean bringing the timetable forward by a few hours but it might just work out. It was just as well Pallisani was stuck on the chairlift, he thought. He didn't want the ex-mafioso privy to the conversation he was about to have.

He glanced over his shoulder to make sure none of his men was within earshot, then lifted the phone from its cradle and pressed nine. There was slight delay and he heard the low warble that told him he had an outside line. Quickly, he punched in the numbers for a cell phone. A voice answered on the first ring.

"Hello."

"It's me," he said quickly. There was no need to identify himself any further. Nobody else had the number to call. "In twenty, okay?"

"I thought—" the voice began, sounding concerned. They weren't supposed to be doing this in daylight. Kormann cut him off quickly.

"Don't argue. In twenty." He waited, willing the other man to acknowledge and get off the line. He was sure the calls on this line would be being monitored by the FBI but he figured they'd have little idea what the cryptic message "twenty" would mean. They might suspect something but they couldn't be sure. He had no idea that his previous call to the same number had been overheard and passed on to the agent-in-charge at Canyon Road.

"Okay. Understood," the pilot said and broke the connection. Kormann replaced the phone in its cradle and smiled to himself. Maybe things were working out after all, he thought. His client wanted the senator dead. That was what this had all been about, right from the get-go. Maybe he wanted it to appear as a tragic accident in the course of a terrorist situation, hiding one murder among many. Hiding one tree in a forest.

This wasn't exactly the way Kormann had planned things. But the main point was, he could still fulfill the contract and get himself out of here.

Twenty minutes gave him time, he thought. It was ten minutes to the top by the cable car. From there, if he detonated the charges set in the mountain, the resulting confusion would give the chopper an opportunity to come in low over the back ridges and get him out. There was even a chance they wouldn't be seen: the helicopter was painted all white and the pilot was an expert in following the terrain and using the mountains and ridges to mask any radar in the area. They'd practiced the approach to the cable car station on a remote mountain in Wyoming several weeks before, finding a series of mountains, ridges and valleys that pretty well matched the situation here. After four days' practice, the pilot had managed to fly the approach with only one brief, two-second appearance on a radar screen. Chances were good that in the confusion caused by the mountain coming down, even that would be missed.

He wished he'd had the time to get the captives into the Atrium restaurant, where the two-story-high glass walls would have exposed them more fully. Still, he figured, the calculations were that the hotel would be buried up to the fourth floor level, and there were sufficient window openings in the gymnasium to ensure that the rock, snow and ice would smash its way in, burying anyone inside. He smiled grimly. The hostages' action in barricading the doors only served to contain them in the danger area. His only possible problem was how to keep his men occupied while he made it to the cable car.

While he was thinking about it, the problem solved itself. One of the men from the roof came into the room, hesitating at the door until Kormann saw him and gestured him in.

"I've been thinking," he said. "We need to get that door open if we're going to get them out of there."

Kormann nodded agreement. "The glass is pretty well bullet-proof, and unless you want to be shot to pieces while you're moving all that furniture they've piled against it, I don't see how you plan to accomplish it," he said. The man waited till he'd finished, as if he'd foreseen the answer. Then he said simply:

"Why not use one of the Stingers?"

Kormann looked at him in admiration. It was a brilliant piece of lateral thinking.

"I can bypass the heat seeker so that it'll fire on command," the man added. Kormann nodded. He knew that under normal conditions, the Stinger needed to have its infrared seeker head locked onto a heat-emitting target before the launcher would fire.

He had no idea if the explosive warhead on the Stinger would arm in the short distance it took to reach the glass doors. But the effect of a rocket-powered missile on the double doors and the hastily erected barricade behind it wasn't hard to imagine. The damn thing would probably tear around and around the room, ripping the place to shreds. In addition, it would keep the men here occupied while he made a break for it.

"Do it," he said, rising from the chair beside the phone. "I'm going to the lobby to make a call to that FBI guy—keep them off our backs." He saw the man's eyes drop to the phone on the bedside table. "This one's screwed," he added in explanation. "I can't get a line on it."

The man nodded. There was no reason why he should question the statement.

"One thing," he said. "Mosby won't like me taking one of the missiles. He looks after them like he paid for them."

Mosby would complain, of course, because the Stingers were intended for anti-aircraft defense. But they had fifteen of them and they could spare one. Not that it mattered if they couldn't, Kormann thought grimly.

"I'll radio him," he said, reaching for the walkie-talkie at his belt. "You get going."

FORTY-SIX

Agent Colby!" The door to the communications van flew open, slamming back against the aluminium side of the vehicle and the technician came out running, yelling for Dent.

The agent-in-charge was making a last-minute check of the line of choppers, ready and laden with grim-faced armed men. The engines were spooled up and turning over, the choppers ready to launch immediately. At the head of the line were the two angular Apache attack birds, hung all over with weaponry. Maloney was in the lead Blackhawk troop carrier, while three other Blackhawks carried the rest of his assault team. Dent would ride in the second of the troop carriers. The idling turbojets masked the frantic calls from the communications tech and it was Cale Lawson who saw him running down the line of helicopters parked along the road.

"Looks like someone wants your attention," he said, touching Dent's arm. Colby turned as the technician pounded up to him, breathless in the thin, cold mountain air.

"Agent Colby . . ." he gasped, "we've . . . monitored a . . . call from . . . Kormann."

"He wants to talk?" Colby asked. He had a moment's illogical fear that Kormann had got wind of the preparations here, that somehow, he was aware of the line of choppers ready to take off. The technician shook his head, speaking more easily now as he got his breath back.

"No. It was to someone else. He just said: 'It's me. Twenty.' Then, when the other guy sounded like he was questioning it, he repeated it: 'twenty.'"

"Twenty?" Colby repeated. "Twenty what?"

Again the technician shook his head. "That was all he said. Just 'twenty.'"

"Twenty men?" Maloney suggested. "Twenty miles?"

The technician held up a hand, remembering a small detail. "'In twenty,'" he said. "He spoke to the other guy and said 'In twenty.' Then the other guy sounded like he was going to argue and Roger repeated it: 'In twenty.'"

"Twenty minutes?" Lawson suggested. "Maybe he's pulling the plug, calling for his pick-up."

"Jesus," said Maloney softly, instinctively looking around to his Blackhawk. Colby hesitated.

"We haven't heard from Jesse . . ." he said uncertainly. He couldn't order the attack on such indefinite evidence.

"Maybe they caught him," Lawson said. "Maybe that's why Kormann's in a rush all of a sudden. He might know we're onto him."

"How did he sound?" Colby asked the technician. The man faltered. "He sounded . . . I guess . . . how do you mean?" he said finally. Colby tried to disguise his irritation.

"Did he sound panicky? Excited? Was he yelling or anything?"

"No. He didn't yell. He sounded pretty normal, I guess," the man replied, feeling guilty that he couldn't add anything useful to the conversation.

"Damn!" said Colby with sudden venom. He felt totally helpless, totally powerless. His fists clenched and unclenched without his being aware of the fact. He'd just like five minutes with that bastard Kormann, he thought. Two even.

"Agent Colby?" It was Maloney. Colby turned to the marine to hear what he had to say.

"I suggest we launch these birds and hold at a point just short of the ridge, where their radar can't see us. Then if Parker makes a call, we're that much closer to the action."

Colby looked at the man gratefully. At least it was something positive he could do. He nodded agreement.

"Okay, let's go." He turned back to the technician. "If you hear anything from Parker, patch him through to me immediately."

"Yessir."

"And put someone watching that remote camera monitor. If anything moves up there, I want to know."

They ran for the choppers, Maloney and Dent angling off in different directions to the two lead Blackhawks. Dent glanced back and saw that Lawson and Lee Torrens were also running, and that the sheriff's department's Bell 206's single rotor was beginning to rotate slowly as well. The small chopper, sleek and pristine in its blue and white paint job, looked incongruous compared to the ugly, drab camo-painted military machines but the two sheriffs didn't plan to be left out of the final phase, Dent knew.

The loadmaster was holding out a hand to help him aboard as he reached the second Blackhawk in the line. Maloney was already aboard the lead ship and, with a hastily donned headset, was giving directions to the six pilots. Move up to the ridge line and hold there for further orders. Do not cross the ridge. Do not expose your aircraft to the watching radar up the valley.

Do not pass Go. Do not collect nine point seven million dollars, thought Colby, donning his own headset in time to hear the final words of Maloney's orders.

At least the falling snow would mask the clouds of windblown snow that their rotors would kick up. Typhoon George had sent the weather front across the northwest right on time—just as Kormann had been hoping.

He dropped into the pipe-framed webbing seat that was bolted to the bulkhead behind the two pilots. There was a small communication hatch between the troop compartment and the cockpit, just a few inches away from him. He felt the floor of the Blackhawk tremble and heave slightly and then they were airborne, taking their part in the slow procession to the holding point.

He glanced around at the faces in the troop compartment. Grim. Ready. Tense. This was what they trained for but no amount of training could really simulate the real thing when it came. Glancing at the selection of automatic weapons they carried—standard issue M16s for some, B-40 grenade launchers for others and H&K submachine guns to round out the picture—he felt somewhat undergunned. His Smith and Wesson Masterpiece .38 was in a shoulder holster under his flak jacket and it seemed slightly inadequate among all the firepower he could see around him.

"Let's hold it here," Maloney's voice crackled in his headset. The lead Apache had reached the furthest point. To go any further would be to risk discovery. He felt the floor tilt as the Blackhawk reared back slightly to hover, heard the sound of the rotors change to a heavy whack-whack-whack as they angled to catch the air more forcefully and hold the big chopper motionless. Craning to look out through the windscreen, Colby could see the two Apaches ahead, and Maloney's Blackhawk out to the side and slightly ahead of the chopper he was in. The other three choppers were all hanging motionless in the air. Thirty feet below them, the massive rotor washes were kicking up mini-snowstorms.

"Set 'em down, pilots, but keep them turning," Maloney said after a few seconds. Gingerly, the helicopters settled to the rough ground, bumping gently as they touched down and the wheels took the weight. The engine sound and rotor noise promptly dropped as the pilot cut his throttle back. Just fifty yards ahead, Colby could see the ridge that marked the final obstacle between them and the hotel. If the call came, they could be up off the ground and powering over that ridge in a matter of minutes.

Straight into the teeth of the radar controlled triple-A and the Stingers.

THE ROOF
CANYON LODGE
WASATCH COUNTY
1143 HOURS, MOUNTAIN TIME
FRIDAY, DAY 7

The Korean radar specialist emerged from the canvas hutch where he spent the greater part of each day. His head was cocked toward the north, and he sniffed the air experimentally.

"Do you hear that?" he asked.

Mosby turned to him curiously. "Hear what?" he asked. He'd heard nothing but he knew the Korean had keen ears. More important, he had instincts for trouble and Mosby knew they could be invaluable in situations like this. The men posted around the roof fingered their weapons. They were edgy, he knew, and they'd been that way ever since they'd spotted the unknown man breaking cover from the hotel and skiing across the clear ground below. Mosby still felt a stab of annoyance at the fact that they'd all missed hitting the lone skier.

"I thought I heard choppers," the Korean said, peering thoughtfully toward the ridge, three miles away. Mosby was instantly fully alert.

"You see anything on your screen?"

The Korean shook his head and made a sign for Mosby to remain quiet while he listened further. He cursed under his breath after a few seconds.

"It's gone now."

"If it was there," Mosby replied. He'd heard no sound of choppers. He'd heard nothing but the wind moaning around the top of the building. Up here, eight stories from the ground, the wind was a constant companion. He thrust his hands into his parka pocket. The Korean hesitated, uncertain whether to get back to his screen.

"Keep your eye on the ridge," he said finally, and turned back into the radar shack to check the screen once more. Mosby moved to the edge of the rampart that surrounded the roof. He had an uneasy feeling about the way things were going. When a situation started to unravel in one direction, it often let go all over, and that's what seemed to be happening here. He'd heard no more from Kormann about the prisoners in the gym—except that he'd been ordered to turn over one of the precious Stingers to try to blast them out of their barricade. It was a mistake, he felt. Their supplies of the Stingers were strictly limited and he'd counted on needing them all if push came to shove. Then there was the unknown intruder whom Pallisani had gone after. Where the hell had he come from? And if one man had managed to penetrate their surveillance, who was to say that there weren't another dozen somewhere about?

Every one of the mercenaries recruited by Kormann for this operation knew that their security depended on a gigantic bluff. The authorities had to believe that they were terrorists, ready to destroy themselves alongside the hostages for the sake of their beliefs. As long as they maintained that scenario, the army couldn't come storming in here on a rescue mission. But the hostage card could only be played once or twice. Sure they could kill one or two of them to keep the authorities at bay, but sooner or later that would become a problem of diminishing returns. The government could not afford to stand by while hostages were slaughtered one at a time. They would have to act. The secret in these situations, Mosby believed, was similar to chess. You had to maintain the momentum. You had to make the moves and force your opponent to react to you—and not make the move he might have chosen for himself. For the past six days, they had managed to do that. Now, it seemed, the momentum might be moving away from them. They were reacting and that was raising large danger signals in his mind.

He shivered, not entirely from the cold, and raised his binoculars to scan the far ridge once more.

GROUND LEVEL
CANYON LODGE
WASATCH COUNTY
1146 HOURS, MOUNTAIN TIME
FRIDAY, DAY 7

"Kormann! Wait up!"

Kormann had paused to collect the remote-control triggering device. Now he was jogging toward the cable car terminal when he heard his name called. He turned and saw Harrison, the man who had been patrolling the first floor, hurrying to catch him.

Harrison was a big man, fit and well muscled. Kormann had looked for big men when he had been recruiting. He wanted the captives well and truly cowed and having men who towered over them was one way of achieving it. He waited till the other man caught up to him, noting that the Ingram was slung across his back, out of immediate reach. He felt his own fingers close around the butt of the Beretta in his jacket pocket, felt for the grooved safety with his thumb and slowly released it.

"What's the panic?" Harrison asked. Kormann gestured with his left hand toward the hotel behind them.

"The prisoners," Kormann said briefly. "They took out Clark, Washburn and Gibson and they've barricaded themselves in the gym."

Harrison's eyes widened with surprise. "Jesus," he said softly. "So what are we going to do?"

"Alston and the others are going to blast them out with a Stinger," Kormann told him, cursing the delay but realizing he had to get rid of the other man before he could move to the cable car. "Maybe you better get up there and give them a hand."

Harrison nodded several times as he thought about it. He started to turn away, then another thought struck him and he stopped, turning back to Kormann.

"Where are you going?" he asked. And that was the problem. There was no logical reason why he should be here, outside the hotel, heading in the direction of the cable car, when there was an emergency situation at the gym.

And unfortunately, Harrison was the sort of guy who would argue the point if he gave him a half-baked reason.

Unfortunately for Harrison.

Kormann nodded, pointing with his chin toward the wide ski slopes at the bottom of the homeward run, behind the other man.

"I'm going to take care of those guys," he said. And as Harrison's head turned to look in the direction he'd indicated, he drew the Beretta from his pocket and fired one shot.

Harrison lurched away from him as the slug hit him in the back, turning slowly as he sank to his knees, clawing vainly for the sudden, burning pain behind him that he couldn't reach. His eyes were puzzled.

"Kormann?" he said hesitantly. "What are—"

He died before he could finish the question. Kormann looked down at the body in the snow.

"Why didn't you just shut up and do as I said?" he asked the dead man. Then he turned and headed for the cable car again. Unlike the chairlift system, the cable car engine didn't kick in automatically each morning. He checked his watch. Time was slipping away and he was going to have to sort out the controls, start up the main motor, let the system warm up and get the car underway. It would all take time and that was getting to be in short supply.

FORTY-SEVEN

The hostages, under the direction of Senator Carling, had dragged bedding and exercise equipment into place to barricade an oblique corner of the room. Now most of them huddled behind the makeshift shelter, while Tina, Nate Pell and several others stood guard at the barrier by the door, waiting to see what the guards' next move was going to be.

Ralph, the chef, had remained in his original position, crouched among the weight benches and heavy bags, with the muzzle of a Beretta protruding through the narrow gap between the doors. Tina eyed him with some surprise. The chef's previous attitude toward his captors had been anything but belligerent. Maybe, she thought, he was making up for it now. He was still disgusted with himself that none of the shots he'd fired had gone close to hitting Kormann and, despite her repeated suggestions that he move back from the doorway, he had remained there, possibly hoping for another shot at the leader of the mercenaries.

Occasionally they saw a quick glimpse of a head thrusting around the edge of the anteroom doorway, moving out and in so quickly that there was no time to get a shot off. Once, in frustration, Ralph had sent a further fusillade of bullets hammering off the concrete walls, just in case anyone out there was planning on looking around the doorway again. With a view to their limited ammunition supply, Tina had ordered him curtly to stop wasting bullets. Reluctantly, he agreed.

The uncertainty of the situation gnawed at them. Tina had seen no point in keeping Jesse's presence a secret from her fellow captives any longer. After all, she had shot the two guards in the hope that Jesse would hear the shots and call Dent Colby. After she had filled them in on the background details, Markus, Pell, Carling and Aldiss had all agreed that the terrorist scenario being played out for the benefit of the FBI was phony. Nothing that they had seen over the previous six days jelled with the impression that their captors were politically motivated. There was a general consensus of opinion that this group were highly unlikely to set off the explosive charges in the mountain if the resulting avalanche was going to bury themselves along with the hostages.

From their position by the gymnasium doors, the occupants could see the entire anteroom, with the doorway to the gym administration office to the right, and the outer door that led to the corridor. The door was open so they could see ten to twelve yards of the corridor, until there was a right-angle turn to the left. It was around that corner that they saw occasional glimpses of the guards as they kept an eye on things.

"We've got a stalemate," Tina told the others. "They can't approach down that corridor without giving us a clear shot at them."

"So we're safe enough," the Senator said, "as long as they don't have any way of blowing us out of here. They can't get in as long as we hold this position here."

"Mind you," Carl Aldiss put in, "it cuts both ways. There's no way we can get out while they're out there."

"The difference is," Tina told them, "they don't have reinforcements on the way. All we have to do is sit tight until the FBI get here."

"If they're coming." That was Nate Pell, pointing out the one possibility they all wanted to ignore.

WHITE EAGLE CHAIRLIFT
SNOW EAGLES RESORT
WASATCH COUNTY
1153 HOURS, MOUNTAIN TIME
FRIDAY, DAY 7

Jesse wriggled his butt forward on the chairlift seat as the chair came into the unload area. As soon as it disconnected from the main cable, he was up and on his feet, poling strongly and skating to get speed up as he moved away from the chairlift line. He glanced back once over his shoulder to see if he could spot the four men who were pursuing him but the line of bobbing, dancing chairs obscured them.

He skied quickly into the thick, ungroomed snow among the trees behind the unload point and began side-stepping smoothly up the mountain. It was hard work, and the tension of the situation combined with the physical effort to drain his strength and leave him gasping for breath. But still he kept on. He had moved perhaps fifty yards from the chairlift when he realized the opportunity he'd missed.

The lift attendant's cabin at the top of the chair, like lift attendant cabins everywhere, was fitted with an emergency stop button, which could be used to bring the chairlift to an instant halt in the event of an accident, or if a skier fell dismounting from the chair. It would have taken him maybe twenty seconds to break the glass windows on the cabin and hit the stop button, leaving his pursuers stranded on the chair, twenty or thirty feet from the ground. Now, of course, it was too late to turn back and try it.

He cursed his own stupidity, then a cold hand clutched his heart as he realized that his pursuers could have done exactly the same thing to him at the bottom of the chair. He uttered a few brief words of thanks that they hadn't done so—whether due to ignorance of the chairlift controls or in the confusion of the chase, he didn't know.

He redoubled his efforts, climbing higher. He was only a few yards from the groomed trail and once he reached that, his progress

would be easier. Below him, he heard the voices of the men following him as they encountered the deep snow and plunged thigh deep
into it. He smiled grimly. If the going was tough for him, it would
be three or four times as bad for the other men, without skis to
spread their weight. With each step, they'd sink deep into the soft,
piled snow.

BLACKHAWK HELICOPTER
TAIL NUMBER 348821
WASATCH COUNTY
1159 HOURS, MOUNTAIN TIME
FRIDAY, DAY 7

In the lead Blackhawk, Colonel Evan Maloney hit the transmit
switch on his headset.

"Colby, you read?"

There was a momentary pause, then he heard the FBI agent's
voice in his earphones.

"I read, Colonel. Still no word." Dent knew what the marine
colonel was calling about but there was still no word from Jesse. He
could sense the soldier's frustration, mirrored by the marines around
him in the Blackhawk, but there was nothing he could do about it.
He had to hold until he heard from Jesse, one way or the other. He
thought of telling the colonel so, then shrugged. Maloney knew it.
Stating the obvious wouldn't make matters any better. The line of
choppers, rotors turning at idle speed, stayed where they were on
the low ground behind the ridge.

THE GYMNASIUM
CANYON LODGE
WASATCH COUNTY
1159 HOURS, MOUNTAIN TIME
FRIDAY, DAY 7

You could almost touch the tension in the big room, Tina thought. The uncertainty of waiting, and the conviction that Kormann would not be content to allow matters to remain as they were, rubbed the raw edges of the nerves like sandpaper on flesh.

"Elevator just came in," Ralph said from his position behind the barricade. Tina looked at him interrogatively and he shrugged.

"I heard the chime," he told her. Almost at the same moment, they saw sudden movement at the end of the corridor, as a figure darted across the opening, wasting no time getting behind cover. But quick as the movement had been, they had all seen what the figure had been carrying—a khaki-colored tube, some four feet in length and maybe eight inches in diameter.

"They've got some kind of missile out there," Nate Pell said suddenly, and began waving them back behind the second barricade. "Get back behind cover! Get back!"

From the corridor, Tina heard the unmistakable double clunk sound as the outer cover was discarded and the firing tube armed. In her time in the service, she'd handled and fired shoulder-mounted missiles, most of them anti-tank weapons, and she'd heard that sound before. She felt panic begin to take hold of her as she backed away from the doors, following Pell, Aldiss and the senator. She went slowly at first, then with ever-increasing urgency. Only Ralph remained by the tangle of equipment, his automatic pressed to the gap between the doors.

"Ralph!" she called. "Get back here."

The chef didn't look around, his gaze fixed on the corner where he knew the missile launcher would reappear. She could see he was shaking his head, refusing her instructions. He had the muzzle of the Beretta pressed against the narrow gap between the doors once more, holding it in a two-handed grip, his upper body sprawled across two of the heavy punching bags that formed part of the door barricade. Tina started toward him, then felt a firm hand on her arm, stopping her. She turned to meet Nate Pell's unwavering gaze.

"If they fire that thing, all hell's going to break loose in here. He's made his choice and there's no point both of you being killed."

Alston, eager to make amends for his earlier failure, had taken control of the Stinger when it had arrived. He discarded the fiber-glass carrying case and shucked the tube open, arming the batteries, bypassing the infra-red guidance system. Then, hesitating, he wondered if he should wait for Kormann to return. He gestured toward the radio clipped to Harrison's belt—his own was halfway along the corridor, lost when he had dived for cover after the first volley of shots nearly nailed him and Kormann.

The other man handed him the radio and he hit the talk button.

"Kormann. This is Alston. We're ready with the Stinger."

There was a pause, extending so long that he was about to try again, then Kormann's voice came over the little speaker.

"Go ahead. Blow the door. Then move in and clean 'em out."

Alston shrugged. It seemed logical to him. When the missile hit the door, there would be confusion and pandemonium inside the gym. It was the obvious time when they should follow up, rather than wait for Kormann to return and give the hostages time to regroup and redeploy their defenses. He glanced at the other men. One of them nodded, patting the Ingram in his hand.

"Blow that mother and let's go," he said quietly.

Alston hefted the tube onto his shoulder, flicked up the optical crosshair sights and moved toward the corner.

FORTY-EIGHT

FLYING EAGLE CABLE CAR
TOP STATION
SNOW EAGLES RESORT
WASATCH COUNTY
1159 HOURS, MOUNTAIN TIME
FRIDAY, DAY 7

With one final, exhausted heave of poles and legs, Jesse skied onto the level ground at the top of the cable car. He knew the other men were still pursuing him, knew they must have fallen far behind as they struggled through the thick, ungroomed snow above the chairlift. Once they reached the access path they'd make better time, of course, but they still wouldn't move anywhere near as fast as he could on skis.

He let the skis glide him to the terminal building and fell, exhausted, onto the bench. He waited a few moments for his breathing to settle down, then reached for the cell phone, punching the memory button for Dent's number. As ever, the comms technician answered.

"FBI."

Slumped against the cold metal of the building, Jesse replied curtly. "This is Parker. Get me Colby."

He was surprised at the reaction his words evoked. Instantly, the technician was all attention.

"Yessir, Deputy Parker! Agent Colby told me to patch you straight through. Just a moment."

There were several clicks and a whirring of atmospherics, then Jesse heard the tone of a phone ringing. It hadn't completed its first cycle before Dent's excited voice was on the line.

"Jesse? Is that you?"

Suddenly, he was very, very tired. "It's all started, Dent. I've been spotted. I'm at the top of the cable car and I've got four guys coming up the hill after me."

"Jesse, what about the hostages? Where are they?"

Jesse frowned. "Still in the gym as far as I know."

"We've been told they're in the Atrium restaurant." Colby's voice was urgent. Even though he couldn't be seen, Jesse shook his head.

"No way. I've been on the stairwell since early morning. They couldn't have moved them without my knowing. Sorry about this, Dent," he added, "I guess I've kind of blown it."

There was a momentary pause as Colby thought over the information. Then he asked the vital question: "Jesse, has the girl done anything yet? Are the hostages still safe?"

"I don't know. I didn't hear anything. She thought Kormann might be planning to move them but so far nothing . . ." he stopped. The wall of the building was vibrating and there was a heavy thud of machinery from inside.

"Just a minute, Dent," he said urgently and, heaving himself to his feet, skied to the edge of the unloading platform.

Someone had switched on the massive electric motor that powered the cable car. Far below, he could see the car at the bottom station, a tiny figure emerging from the control room. Jesse dropped the phone and scrambled for his binoculars, focusing them quickly on the platform. The eight times magnification suddenly swam into view and he could recognize the dark-haired, sunglassed figure he had seen previously, boarding the cable car and moving to the internal control console.

The controls were at the very front of the car and he could see clearly through the large windows. It was Kormann. Jesse dropped to his knees and grabbed for the phone again.

"Dent? You there?"

"What is it, Jesse?"

"It's Kormann. He's in the cable car and he's on his way up. It's started!"

"Hang tight, Jesse. The cavalry's on the way."

BLACKHAWK HELICOPTER 2
TAIL NUMBER 348719
WASATCH COUNTY
1203 HOURS, MOUNTAIN TIME
FRIDAY, DAY 7

Dent passed the cell phone to the marine sergeant beside him, then pressed the transmit button on the headset that connected him to Maloney.

"Colonel, this is Colby. He's making his move. Let's go!"

His voice was a gabble of excitement and instantly Maloney's voice came back at him. "Confirm we are go." The marine wanted to be absolutely sure of what he'd heard, Colby knew. He spoke clearly and slowly this time.

"This is Agent-in-Charge Colby. On my authority: Begin the assault. Go! Go! Go!"

"Roger, go. All units: launch and attack your targets."

Colby felt the floor lurch under his feet again as the Blackhawk rose to ten feet above the ground. Then, fourth in line behind the two lead Apaches and Maloney's Blackhawk, it skimmed over the ridge. Now only open ground lay between it and the hotel.

FLYING EAGLE CABLE CAR
TOP STATION
SNOW EAGLES RESORT
WASATCH COUNTY
1203 HOURS, MOUNTAIN TIME
FRIDAY, DAY 7

Jesse, from his vantage point above the hotel, heard the choppers first—a rising roar of jet engines and whacking rotors. Then he saw the first of them, the two narrow-bodied Apaches that were to clear the way for the troop carriers.

The cable car had passed the first pylon. It was almost a quarter of the way up the mountain and Jesse watched as it slowly hauled itself up the thin wire cable. Already, one of the Apaches was moving to intercept the cable car. The thin-bodied attack helicopter was armed with missiles and a rotary-barreled mini-gun and he watched it rapidly moving in for the kill.

The four drab-painted Blackhawks had cleared the ridge now. They fanned out in a line abreast, jinking to throw off the aim of the gunners on the roof. The first hammering rattle of the fifty calibers opened up and Jesse saw pieces fly from the ship second from the left in the line. Black smoke poured from the cowling below the big rotor blades and instantly the chopper began to lose height. It landed heavily on the uneven slope, about a mile out from the hotel, enveloped now in the black smoke that welled from its ruptured oil lines. He could see tiny figures running from the downed aircraft.

A second Apache was closing on the hotel, smoke pouring back from the rotary mini-gun slung beneath its chin. There were bullet strikes on the concrete balustrade around the roof, then Jesse saw a flash of light and a line of white smoke curved toward the helicopter as one of the Stingers fired.

The pilot had been in the act of firing off a volley of rockets as he saw the missile fire. He jerked the Apache into a hard right break, the salvo of rockets sent screaming over the top of the hotel building to explode harmlessly in the canyon wall half a mile away. A small section of the hill collapsed and slid slowly down into the canyon. It was a warning of what could happen if too many shots went astray.

As the Apache curved away from the Stinger, hugging the canyon wall, banked almost ninety degrees, the fifties opened up again on the incoming Blackhawks. Another troop carrier was trailing a thin banner of smoke but the remaining three kept coming into the face of the fire. Then another flash of light signaled the launch of another missile from the roof—but this time, the target wasn't heading for the hotel.

The lead Apache, swinging wide to intercept Kormann in the cable car, had presented a clear view of its hot jet exhaust to one of the Stingers. It was a target that the heat-seeking missile couldn't resist and its operator heard the lock tone rise to a warbling shriek, while the red "locked on" light beside the sight burned brightly. He squeezed the trigger and the missile arced away.

Jesse watched in horror as the white smoke trail seared toward the Apache, unseen by the pilot or gunner. It seemed to hesitate for a moment, as if making a last minute course correction, then flew straight into the jet tailpipe where its warhead exploded, showering shrapnel fragments into the interior of the engine.

The disintegrating engine components, whirling at several thousand RPM, added to the destruction and the Apache staggered, then seemed to tear itself apart in midair. Like a shot bird, it lurched to one side, then fell into the valley below, spilling burning jet fuel in a large circle around the wreck as it hit the ground.

He grabbed the phone again. He was still connected to the FBI agent. "Dent! Dent!" he yelled, then Colby replied, also yelling to be heard over the racket of the Blackhawk's straining jet engine.

"Jesse! I hear you!"

"The Apache's down, Dent. They got it before he could stop Kormann. The cable car is still coming!"

In the Blackhawk, Dent Colby ducked instinctively as heavy caliber bullet strikes slammed into them. The shooting from the roof was too good and they'd need the remaining Apache's covering fire to make it to the ground below the hotel, where the fifty calibers couldn't depress far enough to reach them. Also, he realized now, if he ordered the attack helicopter to go after the cable car, it would expose itself to the same tailpipe shot from another Stinger. He could lose both attack birds.

"Jesse! Can you stop the cable car? If he's left hanging up there, he can't blow the charges. The avalanche will sweep away the pylons and take him with it. Just buy us some time then we'll take care of him."

Jesse glanced through the small window beside him. The operator's hut was on the far side of the terminal building and there was bound to be an emergency stop somewhere in there. If all else failed, he'd simply take out his .45 and blow the control panel away.

"You've got it," he replied grimly.

The entry door to the terminal was fifteen yards away, uphill. He turned, clumsy in the skis, and bent to release one, setting the phone down on the bench as he did so. The movement saved his life.

A line of ragged holes punched into the shaped metal side of the building. At the same moment, he heard the rattle of an Ingram, and looking up, saw Pallisani and his three companions running from the trees toward him. The doorway was between him and them and he knew he'd never have time to get his skis off and reach safety.

Pallisani fired again and the bullets whipped all around him. They were still at extreme range for the short-barreled machine pistols but they were closing by the minute. He had to move, and move fast. Instinctively, he jump-turned in the skis and skated desperately away, heading downhill to where the ski runs started, opening the distance between himself and the shooters. He heard yelling behind him and more shots, and two or three of the 9 millimeter slugs cracked the air above his head like whips. Below him, the cable car continued to make its way up the mountain.

FORTY-NINE

Alston signaled to the two men beside him. All three of them were mercenaries, with long experience in close-quarter combat like this. At his signal, they broke cover and dashed to the far side of the corridor, spraying shots in the direction of the gymnasium doors some fifty feet away. There was a rapid volley of return fire and 9 millimeter slugs tore chunks from the rendered concrete walls. But their sudden movement had caught the lone shooter by surprise and neither man was hit.

The three mercenaries were under no delusions as to what they had to do, Kormann or no Kormann. The radio was alive with reports of incoming choppers and the sound of machine-gun fire. Their only chance of survival was to get the hostages under their control once more, to hold them as a bargaining chip for their own escape. If the rescue team arrived and found the current stalemate, Alston and the others were toast, and they knew it.

Alston looked across to the opposite corner, caught Milgate's eye and nodded. The other man leaned around the corner and sprayed the door with a burst from his Ingram. As he did so, Alston, knowing that the shooter at the door would be concentrating on the opposite side of the corridor, stepped half clear, the Stinger tube already on his shoulder.

There was no lock-on light or tone because with no heat source, they had disconnected the infrared seeking head. But the target was one he couldn't miss—a double set of doors fifty feet away. He centered the crosshairs on the door and pressed the trigger. The pause before the rocket launched was only half a second or so but it seemed forever to him as a bullet slammed the wall beside him, showering him with concrete chips. He flinched and the crosshairs moved fractionally, then the launcher fired, throwing the missile clear of the tube. Halfway to the door, the main rocket motor ignited and the corridor was full of acrid smoke and howling noise.

Ralph, emptying the Beretta at the machine-gunner, saw Alston too late. He saw the Stinger leap clear of the tube and scream toward him as if in slow motion, the vast smoke trail behind it obliterating everything else from sight. Then the rocket slammed into the right-hand-side door, smashing it into huge shards of toughened glass and hurling it open, scattering the hastily constructed barricade with the sheer force of its momentum. The warhead didn't explode—the oblique impact wasn't enough to crush the detonator. But the out-of-control rocket, capable of reaching out and nailing a fast-moving jet, transformed its speed and energy into an irresistible battering force as it slammed through the doorway, scattering the barricade and hurling Ralph to one side, slashed cruelly by the broken safety glass and already dying from horrific burns as the white-hot exhaust flame flayed the clothes and flesh from three-quarters of his body.

The last-minute wavering of Alston's aim meant the rocket hit the right-hand-side door, not the center gap. So it was deflected slightly as it smashed through the glass, then more so as it hit the chrome uprights of a Nautilus weight machine. It toppled end over end, the rocket motor sending a deafening scream through the room, caromed off the floor, spinning for a moment like a giant Catherine-wheel, then slithered at blinding speed toward the outside wall, slamming into the painted concrete, crushing the nose-cone and finally, finally tripping the detonator inside.

The three-kilogram warhead exploded in a flash of orange flame and a cloud of white-hot metal shrapnel.

There were fifty people huddled behind a hastily erected shelter within thirty feet of the explosion. The shrapnel ripped through the blankets and exercise machines. Four of the hostages died almost instantly. Another eight were injured by the shrapnel, Senator Carling among them.

Nate Pell, Tina Bowden and Carl Aldiss all survived. Blinded and coughing from the choking smoke, which would account for another two lives within the next eight hours, they huddled together behind an upturned weight bench, flinching as shrapnel rang against the metal base. Then Pell, coughing, was on his feet, pistol in hand, as he yelled to them.

"They'll hit us in the smoke! Get up! Get up!"

His battle-hardened instincts knew that the guards would follow up the confusion caused by the explosion. He staggered toward the doorway, sensing Tina behind and beside him. He thought he saw a shadowy figure in the smoke ahead of him and fired twice. Somewhere close at hand he heard an Ingram's tearing rattle. Whether it was Carl Aldiss or one of the mercenaries, he had no idea. His eyes stung, streaming tears and he felt a savage hammer blow in his right leg, felt himself falling, felt the sickness and nausea of shock welling up inside him as he hit the hard nylon carpet.

He sensed a figure above him and tried to raise the pistol, but a soft hand touched his face and he realized it was Tina, crouching over him to protect him.

"It's okay!" she was saying, her voice racked by a fit of coughing as the smoke seared her throat. "It's okay!" then he heard the sharp bark of her pistol and he felt his eyes closing.

THE WALL
SNOW EAGLES MOUNTAIN
WASATCH COUNTY
1208 HOURS, MOUNTAIN TIME
FRIDAY, DAY 7

It dropped away before him. Steep. Impossibly steep. Unforgiving and undefeated.

Fear and self-doubt made the near-vertical snow face seem even steeper as Jesse hesitated at the top of The Wall.

The four gunmen would be after him any minute. He could ski down Drifter and leave them behind, take cover in the trees and hope that everything worked out all right. Odds were he'd survive. Even if Kormann set off an avalanche, Jesse could ski out of its path, back into the center of the canyon. The danger area lay between the top station and the hotel itself, he knew, and he could avoid that, given the time.

But below him lay the means to stop Kormann. All he had to do was reach it. And to reach it, he had to ski The Wall.

Not just ski it, but stay on his feet and stay in control, because if he fell, he'd slide and tumble all the way to the bottom. He took a deep, shuddering breath. This was more than a simple personal test of courage and commitment, more than a battle with his own fears. If he surrendered to the fear this time, he was surrendering the lives of the fifty hostages, condemning them to a thundering, suffocating, crushing death.

He hesitated, breathing deeply, gathering his resolve. Fittingly, the steep wall of snow that stretched below him was in shadow, dark and cold under the close-growing trees that lined either side of the narrow chute. He glanced quickly back up the track to the top station. His pursuers were just visible a hundred and fifty yards away, rounding a bend in the trail, floundering on the uneven snow. Out to his right, the cable car continued to climb inexorably up the mountain, now nearly halfway through its journey.

Behind him, a rattle of automatic fire, but no sound of the bullets passing nearby. The range was still too great for that. He took a deep breath, flexed his legs, bent forward, willing himself to go, yet, at the last moment, unable to commit himself.

Go! His mind screamed. Go now!

And then he did, the scream torn from his mind and emerging from his throat as a high-pitched keening yell and he thrust up and out with his legs and thighs, angling his body out over the giddying drop below him, plunging fifteen feet down through the cold air and then feeling the impact of skis against the soft snow, feeling them dig in and hold as his knees flexed to absorb the landing, feet and skis at forty-five degrees to the fall line and his mind screaming at him: Stay out with the upper body! Stay out!

Then reach far down the face and plant the pole . . . slamming it in too hard but never mind style, he'd reached far enough to keep his upper body facing the terrifying slope . . . now thrust with the knees and thighs and spring high and clear, letting his legs rotate back through one hundred and twenty degrees, while his upper body hardly moved . . . and down again! Feel the skis thrusting into the snow, the edges biting and controlling and holding him as he maintained that vital upper-body position.

Scream and jump again! Up and out and down again, thrusting, controlling and Christ don't lean back into the mountain! Leap out and up again, fighting the urge to rear back, away from the steep, dizzying drop below, getting it under control again and now a rhythm was beginning to assert itself: jump and turn and jump and turn and he felt an almost primal surge of satisfaction at being in control, of giving himself over to the rhythm as his fears scuttled back into the dark hole from which they had emerged.

Don't turn when you want to, he'd been told years before, turn when the rhythm wants to. And now he did that, obeying the rhythm, leaping, twisting, regardless of the fact that every time his skis drove into the snow face they set off mini-avalanches of their own, falling through fifteen to twenty feet of space with each jump before his skis made their tenuous contact once more on the near vertical slope.

And there was the timber platform, just below him, and he dug in with the skis and threw arms and upper body way, way out over the abyss, holding them there against all seeming logic and every demand of intellec , as he felt the exhilarating downhill rush slowly dragged to a halt by the resistance of the skis in the thick, powdery snow.

And it was over.

He'd dropped a few feet below the platform and now he shuffled hurriedly back uphill, sliding forward until his skis grated on the rough, untrimmed planks beneath the covering of snow. He released his bindings and stepped clear of the skis, running the few steps to the canvas-shrouded shape at the outer edge of the platform.

He tore at the lacings and threw off the canvas storm cover that protected the oiled, well-maintained 75 millimeter recoilless rifle. A quick glance across the valley told him that Kormann was two-thirds of the way to the top station. He looked for the ready-use ammunition locker, saw it to one side—padlocked, of course. He took the .45 from his inner pocket and jacked a round into the breech. There was a moment when he hesitated, considering the folly of firing a shot into a wooden chest full of high explosive projectiles. Then, realizing he had no other choice, he aimed carefully at the padlock and squeezed off a shot.

The force of the heavy slug tore the lock hasp clear of its restraints. Thankfully, the bullet ricocheted away from the ammunition locker, howling as it tumbled end over end into the clear air beyond the platform. He wrenched the lid of the locker open and found himself staring at two neat rows of projectiles, stacked nose to tail. He took one, cradling it carefully, and moved to the artillery piece. There was a crank-handle-shaped lever on the breech end and he turned it to allow the breech to swing smoothly open. The projectile slid in easily and he slammed the breech shut and locked it, dropping to his knees behind the gun, searching for the sights.

They were simple open sights—rear sight V and front sight leaf. He swung the gun experimentally on its tripod. The movement was easy and smooth, obviously the Avalanche Patrol kept it well maintained. He had no idea of the speed or trajectory of the shell's flight so he'd have to experiment. Figuring there'd be some drop, at least, he raised the barrel until he was sighted on the top of the giant claw holding the car to the cable, then swung to the right to lead it by about ten yards.

A squeeze of the handgrip trigger was followed by a loud WHOOMP! as a huge burst of propellant gas was released from the breech behind him. The projectile leapt away from the barrel, arcing up and across the valley. The avalanche patrollers used tracer rounds, fortunately, and he could follow the glowing projectile easily in the dull, overcast light. By the time it was halfway, he realized he hadn't allowed enough for drop. It was beginning to arc downwards and he knew it would never reach the cable car. The shell slid under the car by about ten feet, and about five yards behind, fountaining up a small burst of snow and smoke when it detonated on the hillside. Unlike the avalanche patrol, he hadn't fired into a carefully plotted fault line in the snow. Nevertheless, a small avalanche slid away from the point of impact.

Jesse turned back to the locker and carried four shells to the gun this time. He didn't have time to keep going back for each one—the cable car was on the last quarter of its travel. He realized it was higher now, further above him than before, so he raised the aim point even further, and led the car by a greater margin.

Another bang and another glowing tracer round curved across the valley. This time, for a few seconds, he thought he had done it. But at the last minute the shell slid behind the cable car again.

The third shell was perfect for line but low once more. Jesse rammed the last shell into the breech. He didn't know if he'd have time to fetch more before the cable car reached the safety of the top shelter. Getting the elevation right was incredibly difficult due to the fact that the cable car was climbing all the time. He adjusted the sight picture until he felt it was the right combination of horizontal and vertical aim off, then, in a last minute flash of indecision, he raised the barrel even further, to a point that felt wrong. He reasoned that, working by instinct alone, he had continually underestimated the elevation. So it only made sense to do what his instincts told him was wrong. Before he could argue himself out of it, he fired.

And realized, almost immediately, that he had aimed too high.

The shell arced across the valley, its path and that of the cable car converging with each second. He was right on line, he thought, but the projectile would miss the top of the cable car by a dozen feet or so. He cursed himself furiously, realizing that his initial setting had been correct.

He turned desperately to the ammunition store, knowing he would be too late, when he heard the blast of an explosion across the valley. This time, it wasn't the muffled crump as a shell buried itself in the snow and exploded below the surface. This time, it had a hard, ringing quality to it.

The shell, missing the top of the cable car by a dozen feet, impacted instead on the steel framework support structure that attached the car to the cable. The impact fuse exploded as it slammed into one of the steel girders, blasting it and several of its smaller support pieces to atoms. The cable car sagged dangerously, swaying crazily under the impact and the loss of support on one side, then the remaining steel support arm began to buckle and the claw assembly, shattered by the force of the explosion just below it, slowly gaped open, releasing its hold on the cable.

The cable car, seeming to move in slow motion, dropped clear of the cable, which jerked upwards like a plucked guitar string as the weight left it. Slowly toppling, the car gathered speed as it fell fifty feet to the snow-covered slope below. It hit the slope and rolled over and over, gathering speed and momentum as it tumbled down.

Jesse watched, fascinated, as it hit a slight hump in the mountainside and bounced clear of the ground, spinning like a top, battered out of all shape, before it slammed back down again, rolling and sliding, accompanied now by its own wall of tumbling rock and snow. For a moment, he thought it would slide and tumble all the way to the bottom of the valley, but there was a major obstacle in its way.

The number one pylon supporting the cable was made of solid steel and concrete. The cable car was lightweight aluminium and plastic. It struck the pylon almost dead center and was virtually torn in half in an instant. Bent back double over itself around the base of the pylon, it was transformed into a pile of twisted, tortured, crushed metal. It hung there, trapped against the concrete.

Then the roaring wall of tumbling snow that it had created slammed into it and within seconds, it was hidden from sight, buried under a hundred tons of rock and ice and snow.

The small, localized avalanche continued past the pylon for another three hundred yards, gradually petering out as the slope lessened. It rolled to a halt against the west-facing wall of Canyon Lodge, the snow, its last gasp spent, banked up against the wall a matter of a few feet.

Jesse stood from behind the gun, his knees unsteady. Below him, he could see troops deploying from the Blackhawks on the clear ground beside Canyon Lodge.

The fifty calibers on the roof, no longer able to bear, had fallen silent and Maloney's troops had set two M60 machine guns to spraying the roof parapet, encouraging the men there to keep their heads down. Now the distant pop of small-arms fire could be heard, carried on the slight wind, and hearing it, he hoped dully that Tina Bowden was all right.

FIFTY

Dent Colby leaned against the side of the Blackhawk and unfastened the velcro straps that held his flak jacket in place. The hotel was thirty yards away and the main force of Maloney's marines had gone in some five minutes ago. The next few minutes would tell him whether he had acted correctly, he thought, or whether he had caused the deaths of fifty unarmed hostages.

It would also decide whether he still had a career with the bureau, he thought dully, but that was an insignificant consideration right now. He glanced around to see Cale Lawson and Lee Torrens studying the wrecked remains of the cable car some two hundred yards up the mountain.

"Your boy did good," Lawson said and Lee nodded.

"Yeah. He usually does." They all knew that it could only have been Jesse who had taken out the cable car. Somehow, Dent figured, he must have gotten ahold of some of the Stinger missiles. Cale Lawson went to say more but the earphone on Dent's headset chirped and he held up a hand to stop him.

"This is Maloney. You copy, Colby?"

"I hear you."

"We've secured the gym. Most of the hostages are okay. There were five killed and another half dozen or so wounded. My medics are attending to them now. The enemy took four casualties here, all KIAs."

Dent Colby felt an enormous sense of relief wash over him. Five hostages dead was bad news, he thought, but it was a damn sight better than fifty. The radio chirped again; this time another voice spoke.

"Colonel Maloney, this is Rapper."

Emil Rapper was the captain leading the roof assault team. Maloney acknowledged the call.

"Go ahead, Rap."

"Roof's secured, sir. One enemy wounded, seven KIA. We called on them to surrender, sir, but they didn't seem interested."

"You gave them the chance though?"

"Just the one, sir," the captain's voice was flat and unemotional. Colby guessed you didn't give too many chances to a group of mercenaries armed with multiple fifty-caliber machine guns. Apparently, Maloney agreed.

"Good work, Rap. Look after that prisoner. We're going to want to know what this was all about."

"Affirmative, sir. Rapper out."

"You hear that, Colby?" Maloney spoke again.

"I heard. Your boys do good work, Colonel."

"It's what we train for. We've accounted for fourteen of the enemy but according to witnesses here, there may be still four or five wandering around somewhere. So keep your eyes open. In the meantime, you'd better get your boy down off the mountain."

"We'll do that," Colby told him. Then, as a thought struck him, he added, "Colonel, how's the girl"—he thought for her name for a moment, then added—"Bowden?" There was a just discernible pause before the marine answered.

"She was one of the five who didn't make it. Apparently, she did a hell of a job in here."

Dent shook his head sadly. He'd hoped she'd be one of the survivors. She deserved to be.

"Damn," he said quietly. Then he continued. "Thanks, Colonel. We'd better go get Parker. He'll be up the mountain somewhere."

Cale Lawson jerked his head toward the sheriff's department Jet Ranger.

"We'll take my chopper," he said. "The Blackhawks might still be needed here."

*   *   *

Painted all white and traveling low over the snow-covered terrain, the Squirrel helicopter was almost impossible to see. The pilot, hunched forward and eyes squinted against the dull light and falling snow, looked anxiously at the rising pillar of smoke from over the next ridge. He eased the cyclic forward and the Squirrel hugged the contours of the ground a little closer. He didn't like the look of this. Not at all.

The Squirrel's radio had one channel dedicated to a cell-phone circuit and he hit the redial key, sending out a signal to Kormann's phone. The headset earphone buzzed for a second, then a flat, emotionless female voice spoke.

"The cellular phone you are calling is either out of range or switched off."

He thumbed the switch to cut the contact and glanced at his watch. Twenty-one minutes had elapsed since Kormann's phone call and now the rising bulk of Eagle Ridge loomed ahead of him. Once he crossed the ridge, the horseshoe-shaped area of Snow Eagles Resort would lie spread before him. Again, he frowned at the thin column of smoke.

He hesitated, his left hand on the collective pushed down and twisted, changing the pitch of the rotor blades and raising the RPM of the jet turbine engine.

A slight back pressure on the cyclic raised the Squirrel's blunt nose and the little helicopter hovered below the ridge line, close enough to the ground for its rotor downwash to send a cloud of blown powder into the air around him. That was probably what saved him from being seen. The white cloud of snow rose up around the white-painted helicopter so that it merged into the background of falling snow and snow-covered pines. Then a blue and white-painted Jet Ranger soared briefly above the ridge line, wheeled and turned to head back into the valley on the other side.

He'd seen the gold sheriff's star painted on the side of the fuselage and that was enough for him. Kormann wasn't answering. There was smoke coming from somewhere in the valley and now the cops were flying over the ridge line, uncontested. His fee for the pickup was fifty thousand, half paid in advance. His fingers clenched and un-clenched on the collective as he made his decision.

Twenty-five thousand was better than nothing, he thought. Certainly better than ninety years in the pen. He wheeled the chopper through an in-place one-eighty, easing cyclic and collective as the nose came around, and headed off, nose down, hugging the terrain contours, back the way he'd come.

In the Jet Ranger, Lawson's deputy hurled the chopper into a tight, diving turn as they felt the unmistakable sensation of bullet strikes on the underside. The Jet Ranger wheeled and dived back down toward the valley, the occupants craning to see where the shots had come from. There was nobody visible, and Cale Lawson pressed the transmit button on the floor in front of him.

"Colonel Maloney?" he said into the boom mike on his headset. There was a brief pause before the marine leader answered.

"This is Maloney."

"This is the Wasatch County sheriff's helicopter, Colonel. We think we've found your missing four bandits. They're somewhere in the trees on top of the ridge here, shooting at us. I'd appreciate it if you'd send some of your fire eaters up here to teach them some manners."

"On the way, Sheriff." the colonel replied briefly. Cale Lawson turned to Dent and Lee in the rear seat and shrugged.

"No sense getting ourselves shot at when the marines are drawing combat pay," he said, and Dent grinned at him in return.

"Couldn't agree more, Sheriff," he said, then the grin faded as a thought struck him.

"I just hope Jesse hasn't run into those guys," he said. But the older man was already pointing to the trail leading down toward the hotel, where the slope lessened and the tree line ended.

A single figure was skiing smooth and fast out of the trees. As the chopper flashed above him, barely a hundred feet up, he looked up and waved one hand.

"Could be that's our friend right there," he said. Lee was sitting on that side of the little aircraft and she took one glance at the easy grace and smooth-flowing style.

"That's him," she said. Then, as the lone skier went into a tuck and began a straight run down to the flat land below, she added with a relieved grin: "We better haul ass if he isn't going to beat us down."

FIFTY-ONE

Linus Benjamin was ushered into the Oval Office by one of the president's two secretaries. President Gorton was behind the desk, framed by the late morning light streaming through the French doors. Pohlsen, as ever, hovered close by. The president smiled and rose, extending his hand as the FBI director entered the room.

"Linus! Come in, won't you? Take a seat."

The handshake was brief and firm. A politician's handshake, Benjamin thought wryly, then instantly regretted the thought as the president continued.

"Your people did a good job on that Utah business. I want you to know I'm grateful."

Benjamin took one of the seats opposite the president. Gorton sat as well. Pohlsen remained standing, moving restlessly to one side of the desk and surreptitiously checking his wristwatch. The president's day was measured in five minute blocks and his chief of staff was a jealous guardian of the timetable. Benjamin shrugged diffidently in reply to the president's compliment.

"Seven hostages dead," he said bitterly. "I would like to have done better."

"Seven?" The president's forehead creased in a frown. "I thought there were five casualties?"

"Two more died subsequently. One from burns and one from severe lung problems caused by smoke inhalation. Plus the pilot of the Apache. His gunner survived, somehow. I wish we had done better," he repeated. The president lifted his shoulders in a slight shrug.

"You could have done a whole lot worse," he told the director. "We all could have. We could be looking now at a figure of fifty dead. Seven is regrettable, naturally. But on balance, I don't know that you could have done better."

Benjamin accepted the assessment. In his heart, he knew the president was right. They had been in a no-win situation from day one. The best they could have ever hoped for was to minimize their losses.

"It seems Emery's theory was correct," he said, looking carefully at the man opposite to see what effect the words would have. To his surprise, the president grinned ruefully.

"The damned man usually is," he said. "That's one of the reasons why I find him so insufferable. Still, I suppose we do owe him a debt." He dismissed the former professor by moving onto another subject. "Your man on the spot handled the situation well. Colby, was it?"

Benjamin nodded. "That's right, Mr. President. He had to make a tough decision on the spur of the moment and he made the right one. And thank God for that."

The president nodded several times. "I was thinking that some gesture on my part might be appropriate—some kind of citation perhaps?" he suggested. Benjamin grinned slightly.

"A presidential citation in his personnel file never did any FBI agent harm, Mr. President," he replied. Regardless of your political leanings or personal feelings about the man in the White House, a presidential citation was a certain aid to rapid promotion.

"Then there's the matter of the girl"—he glanced down at a legal pad on his desk—"Bowden. Tragic that she should be among the casualties."

Benjamin said nothing. The president had summed it up. The eyewitness accounts, particularly Nate Pell and Senator Carling, left no doubt that all the survivors were indebted to Tina Bowden for their lives. The president was shuffling a few papers on his desk until he found the one he was looking for.

"It seems that Ms. Bowden was still on the Marine Corps reserve list," he said. "That means it's within my powers to recommend her for a decoration. I've spoken with the marine commandant and we feel the Navy Cross might be appropriate."

"I'm sure her family would appreciate that, Mr. President," Benjamin replied and again, the president's reaction caught him by surprise.

"Not as much as they'd appreciate having their daughter still alive, I'm sure. I thought maybe a private ceremony here at the White House. No press. Just an informal presentation to her parents."

Benjamin noticed the quick sidelong glance that Gorton directed at his chief of staff as he said the words "no press." He guessed that had been a matter of disagreement between them. Pohlsen would have hated to see a photo op like that pass by.

"I'm sure it would mean a lot to them, sir," he said. He was a little bewildered by this conversation. He had assumed there would be an official debriefing at some time in the next week, not this informal and undeniably friendly chat.

"And how about the other guy—the deputy from Steamboat Springs? You think maybe we should do something for him?"

Benjamin hesitated. He didn't want to deny Jesse Parker his moment in the sun but Dent Colby had discussed the matter with him at some length.

"Parker has been helping Dent Colby with the debrief, sir. Then he plans to go back to Colorado as soon as possible. I believe he was pretty torn up about the girl's death. Took it hard, Colby tells me."

The president raised an eyebrow at the news. "Is that right? Something between them, was there?" Benjamin shook his head.

"Not really. Agent Colby feels it was more a case of the two of them being thrown together as they were, each being the other's only contact during a high stress time. Besides, I believe that Parker has a relationship with the sheriff back in Routt County."

The president's eyebrow soared at that and Benjamin hurried to correct the impression. "The sheriff is a woman, Mr. President. And from all reports, a very attractive one."

President Gorton shook his head. "That's a relief," he said. "The alternative was too complicated to consider."

"I think maybe a personal letter of gratitude and commendation from you might be enough there, sir," Benjamin concluded and the president made a note on the legal pad.

In the background, Pohlsen cleared his throat apologetically and Gorton rose from behind the desk. Taking his cue, Benjamin rose also, preparing to leave. The next words stopped him.

"Take a quick turn in the Rose Garden with me, Mr. Director," said the president. Terence Pohlsen glanced at his watch and the clipboard that held Gorton's list of appointments.

"Mr. President, you're already overdue for your meeting with the delegation from Lagos—" he began, but Gorton cut him off.

"They can wait, Terry," he said with some asperity. "Christ, we're giving them a hundred million dollars worth of aid. That should be worth five minutes of their time!"

Pohlsen shrugged, defeated. He glanced at the list, mentally juggling appointments for the rest of the day as he planned how to make up the lost time. Automatically, he began to follow as Gorton ushered the FBI director through the French doors into the crisp spring sunshine.

"No need for you to bother, Terry," the president said quietly and the chief of staff stopped, puzzled. Outside, two ever-present secret service agents fell into place behind the president and Linus Benjamin. One of them raised his sleeve mike to his mouth and spoke into it. Linus could imagine the exchange.

"Banjo is leaving the Oval Office. In the Rose Garden with Director Benjamin."

When Gorton had been sworn in, he had made it clear that he would not be referred to as POTUS (President of the United States). The name, he said, sounded like some kind of a soup and he had instructed the service to use the code name assigned to him as VP. "Banjo" was the result, created after he confessed to a weakness for Dixieland jazz. The agents followed, just out of earshot and as he noticed them, Benjamin understood the reason for the move from the Oval Office. There were no microphones out here. Their conversation would not be recorded.

Gorton nodded to the bare rosebushes. "No roses to show you, Mr. Director, I'm afraid," he said in a bantering tone.

"I'll try to live without them, Mr. President."

"So, our best guess is that this drug lord was behind the whole thing, is that right?" the president asked thoughtfully.

"We've no solid proof, Mr. President. Only one of the gang survived and he knew nothing beyond the facts of the kidnapping. There were another four that the marines caught up with on the mountain—the ones who went after Jesse Parker. But they died in the shoot-out as well."

"Probably cleaner that way. The last thing we want is more terrorists trying to blackmail us into setting prisoners free."

"From all we can see, they weren't terrorists, Mr. President. At least, not in the sense that they were politically motivated. We've identified six so far and they were all mercenaries—American, Rhodesians and one Italian. One of the guys on the mountain was an ex-mobster named Pallisani. He had no political connections that we're aware of."

"So, on the face of it, it was all about money."

Benjamin nodded. "Except when you go below the surface, Kormann was obviously prepared to kill the hostages at the last moment while he tried to make his getaway. If it was all about money, why do that?"

The president pondered the matter for a few seconds, staring unseeingly at one of the bare rosebushes in the garden.

"Unless someone else was paying him to do it and that was the plan right from the first moment?" he said, and Benjamin nodded agreement.

"That's pretty much the way we see it. And of course, there's a reasonable amount of evidence to suggest that the 'someone' is Estevez." He paused, then went on. "As a matter of fact, we're starting to think it wasn't the first time he's tried to have the senator killed."

Gorton stopped and turned toward him. "He's tried before? When?"

"The Atherton shooting, sir. Carling was with him that night. At the time, everyone assumed that Atherton was the target and the shooter was some gun crazy right to lifer. Now we're starting to think that maybe Carling was the target. They both stooped to pick up the glove at the same time. But Carling was on the side closest to the sniper."

President Gorton sighed deeply. He was an ordinary man, he knew, thrust into an extraordinary position. "It's kind of frightening, isn't it, that there are two equally plausible reasons behind that shooting?" he asked. Benjamin had no answer to that and guessed that the president wasn't asking for one. The silence between them grew. Finally, it was the president who broke it.

"You did a good job, Benjamin. I want you to know I appreciate that."

Benjamin nodded his acceptance of the compliment. He sensed there was more to come and the president's next words proved him right.

"I've got a hell of a job making this office my own, you know?" he said, half to himself. "This presidency is still seen as belonging to Adam Couch and I'm just an accidental blow-in. Well, if I'm stuck with the job, I plan to make it my own."

He paused and looked meaningfully at the director. Benjamin shrugged. He couldn't argue with that.

"You were a Couch appointment, Director Benjamin. You were part of his administration and I want to make changes so that this becomes my administration. Do you follow where I'm going?"

Benjamin nodded carefully. "I think so, Mr. President. The last director with permanent tenure was Hoover, I guess," he replied. Gorton nodded once or twice.

"I felt I owed it to you to tell you to your face," he said, eventually. "I'll be making changes to my emergency council because I need them. Not because you haven't performed and not because I think you wouldn't perform in future. But be honest with me, you'd always look on me as a second choice to Couch, wouldn't you?"

It was on the tip of Benjamin's tongue to deny the suggestion. Then wryly, he realized that the president was correct. His opinion of Gorton had improved in the previous week, but he still saw him as a second choice, and way behind Adam Lindsay Couch, he realized.

"I guess I would at that, Mr. President."

Again, Gorton nodded. "I appreciate your honesty. We both know it's the truth. And one thing I've learned is that I cannot carry out this office unless my inner group of advisers are committed to me—totally and absolutely. And not to the ghost of some former incumbent."

"I understand, sir," Benjamin replied. He felt a twinge of disappointment at the thought of leaving the Bureau. But then, he thought, he'd only been in the job six months. He guessed it wouldn't be too big a wrench to leave.

"Any other way we can help you, we'll be glad to," Gorton continued. "There's a vacancy coming up for state's attorney general in New York. I can almost guarantee you'd have it if you wanted it."

Benjamin shoved his hands in his pockets and gazed across the White House lawn. It was a crisp spring day in Washington, with a slight haze in the sky and a chill still in the air.

"I'd like to think it over, sir," he said and Gorton nodded repeatedly once more. Benjamin was beginning to realize that this was a mannerism of the president's.

"Think it over. Think it over. Let me know. It's not a punishment, Benjamin, I want you to know that. It's not some kind of revenge. It's what I need if I'm to do this job halfway decently, is all."

He glanced at his watch. "Now I guess I'd better get back to these people from Lagos. What the hell do you call them—Lagotians?"

Benjamin couldn't help grinning. "I guess that's as close as anything, Mr. President." He added, "Thanks for taking the time to explain."

Gorton waved a hand in dismissal. "It was the least you deserved. I'm sorry things turned out this way. Damned sorry. But . . ." he shrugged. Everything had been said and he turned away again, heading for the French doors. But Benjamin had one more thing to say.

"Mr. President?" he said again and Gorton stopped, turned back to face him, eyebrows raised in a question.

"I want to thank you, sir. For your directness . . . and your honesty."

Gorton allowed a trace of a smile to lift the corners of his mouth. "I could say the same for yours, Mr. Director," he replied and Benjamin shrugged.

"I owe it to the office, sir," he said and the smile widened a trifle.

"Just to the office, Mr. Director? Not to the man as well?" the president asked.

Benjamin hesitated then replied, knowing he was speaking the truth. "Maybe to him as well, Mr. President."

FIFTY-TWO

It fell away below him. Steep. Impossibly steep. Seeming almost sheer as he stood at the edge looking down.

It had snowed the day before and the fresh fall had covered all traces of his last run down The Wall with a thick blanket of fresh Wasatch powder. The mid-morning sun shone on it now, reflecting fiercely so that even behind his dark glasses, his eyes narrowed.

Below and beyond, the various ski runs of Snow Eagles Resort stretched out to the hotel. It was empty now of skiers as the resort was closed while Dent's people carried out their final investigations. The snowfall had almost covered the traces of the burned out Apache as well. A little later in the day, a big Boeing chopper was due to come in and lift the wreckage out of the valley.

His breath clouded on the clear, frigid air. It was a perfect day. Clear sky, bright sun, no wind and the air so cold it cut like a knife into your lungs as you breathed it in. It was the sort of day Jesse lived for and he wished that the sadness weighing down upon him would lift.

Odd that he should grieve so deeply for Tina Bowden, he thought. After all, there'd been just that one night between them. He had liked her, and enjoyed her company. But it went no further than that. During the siege, they had met less than half a dozen times, exchanging hurried words as they kept one fearful eye on the door to the kitchen, speaking in whispers, trying to make sense of the whole crazy situation. And yet he felt a deep sense of loss—and had done so since the moment when the marine light colonel had told him that she had been killed at the end. She'd died protecting one of the hostages, standing over him and facing a mercenary armed with a machine pistol. He didn't care about the other casualties. They were just names and there was no face to any of them—no connection to him. But Tina Bowden he had known, even if it had been for such a short time.

He'd spoken about it with Colby. The FBI agent had a psychology degree, after all, and he suggested that the pressure of the situation in which they had met had accelerated their relationship, making them interdependent and creating a bond similar to that formed between soldiers in combat. Jesse thought maybe he was right.

Whatever the reason, he wanted to say his own good-byes to her before heading back to Colorado and this had seemed the right place to do it. The hotel was still crowded with people and the gym where she had died was scorched by the flames of the Stinger's exhaust and scarred with bullet holes. Technicians and forensic crews crowded one another, sifting evidence, looking for some clue as to the reasons behind the whole affair.

Here there was silence and the solitude he wanted. He rode the chairlift to the top as he had done before, then skied up to the crest, passing the spot where Pallisani and his men had finally been cornered by the squad of marines. The snow had covered all traces of that battle as well, he noticed.

Now here he was, above The Wall, staring down at the perfect snow below, smiling wryly to himself as he remembered how it had become a symbol for him—a crystallization of his efforts to regain his former self. Looking at it now, it was just a ski run, he thought. Steep. Sheer, almost. But skiable. And well within his capabilities. Behind him, Drifter curved away into the trees, emerging several hundred feet lower down, where it joined back into Broadway for the run home to the hotel. In front of him was The Wall. Double Black, experts only. A mental as well as a physical barrier to him. He reached into his side pocket and took out a single red rose.

He turned it in his fingers, letting the sun play on the lustrous red petals, then tossed it underhand, out onto the snow.

It landed ten feet down and rolled, bouncing lightly until it came to rest twenty-five feet below him, in the bright sunlight that speared through a gap in the trees. It looked to him like a single drop of dark red blood on the perfect white of the snow, and he thought that was fitting.

"*Semper fi*, Tina Bowden," he said softly.

Then he kick-turned one-eighty degrees and skied off down the gentle, even slope that was Drifter. He didn't want to disturb the rose in the snow and he had nothing to prove to himself anymore.

EPILOGUE

Linus Benjamin rose from behind his desk to greet his visitor, reaching forward to shake hands. The woman had a surprizingly strong grip, he thought. He gestured to the visitor's chair.

"Sheriff Torrens, please take a seat. Would you like coffee? Water?"

Lee shook her head, smiling briefly. "No thank you, Mr. Director."

Benjamin smiled in turn at the title. "Not for much longer, I'm afraid. My replacement takes over in two weeks."

"So I'd heard. That's why I wanted to see you."

She was a very attractive woman, he thought. Tall, long-legged and with an excellent figure. Her hair was shoulder-length blond, she had high cheekbones and her gray eyes were slightly uptilted. He placed her age as late thirties, possibly early forties. He revised his first judgment. More than attractive, he thought, quite beautiful in a natural, outdoors way.

"I've never had the chance to thank you for your help with the Snow Eagles affair," he said and she shrugged, dismissing her part as unimportant.

"I was just a communication link," she said. "It was Jesse who did all the hard work."

Benjamin inclined his head a little. "He did at that. So why did you ask to see me?" He sensed she was a person who would prefer to get right to the point. "Is it to do with your deputy?"

She hesitated, then replied. "It is," she said. "But I don't want him knowing about it. I wanted to ask you about Estevez."

"The man we believe was behind all this?" he said and she nodded.

"Way I heard it, he's a vengeful kind of character," she said, and he agreed with her.

"That's Emery's theory. This whole thing was about revenge. Back when he was a presidential assistant, Senator Carling authorized a raid that cost Estevez a lot of money—and set his operation back by at least six months. He wanted Carling dead because of that. In fact," he continued, "we now believe that this wasn't the first time he's tried to have him killed. Emery's been squirreling around on this and he's unearthed some interesting facts. There was a bungled shooting some years ago, when Carling was meeting with a Senator Atherton. At the time, everyone assumed Atherton was the target. Now, we're not so sure. We've also noticed that the men who betrayed Estevez in the first place all seemed to have dropped off the radar over a period of years. Now we've had another attack on Carling at Snow Eagles. So yes, I think your description of him as a vengeful man is accurate."

"And he hasn't achieved his principal aim. Carling is still alive," Lee said, and again Benjamin nodded agreement.

"That had occurred to us," he said.

"And Jesse is the one who threw a spanner in the works," Lee continued, and now the FBI director started to see what was behind her request for a meeting.

"Ye-es," he said thoughtfully. "That hadn't occurred to me."

"It's occurred to me," Lee told him. "And it's occurred plenty to the press. Jesse's name and face have been splashed all over the papers and the TV from one end of this country to the other."

"Your point being?"

Lee took a long breath. "Mr. Director, I was raised on a ranch. On a ranch, if you've got a predator that kills your stock, you don't wait for it to come back and do it again. You go out and hunt it down. I've been a hunter since I was fourteen years old. It's kind of why I do what I do now, as a matter of fact."

"And why are you telling me this, Sheriff Torrens?" Benjamin regarded her carefully. Lee met his gaze squarely.

"I figure with all the facilities you government agencies have, and with the threat to Senator Carling still very much alive, you might have been looking to get a line on where this Estevez person goes to ground," she said.

Benjamin leaned his chair back and looked out the window, waiting to see if she'd say more. It was usually an effective technique. Most people eventually felt obliged to fill the awkward silence and would expand on what they'd already said. But the tall, blond woman didn't fall into the trap. She watched him impassively through those uptilted eyes. There might be Native American ancestry there, he thought. Eventually he had to break his own silence.

"And if we did?" he said, and she shrugged her shoulders.

"I'd be interested to know where he could be found. As I said, I'm a hunter and I don't wait for trouble to come to me."

"What about your deputy?" he asked, and she shook her head immediately.

"Jesse doesn't know I'm here. He doesn't need to know about any of this. He'd figure he could take care of himself."

"And you figure he can't?" he asked, but she shook her head again.

"No. I figure he probably could. But probably isn't good enough. And I don't want to spend the next five years or so waiting for Estevez to drop the other shoe."

The director leaned forward and steepled his fingers, resting his chin on them, then replied.

"As a matter of fact we do have a line on Estevez. Several, in fact. He has a fondness for vintage planes and cars and boats, and that's helped us track him down. Seems that someone who sounds very much like him has residences in Panama, Thailand and in Marseilles."

"He does get around. I'd appreciate knowing where he might be at any particular time."

"Thailand would be best. More secluded than Marseilles and easier to go unnoticed there than in Panama," Benjamin mused. "And if you planned to, say—visit Thailand, I'm sure we could help with any special needs you might have. Mind you, I'll be leaving this office in a week or two. But I'll speak to my successor. I'm sure he'll be only too willing to continue the arrangement."

She rose from the chair, a graceful feline movement, and extended her hand across the desk.

"I'm glad we understand each other, Mr. Director," she said. Benjamin took the hand, remarking once more on the strength of her grip.

"The pleasure's all mine, Sheriff," he said.

KOH LARN ISLAND
THE GULF OF SIAM
THAILAND

"Paolo! There's someone on the beach. Get rid of them!"

A tall figure, silhouetted by the late afternoon sun, was moving down the beach from the headland. Estevez watched as Paolo emerged from the villa, glanced up the beach and hurried down the three steps on to the sand, trotting toward the interloper.

Estevez turned back to the lounge chair he'd been reclining on. Then he paused and looked at the two figures, now growing closer together. He reached to the table beside the lounge and picked up the ten-by-fifty Nikons that he kept there. He raised the glasses and focused them. Then he smiled.

Tall, shapely and blond. She stopped as Paolo called to her. She carried a beach towel over her left shoulder and a large raffia beach bag in her right hand. She was wearing cut off denim shorts that revealed the lower curve of her buttocks and displayed her fine legs to full advantage. Other than that, she wore only a brief bikini top. He zoomed the binoculars onto the full, firm breasts, barely contained by two small triangles of yellow and red fabric. He fancied he could see the slight bulge of the nipples there. She wasn't a girl, he thought. She was a woman. And she was at that age where a beautiful woman realizes her own sexuality and the power of her own body. She stood waiting for Paolo, her hips thrust slightly forward in an unconsciously provocative pose. He ran the glasses over the smooth, rounded belly above the shorts. Unconsciously, his tongue passed across his lips, moistening them. He saw Paolo gesturing for the beach bag and nodded agreement. Even a beautiful woman like this could have a nasty surprise in a harmless looking bag like that. Still, once Paolo had checked her out, there was no need to get rid of her. Maybe he should ask her up to the villa for a drink. Then dinner. Then who knew what? He set down the Nikons, slipped the Walther P5 that he always kept nearby into the rear pocket of his linen slacks and walked briskly across the patio to the beach.

Let me see the bag," Paolo demanded, holding out his hand. Lee took half a step backward.

"Why?" she asked. Paolo snapped his fingers impatiently. "I told you. This is a private beach. You're trespassing."

"Then I'll leave. So there's no need for you to see my bag," she said in a slightly annoyed tone.

"You'll leave all right. But I'll see the bag first," Paolo told her. "I want to be sure you're not planning on coming back later."

She snorted derisively. "Bet your ass I'm not. And I'm damned if you're putting your paws all over my bag."

"One way or another, I will see it," Paolo told her. He flicked up the tail of his beach shirt on the left-hand side to reveal the grip of the large automatic in his waistband. Lee allowed her eyes to widen a little.

"Hey! Hold on a minute, feller! There's no need for that! Take the bag!" She passed the bag to him. He took it and rifled through it. There was very little in it. A pink T-shirt, sun lotion, Nokia cell phone, a plastic bottle of water, now lukewarm, Bolle sunglasses and a worn leather billfold. His eyes kept darting down to the bag as he examined it, then back up to the blond woman.

"This your boss?" she asked, looking over his left shoulder. But Paolo's gaze wasn't diverted. He heard the soft whisper of footsteps in the sand. It could only be *El Jefe*, he reasoned.

"Good afternoon," she said and, from a few yards away, Estevez replied, his voice friendly.

"*Buenas dias.* Paolo, is the young lady carrying anything we should be concerned about?"

Now Paolo glanced quickly behind him and, as he did, Lee's right hand moved smoothly to the heavy towel draped over her left shoulder. The night before, she'd turned up the bottom six inches and sewed it into a pocket. Her hand went into it and closed over the checkered butt of the Ruger .22 automatic concealed there.

"Everything is in order, *Jefe*," Paolo said. Then he saw the look of alarm in Estevez's eyes and he swung back, dropping the beach bag, reaching across his body for the Browning Hi-Power.

Crack-crack!

The two shots were so fast they almost blended into one sound as she put two of the hollow point Long Rifle .22 slugs into his wrist, smashing into the junction point of bones, nerves and tendons. The Browning, half-drawn, fell from his suddenly limp fingers. His wrist felt as if someone slammed it with a hammer, the painful buzz of injured nerves ringing up his arm.

He made a choking noise of pain and doubled over, his left hand clutched to the destroyed right wrist.

"Hold it!" Lee called as Estevez started to turn away. He froze in place, looking into the barrel of the Ruger. It wasn't a big gun—a .22 or a .25 at most—but it was only a few yards away and the woman had already proven she would hit what she aimed at. Right now, she seemed to be aiming at his left eye, and the barrel of the gun was steady and unwavering. A headshot from a .22 would be lethal at this range.

"Get on your knees," she ordered, and when he hesitated, the barrel of the .22 made a quick gesture downward. He sank to his knees in the hot sand.

"Don't want you running off on me," she said. Then she glanced at Paolo, still doubled forward over his wounded hand.

"You," she said, and when he didn't answer: "You with the broken wrist!" At that, he looked up at her. He saw the Ruger was still trained on Estevez, still rock-steady.

"I've got no argument with you," she said quietly. "You can stay or go, it's your choice. But if you stay, you'll get what he gets."

"Paolo!" Estevez's voice cracked like a whip. "You know what happens to those who betray me!"

For a moment, Paolo hesitated. Then Lee smiled grimly.

"Hear that?" she said. "That's the sound of a dead man making threats. Now stay or go. You choose."

Paolo chose. Still hunched over and nursing his shattered wrist, he turned away and began to shamble up the beach, leaving Estevez behind.

"Paolo!" Estevez shouted after him, his face darkening as blood rushed to it. "You'll pay for this! I swear it!"

"Shut up," the woman said. He swung his gaze back on her now and noticed that her eyes were following Paolo as his stumbling figure moved further away. Estevez's right hand began to steal behind his back to the Walther in his back pocket.

Seemingly intent on the deserting bodyguard, Lee felt a small glow of satisfaction as she saw the movement. She'd assumed Estevez would be armed. She'd hoped so. She didn't like the idea of shooting him in cold blood—although if it came to that, she would do it. The Ruger was loose in her hand, held lightly. She waited until Estevez took a grip on the Walther and began to bring it around from behind his back.

He had the gun halfway leveled when the woman looked back at him. In the same instant, the barrel of the automatic in her hand swung, foreshortened in his gaze, and spat out the same spiteful double crack.

Compared to the Blackhawk .44 she normally carried, the .22 had virtually no recoil. And it was much lighter and easier to conceal. That was why she had chosen it. She was used to the gun. She kept one at home for varmint shooting, which was pretty much what she was doing now, she thought. The two bullets struck Estevez in the forehead, a fraction above the left eyebrow and barely half an inch apart. His body went limp instantly and he slumped forward like an empty bag, dead before his face hit the sand.

She looked down at him dispassionately. The Walther was close by his outflung hand, half-buried in the sand.

"I'm so glad you tried," she said.

She turned and walked back the way she had come. Her hired runabout was beached around the next headland and on the brief trip back to Pattaya Beach, she'd lose the Ruger overboard. It had come into the country in the diplomatic bag and now it was time to get rid of it. She'd picked it up when she first arrived, using the fake passport supplied by the FBI. That, she would burn once she was back home.

Later that night, she called an unlisted number in Virginia. The man who answered—Linus Benjamin's replacement—spoke with a pleasant southern accent. She identified herself, using the name from the fake passport.

"This is Laura Templeton," she said, giving him a second to recognize the significance of the name. "It's done." There was a slight pause and he replied.

"That was quick," he sounded impressed. "Any problems?"

"None. It's done and I'm going home."

"Well, stay in touch, Laura. Maybe we could do business again," he said.

Her reply was cold and uncompromising. "I don't think so. I don't make a habit of this sort of thing."

She hung up, leaned back and sighed. Her bag was packed on the bed beside her and her plane was leaving in three hours. It was time to get back to Steamboat Springs.

And Jesse.

ABOUT THE AUTHOR

John A. Flanagan, now a full-time author, is a former advertising and television writer. His adventure series for young adults, Ranger's Apprentice, has spent more than a year on the *New York Times* bestseller list.

Background for the Jesse Parker series came from his many visits to the ski resorts of Colorado and Utah. *Storm Peak* was published in 2009.

John lives with his wife, Leonie, in Manly, Australia, on Sydney's northern beaches.